PASSION'S SURRENDER

Maria looked up at Shadow again, questioning him with her eyes. Why, oh, why couldn't she fight him? She should show some sort of protest, yet she could not. A side of her that she had never known before would not allow her to deny him . . .

Her pulse raced as his face drew closer, her eyes became wild, her knees weak. She did not truly want to feel this need that ate away at her heart. Never in her life had she been rendered so helpless.

A sensual tremor coursed through Maria at the first contact of his mouth on her lips. A throaty moan frightened her when it rose from deep inside her. The pleasure of his kiss was so profound and the touch of his hands, now cupping her breasts through the soft buckskin blouse, was so beautifully sweet. Never in her wildest dreams had she thought any man could steal away her ability to think.

But it was happening . . .

SAVAGE DREAM

CASSIE EDWARDS

CHARTER BOOKS, NEW YORK

SAVAGE DREAM

A Charter Book / published by arrangement with
the author

PRINTING HISTORY
Charter edition / June 1990

ISBN: 1-55773-345-7

Charter Books are published by The Berkley Publishing Group,
200 Madison Avenue, New York, New York 10016.
The name "CHARTER" and the "C" logo
are trademarks belonging to Charter Communications, Inc.

PRINTED IN THE UNITED STATES OF AMERICA

10 9 8 7 6 5 4 3 2 1

AUTHOR'S NOTE

The Navaho were once the largest Indian tribe in the United States, a vigorous, proud people, full of life. Uniquely outstanding sheep raisers, they love horses as well, calling the horse "the animal of the mountain."

The Navaho call themselves *Dineh*, the People. "Navaho" was the name given to them by the Spaniards.

The Navaho's primary concern was, and still is, to keep themselves harmonious with God and all his creations.

For several special people:

Nancy Demuth
Pat Sargent
Virginia Knight
Donna Combs
Donna Burgee
Deborah Abrams
Nancy Nelson

Jim and Mary White
Irene Manchester
Mickey Brannan
Ava Janson
Karm Cook
Nancy Waltrip
Daphna Williams
Dean and Wes Nelson

CHAPTER
1

Voices came louder through the door as Maria Zamora stood listening close behind it. She had watched the arrival of the Navaho Indian chief, Shadow, and having been entranced by him since the first time she had seen him many years ago when she was ten, could not help but stay to listen to his deep, fine voice, though she longed to see him face to face instead of from a distance, as was usually the case.

Now a ravishing beauty at eighteen, Maria was forbidden by her father to be within viewing range of the Indian leader whenever the two men transacted business. Usually the meetings were held away from their plantation.

But today, since Governor Castillo was also present for this meeting between two powerful landowners, it seemed only appropriate to gather in the comfort of Esteban Zamora's mansion. Maria's father had ordered her to stay in the sewing room at the back of the house.

But Maria couldn't! Never had she been this close to Shadow! And because this might be her last opportunity she had disobeyed her father.

When the voices grew more and more bitter in the study, Maria became uneasy. She swept her long and flowing, bright calico skirt around and moved farther into the parlor adjoining the study where the argument was taking place. Through the plaster wall she could still hear the determined

1

voices, first her father, then Shadow, and then Governor
Castillo.

Accusations were being tossed about from man to man
and she understood them all, having heard them discussed
so often at the dinner table between her father—the wealthy
owner of a *plantación* and a grand *cortijo*, or manor
house—and those who would come to discuss the matters of
the Indians with him.

She turned and stared at the closed door when her father's
voice became dominant in the study. When she heard him
offer a bribe to Shadow, a bribe that could eventually force
Shadow to relinquish his land and sheep, Maria cringed and
tried to focus her thoughts elsewhere; she knew without a
doubt what the reaction of the handsome Indian would be.
He was a man who had not yet been corrupted by bribes.
She knew not to expect him to be fooled into accepting this
time!

Yet she feared hearing his answer. If he did accept the
bribe, he would not be the man that she had always
envisioned . . . a man of pride and distinction, a man
who would let no one rule him.

A silver necklace with soft highlights and deep shadows
glowed against the deep blue of Maria's velveteen bodice;
oval medallions of silver adorned her waist. She began
pacing the full length of the room, her skirt swinging over
her short, calculated steps, a froth of petticoats at her ankles
sounding like light-falling rain.

Maria's reflection in a large mirror mounted over the
fireplace revealed a shapely young woman with dark,
flashing eyes and luxuriant waist-length coal-black hair
drawn back from her delicate, lovely face with combs
encrusted with jewels.

She was a five-foot tall, one-hundred-pound whirlwind of
energy, who felt imprisoned by her overprotective father.
She hungered to be free. She longed for excitement! She
didn't want to end up like her mother, an empty woman
merely existing from day to day with no outlets for any
feelings. Her mother seemed only half alive.

Maria wanted more out of life than that. It was her dream

to become a highly acclaimed seamstress. She wanted to experience the vibrancy of life, to fully take part in it!

But . . . how?

Her father guarded her as though she were one of his prized Arabian horses!

Disconsolately, Maria looked around her, having finally grown used to this house after having spent most of her childhood in Valencia, Spain. She lifted an eyebrow and tilted her head, sighing. It was true that her family lived a luxurious life. The parlor was filled with elegantly carved Spanish tables, plush velveteen-upholstered chairs and sofas, and priceless Turkish rugs. A tremendous fire was burning in the fireplace, blazing logs three feet long lying across massive brass andirons.

Maria's parents had brought their love of Spain with them to this land of New Mexico. Zamora Manor was a near duplicate of the home they had left behind, with its Spanish tile roof suspended like an umbrella over wide porches called galleries. The galleries surrounded the house, protecting the interior from sun and rain. The windows were as wide and tall as the doors and had louvered shutters, jalousies. Wrought iron was used lavishly throughout the structure for the staircase, balconies, decorative lanterns, latches, door handles, and keyholes. It was lovely but stood in a desolate area, with no neighbors for miles.

Maria went to the window and lifted its sheer curtain to peer outside. To avoid unnecessary heat in the house during the summer months the kitchen was in a separate building. Zamora Manor stood near the front of the property, with the slaves' quarters and bunkhouses for the vaqueros, or cowhands, behind it. Beyond these quarters were verdant fields and pastures in which horses and sheep grazed peacefully as far as the eye could see.

Maria turned and gazed at the gilded pier glass at the far side of the room. There was also a grand piano, and, oh, so much more that spoke of the riches her father had acquired over the years during his illegal raids.

Being a retired Spanish army officer was a position that only made him look respectable. It was the stolen horses, slaves, and sheep that made him a wealthy man. Now he was finding devious ways to wrest land away from the Indians!

Maria felt dirty because of this criminally acquired wealth. But he was her father and she knew that respect must be paid him for that reason if no other.

Yet, sometimes it was so very hard!

Like *now*!

Her hand formed a tight fist at her side as she stepped up to the closed door and resumed listening. She sensed the explosive atmosphere in the study and knew that she should return to the privacy of the sewing room, but she could not pull herself away. The dispute in the adjoining room was too interesting; her curiosity about what Shadow was going to do was too compelling. His voice reached her heart, making it pound so strangely! What if she did actually meet him? Could she bear the joy of that moment?

Maria listened, trying to envision Shadow in his anger . . .

"*E-ya*, I did not come here to be bribed," she heard Shadow say. "I have come in peace to see if you know anything of my missing people. Never would I have come had I known you were planning to trick me with this man you white men call governor. Your time is wasted, Señor Zamora. *E-do-ta*! No. You waste my time!"

"*Lo siento*, I am sorry, I know of no missing slaves," Zamora said, his voice filled with mockery. "*Amigo*, I am not guilty of slave raids. Do you not know? Have you not heard? Slavery has been forbidden by the Spanish crown since 1530! And what I have offered you is not a bribe. *Sí*, it is an honor that Governor Castillo has chosen you above all other Indian chiefs to receive such a lovely costume today. Look at the red velveteen breeches, Shadow. Look at the silver buttons! Even a scarlet headband is offered to you to replace the one you wear, which is soiled by dust and sweat. And these are only the beginning! There will be many more gifts. How can you refuse?"

"You think Shadow is so poor that he must accept such gifts from you? It is because I am not poor and because you have done this before with other powerful Navaho leaders who have become weak by you that Shadow refuses!" Shadow said heatedly. "After a chief receives gifts from such as you, he takes his people away from their homes, leaving the land for your people. *E-do-ta*! No. Never will I accept this gift. Never!"

"Never is a long time," Zamora said in a low growl. "And as for those missing slaves? Perhaps you will soon discover more missing if you do not accept the gifts offered to you today!"

"You threaten Shadow?" the proud Indian hissed.

"If that is what you wish to call it, well, *sí*, I guess you could say that I am threatening you," Zamora said, laughing softly. "Did I not detect a threatening tone in your voice? One threat is followed by another!"

"You are *hogay-gahn*, bad. Your words are all mockery. You speak with a forked tongue, always," Shadow said stiffly. "First you deny that you raid, and then you threaten to raid. How many of my people do you house in your slave dwellings? How many?"

Maria paled, realizing where threats could lead between Shadow and her father. She had seen it before. Many had been slain on both sides when each had gathered enough men to display a show of force.

Maria found herself sympathizing with Shadow. She knew that few paid servants were to be had by the Spanish, for all those who came to the new world wanted to be masters and make their own fortunes. The best way to get help in house and field had been to raid the Indian villages, taking captives and forcing them to work in the Spanish households.

Most Spaniards considered this custom proper and fair to the Indians. While living with the Spaniards, the Indians were taught the civilized ways of the white man and the Christian religion. As if they should be grateful!

A bitterness about what the Spaniards had done to the Indians swept through Maria. She knew that the white conquerors were worried about the Navaho, who were spreading through the territory, growing rich and strong.

People like her father resented the fact that the chiefs reigned like kings and could make treaties for their tribes just as kings in Europe did for their sovereignties.

But she had found out by talking with various Indian slaves that each Navaho tribe had not only chiefs but also local leaders who acted as guides and advisers. Each part of Navaho country had two or three prominent men who were rich and wise and therefore were listened to by the people. These men were very influential with their groups. But they became headmen, who led a warrior group of raiders, only when they formed their own small groups to defend or reclaim the rights of their people.

Shadow was such a powerful man, who had at one time led such a group of marauding Navaho. He was now rich and he no longer led raids, but he retained his position as chief.

Was Maria's father going to incite him to action with threats?

It was true that slavery had been officially forbidden by the Spanish crown, but even the Spanish governor of this territory still had Indian slaves.

Maria tensed when she heard Shadow speaking passionately to her father.

"I have already earned all the wealth I need, and now I share my riches with my beloved people, never with *anaye*, strangers!" he said. "I do not want to lead my people into war. They have enjoyed peaceful lives. But if any more of my people are captured prey, you can expect blood to be spread on the land as far as you can see. Remember that, white man, when you send vaqueros to rob my stronghold! Remember that! *Niye tinishten*, as far as man can see there will be blood!"

Suddenly the door was jerked open, startling Maria. When she saw Shadow standing there, she became weak all over. As he stared down at her from his powerful six-foot frame, her breath was momentarily stolen; she found herself mesmerized by his dark, fathomless eyes, his strongly sculpted face, and the somehow seductive curve of his brooding hard-pressed lips and set jaw.

In her dreams she had envisioned a moment when they might meet, but she had never imagined that it would be so totally disarming! In reality, he was even more handsome, with his smooth bronze skin and striking Indian features. He was breathtakingly, ruggedly handsome, his sleek black hair worn long and loose over his broad shoulders, a folded bright red handkerchief tied around his brow.

She didn't have to look lower to see how he was dressed. From her upstairs bedroom window she had seen him arrive and had noticed that he was dressed as he had been the other times she had seen him from afar. He wore a buckskin shirt, deerskin breeches, and moccasins that were adorned with silver buttons. Since he needed protection as he traveled among rocks and bushes, Shadow had wrapped flat pieces of hide around his legs in a stovepipe shape. He had tucked them inside his moccasins and tied them at his knees with strips of leather that served as garters.

Around Shadow's left wrist was a tough strip of leather decorated with porcupine quills, to protect his skin from the snap of the bowstring. A quiver made of mountain lion skin, with tail and fringes for decoration, was strapped over his right shoulder so that it hung down his back. The quiver had two compartments. In the longer compartment on the right side he carried his short bow, shaped in a double curve and wrapped with sinew. The shorter compartment at the left was for his arrows. Joining them was a strip of wood.

Maria became unnerved as she met Shadow's questioning eyes. As he gazed down at her, his surprise was obvious.

"Maria, go to your room," her father ordered, speaking from behind Shadow. "Now!"

Shadow flinched, hardly able to believe that this was the conniving Spaniard's daughter. She had been a mere child the last time he had seen her, and though she was still only a wisp of a lady, she was now a mature woman, beautiful in every sense of the word. Her eyes were wide and dark, intense enough to completely absorb a man.

Shadow ignored the harsh breathing of Maria's father, who now stood beside him. For at this moment there was only Maria and the delicate texture of her skin, her beautiful features, those seductive lips, and her meaningful expression as she returned his steady gaze.

Something stirred within him, something Shadow sensed as dangerous. This woman was kin to a man Shadow despised. Surely she was as despicable and scheming as her father.

Yet Shadow could not keep his eyes from savoring every feature of her face and every curve emphasized by the velveteen blouse that was clinging to her breasts.

"Maria! Go to your room," her father repeated, stepping between Shadow and his daughter. "Pronto!"

Drawn forcefully from her hypnotic state, Maria brushed a hand across her brow as she looked up at her father with annoyance. "*Sí, padre mío*," she murmured. Yanking the tail of her skirt around, she fled across the room.

Half stumbling in her flight, she rushed up the stairs. Once in her bedroom, she rushed to the window. Breathing hard, excited that Shadow's eyes had mirrored her own feelings, she watched him mount his horse. Alongside an Indian companion, he rode away from the plantation.

Her heart skipped a beat when she caught sight of the many Navaho warriors awaiting Shadow on a slight rise of land overlooking Zamora plantation.

"Shadow could overpower my father even now if he wished," she whispered, then spun around when heavy footsteps sounded behind her.

"You have been disobedient, Maria," Zamora said, moving into the room. He stopped next to her, tall and lean in his dark brown suit. "You made it awkward for me. Never do that again."

He nervously twisted one end of his tapered black mustache between the tips of his fingers. "You must remember at all times that you are of the fair sex and your only duty is to please," he said blandly. "Today you pleased no one but yourself."

Maria's eyes wavered, and then she found courage building within her. She wanted to lash out at him and tell him that she could not be docile and passive. She hoped she had given pleasure not only to herself but also to Shadow, by offering him something besides her father's crudeness to think about. She had seen the look in Shadow's eyes when he paused to gaze down at her. She hoped Shadow would remember her forever . . .

Even though no future was possible between her and Shadow, it was wonderful to fantasize. Daydreaming sometimes helped to ease the loneliness. She had only one true friend, and her father limited even their time together. There was so much mistrust among the people in the Spanish community that daughters were not allowed to become close!

"*No se preocupe*, don't worry, *Padre*," she finally said, her courage waning. "I shall return to my sewing."

Her father's full lips lifted in a smug smile. He stroked Maria's hair. "*Gracias, hija*," he murmured. "That's good. Working with lace is much safer than sneaking around listening to your father's conversations with savages."

He stepped to the window and drew back the curtain to watch Shadow ride away with his warriors, fear striking his heart at the sight of so many. "Don't forget that, Maria," he snarled. "Shadow *is* a savage. A no-good savage. And so is his best friend, Blue Arrow, who rides alongside him."

He turned slowly around and faced her. "I saw the way you were looking at Shadow," he said thickly. "Of course you would be intrigued by the likes of him. But let those feelings go no further."

He walked square-shouldered toward the door. "*Adios*, Maria," he said smoothly. He looked over his shoulder at her. "You continue to be a good girl, *sí*?"

Maria gave him a surprised look. Had her father sensed the attraction she and Shadow had for each other? Had he seen it in their eyes?

Maria felt in her heart that something indefinable had happened during those brief moments of wondrous eye contact with Shadow.

But how could her father even think that something could come of it? She knew the impossibility of the situation and, though she didn't want to, accepted it!

"*Espere un momento*, wait a moment," Maria said,

rushing to her father, suddenly afraid of her feelings and of her sudden desire to go against everything he had taught her! Obedience to him was to come first and foremost! At this moment, because of an Indian, she was ready to challenge this ruling and it frightened her!

Stepping in front of her father she stopped his exit from the room and twined her arms around his narrow chest.

"*Lo siento*, I am sorry if I disappointed you, *mi padre*," she said, hugging him tightly. "But it does get so boring here at the plantation. I could not help myself this time."

Her father caressed her back. "*Sí, sí*," he said softly. He held her away from him and stared down into her luminous eyes. "Shall I send Pleasant Voice up from the slaves' quarters to spend time with you? She being of your age, you seem to get along so well."

"*Sí*, please tell Pleasant Voice that I would like to teach her more about sewing with fine lace," Maria said in a slight purr, knowing that she intended to do more than teach today. She would confide in Pleasant Voice! She would tell her friend that she had just met the most handsome man in the world and that the Navaho visitors had been so close to Pleasant Voice that she could have reached out and touched them if her father had not ordered all the slaves locked away.

"As good as done," her father said, nodding.

Maria's heart raced as she went to the window and watched Shadow and his warriors getting smaller in the distance. It was like looking upon small moving dots, hardly distinguishable from the sheep grazing on the hillsides.

Then she looked at the slaves' quarters and saw Pleasant Voice watching eagerly through a window. She had also seen! She already knew that she had come so close to being with her people again! Surely her heart was being torn to shreds!

Maria cast her eyes downward, ashamed. Wasn't there any end to these punishments in life?

CHAPTER
2

Many bolts of Valencia lace lay on the shelves in the sewing room along with colorful fabrics and ribbons. A loom stood in one corner of the room beside a wide curtainless window with a view of gray bluffs, gray rolling plateaus, and harshly monotonous distant mountains.

A fine collection of comfortable chairs stood around the room on waxed hardwood floors where light was accessible from hanging lamps over them. Maria sat in one of the most comfortable seats beside a table whereupon sat a cup of hot tea in a delicate Chinese porcelain cup.

Maria concentrated on the lace that she was gathering for a velveteen blouse she was making, but her patience was running thin. Her father had promised to send for Pleasant Voice several hours earlier. Since the sewing room was the only room Pleasant Voice was allowed to enter in this palatial mansion, Maria had wasted no time in getting there.

But where was Pleasant Voice? Had she been too upset from having seen Shadow and his warriors to come and be with her friend? Had seeing her Navaho people made Pleasant Voice suddenly resent Maria because of her father and what he stood for?

Moody, not wanting to think of the terrible habits of her father or of possibly having lost her only friend in this desolate land because of him, Maria laid her gathered lace aside. She rose from the chair and went to the window and looked toward the mountains, wondering where among them Shadow had built his stronghold for his people. Thus far no Spaniard had found it.

But Charging Falcon, a Pueblo Indian, knew where it was. Pleasant Voice had told Maria that Charging Falcon and Shadow had at one time been good friends, having come to know each other when they were children. During earlier times, after the Spanish invasion, many Pueblo had taken up residence with the Navaho to escape Spanish cruelty. The Pueblo villages had been in the fertile valleys the Spaniards wanted. The Pueblo were forced to pay taxes to the Spaniards and to swear their loyalty to the king of Spain. Running away had meant starvation; resistance had meant death. Some had been killed . . . even burned alive.

Charging Falcon had escaped with his family and had been taken in by Shadow's people, but now Shadow and Charging Falcon were enemies because Shadow had been more cunning in accumulating wealth, and Charging Falcon resented his good fortune.

Friends had become enemies when jealousy came between them!

"And now Charging Falcon works for my father," Maria whispered. "By doing this he is accumulating his own measure of wealth, for my father's bribes have worked quite well with him."

"Maria?"

The tiny voice behind Maria made her turn with a swirl of skirt and petticoat and look toward the open door where Pleasant Voice stood with her head humbly bowed. Though Maria could not boast of being more than a slight lady herself, Pleasant Voice was even more delicate and fragile. At twenty, her copper face displayed large, dark, slanted eyes, her nose was slightly curved, and her lips were full. Her dark hair was combed straight back and gathered into a roll at the nape of her neck. She wore a simple buckskin skirt and blouse, and moccasins.

"Pleasant Voice," Maria said, rushing to her. She took

her friend's hands and led her into the room. "What took you so long? I didn't think you would ever get here."

Pleasant Voice's eyes pooled with tears. "I did not come as soon as I could," she murmured, imploring Maria with a sad stare. "After being locked away I know I should have welcomed the open door. But my heart would not carry me away. It was too troubled by having seen Blue Arrow and not having been able to go to him and be held in his arms." She blinked tears from her thick eyelashes. "Did you see him, also, Maria?" she asked, her voice breaking. "Did you see him with Shadow?"

"Blue Arrow?" Maria said softly. "I heard my father mention his name. What is he to you?"

"Shadow and Blue Arrow only recently became acquainted and became best friends before my abduction," Pleasant Voice said, looking past Maria, out the window. "Blue Arrow is as wealthy as Shadow. He has his own stronghold. I was to live with him as his wife, but then I was abducted from the fields while I was tending our people's beautiful sheep, and I was brought here! Blue Arrow does not know that I am here! He would have come and stolen me away!"

Maria eased her hands away from Pleasant Voice and led the slight Indian to a chair and guided her down into it. Distraught, she looked even more fragile!

"*Lo siento*, I am so sorry. But perhaps no one has come to rescue you here not only because Blue Arrow obviously does not know where you are but also because of the struggles for peace between the Indians and my people," Maria said, settling down into a chair opposite Pleasant Voice.

Pleasant Voice wiped tears from her eyes and looked sourly at Maria. "Your father does not live in peace," she said icily. "You know that as well as I. He steals Indian children and women and brings them here all the time, and that corrupt Charging Falcon helps him! He should die!"

"*Sí*, I agree that he is responsible for much of the tragedy in the Navaho communities," Maria said, sighing disconsolately. "Perhaps in time Shadow and Blue Arrow will catch him and stop his vicious acts against your people."

"Against his own people as well! Many Pueblo live with the Navaho now!" Pleasant Voice said, shuddering at the thought of an Indian doing such harm against others of his own kind. "*E-ya*, Charging Falcon is *hogay-gahn*, bad!"

Pleasant Voice rose from the chair and went to the window to stare at the mountains. She lifted a hand and gestured toward them. "*Daltso hozhoni*, all is beautiful where my people dwell," she said, her voice thin. "Pleasant Voice longs to be there and become wife to Blue Arrow and bear his children!"

Maria went to Pleasant Voice and stood beside her, also again looking at the mountains. "Pleasant Voice, for so long I have wanted to meet Shadow," she murmured, recalling his fathomless eyes, the magnetic pull of them as he had looked at her with an intense interest. No conversation had been exchanged between them, but their expressions had said much. "Today I did get to meet him, if only for a brief moment."

Her cheeks were flushed with passion for a man for the first time in her life. She turned to Pleasant Voice and smiled. "Though we weren't formally introduced, we came this close to touching!" she said, measuring with her hands so that Pleasant Voice could get the general idea. She dropped her hands to her sides and sighed heavily. "Oh, Pleasant Voice, I have never seen such a handsome man in my entire life!" She lifted her chin, shook her long hair down her back, and closed her eyes in ecstasy.

Then she lowered her chin and met Pleasant Voice's steady stare and was embarrassed. Surely Pleasant Voice did not approve of a white woman making such a fuss over the Indian who was in charge of her clan's destiny! Even though Maria and Pleasant Voice were good friends, it was surely different where admiring an Indian chief was concerned!

Suddenly Pleasant Voice giggled. She covered her mouth with a hand and laughed harder. Then she grabbed Maria by the hands. "My friend!" she said, her dark eyes dancing.

"You surely are part Indian to have such devotion to them! And to have fallen in love with Shadow? It's wonderful, Maria! Wonderful!"

Maria's eyes were wide, stunned by Pleasant Voice's reaction, yet very grateful. "You think it is?" she said, a smile quivering on her lips. "Truly? And you do think that what I feel is love? Can a woman fall in love instantly?"

"It was not instant," Pleasant Voice said, sobering. "You have spoken of Shadow many times in passing. You have seen him from afar and have been intrigued by him. Even years ago you were in love with him, but you did not know how it should feel to be in love!"

"But I was so young."

"Love does not choose an age."

"And you? How long have you been in love with Blue Arrow?"

"I did not meet Blue Arrow until just before my abduction," Pleasant Voice said, once more gazing toward the mountains. "Blue Arrow came from far across the mountains to seek wealth. He and Shadow became close friends. Blue Arrow and I had just begun talking of marriage when I was stolen by Charging Falcon and brought here."

Maria paled. "You never told me before that it was Charging Falcon who abducted you," she gasped. "Shadow must not know how much of an enemy Charging Falcon has become!"

"One day he will know, and Charging Falcon will pay with his life!" Pleasant Voice hissed.

"But if Charging Falcon and Shadow were once such good friends, why is it that they have turned into such intense enemies?"

"Greed, Maria. Greed," Pleasant Voice said, her dark eyes snapping.

Maria stepped closer to the window when she heard horses approaching. They sounded close, but she was in no position to see them, for the sewing room was at the back of the house. "I wonder who is arriving this late in the evening," Maria said, lifting her skirt into her arms as she

turned and began hurrying toward the door. She beckoned
to Pleasant Voice. "Come on. Let's see who it is."

Pleasant Voice's eyes widened and she hesitated. "But I
am forbidden to enter any room other than this one," she
said, her voice shallow. "I mustn't, Maria. What if your
father . . ."

"Pooh on Father," Maria said, laughing over her shoulder. "Anyhow, he will be kept busy with whoever is
arriving. He won't know you are watching with me from my
bedroom window."

Giggling softly, they went to Maria's bedroom. A four-
poster bed covered with a satin comforter and a lacy dust
ruffle stood in the center of the room. A thick carpet
cushioned their footsteps, silencing them, as they hurried to
the window.

"Stand back somewhat," Maria whispered, slowly drawing the sheer curtain aside. "Don't take a chance of being
seen, even though no lamps are yet lit in my room."

"I shall be careful," Pleasant Voice said, tiptoeing to the
window. She giggled. "Maria, this is such fun! It is helping
me forget my sadness, at least for a while!"

Maria smiled at Pleasant Voice, then leaned close to the
window and looked down at a congregation of Indians on
horseback who had stopped just in front of the wide porch
of the mansion. The hair bristled at the back of Maria's neck
when she recognized the lead rider, who was just now
dismounting.

"Charging Falcon!" she whispered harshly. "I've seen
him here many times, and I would never mistake him.
Pleasant Voice, Charging Falcon is surely going to be paid
to lead another raid tonight!"

"*Hogay-gahn*, bad," Pleasant Voice whispered, doubling
her hands into tight fists at her sides.

Maria scurried from the window. "I'm going to go and
see just what this is all about," she said in a rush of words.
"Pleasant Voice, go back to the sewing room while I once
again listen through a door."

Pleasant Voice rushed after Maria and grabbed her hand.
"*E-do-ta*! No!" she warned. "Should you be discovered—"

"I shall be more careful this time," Maria reassured. "Anyhow, I'm glad I was discovered when Shadow was here. How else would I have had the opportunity to meet him eye to eye?"

She laughed softly and rushed on from the room, her heart thundering inside her, having found more excitement today than she had in months. Perhaps this was the beginning of more daring ways. Staying in her room or in the sewing room had become tedious, to say the least. Now she knew that adventure was only footsteps away, and she would not deny herself any of it!

After sneaking down the stairs, she listened to voices coming from the study. One was clipped, speaking half in Indian; the other spoke in a mixture of Spanish and English. She crept to the closed door and listened, paling at what she heard. Her father was giving Charging Falcon instructions to raid Shadow's stronghold tonight! If the raiders were lucky, Shadow would make camp before traveling on to his stronghold. While he was sleeping, death and destruction would come to his people!

A sick feeling invaded the pit of Maria's stomach. Her knees grew weak at the thought of what her father was planning. Listening further, she heard Charging Falcon accept the bribes being offered him for his troubles!

Turning, she ran back up the stairs to her bedroom, torn with feelings about her father and dreading what tonight would bring to Shadow and his people. Her heart went out to him. She only wished there was some way to warn him!

But there wasn't. She would just have to sit and wait to hear the arrival of new slaves to the plantation tonight . . . slaves taken from Shadow's stronghold!

"Maria?"

Pleasant Voice broke through Maria's troubled thoughts. Maria turned and saw the slight Indian daring to be caught by coming to Maria's bedroom again.

"Oh, Pleasant Voice," Maria cried, going to her friend, embracing her. "It's so horrible! Wait until I tell you what I have found out!"

Pleasant Voice grew tense within Maria's arms. "*E-*

do-ta, no," she whispered, feeling cold inside. "I don't want to know."

A late moon rose, cool and remote. Shadow was reclining on sheepskins on the ground before a campfire while ears of corn were roasting in the hot ashes at the edges of the fire. No breeze stirred. There were no details to be seen in the cliffs or the valley around Shadow, only distant silhouettes against the dark sky.

"You are in such deep thought," Blue Arrow said, easing down on the spread sheepskins next to Shadow. "Is it because of the white man? Or is it the white woman you told me about?" he questioned softly. "It is dangerous, Shadow, to think of her at all. She is the daughter of the Spaniard you had bad words with. It is best that you do not think of her in any capacity!"

"Shadow knows this," he said in a grumble, looking at Blue Arrow, seeing much in his friend's features that matched his own, except for a long slant of a scar that marred his right cheek. "Many things trouble my heart tonight, not only the woman. Raiding may become necessary again. What will my people think of this? Will they accept my decision? Except for the few women and children who have been abducted from the fields where they wandered for relaxation, there has for the most part been peace at both our strongholds, Blue Arrow. Yours and mine. Though our people hate the Spaniards for stealing even one person away, they know that to rebel would mean war, and they are afraid of war! The Anaasazi, ancient people, remember all too well what it was like to have blood spilled at their feet."

"But those who took part in the raids have surely missed the excitement of raiding," Blue Arrow, his copper face golden in the fire's glow, tried to reassure his friend.

Shadow gazed at his friend, seeing determination in the set of his jaw and in the fire of his dark eyes. He knew that Blue Arrow was hungering to raid again. Even Shadow himself had missed the excitement of the raids!

What would be best for his people?

He gazed into the fire, reaching out to remove an ear of

corn from the ashes. The husks were hot against his fingertips, and he quickly shucked it, then began nibbling the tender kernels.

"We will just have to wait and see what Zamora's next move is," he grumbled, chewing. Out of the corner of his eye he watched Blue Arrow reach for an ear of corn and quickly shuck it. He saw him take several bites of the corn and chew angrily.

It was obvious that Blue Arrow was thinking about Pleasant Voice, who had been missing for some time now. A thorough search had been made for her; the Indians had done as much as they could do, had tried everything but an actual raid on the Zamora plantation, but not one sign of her had they found.

Often Shadow had wondered if she was at the Zamora plantation.

But he had restrained himself from going to search for her there! She was only one of a few who had disappeared over the years since a truce had been made between the Navaho and Spaniards. There were more Navaho to protect in the various strongholds by *not* going to war against the whites again.

Shadow turned his eyes back to the fire and watched its curling flames, seeing in them a lithe, dancing figure of a lady. He could even make out her facial features and understood that his mind was playing tricks on him, for it was the Spanish lady who was teasing him in the fire, beckoning to him to follow her into the flames to dance with him!

Blinking, rubbing his eyes with his free hand, Shadow felt foolish, yet Maria Zamora had been on his mind more than not this evening. Hadn't she been one of the reasons he had not raided the Zamora plantation through the years? Though he had only seen her from afar and had not until today seen her as a grown-up woman, there was something special about her that he wanted to protect by not raiding her plantation, maiming, killing, and stealing!

Now he understood why! After coming face to face with her today, seeing so much in her expression as she gazed up at him, he knew that destiny was theirs for sharing! Somehow! And this was why he had refrained from harming her plantation and those who loved her. She might be harmed, also, in the frenzy of an attack!

"This day has been long and tiring," Blue Arrow said, tossing the stripped corncob into the fire. "It is best that I go to my own pallet of sheepskin. If I continue to talk of raiding I shall encourage it with all of my might! I have many reasons to raid Zamora's land."

Shadow tossed his corncob into the fire, then rose to his feet and warmly embraced his friend. "Tomorrow will be brighter, my friend," he said, to reassure him. "Perhaps you might even want to bring your people to my stronghold and we will have a celebration of love?"

"A celebration of love," Blue Arrow said, slipping from Shadow's embrace, "but perhaps no longer one of peace! I do not trust the Spaniards any more than I trust the Ute Indians! And you know how little I trust them."

Shadow sighed and nodded. "I, too, trust them so little," he said, looking into the distant hills. "It is because of the Ute that we are in New Mexico. They are a warlike people. Many of the Navaho died because of them!"

Blue Arrow clasped Shadow's shoulders. "Tomorrow will come soon," he said. "Lose yourself in sleep tonight, Shadow. There is always peace in sleep, is there not?"

Shadow chuckled. "Sometimes not even then," he said, then settled back down on his sheepskins as Blue Arrow went to his pallet and stretched out, covering himself with skins.

Again Shadow's thoughts turned to Maria Zamora . . . to her loveliness and the innocence he had seen in her wide dark eyes. Surely she was not like her father in heart and deed! True, she was his daughter, but that did not mean she had the same evil flowing through her veins.

He stretched out on his side and drew a sheepskin up over his body, feeling the lethargy of sleep slowly claiming him. As his eyes closed, he was still thinking of Maria. How could he see her again? Should he steal her away?

No! It would cause a war between his people and the Spaniards. There was peace now except for a few minor raids! He could not place his selfish desires before the welfare of his people.

After falling into a restless sleep, Shadow carried Maria with him into his dreams . . .

Maria, with her soft ringlets framing her delicately chiseled features, was lying beside Shadow beneath a full moon. He looked into her lustrous brown eyes as he lowered himself over her, his muscled arms drawing her into his embrace.

With his mouth he touched her lips wonderingly, a raging hunger eating away at his insides. His loins were on fire with desire he could not hold back any longer. He kissed her savagely, familiarizing himself with the delicate texture of her skin as he disrobed her until she lay silkenly nude against him.

Wanting to taste her flesh, to become a part of it, Shadow trailed kisses from her mouth down to her breasts, which were swollen with need. His lips moved lower, across her abdomen, which quivered beneath his kisses, and then lower, to where the forbidden triangle of hair at the juncture of her thighs beckoned to him.

But Maria's hands on his shoulders, urging him not to take her that way, caused him to brush sensual kisses upward on her body until he was kissing her lips once again.

As she clung ardently to him, returning his kisses, clinging to him and arching her hungry body upward, Shadow lowered his buckskin breeches. Breathless, his body growing feverish, he tossed them aside and guided his manhood downward . . . downward . . . downward . . .

Shadow awakened with sweaty palms and brow. He inhaled deeply and stared up at the stars overhead, realizing that though it was only a dream, he had experienced all the emotions and desires as if it had been a reality!

He now knew that he must have Maria!

Somehow!

If not, he would never have a restful night of sleep again!

He did not want to take a wife, however, for among the

Navaho, women could own the house, land, children, and sheep and could divorce a man simply by placing his personal property outside the house! Shadow wanted no woman to have that much power over him. He needed women only for sexual pleasure.

A slow smile lifted the corners of his lips as he turned on his stomach to stare into the fire. Whenever he got the opportunity, he would steal Maria from the *cortijo*! She would be his love slave!

But never would he marry her!

CHAPTER
3

Maria squirmed uneasily beneath her comforter. Her sleep was restless, for she continued to dream about Shadow. He was riding his horse, the silver ornaments on his elaborate Navaho saddle glittering in the sunshine. He was riding toward her as she stood beside the road in a sheer, billowing chemise, her hair wind-whipped by the breeze that blew steadily around her.

A sensual tremor coursed through her as Shadow came closer, his dark eyes branding her as his. With one sweep of an arm he plucked her up from the ground and clasped her within his muscular embrace, riding away with her as she twined her arms around his neck, reveling in his closeness . . .

A scream pierced the air, awakening Maria from her pleasantly sweet dream with a start. She felt the numbness that she always experienced when she knew that captives were being brought to Zamora plantation to be enslaved. Nibbling nervously on her lower lip, she listened to the pounding hooves of the horses, the sound of children crying, and the hysterical cries of women.

Unable to stand it any longer, Maria bolted from the bed and went to the window and gazed toward the slaves' quarters. The morning sky was light enough for her to see the activity there.

A coldness swept through her when she saw how many captured women and children were being herded into the slaves' cabins while many Indian warriors sat on their horses watching, arrows notched onto their bows.

"Charging Falcon!" Maria gasped, placing a hand to her throat, knowing that he was the leader of this group of Indians responsible for this ghastly deed. She had heard the agreement between her father and the Pueblo Indian.

Her eyes moved to another man . . . her father. He was among those who were watching the innocent Indians being forced into slavery like animals!"

"How can Charging Falcon do this to his Indian people? How?" she whispered harshly. "How can my father be so unfeeling?"

Sick at heart, Maria turned her eyes from the pitiful sight, appalled by her father's participation in what was happening tonight. And these people had to be from Shadow's stronghold! Wouldn't he retaliate, *soon*?

Was this what her father wanted? Or did he think that Shadow would not carry out his threat against him?

Maria had heard the venom in Shadow's voice!

He had meant every word of that threat!

Zamora held a lantern up, lighting the tear-streaked faces of the women who were passing before him on their way into the cabin with the others, who had been abducted earlier.

"Charging Falcon, can't you do something about these women who are causing such a commotion?" he growled, raising the lantern so that it lit up Charging Falcon's long, narrow face framed by wild, dark hair. "I didn't want anyone at the house to hear. My wife and daughter don't approve of these raids. It's best they don't actually see it happening right beneath their noses."

Charging Falcon, attired in only a breechcloth and moccasins and with his bow slung across his shoulder, dismounted and stepped closer to the Spaniard. "You did not pay me to silence the women," he said blandly. "Perhaps you want me to kill them, for that is the only way these women who have been stolen from their beds this night are going to cooperate in any way with you or me."

Zamora looked uneasily toward the house. He tightened his grip on his whip. "*Más aprisa*! Faster!" he ordered flatly, lifting his whip threateningly. He poked first one woman and then another with the handle of the whip, causing a quick silence and making the women cower as they hurried their steps.

Pleasant Voice stood in the darkness of the cabin, watching as the women crowded in around her. She began edging her way past them, her eyes firelit as she looked toward Charging Falcon. Hate ate away at her insides for the man, and though she could be whipped by Maria's father, Pleasant Voice was driven to let the Pueblo Indian know how much she hated him. In a sense she would be speaking for all of those who had been swept from their beds tonight or, like herself, abducted from the fields as she walked innocently among the sheep, admiring them!

Her heart racing, her knees weak with building fear, Pleasant Voice moved through the clamor of the women pushing their way through the door and defied both Zamora and Charging Falcon with an audacious stare.

"*Qué es eso*? What is the matter?" Zamora said, forking an eyebrow as he watched Pleasant Voice stop before Charging Falcon to glare up at him. "Pleasant Voice, what are you doing?" He gestured with a wide swing of the hand. "Get back inside with the rest of the women. Hurry along, now!"

Her chin held stubbornly high, her dark hair loosened from its bun and rippling down her back, Pleasant Voice ignored his command. She stepped closer to Charging Falcon, the lamplight from Zamora's lantern lighting up the Pueblo Indian's eyes, which revealed a sudden uneasiness.

"Charging Falcon, you are a traitor to your people and to Shadow's tribe!" Pleasant Voice cried. She rose up on tiptoe and spit in his face. "You are *hogay-gahn*! Bad!"

Charging Falcon took a shaky step backwards, wiping his face with the back of his hand. He flinched when Zamora grabbed Pleasant Voice and swung her away from him.

What she had just done to him had been worse than having been stung by many arrows! It awakened shame in his heart for what he had been led to do by his desire to be as rich as Shadow!

Yet, now that he had tasted a portion of such wealth, he could not curb his desire to have everything! And to accumulate more, raids were necessary! Seeing Pleasant Voice's anger had made him realize how dangerous she could be to him and his future dealings with the wealthy Spaniard! If ever she managed to escape, she would tell Shadow about Charging Falcon's involvement with the Spaniard! This could not be allowed to happen! Shadow would hunt Charging Falcon down and kill him!

"Pleasant Voice, what has gotten into you?" Zamora growled, worried that he might have to make an example of her, knowing that if Maria found out she would never forgive him! Pleasant Voice and Maria had become too close. He now understood the danger of this and could not allow it any longer!

"*E-ya!*" Pleasant Voice screamed, afraid of the whip that was used against those who were disobedient.

Charging Falcon cleared his throat nervously as he wiped the spit from his face. His dark eyes deepened in intensity as he moved closer to Pleasant Voice. "*Senōr*, tonight I ask for added payment for what I have brought you," he said in a deep growl, glaring down at Pleasant Voice. "Tonight I ask for *her* as payment. In many ways she is dangerous to Charging Falcon! I must make sure I, personally, can keep watch on her! She will be my slave!"

Zamora tightened his grip on Pleasant Voice's wrist, looking from her to Charging Falcon. What Charging Falcon suggested would allow him to solve the problem he had just been awakened to. It would be easier to forbid Maria to see Pleasant Voice if her friend was no longer around. If Pleasant Voice was with Charging Falcon, she would be his responsibility!

A slow smile lifted Zamora's wide lips. His mustache quivered as he nodded at Charging Falcon. "*Sí amigo*, she is yours," he said, shoving Pleasant Voice toward the

Pueblo Indian. "She is of no use to me any longer. She is only trouble!"

Wild-eyed, Pleasant Voice looked disbelievingly up into Zamora's face, her pulse racing. Going with Charging Falcon would surely mean death for her! She knew too much. She could be the cause of Charging Falcon's death at the hands of Shadow! She would not be a slave for long! She would . . . die!

Grabbing Maria's father, she clung to his arm. "*E-do-ta*! No!" she cried. "Do not send me away. Charging Falcon will kill me!"

Zamora ignored her and turned his back on her. He closed the slaves' doors and bolted them. His heart was thundering inside him; he hated to do this to Pleasant Voice, for he had grown fond of her.

But she was a bad example for the other slaves. She had been defiant, and if he did not send her away, especially after Charging Falcon had asked for her, it would give the others cause to believe they could rebel at any time and get away with it!

"Please!" Pleasant Voice pleaded, but was once again ignored. She looked up at the house, at Maria's window, then broke into a mad rush toward the mansion. "Maria!" she screamed, waving her hands. "Maria! Save me! Your father is sending me away! Charging Falcon will kill me!"

Maria stood to one side of the window cowering against the wall, no longer watching, not wanting to see any more of the transaction between her father and Charging Falcon.

But when she heard her friend crying her name, a shock of horror went through her. She turned on her heel and brushed aside the sheer curtain and grew numbly cold inside when she saw Pleasant Voice racing across the courtyard, waving and shouting her name. She sucked in her breath and grew light-headed when she saw Charging Falcon run after Pleasant Voice, grab her, and wrestle her to the ground!

"*Dios mío!* Good Lord!" Maria gasped, paling.

Not giving herself time to see what then transpired, only feeling a desperate need to stop what was happening to her dear friend, Maria pulled on a robe and ran from the room.

Her bare feet barely made contact on the steps as she moved from the second floor to the first. Her breathing was harsh, her heart was beating rapidly as she rushed outside into the twilight of morning, feeling desperation rise inside her when she saw Charging Falcon roughly fling Pleasant Voice onto his fancy saddle and quickly mount behind her, then held her in place against his body while one of his warriors blindfolded her.

"Pleasant Voice!" Maria shouted, sobs of fury almost strangling her. She ran toward Charging Falcon's horse, then felt strong arms stopping her. Wildly, she looked up at her father. "What is happening? Why is Charging Falcon having Pleasant Voice blindfolded? Why is he going to take her away? Why, Father? Why?"

Zamora looked down at Maria, his eyes registering shock. "*Caramba*! What are you doing here?" he gasped, his voice sounding strangled. His gaze swept over her, seeing that she wore only a thin robe over her chemise and was barefoot.

"I heard the commotion out here," Maria cried. "I *always* hear it. Do you think I am deaf? Do you think I am blind?"

Her father paled. He motioned toward the house with a flick of the wrist. "Go back to your room," he growled. "*Pronto!*"

"Where is Charging Falcon taking Pleasant Voice?" Maria cried, blatantly ignoring her father's orders. "*Why* is he taking her away? *Padre*, answer me."

Zamora's eyes wavered. "Maria, it is best this way," he said at last. "I am sorry, but Pleasant Voice was rebellious tonight. The other slaves saw her. She sets a bad example. Try to understand!"

Tears ran in streams down Maria's face as she looked over her shoulder at Charging Falcon, now riding away with Pleasant Voice, then pleaded with her eyes up at her father.

"*Padre*, don't do this!" she cried. "She is my best friend. You know that! You punish not only Pleasant Voice but also your daughter. *Por favor*? Please reconsider. Did not you see her fear? She is afraid of Charging Falcon and she has a right to be! Nothing he does is good, *ever*!"

Now that Charging Falcon and his warriors were far enough away so that Maria could not catch up with them, Zamora loosened his grip on her waist. He looked her up and down, again aware of her scant attire.

"We will talk no longer of Pleasant Voice," he said. "You must return to the house, pronto! The morning air will give you a chill."

Maria doubled her hands into tight fists at her sides. "Do you think I care if I take a cold?" she said, her voice breaking. "I care only about Pleasant Voice!"

Her father's face became drawn and lined as he frowned. "Well, Maria, you mustn't," he said darkly. "She is no longer our concern. She now belongs to Charging Falcon. And none too soon, as I see it. Being given the privilege of becoming your friend made her set herself apart from the other slaves on our plantation. When a slave does this it becomes dangerous."

He gestured toward the house again. "Go to your room and stop making a scene," he said. "You are setting almost as bad an example as Pleasant Voice by expressing disagreement with me."

Maria wiped tears from her eyes. She sniffled, then squared her shoulders and glared up at her father. "How will you punish me for *my* disobedience, *Padre*?" she said. "Will you send me away too? Will you?"

She held her head high, then turned and stomped away from her father, cringing when she heard him gasp at her hate-filled comment to him. Never had she been so rebellious. Never!

But there was no denying how good it felt. Selling Pleasant Voice to Charging Falcon was unforgivable as far as Maria was concerned!

Pausing in mid-step, Maria looked toward the mountains. Oh, if only she had a way to communicate with Shadow! He would save Pleasant Voice.

Tears once again flooded her eyes when she looked into the distance, toward the parade of warriors following

behind Charging Falcon. They were too far away now for
her to see Pleasant Voice.

Sobbing, she ran toward the house . . .

Shadow stretched and yawned as he walked toward his
horse. He watched his warriors saddle their mounts, then
looked toward the horizon. At first light the desert was
intimate, and somehow Shadow felt the presence of others
as an intrusion this morning. He had just awakened from
another dream of Maria Zamora and he wanted to carry the
thought with him for as long as possible.

He went and saddled his horse, passing the cinch strap
through the rings, then up to the horn, where he would hold
it fast with one hand, a finger of which would also hold the
reins, but he could not concentrate on the business at hand.
The loveliness of the morning touched him, heart and soul,
for the blinding light of full day had not yet supplanted soft
grays of dawn, the uncertain forms and shapes of the cliffs
had not yet become harsh with daylight, and the canyons
were still soft with wells of coolness.

The world was a secret place to each man, and it was this
intimacy that Shadow enjoyed most about the mornings.
Still, he could not help thinking of Maria, and a slight
uneasiness kept creeping into his consciousness whenever
his thoughts strayed to his stronghold.

Had something happened to his people during the night?
Had he been lax by taking time to stop and make camp
instead of traveling on to the stronghold the last evening?
The Spaniard was a man who could not be trusted. And
hadn't Zamora made threats that could have been carried out
even this quickly?

"It is a good day for traveling," said Blue Arrow,
suddenly at Shadow's side. He began readying his horse. "I
shall accompany you to your stronghold, and then I must
return to mine."

"You will bring your people soon for a celebration of
love?" Shadow asked, recalling their talk of celebrations
while at the fireside the previous night.

"Soon," Blue Arrow said.

"That is good." Shadow nodded. "My people need such a diversion once in a while. It is good for the soul!"

While waiting for the rest of his warriors to finish saddling their horses, Shadow comforted his mount. He rode a fine chestnut stallion trained for war. The horse was swift and clever as a snake, so Shadow called him Racer, after the fast-wriggling snake of the same name.

Shadow gazed with admiration at Racer, at his sleek, gleaming haunches, the bunched muscles at the juncture of his shoulder and chest, the ripple of light and shadow on his withers, his arched neck and smooth head, and the character and intelligence of his eyes.

Shadow ran his hands over Racer's withers, feeling the lean, powerful muscles. He had selected him, trained him, and now felt that the horse was his own creation, like his bow guard. Little and compact, he was like an arrow notched to a taut bowstring. A movement of the hand would send him flying swiftly to a mark.

Shadow passed his hand along the stallion's neck, along his back, feeling the tough muscles there. He was proud of his horse . . . the animal of the mountain.

Seeing that his men were ready to travel, Shadow swung himself into his high-cantled Navaho saddle with its seat of stamped leather held together with silver nails and draped with a dyed goatskin. As he broke into a gallop, round silver ornaments jangled on the bridle, ornaments that the Spaniards called *conchas*, or shells.

"*Ei-yei!*" Shadow shouted, raising a fist in the air, laughing with Blue Arrow as he led his horse challengingly alongside his friend's mount. "Ride long! Ride hard!"

As the insides of Shadow's calves touched his horse's barrel, he felt a current run through them and felt at peace with himself . . . at home.

He was a skilled horseman, having spent half of his waking hours on a horse's back. Not even the longest day of riding had ever destroyed his pleasure in the mile-eating lope of his stallion.

His hair lifting from his shoulders as he rode faster, Shadow watched a flock of sheep running down a hillside.

Two goats were leading the sheep and a small dog ran barking alongside. Shadow grew bitter. Spanish ranchers owned enormous tracts of land in the mountains and valleys, land that provided grass for every season. Their sheep grazed over this great domain in flocks of thousands, guided by a shepherd who camped among them with his dog and took his pay in lambs.

The sheep were called *churros* by the Spanish and were wild animals, thin and light with long legs and coarse, smooth wool that was often brown. They sometimes had four horns and were suited to life in the bare rocky hills and dry plains.

The Navaho had their own livestock and land, but had to keep their sheep near them to protect them from the greedy Spaniards. The flock was driven out to graze every day and brought back at night to a corral of boughs in the stronghold.

Shadow had fewer fields and fewer slaves to care for them than the Spanish landowners, but what he had was enough for him. Why couldn't the Spaniards be content with the wealth they had amassed over the years? Surely they never would be happy until all Indians were run out of this land of New Mexico!

Peace seemed to be growing dimmer and dimmer in Shadow's heart. If Zamora stole any of his people again, there would be a war of wars!

With worry mounting inside him, Shadow rode his horse hard through wooded hills and deep canyons, then up into the mountains and through hidden valleys that had at one time been used to hide the sheep the Navaho had taken from Spanish ranches.

Beyond were red-brown cliffs, dull orange bald rock, and yellow sand, leading away to blend into a kind of purplish brown with hazy blue mountains for background. He led Racer to a clump of scrub oak clustered beside a cool stream, a place full of shadow. Looking up, he saw magnificent dark firs growing along the ledges. Up there, the ruddy rock, touched by sunlight, became dull orange and buff with flecks of gold and a golden line where the earth met a cloudless sky.

After Racer had been watered and rested, Shadow urged him upward in a fatiguing, scrambling climb, around a thick growth of jack pine and spruce. He then followed a winding path over a short stretch of broken ground studded with gray, knobbed rocks and thick with oaks whose branches he had to duck. At his left was a shallow gorge split by a tumbling stream.

Racer's hooves made a tiny, soft noise in the sand as Shadow entered a canyon shaped like a long *Y*, with walls so steep and solid a horseman could find no way out without riding from one end to the other.

Fear seized his heart when he did not see any sign of the sentries he had left posted at the stronghold, and Shadow urged his horse into a slow, cautious trot.

He gave Blue Arrow a sideways glance. "It might be best if you drop back and keep watch on the rear," he said flatly. "There may be an ambush. Nothing is right. I smell danger!"

Blue Arrow nodded in compliance, swung his horse around, and rode away. Shadow removed his bow and grabbed an arrow to notch into the string. His eyes were lit with fire as he gazed from place to place, now knowing that something was wrong. His sentries were always posted on the cliffs above the canyons and when they gave the signal, women and children and old people dashed from their homes and hid in holes in the rocks, crouching like rabbits, until it was safe to return to their homes.

Never would his sentries desert their posts!

Unless they . . . had been killed!

He rode onward, now seeing the rim of the canyon that housed his village. Where the walls widened, stone houses could be seen built in the shallow caves. Everywhere Shadow looked he saw death and destruction! Only the sheep seemed to have survived the raid of the previous night, for they grazed peacefully within their fence made of boughs!

Shadow quickly dismounted when he saw people scrambling from hiding places among the rocks. Some had survived!

But how many had not? How many had been stolen and taken away to be used as slaves by the Spaniards in the valley?

Shadow had had reason to be uneasy upon awakening this morning! The raid that he so feared had come about! Had he also been right in suspecting that the Spaniard Zamora had ordered this raid? And how had he found the stronghold so easily? Always before, the raids had been on the innocent Navaho who had chosen to wander away from the stronghold for whatever reasons.

Only one person who could be an enemy would know of the stronghold . . .

"Shadow!" an elderly Pueblo woman said, half stumbling toward him. She reached for him and fell to her knees, grabbing him by the leg, hugging him to her. "Charging Falcon!" she wailed, looking remorsefully up at him. "He came and he killed! My own nephew, Charging Falcon, did this! Oh, what has changed him so, Shadow? He has become someone I don't know!"

Shadow flinched as though shot, yet had he not already known that only Charging Falcon could have done this? Did the Pueblo brother resent him this much?

He patted the woman's wiry gray head. "Little Doe, he is someone no one knows any longer," he said, his voice thick with emotion. He helped Little Doe up from the ground, giving Blue Arrow troubled looks as he dismounted and came to stand beside him.

"Charging Falcon?" Blue Arrow growled, his eyes narrowing as he looked around him at the death and destruction.

"Yes, Charging Falcon," Shadow growled, his jaw tightening. "And he must *pay*."

He looked into the distance. "But first, someone else has to pay," he said smoothly. "You see, Charging Falcon would do this only if he was paid well enough for it. And I know just who would go to such lengths as this to prove a point!"

In his mind's eye he was seeing Maria. Oh, how dearly Señor Zamora was going to pay for doing this to Shadow's beloved people! The Spaniard's daughter would be only *one* way that Shadow would seek vengeance against the greedy, evil Spaniard. Señor Zamora would never see his daughter again after tonight!

Never!

CHAPTER
4

The moon cold and remote overhead, Shadow rode stiffly in his Navaho saddle, hate searing his heart. But tonight the Spanish landowner would be spared his life. He would begin experiencing many agonies upon the rising of the sun! First the loss of his daughter, then that of his sheep, and then . . .

A slow smile flickered along Shadow's sculpted lips. "And then Charging Falcon will pay for what he has done," he whispered.

Shadow's long hair flew wildly in the wind as his chestnut stallion thundered across the yellow sand where the land was studded with solitary peaks, weird and lonesome in the night. He had reclaimed the title of headman; his warrior band had re-formed and now rode behind him under his command.

His eyes wavered as he glanced over at Blue Arrow who rode with him this night, devotedly his friend. The strength of Blue Arrow's warriors would increase the misery of the Spaniard this night.

Then Shadow peered straight ahead with a slight ache in his heart. He had wanted nothing more than to keep his people safe in a hidden canyon. He had built the stronghold in the mountains, wanting to live in peace. The Spaniards had promised peace but they had spoken with forked tongues!

Though he hoped that no violence would be required this night to prove a point to the evil Señor Zamora, he feared retaliation against his men that they did not deserve, and so his warriors were dressed for battle in shirts of the thickest buckskin. Shadow, being a wealthy man, had glued four thicknesses together with sticky gum from the leaves of the wide cactus, sometimes called the prickly pear. The shirts were made in poncho style but sewed up the sides with sleeves to the elbow in one piece with the shirt. They were tight around the neck and laced down the front. The warriors wore moccasins and skin leggings tied with garters.

Their bows were like the ones they used in hunting, but the warriors had put new sinew backing and new bowstrings on their warring equipment. Each man carried fifty arrows tipped with various deadly poisons. One Navaho poison was made with rattlesnake blood and the stingers of ants and bees. Another poison was made of rattlesnake blood mixed with yucca juice and pith from the prickly pear. A third was made from juice from a yucca leaf and charcoal from a tree that had been struck by lightning.

For close-range attacks, which might be required tonight to kill sentries posted around Señor Zamora's dwelling, each Navaho had brought a club with a stone head and wooden handle.

Blue Arrow edged his horse closer to Shadow's. "My friend, you are troubled," he shouted over the thundering of the hooves. "I am troubled also, but what we do tonight is required, to show the Spaniards that we do not sit politely by while they steal our loved ones. We should have retaliated earlier. When Pleasant Voice was abducted it took all that was in me not to burn every Spaniard's house to the ground! Only because I feared for the rest of our people did I not do this. I hoped to get her back by peaceable means . . . by bargaining."

"But you found no one willing to listen to your bargains, did you?" Shadow said bitterly. "The Spaniards want to have full power to decide what will and what will not be bargained for. Pleasant Voice was from *my* stronghold. I have also tried to bargain for her, but no one has listened. No one will admit to having her in their slaves' quarters! That would be admitting too many things, would it not, my friend?"

"Tonight we shall rescue her if she is among Zamora's slaves!" Blue Arrow said, laughing sourly. "If she is there, I shall cut the heart from the Spaniard!"

Shadow looked quickly over at Blue Arrow, seeing the hate in the depths of his eyes. "It is understandable why you should want to do this," he said, his jaw firm. "But we do not want to give cause for the Spaniards to label us as savages. We will kill only those we have to dispose of to get to the slaves' quarters, take our people, then flee into the night! Nothing more, Blue Arrow. It is best that way."

Blue Arrow nodded, then smiled over at Shadow. "But my friend, you failed to mention that someone is to be taken besides our people tonight," he said. "Are you not planning to take your own slave, Shadow? The pretty *señorita* will most surely make an interesting love slave, don't you think?"

The beautiful face of Maria flashed before Shadow's eyes, momentarily unnerving him; then he smiled back at Blue Arrow. "Yes, it is in my plan to abduct her," he said smugly. "You heard me command one of my warriors to ride ahead earlier in the day and stand watch close to Señor Zamora's luxurious dwelling. He will look into window after window as lamplight floods them, to see which one the lovely Spanish lady casts her tiny silhouette against. This will allow him to determine which room is solely hers. Knowing this will make her abduction more simple."

His eyes filmed with desire. "Blue Arrow, she is so pale and slight; she is hardly more than a wisp of grass!" he said thickly. "My friend, she is so lovely that my gut aches with want of her!"

Blue Arrow frowned. He pressed his knees to the sides of his horse, pouring leather into his horse as he rode briskly away from his friend. Shadow watched him, understanding that Blue Arrow did not like to hear a Navaho speak favorably of anyone with the white skin. And Shadow felt guilt for these feelings tormenting him! Surely Maria Zamora would prove unworthy of such feelings.

She would be his love slave.

Nothing more!

Worried about Pleasant Voice, Maria was finding it hard to sleep. She drew her satin comforter up to her chin and looked across the room to peer through her bedroom window, seeing how the moon had descended in the sky. Soon it would be dawn and she had hardly closed her eyes the entire night! But she could not stop worrying about Pleasant Voice! Where was she? Was Charging Falcon mistreating her? Was he possibly even . . . raping her?

A soft cry of grief rose from deep within Maria at such a thought. She turned on her stomach and tried to get comfortable in that position and felt herself finally slowly drifting off to a realm of unconsciousness that might offer a few moments' peace for her—unless she had disturbing dreams of Shadow again.

She had seen her friend roughly carted off by an Indian. Surely Shadow was no less cruel and heartless! She knew that in the past he had stolen slaves, horses, and sheep. That was how he had amassed his fortune.

She turned to her side and lay in a curled-up position, still thinking of Shadow, her troubled thoughts still preventing the lethargy of sleep.

How could she condemn the Navaho warrior for having done what her own father was guilty of doing? Should she even condemn Charging Falcon?

Stealing people and bargaining for their release seemed to be the way of life in this new world. Shadow himself could have been stolen as a child and forced into slavery. If he had been so unfortunate as that, he would never have had the opportunity to be the powerful, wealthy leader he was today.

"I must get some sleep," Maria whispered, willing her mind to clear itself of its muddled thoughts. "I must. I must . . ."

Her breathing became smooth and even as she drifted off

into sleep. She rolled over and lay on her side facing the window, the moonlight filtering through the sheer, lacy curtain and casting a silver sheen on her face. Her dark, thick eyelashes lay against her cheeks; her sultry lips were parted as in her dreams she melted into Shadow's embrace . . .

Then a sound outside on her balcony drew her quickly awake. When she saw a powerful shadow against the French doors, her whole body turned weak and her voice froze in her throat, rendering her so helpless she could not cry out.

The doors eased slowly open. Maria drew the comforter up to her chin and sat up straight, her heart beating so rapidly she could hardly get her breath. But still she could not cry out!

Suddenly the moonbeams caught the intruder square in the face and Maria's heart skipped a beat. The man who had just entered her room was Shadow! Stunned, she stared up at his sharply chiseled masculine features, at his strong and determined face and hard cheekbones. He was tall and muscular and so handsome it made her fear him less than she feared her own reaction to him!

He had moved stealthily toward her through the darkness, but when she recognized him, his movements became as swift as those of a bird in flight! He was suddenly on the bed beside Maria, wrapping a strip of buckskin around her mouth, gagging her. Without saying a single word to her he secured her wrists behind her back while she tried to fight him, mumbling into the foul-tasting fabric that pressed hard into her lips.

Shadow glared down at her. "Do not fight me," he whispered harshly. "You will only make your wrists raw from the rope. Woman, your father is paying for what he has done to my people! Even now he is becoming a man who owns no slaves. They are being set free and returned to the land of the Navaho!"

Maria's eyes widened over the gag. She was suddenly not so concerned about herself as she was Pleasant Voice. Shadow must be told that she had been taken by Charging

Falcon. Perhaps even this moment Charging Falcon was defiling her sweet, innocent body!

She began mumbling harder against the gag in her mouth, pleading with her eyes. Somehow he must be made to understand that Pleasant Voice was in more danger than she was. Though Maria was being abducted, she was not afraid. When she had made brief eye contact with Shadow outside her father's study, she had seen enough gentleness in his eyes to know that he would not harm her. Even now as he bound and gagged her he had done it with a keen gentleness! His eyes, as the moon revealed them to Maria, spoke of much that touched her heart and unleashed her passion!

Sí, though she was being abducted, she did not feel threatened.

But what of Pleasant Voice?

How could Maria make Shadow understand that her struggles to get free were to tell him that Charging Falcon had taken Pleasant Voice as payment for this latest exchange of slaves with her father? When Shadow hadn't seen Pleasant Voice in the slaves' cabins, did he think that she had been sold as a slave to another Spaniard?

In truth Pleasant Voice was a slave to a Pueblo Indian!

Shadow ignored Maria's continued attempts to speak while gagged, but he could not help being entranced by her large, dark, and liquid eyes as she looked up at him, and by her soft and brilliant glossy dark hair as it swirled around her bare pale shoulders.

His nose twitched and he enjoyed the sweet scent of her perfumed body as he peeled the satin comforter away from her. As the moon spilled its silver beams upon her, Shadow felt a burning in his loins as he gazed at her with a hunger never before known to him. Beneath her sheer chemise, cut low to reveal the soft swells of her breasts, he could see her nipples peaked beneath the filmy white fabric, and the dark triangle of hair at the juncture of her thighs.

He had to fight the urge to touch her wondrous curves, to sweep the nightwear away from her, to take her boldly and without delay. But he was going to wait for that pleasure until it could be done slowly and leisurely. He would arouse the same passion in her that he was experiencing, for there was more pleasure in a seduction if the passion was a mutual one between a man and his woman!

Not wanting his warriors to see the wonders of her body, wanting her all to himself, Shadow grabbed a blanket from the foot of the bed and wrapped it around Maria.

"You will come with me peacefully," he whispered. "If your father or mother awakens, it will be necessary to silence them. Thus far all deaths tonight have come silently. The poison on the tips of my warriors' arrows killed swiftly and very quietly. Only the sentries were killed. No one from your dwelling is even aware of the raid. Let us keep it that way, woman. I have much planned for your father that does not include immediate death for him!"

Maria grew numb inside. She gave Shadow a questioning look. Then her head jerked back as he lifted her in his arms and carried her toward the open French doors.

"You might as well accept your fate, Maria," Shadow whispered harshly. "From this night forth you are *mine*, in every sense of the word!"

The thought of being a slave, no matter whose, filled Maria with a sense of foreboding. Did that also mean that she would be his love slave? She had heard tales of such slaves in the Indian strongholds. It was common knowledge that Shadow did not have a wife. Perhaps he had no need of one because he had many women at his beck and call. Was she going to be one of those women?

She was torn between curiosity about how it would feel to be with him sensually, and dread of having such intimacy forced upon her!

Shadow carried her out onto the balcony, set her on her feet, and leaned down into her face. "You will climb down the trellis before me," he flatly ordered. "When you reach the ground, do not run away. Remember that your father and mother have not yet awakened and do not know what is happening here tonight. Should they try to interfere, they will be killed."

Believing Shadow, Maria turned and showed him that her wrists were still tied behind her, showing him how impossible it would be to do as he ordered if her hands weren't free.

His warm fingers brushed against her flesh as he loosened her bonds, then stung her as he grasped hard onto her wrists and turned her back around to face him.

"As long as you behave, you will not be bound," he said harshly.

She mumbled something beneath the gag, wanting to ask him to remove it. If he didn't, she would! With her hands free she was capable of doing many things when he wasn't looking.

"Be quiet!" Shadow hissed, tightening his grip on her wrists, paining her even more.

He released her hands and nudged her closer to the railing, then lifted her and placed her close to the trellis. She motioned toward her gag.

"You cannot remove the gag until we are far from this place," Shadow said, lifting her up by the waist, bodily placing her on the trellis.

Maria held on to the crisscrossed slats of wood on the trellis, moaning when a thorn from the rosebush pierced the tender skin of her thumb. She winced when another thorn caught the fabric of her chemise, then with one hand caught the blanket as it began slipping from her shoulders.

She gave Shadow an annoyed look, wondering how he could expect her to keep hold of the blanket and climb at the same time, *and* not be pierced all over by the thorns. Little did he care, for he was well protected with what appeared to be layers of clothing!

"Go! Now!" Shadow said, swinging a leg over the railing, ready to climb onto the trellis above her.

Afraid that he would push her to the ground, fearing the fall more than the thorns, Maria began climbing clumsily from one wooden slat to another, her bare feet stinging from splinters and thorns. If she survived this night she would be surprised!

Yet there was more at stake tonight than scars caused by thorns and splinters and her father awakening to discover the Navaho in the midst of their abduction. Maria feared being alone with Shadow for any length of time. This was much different from her dreams. This was reality. A reality that was threatening her entire future as a woman. She was going to be imprisoned!

Yet, looking up at Shadow, at his litheness and eyes of fire as he looked over his shoulder at her, she did not feel any true fear of what was happening. Instead, she was filled with a strange sort of excitement and anticipation! These feelings puzzled her. She should hate Shadow. But her feelings for him were unrelated to hatred. His mere presence made her feel foreign to herself . . . like a new person.

Finally reaching the ground, Maria had no choice but to step aside as Shadow climbed down beside her. Again he swept her up in his arms. He held her close as he ran with her to his horse. Placing her in the saddle, then mounting behind her, he waited for the rescued Indians to mount the horses they had stolen from Maria's father.

Then, leaving only a few slain Spaniards behind in the wake of the rescue of the Indian captives and the abduction of Zamora's daughter, the horsemen slipped away into the night, heading toward the mountains that had just begun to be visible in the distance. They rose like great purple masses along the horizon as dawn began to break.

Maria took a last glance at Zamora Manor over her shoulder, finding her parents' bedroom window. As her mother and father peacefully slept, their lives had been changed forever.

Shivering from the cold, the desert wind sharp at this hour of twilight, Pleasant Voice crept closer to the base of the steep rocky cliff that loomed over her like a deep shadow in the night. The campfire had burned down low and all of Charging Falcon's warriors were spread out across the land, asleep on their sheepskin pallets.

Glaring over at Charging Falcon who lay close to her on the ground, snoring loudly as he slept, Pleasant Voice began rubbing the ropes at her wrists on jagged rocks where her hands were tied behind her. Determined to free herself, she moved them back and forth across the rocks, watching around her for any signs of movements. But even the sentries had succumbed to their need to sleep.

If she could cut the rope, she could attempt to escape. Thus far Charging Falcon and his raiders had not approached her or tried to seduce her. Perhaps Charging Falcon knew that rape was the one unpardonable sin that could get him slain if Shadow ever found out. She was a virgin, a highly treasured commodity in the eyes of the unmarried Navaho warriors.

Moreover, she was already spoken for, and she wanted to remain virginal for Blue Arrow. She wanted him to teach her the mysteries of being a woman. She wanted him, only him, to awaken her to all feelings of a woman.

Her body jerked as her wrists separated when the rope snapped. Her dark, slightly slanted eyes widened with surprise and happiness. Then she once again appraised the situation around her. Flexing her hands and rubbing her raw wrists, she studied the warriors as they slept soundly. Her fingers trembled as she raised them to her mouth and worked at the knot that had tied the buckskin gag to her mouth.

And when even that was removed and tossed aside, again she checked to see if it was safe for her to attempt her escape. She knew this wild, treacherous country, for as a child she had been taught the art of survival, as were all Navaho children. To the south were forested canyons that would lead her to Tsegi, the canyon where Shadow had thought that his people would be safe and happy. Had it not been for the deceit of Charging Falcon, that would still be true!

As it was, death and destruction had come at the hands of Charging Falcon, who had gone to the Tsegi and stolen so many of Shadow's people away! Pleasant Voice dreaded finding out the true facts of the extent of his thievery in the night!

What of her own family? How many of them had died in that raid? Was her mother alive? Her father?

None of those captured and placed in the slaves' quarters

with her had known the answers to those questions. They had been whisked away in the dark before even knowing of their own relatives' fate.

Chilled to the bone, dressed only in her buckskin outfit, Pleasant Voice crawled into the gloomy shadow of the cliff, away from the fire. And when she felt that she was safe enough she rose quickly to her feet and began to run toward the horses that were grazing beside a swift gray river that flowed downward and through the valley below.

Weak from fear, yet knowing this was her only chance to escape, Pleasant Voice placed a hand on one horse's side and urged it away from the others. When she was far enough away so as not to cause a commotion, she pulled herself up onto the horse bareback and lay low over its neck, clinging to it, and began riding away in a quiet lope.

Her heartbeat was wild as she rode farther and farther away from the campsite, and when she knew that she was beyond hearing range of the raiders, she thrust her knees into the sides of the horse and held on to its mane as it galloped toward the distant mountains.

Fear ate away at her insides for what she was going to find once she arrived at the stronghold. Would she even be given the chance to arrive? When Charging Falcon discovered her missing, he and his warriors would know exactly which route to take to find her.

"I must get to the stronghold before Charging Falcon finds me!" she said aloud. "I must! Oh, Shadow, please be there! Please!"

CHAPTER
5

The miles stretched out before Maria during the long ride in the hot sun and wind. It was now late afternoon and sandy dust was rising from the trail in clouds. Silent, Maria clung to the blanket around her shoulders to hide her body, which was covered only by a sheer chemise. With the gag now removed from her mouth, she licked her parched lips. She was thirsty from the dust, and this, combined with lack of sleep made her limbs sluggish and her eyelids heavy.

Shadow held her against his hard body as his chestnut stallion continued its journey ahead of the other Navaho warriors, but Maria was now only vaguely aware of his arms around her waist. She was in a sort of daze, oh, so sleepy and tired. Strange, this sadness she felt when she recalled the pain she had seen in Shadow's and Blue Arrow's eyes after the gag was removed and she told them of Pleasant Voice's abduction.

Both had been stunned speechless! When they had not found Pleasant Voice among the slaves at the plantation, they had assumed she was a slave to another Spaniard. Maria had seen their keen disappointment when they realized they had come so close to rescuing her. If Shadow had decided to stage his raid one day earlier, Pleasant Voice would have been rescued along with the other captives, for she had been at the Zamora plantation until only a short while ago.

49

Now who could guess what her fate might be?

Blue Arrow was now traveling with his own warriors, separate from Shadow, searching for Charging Falcon and Pleasant Voice. Shadow had his own mission to carry out: returning the people who had been enslaved by Zamora to their homes at the stronghold, and seeing that all wrongs were made right for them and for those who had survived Charging Falcon's recent raid!

Blinking her eyes, fighting sleep, Maria looked around her, having become disoriented long ago. She was not sure where she was or how she had gotten there. They had traveled through wooded hills and deep canyons, up into the mountains and down among the hidden valleys.

Now they were apparently on the mountain where Shadow had built his stronghold. He had brought her to a high place after a fatiguing, scrambling climb, alleviated by the increasing growth of jack pine and spruce. They were following a winding path under firs; warm golden cliffs, painted with red and purplish brown and luminous shadows, loomed straight ahead.

Shadow led his horse closer to the edge of the cliff where it fell away many hundred feet, stealing Maria's breath with fright as she gazed downward. Below, the world was red in late afternoon sunlight where fierce, narrow canyons were ribboned with shadow and the lesser hills were streaked with opaque purple shadows like deep holes in the world.

Suddenly Shadow led his horse down a slope of bald rock into a valley about three miles square surrounded by moderately high cliffs. Water was seeping out under the rocks. There was shade and peace and coolness with a sweet smell of dampness. Strips of irrigated green formed a backdrop for fields of alfalfa, corn, and beans.

Along the cliff was a long ledge, with the rock above it rising in a concave shell of light reflected under shadow. Maria became aware of little groups of hogans nestled in caves and built on terraces above a small winding river. The hogans, forked-stick pointed houses, their frames covered with fine adobe clay baked as hard as brick, were round, symbolic of the sun. Their black doorways faced the east to greet the rise of Father Sun, one of the most revered of the Navaho deities.

And there were people everywhere, scampering from their houses, their expressions eager as they saw that Shadow had returned. Maria swept her eyes around, seeing no sign of the recent raid anywhere. The Indians had already buried the dead and resumed their lives, aware that life would go on, regardless of what fate handed them!

Shadow clung to Maria's waist and held his chin proudly high as some of his people began running alongside his horse, smiling up at him, shouting a welcome, while others embraced their returned loved ones. He was quite observant of how his people were taking the presence of a white woman. They saw her as the slave that she was. But little did they know that she was his . . . only his!

Riding on to his own dwelling, he dismounted and looped his reins over his saddle horn, then lifted Maria down from the horse and carried her toward his hogan. Maria's knees felt rubbery as Shadow placed her on her feet just outside the door. Aware of being watched by the silent Navaho, she drew her blanket snugly around her shoulders.

"Go inside," Shadow said flatly, gesturing with a hand toward the door. "My dwelling is now also yours. You will not leave except with me."

Maria whirled around and glared up at him. "I am not at all surprised," she hissed. "Whatever you have planned for me will not surprise me. Surely you are as my father has labeled you—a heartless savage!"

A shiver coursed through her as the evening breeze lifted her blanket and seeped through the thin material of her chemise, touching her flesh like probing fingers.

Yet she knew that she was chilled not by the air but for wonder of how his seduction would be.

Would he be gentle or fierce?

She knew there would be a seduction. It was evident that she was to be his love slave. His intention had been clear in the sultriness of his eyes and in the thickness of his voice when he talked to her.

Perhaps she had been wrong to call him a savage. Thus far he had been nothing but gentle!

"Men like your father have labels for everyone," Shadow said, taking Maria by the arm, leading her closer to the door. "Even for you, I am sure."

Maria recalled what her father had called her: one of the fair sex whose only duty was to please! That was as insulting as being called a savage. It had its own sinister implications.

"If you will release my arm I shall do as you say," Maria said, giving Shadow a sideways glance. "Haven't I thus far since you abducted me?"

Her face grew hot with a blush, and she hoped she hadn't given him the idea that she would cooperate with *everything* he wanted her to do. She ached to be held in his arms as a man held a woman when they were in love, but she could not imagine being fully intimate with him. She had not been with a man before. She did not even know how it was done, and she did not want to be taken by force. Ever!

No matter how intrigued she was by Shadow, she would fight every inch of the way against being fully intimate with him!

Shadow moved his hand slowly away from her, branding her with his dark, fathomless eyes as he watched her enter his hogan, her chin held high. He followed her inside, then stood towering over her as she looked around at the way he lived.

Following her wondering stare, Shadow could tell that she was not impressed, but of course she would not be. Though he was a wealthy Navaho, just as her father was a wealthy Spaniard, Shadow did not show off his wealth by displaying elegant furnishings and paintings. Instead, he shared his wealth with his people, feeding and clothing them. Until the recent raid he had seen to their complete safety. That was what life was all about, peace and harmony among his people.

Slipping his quiver off his shoulder, Shadow smiled at a middle-aged woman who came into the stone house carrying a wooden platter of food, which she placed on a sheepskin with the wool side down, spread like a tablecloth beside the fire that burned in a round pit edged with stones near the center of the house.

Nodding a silent thank-you to the lady, he watched her quiet departure, then sat down beside the food and took a wooden bowl and spoon from the platter. Maria would eat when she chose to. At least she would have freedom in that respect!

While keeping an eye on Maria, Shadow ate meat from the backbone of a yearling calf boiled with corn, then tore pieces from a flat, round loaf of rubbery bread and dipped them into the meat juices in his bowl.

Sucking the juice from the bread, he became amused at Maria who still stood like a statue looking around her, seeing where she was to spend her days of imprisonment. It would be nothing like the luxury she was used to in the white man's mansion. Her adjustments were many in her new way of life!

But once he got her settled in, he had many chores to tend to outside his dwelling. He had to reassure his people, and even himself, that no more raids would come to them. Once Charging Falcon was found and dealt with, nobody else, especially those who had followed Charging Falcon in these raids, would dare come to the Tsegi! And the soldiers knew not where the stronghold was!

Yes, life would eventually return to normal. Blue Arrow would bring Pleasant Voice home to her family. Then he and Shadow would join forces and resume their planned vengeance . . .

Maria clung to the blanket, her eyes wide as she absorbed the way Shadow lived, having expected more, since he was known to be wealthy. She ignored the food in front of her, even though her stomach was rumbling with intense hunger, and acquainted herself with this jail cell into which she had been rudely forced.

She accepted the warmth of the fire, the heat of the day having been replaced by the cold dampness of evening. Smoke escaped through a hole in the roof of the stone dwelling. The interior of the house was a circle some twelve feet in diameter with saddles, cooking utensils, and blankets filling much of the space. A loom frame hung near the door; on the other side was an anvil.

The place looked comfortable enough, with sheepskins spread around on the floor. Against the far wall, deep in shadows, was a bed piled high with the same soft coverings. The walls were decorated with buffalo hides and Indian trophies, including mounted heads of buffalo.

The smell of the food wafting upward into Maria's nostrils made her lick her lips hungrily. Her full attention was drawn to Shadow and what he was eating. It looked appetizing, and she could hardly hold back any longer. If she did not eat soon, she might swoon from weakness, and she could not have that. She must keep up her guard at all times so that she would be aware of all movements around her. Though she felt that she could trust Shadow, she feared that one of his people might try to harm her.

She was kin to their most hated enemy, a Spaniard.

Famished, Maria settled down on a sheepskin close to where the platter of food sat tempting her. She seized the bowl and spoon that were surely meant for her. Forgetting her blanket in her hunger, she let it tumble away from her shoulders as she reached out to fill her bowl with food.

Without hesitating, she began scooping the delicious meat mixture into her mouth, sighing with relief when its warmth seemed to melt within her, spreading a calm throughout her that she had not felt since her abduction. Hungrily she ate until the bowl was empty.

Then she became aware of something besides eating and realized that Shadow's eyes were on her, lighting fires along her flesh as his gaze moved over her breasts and downward . . .

Maria followed his eyes slowly downward and she gasped when she discovered that the light from the fire was penetrating her silken garment. She knew he could see the darkness of her nipples and the triangle of crinkly curls at the juncture of her thighs!

She gasped with alarm, dropping the bowl and spoon, drawing the blanket back up around her shoulders. Her face was hot as she looked boldly at Shadow, daring him with her snapping dark eyes.

"You cannot go around dressed that way," Shadow said, pushing his empty bowl away from him. "After you have rested from the long ride, you will be given a blouse and skirt to wear on your next journey."

Maria's eyes widened. "What do you mean, my *next* journey?" she said, her voice drawn and thin.

"In a few hours you will ride with me on another raid against your father," he said smoothly. "You will help in the raid. You will steal many of your father's prized merino sheep!"

Maria paled. "No!" she gasped. "I can't. *You* can't. The king of Spain presented those sheep to my father! They are royal sheep!"

Shadow chuckled as he stretched his arms above his head. "Yes, they are royal sheep," he said, smiling at Maria as he eased his arms down. "Because they are so valuable to your father, stealing them will be a special pleasure for Shadow!"

Maria squirmed uneasily. She clutched the blanket. "But why must I go with you?" she asked softly. "Isn't it enough that you have stolen me away from my father and mother? Why must I steal from them myself? I can't, Shadow! I can't!"

"But you *will*," Shadow said darkly, rising to his feet to look down at her. "And this is only the beginning of my vengeance against your father. He has chosen to break the peace! So be it!"

Maria rose quickly to her feet. She glared up at Shadow, then swung a hand in an effort to slap him. But he was much too quick for her. He grabbed her wrist and held it immobile for a moment, then slowly drew her closer to him, his eyes feasting on her curves as the blanket fell away from her and slid to the floor.

"Never do that again," he growled, his face so close to her he was becoming intoxicated by her perfumed scent, which the dust had not bled away from her flesh. "No woman strikes Shadow without having to pay dearly for the act. Do you . . . want to pay?"

Maria was recalling how her father made his slaves pay for disobedience. With the whip! The disfiguring whip! Perhaps Shadow would use the same sort of device. She could not bear to think of the pain or the disfigurement it would cause her!

But how far could she let him go with her without being disobedient to him again? What if he tried to rape her? Was rape the worse of the two invasions of her body?

While standing so near to Shadow in this way, while his breath was hot on her face, she could hardly control her heartbeat. It was not beating from fear! It was behaving erratically because of desire for Shadow!

Oh, what was she to do?

She was trapped, either way she looked at it! She wanted him, but she feared this want! He was no more than a thief! He was a renegade Indian! How could she be filled with such pleasure when near him? Was it because she had allowed herself to dream of him so often and accept his embraces and passionate kisses in her dreams? Had she been foolish to fantasize about him?

At this moment she wasn't sure about anything, except that she was now feeling the same emotions she had felt while dreaming about him.

She wanted him to kiss her!

She wanted him to hold her!

"Woman, you do not answer me," Shadow said, locking his arms around her waist, drawing her body to his.

"I have forgotten what the question was," Maria said weakly, her whole body quivering from his nearness.

"And why is that?" Shadow said huskily, smiling down at her. His loins were on fire with need, but he exercised restraint at this moment. Besides Maria, there was other business to tend to. He could not place his people second to his hunger of the flesh!

Maria's eyes wavered beneath his steady stare. "I guess I am absentminded because I am so tired," she said, smiling sheepishly up at him, lying.

"Or perhaps it is because I am being forced into slavery," she said more determinedly. "How can one stay alert if one's mind is filled with sadness and fear?"

Shadow lifted his hands to her face and gently placed them on her cheeks. He drew her mouth close to his. "You do not tell the truth when you say you are afraid," he whispered, brushing a soft kiss against her lips. "You know that you have no true reason to be afraid while with me. You have felt how gentle I am to you. You can see in my eyes how I feel about you. Woman, I could never harm you." He tantalized her with another fleeting kiss. "I only want to fill you with peace and love. Allow it without fighting me, woman. Allow it."

His lips were warm and soft, and Maria was startled by the intense passion that his kiss suddenly aroused in her. It was as though a rush of spring wind had blown through her, touching her insides all over with a sweet, pleasant warmth.

Something compelled her to twine her arms about his neck and she knew that what he had said was true: She was not afraid of him! It was as though she had known him for all eternity. Her dreams had made it so! This was an extension of those many nights in her bed when she had drifted into a time and place that had been shared with the man of copper skin and hauntingly dark, commanding eyes!

When his hands eased away from her face and moved down to curve over her breasts through the sheer silk of her chemise, Maria's blood quickened. She moaned against his lips as his fingers kneaded her breasts. She had never felt anything so wonderfully delicious in her life. But the feeling was sending messages of danger to her heart! If she allowed him to kiss and touch her, the seduction would be a reality within a few minutes! She was afraid of that. Not of him, but of what completely surrendering to him would mean!

Total enslavement!

Total permission to do as he wished with her!

Jerking herself free, her heart pounded so hard she felt as though she might faint. As a strange light-headedness swept through her, Maria stepped quickly away from Shadow and tried to cover her breasts with her arms. She breathed hard and her eyes were wild as she looked up at him.

"Please don't," she said in a voice unfamiliar to her. "I . . . can't."

His whole body having been infused with searing need, Shadow looked down at Maria, doubting his sanity for not taking her sexually. She was his slave! He had earned the right to do with her as he wished!

The fact that his people needed his attention, combined with the pleading in Maria's voice and eyes, made him decide that he still wanted a mutual seduction when making love with her.

He would make love *with* her, not *to* her.

He had learned something from the way she had returned his kiss and had clung to him while kissing him: Maria wanted him as much as he wanted her. When the time was ripe for loving, it would be something fierce and exciting!

Sweeping her up into his arms, he ignored her gasp, knowing she was thinking that he had ignored her plea. As he carried her to his bed covered with soft sheepskins, she pushed against his chest, expecting to be seduced in a moment's time. When he laid her down and covered her gently with another sheepskin, then smiled down at her, he was amused to see the puzzled look on her face.

"You sleep now," he said, then turned and walked away from her. "As I said, just ahead there is another journey to be made. Perhaps you will even find the raid exhilarating. Surely within your heart you know the evil your father practices! It was he, not I, who broke the truce between his people and mine!"

Trembling from sensations aroused inside her that felt so wonderfully sweet, yet frightening, Maria ignored Shadow's comments about her father and turned her back to him, snuggling the sheepskin up close to her chin. Breathing hard, trying to sort out her feelings, she stared at the stone wall of the house. Perhaps sleep would come quickly. She hoped she would not dream of Shadow!

She needed to escape from him, if not in real life, at least in her dreams!

*   *   *

Pleasant Voice was limp on the horse, the sweat of her legs blending in with the sweat of the horse, every inch of her aching from the long ride. She was lost! How could she have gotten lost when all along she had been so confident that she was riding on familiar land that would lead her to her home? And of late, she had heard the faint sound of a horse not all that far behind her. Charging Falcon was good at tracking. Surely he was taunting her by letting her travel onward, getting more confused, hungrier, and thirstier.

Surely when she dropped from the horse with exhaustion, he would be there to stand over her and laugh!

What then?

Would he steal her away again?

Or would he kill her?

A distant turtledove mocked her and a high-sailing pendent buzzard sailed overhead, frightening against the darkening sky.

And then a strange hissing noise drew Pleasant Voice's head around with a jerk. She felt a sudden sharp pain in her right shoulder. She cried out as the impact of the arrow piercing her flesh knocked her from the horse to the ground.

Writhing in pain, clutching at the arrow, which had gone clear through her upper shoulder, Pleasant Voice moaned, then flinched and grew silent when the horse that had been following her approached and stopped close beside her.

Perspiration lacing her brow, Pleasant Voice heard the grinding of moccasins in the sand as someone approached. She was not at all surprised when she looked up and saw Charging Falcon staring down at her, clutching a bow.

"Charging Falcon, why?" Pleasant Voice managed in a whisper.

"You could have stayed with Charging Falcon and been treated like a princess," he said thickly. "I grow richer each time I get paid to raid! Soon I shall have my own stronghold filled with happy people under my command! But you could not be patient enough to wait! You know that if you stayed with me you would have no set home for a while. You would be traveling from place to place with the other women as their men fight for survival! That was not good enough for you. Well, woman, you are no longer good enough for me!"

The heat of blood was trickling down Pleasant Voice's skin beneath her buckskin blouse. Her shoulder was on fire with pain. "You will leave me to die?" she sobbed.

"You will die, yes," Charging Falcon said, frowning down at her. "There is no other way. I cannot let you go to Shadow and tell him everything you know of my relationship with Señor Zamora and the many other Spaniards who pay me well for my raids."

He sank down on one knee and touched the arrow that protruded from her flesh. "You can thank me that I did not shoot you with a poison-tipped arrow," he said, his wild, dark hair blowing around his thin face. "You would have suffered much more severely from the poison."

"Shadow will find and kill you for everything you have done," Pleasant Voice said, tears cleaning dust from her face as they streamed across her cheeks. "He does not need me to tell him of your treacherous ways. He knows already, Charging Falcon. If you were smart, you would go into hiding for a long time!"

Charging Falcon touched her brow softly, smoothing his hand across it. He nodded. "Yes, of course you are right," he said somberly. "Charging Falcon is going into hiding. Too bad you won't be there to enjoy the nights with me. We could have been good for each other. I have never met anyone who stirs my insides to wanting as you do." A soft sob tore from the depths of his throat. "Why couldn't you have felt the same? Why did you make it necessary for me to shoot you?"

Though dizzy with pain, Pleasant Voice turned her head so that his hand could not touch her face. "Charging Falcon, you do not know how to love," she whispered. "You are filled with hate! Only hate!"

Charging Falcon rose to his feet and took one last look down at her, then swung himself into his saddle. Without another word to Pleasant Voice, he wheeled his horse around and galloped away.

He was glad that Pleasant Voice could not see the tears silvering the corners of his eyes!

A soft film of blackness began to obscure Pleasant Voice's vision. She drew her legs up close to her chest, crying softly as she escaped into a welcome void of unconsciousness . . .

CHAPTER
6

Maria sat on her horse confidently, riding with high bridle hand and slack rein, comfortable in the high-cantled Navaho saddle over which a dyed goatskin was thrown. The buckskin Indian skirt and blouse accentuated her whiteness; her dark hair billowed across her shoulders as the wind lifted and whipped it.

The world was full of the roar of hooves. The saddles and bridles were heavy with silver and brass as the Navaho leaned forward over their steeds' necks, shrieking "E-e-e-e!" as they traveled across a lush green meadow watered by the streams spiraling down from the mountains.

Armed with bows and arrows, wrapped in striped blankets belted at the waist, and wearing deerskin moccasins reaching to the knees, the Navaho were a determined lot, with Shadow in the lead and Maria riding dutifully at his side.

Shadow had left sentries doubled at their posts in the stronghold to keep a keen watch, while he was away. His party had already ridden for a full day to reach the land on which Zamora's prized merino sheep grazed. Now at last they were there! As far as the eye could see, sheep dotted the land!

Maria knew that her father's sheep were divided for grazing into flocks of one thousand. Each flock was under the care of one lone sheepherder. This herdsman was a simple country man who carried a small gun to shoot coyotes. He lived with his sheep far from the ranch where his only companions were his dogs.

The Navaho knew the ways of the Spaniards, and in the past, as now, found the herdsmen easy prey.

The sheep moved along the land, hundreds of dots of thick, curly wool against the plush green meadow. The herdsman with his staff could be seen in the far distance. Having turned his gaze toward the approaching horsemen, he was now aware of the Navaho raiders.

Maria felt like a traitor to her family as she recognized the elderly man's face. It was Manuel. This particular herdsman was one of her father's favorites. He had come to her father's study often enough for her to know him. If he was murdered by the Navaho she would never forgive herself, yet she had to keep reminding herself that she had no control over what was happening today, or perhaps any other day that lay ahead of her.

She had lost control of her future . . . and her destiny, it seemed.

But she did not feel as devastated by the loss of her freedom as she thought she should. Somehow just being with Shadow, no matter the reason, made her feel important . . . special. Did he not treat her in a special way?

Or was that a scheme of his to lure her into his bed without a fight? Dare she take the test all the way? The next time he kissed and touched her in the marvelous way he knew how, could she shove him away again?

Or did her need of him lie deep within her? Did she want him with all of her soul? Would that part of her allow a mutual seduction when she and Shadow were alone again . . . perhaps even tonight?

She shook such thoughts from her mind, knowing this was not the time to worry about anything other than surviving. She was taking life as it was handed her, one moment at a time, and this was a most dangerous moment. If she tried to escape while Shadow was stealing the sheep, she might be shot in the back by one of his warriors!

Fearing this, she followed Shadow's lead, thrusting her heels into her horse's sides, urging it into a gallop toward the herd of sheep. Her buckskin skirt whipped above her knees; high moccasins hid her calves. Silver buttons on her blouse flashed in the sun, her flying hair picked up the red rays of the sun as it sank, brilliantly orange and large, toward the horizon.

Yelping and shrieking, the Navaho made a path through the flock, scattering the sheep in all directions and driving the sheep dogs wild with confusion.

Maria gasped as she watched Shadow notch an arrow meticulously on his bowstring, draw to the head, and release it toward Manuel, who was struggling to remove his gun from a holster at his right side.

The twang of the string echoed over a great distance.

But to Maria's great surprise, the flight of the arrow carried it above the herdsman's head.

Shadow rode forward and stopped only a few feet away from Manuel, another arrow notched. "The second one will find your heart," he growled, aiming at the herdsman. "My fight is not with you but with the Spaniard who pays you to labor for him. Drop the gun and leave this area peacefully." He nodded toward the barking sheep dogs that were yapping at his heels. "Take your dogs with you."

Maria's horse came to a shuddering halt beside Shadow's. She was relieved that he had not killed Manuel. This showed that Shadow held within his heart some compassion!

But how strange it was to her that he would spare the herdsman because he was innocent of the evils her father had wrought upon the Navaho, yet steal her away even though she, too, was innocent.

This proved something to Maria. Shadow had stolen her away for more than one reason. He wanted her not only to avenge his people but also because he had became enamored with her!

Could his caring for her be genuine?

Seeing his compassion made a ray of hope shine within Maria's heart!

Feeling Manuel's eyes on her, Maria swallowed hard and
then breathed nervously when her eyes met and held his as
he dropped his gun to the ground. She had been recognized.
Had Shadow planned this? Did he want the herdsman to see
her riding side by side with Chief Shadow, the archenemy
of her father?

Her hopes dwindled somewhat about Shadow being
compassionate and sincere. He had probably spared the
herdsman his life only so that the man could go to her father
and tell him where Maria was . . . and with whom!
Manuel would tell her father that she was riding with
Shadow and stealing from her own father! Perhaps her
father would not understand that she was being forced! No
one was holding a gun to her temple while she sat on a horse
beside Shadow!

A cold sense of foreboding swam through Maria, almost
dizzying her with worry about how her father would react to
the news about her.

But surely he would understand that she could never steal
from him! Never!

Not having noticed a spare horse riding with the Navaho,
Maria was stunned when it was brought to Shadow. He
looped the reins over his fingers and handed them to the
herdsman.

"It is a long walk back to the Spaniard's dwelling,"
Shadow said, his jaw tight. "Take the horse. The brand it
carries is the Spaniard's anyway; it was stolen in a raid a
few years back. Ride in peace, old man."

Manuel's mouth dropped open in surprise and tears
sparkled in the corners of his eyes. "*Gracias*," he said,
taking the reins in his bony hands. "*Gracias, amigo*."

The sheep dogs were still yapping around Shadow's feet.
"Take your dogs," he reminded the old shepherd. "Hurry
off with them. Now!"

Manuel mounted the horse bareback and whistled a
command to his dogs. As he rode off, the sheepdogs
followed, now silent.

Maria looked over at Shadow, more puzzled than before
by his kindness, yet did it not point to what she had

surmised? He wanted the herdsman to arrive quickly and safely at the plantation so that he could convey to her father the message about her being a part of the raid. Until now her father could not even be absolutely sure who had cleaned out his slaves' quarters.

Now he would be certain.

Did Shadow expect her father to retaliate? Was he luring her father into a trap? Surely Shadow knew that it would take her father many days to round up enough soldiers to defend himself against the many Navaho warriors who rode with Shadow.

And then there was Blue Arrow! Once he returned from his search for Pleasant Voice, he would join forces with Shadow.

An ache circled Maria's heart. Her father would have no chance to survive if he came up against Shadow. Why hadn't he thought of that when he had sent Charging Falcon to steal from the powerful Navaho leader?

Charging Falcon! That was the answer! Her father would depend on the Pueblo raider to do the dirty business for him again. He would not use Spanish soldiers!

In her heart she felt torn. A part of her wanted Charging Falcon to be caught and sentenced to death by Blue Arrow, yet a part of her feared that without Charging Falcon's strength, her father would be unable to defend himself.

Life was suddenly becoming complicated.

She watched silently as the sheep were rounded up by the warriors. She heard Shadow shouting out commands to his men in his Navaho language, rendering her helpless in her need to understand what he was saying.

Almost listless from mixed-up emotions, Maria sat in the Navaho saddle and watched the sheep being herded toward the mountains.

Her pulse raced when Shadow wheeled his stallion around and began riding toward her, having separated himself from the sheep and his men.

"Come with me," he said, still handing out commands, only this time to Maria. "We shall ride separate from the sheep and my warriors for a short while." His eyes wavered as he reached out to touch her cheek. "Woman, you look bone-weary. We shall rest."

Maria stiffened, not daring to believe that he was truly concerned about her welfare. If he was, he would let her return home where she belonged! "You are so generous, *señor*," she mocked. "First you spared the herdsman's life and that of his dogs; then you gave him a horse on which to travel. Now you want me to believe that you are concerned about my welfare?"

She lifted her chin haughtily. "I cannot be fooled so easily, Shadow," she said. "I understand your reasons for doing all of these things."

Her eyes wavered somewhat. "But I will accept your offer of rest before traveling onward," she murmured. She rubbed her bottom, numb from the long ride. "*Sí*, many parts of my body thank you."

Then fire entered her dark eyes. "But do not try to take payment for your kindness while I am resting," she said flatly. "You see, I *do* understand why you and I are riding separate from your men. You hope that a campfire and the stars will stir something within me into wanting to kiss you again. Well, that won't happen. I loathe you. Do you understand? I loathe you."

Shadow chuckled, his eyes dancing. He rode in a slow trot away from Maria. She shook her head in despair then nudged her horse in the sides with her knees and rode along behind him. She had not been convincing enough when she had said that she loathed Shadow and would not allow him to kiss her again! Even now, with every beat of her heart, she ached for his arms . . . his lips.

The stars and moon would make her defenseless.

Totally!

And Shadow knew this. In the short time since she had become acquainted with him, Maria had learned that he planned and schemed everything out carefully in his mind and in his heart.

He knew what the intimacy of night and its dark shadows could bring.

So did Maria, and the knowing frightened and excited her . . .

Maria ducked her head in shame for feeling excited and filled with anticipation.

The moon was high in the dark heavens, illuminating everything for miles around with its silver light. Riding incessantly onward, followed by his warriors, Blue Arrow was weary from searching for Charging Falcon's hideout and afraid for Pleasant Voice's welfare.

There was a hostile fury in the silence of the night, unnerving Blue Arrow. His dark eyes moved constantly around him, seeing the looming shadows of deep canyons that gashed the high plateaus, and lonesome, steep gullies that wound snakelike through the flat bottomland. Clumps of juniper and piñon pine added their dark shadows to the landscape . . .

A silhouette against the darkness just ahead made Blue Arrow draw a deep, shuddering breath. His heart skipped a beat when he drew closer and saw that it was someone lying lifeless on the ground.

Then he felt as though a knife had pierced his heart when, as he led his horse still closer, he saw that it was Pleasant Voice, an arrow protruding from her shoulder.

"*Ei-yei!*" Blue Arrow cried, sliding quickly from his saddle. He ran to Pleasant Voice and fell to his knees beside her. His hands trembled as he reached for her, but he hesitated to touch her. There was much dried blood on her buckskin blouse around the protruding shaft of the arrow. Her eyes were closed as though in a death sleep. Her breathing was shallow and her lips were pale.

"Pleasant Voice," he said, stifling a sob that lay at the depths of his throat. "I'm here. It is I, Blue Arrow. I'll take you home. You will be all right."

When Blue Arrow's warriors came to stand around him, their eyes filled with sadness at the sight of Pleasant Voice, Blue Arrow began handing out orders. He needed water. He needed clean buckskin, some wet and some dry. He needed a knife that had been run through flames to disinfect it.

Silently cursing Charging Falcon, vowing to find and kill him, Blue Arrow wrapped his fingers around the shaft of the arrow that penetrated clean through Pleasant Voice's body and gritted his teeth as he snapped off the arrowhead on one side of her shoulder and slowly pulled the shaft free, saying thanks to the heavens that it had come out clean, without jagged edges ripping her flesh.

Though Pleasant Voice was unconscious, she cried out with pain when the shaft was yanked from her flesh and fresh streamers of blood began to seep from the open wounds.

Damp strips of buckskin were brought to Blue Arrow. He tore Pleasant Voice's blouse away and began treating the wounds, glad that he would not have to use the knife to cut into her lovely, soft flesh. Since the shaft had come out smoothly, the wound would heal quickly. At least that was in Pleasant Voice's favor!

While another warrior bathed Pleasant Voice's perspiration-laced brow, Blue Arrow wrapped her wounds with buckskin ripped from the tails of several warriors' shirts. He watched her sweet face for any sign that she was emerging from the deep sleep she was in, but saw none. It was imperative that he get her to her dwelling so that she could be warmed and given nourishment to enable her to regain the strength she had lost due to her loss of blood.

"One day soon all of this will be behind you and you will be well again," Blue Arrow whispered, brushing a kiss against Pleasant Voice's cheek. "Blue Arrow will see to it that you will be *ka-bike-hozhoni-bi*, happy evermore. As promised, you will become my wife!"

Pleasant Voice stirred, hearing a voice as though it were being spoken from a deep, sunken cave. She licked her parched lips and slowly opened her eyes, blinking when she saw the handsome face of Blue Arrow leaning down so close to hers. She could still feel the kiss that he had just placed on her cheek!

Sobbing softly, she ran her fingers through the wondrous dark hair that hung to his shoulders. "Blue Arrow," she whispered. "You . . . have come . . ."

* * *

Zamora stood at the window of his study, his powerful hands clasped behind him. He glared from the window, awaiting word as to whether or not Charging Falcon had been found so that he could lead another raid against Shadow. Only Charging Falcon knew where the stronghold was. Without him . . .

A voice broke through the silence in the room. Zamora turned with a start and looked at the Pueblo brave who had only recently been hired to work as his scout and informant. The Indian was clothed in only a breechclout and moccasins. His hair was long and smooth over his shoulders, held in place by a bright red handkerchief wrapped around his brow.

"Well? Did you find Charging Falcon?" Zamora growled, nervously twisting his mustache between his fingers. "You are Pueblo. Surely you know where most Pueblos hide when they are on the run."

"Yes, I am Pueblo," Gray Bone said, nodding. He folded his arms across his bare, hefty chest, his shoulders cording, revealing a very muscled man. "But I am only recently from these parts. It will take time to learn the habits of those you command me to watch. Today I shall go and search for Charging Falcon again. He can't be far."

Zamora leaned his hands, palms down, on his desk and leaned closer to Gray Bone's face. "You are sure you do not know where Shadow has his stronghold?" he asked, his lips quivering from nervousness. "If you did know, I would not need Charging Falcon to point my way there. Did I choose the wrong Indian to put my trust in when I chose you to be my personal scout?"

"How many did you ask before you found Gray Bone?" the scout taunted, knowing that most Indians would not work hand in hand with this greedy Spaniard. Gray Bone did so only to gain a small portion of wealth so that his children could be more comfortable in life.

In truth, he hated every minute that he spent deceiving the people of his own skin coloring! He did not call his choice greed. He called it survival!

Zamora clamped his lips shut. He was surprised that this Indian was so smart. *Sí*, he *had* had trouble getting Indians to cooperate with him. Charging Falcon had been willing because of his dislike for Shadow. And Charging Falcon's warriors had cooperated out of loyalty to their leader.

He turned and went back to the window. Times were becoming harder in these parts. If something wasn't done quickly, the Spanish people would have to give their land back to the rich, land-hungry Navaho!

Sí, something *must* be done!

"Send for one of my guards, Gray Bone," Zamora growled. "I'm tired of waiting for Charging Falcon. I want as many soldiers rounded up as possible. I will find Shadow's stronghold! I will lead the attack myself!"

"I don't think that is wise," Manuel said suddenly from behind him, stepping into the room in a slow gait, weary from the long ride.

Paling, recognizing his main herdsman's voice and knowing that he should not have deserted his flock of sheep for any reason, Zamora turned with a start and gazed in wonder at Manuel whose face was covered with dust and perspiration.

"Why are you here?" he gasped. "Why aren't you tending to my prized merino sheep?"

"Shadow came and took them from me," Manuel said, lowering his head in shame. "It was something I had no control over. There were many warriors. There was only me and my dogs."

"*Caramba*!" Zamora said, settling down into the chair behind his desk, hanging his head in his hands.

"I heard you say something about leading an attack against Shadow," Manuel said, stepping up closer to the desk. "As I said, that wouldn't be wise. It must be done more subtly. Señor Zamora, your daughter's life lies in balance."

Zamora raised his eyes slowly, scarcely breathing. "What do you mean, my daughter?" he said, his voice thin and drawn. "How do you know she is missing? How do you know she is with Shadow? She *is*, isn't she? No one else would be brazen enough to come in the middle of the night into my house and take her as he did. But how do you know this, Manuel?"

"Señor Zamora, Maria was riding with Shadow when the Navaho headman came and took your sheep from me," Manuel said, gulping hard when he saw anger flare suddenly in his *patrón*'s eyes. "That is how I know. I saw her with Shadow."

Zamora's burliest guard, brought from his hometown of Valencia, stepped into the room, his wiry dark hair hanging to his shoulders. A bright crimson velveteen shirt worn with skintight velveteen breeches shone in the sun that poured through the windows at his left side.

"William, send for many soldiers," Zamora said. "We have much to do. First I will try to bargain for my daughter's release. If that doesn't work we must find her and bring her home."

"Rounding up enough soldiers for what you are wanting could take days," William said, flexing his muscles as he leaned down against the desk.

Zamora glared up at him. "Do as I tell you," he said hotly. "Whatever . . . however long it takes, do it! Maria is with that bastard Shadow! She's probably already been raped. He *is* a *savage*, you know!"

"*Sí, señor*," William said, his dark eyes wavering. "I will get to it. Pronto."

"*Gracias, gracias*," Zamora said, nodding. In his mind's eye he was seeing Maria defenseless, frightened, hungry, and so many other things that tore at his very gut.

More than likely she *had* been raped. Surely that savage had taken advantage of her sweet innocence, her sultry loveliness? Would she ever be the same again, even if she was found and brought back to her home? Had the damn Navaho headman ruined her for eternity?

Zamora withdrew a pistol from his desk drawer and shifted it from one hand to the other, contemplating how he would use it . . .

CHAPTER
7

Spindly cottonwoods rattled their leaves over the stream, sounding like rain in the night. The moon was high. The grass, on which a sheepskin blanket had been spread for Maria to sit upon, was deep and soft. A lazy fire burned within a protective wall of rock on a patch of cleared ground over which a rabbit simmered on a spit, growing golden from its slow roasting. The evening breeze had not become cool because of the protective high, steep walls of a canyon towering overhead on both sides of the campsite.

Maria looked over at Shadow, who seemed absorbed in his own thoughts, having barely glanced her way since he had killed and prepared the rabbit for cooking. She shivered at the thought of what easy prey the rabbit had been for Shadow. Would she be the same? Was she already?

She turned her eyes away, not wanting to think about how Shadow had frightened the rabbit from its burrow after it had most surely been settled in for a peaceful night of sleep. She did not want to recall how he had bludgeoned the rabbit to death with a curved wooden club, or of how quickly he had skinned it.

But she could not deny how delicious the rabbit smelled and how hungry she was for it. How it was killed should not matter. Eating it was just another part of her survival, a survival that had become more and more tenuous as the hours passed . . .

A warm hand on her cheek made Maria turn with a start. She swallowed hard as she looked up into eyes darker than all midnights, and at a strong, determined face with hard cheekbones, oh, so sharply chiseled and handsome!

Then her gaze lowered and she became aware that Shadow had removed his buckskin shirt, revealing to her the smooth, wide, lean, and muscular expanse of his naked hairless chest.

She looked up at him again, questioning him with her eyes, numb from what she knew would happen in the next moment. Hadn't she known this was part of his plan? Why, oh, why couldn't she fight him? She should show some sort of protest, yet she could not. A side of her that she had never known before setting eyes upon him would not allow her to deny him.

Her pulse raced as his face drew closer and he urged hers nearer to his by the pressure of his thumb and forefinger on her flesh. Her eyes became wild, her knees weak. She did not truly want to feel this need that ate away at her heart for him, but she was becoming consumed by it. Never in her life had she been rendered so helpless.

A sensual tremor coursed through Maria at the first contact of his mouth on her lips. A throaty moan frightened her when it rose from deep inside her. The pleasure of his kiss was so profound and the touch of his hands, now cupping her breasts through the soft buckskin blouse, was so beautifully sweet that the emotion she felt was almost indefinable. Never in her wildest dreams had she thought any man could steal away her ability to think.

But it was happening. As she let Shadow slip his hands beneath her blouse and touch her bare breasts, she knew that anything was possible while she was with him.

She shuddered and let him spread her out on the ground beneath him with the pressure of his lips still kissing and drugging her. One of his hands strayed lower and removed her skirt, but she was too far beyond coherent thought to deny him even this. Her whole body had turned into a wild pulse beat. Delicious warm spirals of rapture were flooding her senses; she wanted everything this man was offering her tonight. At this moment he was not her enemy.

Oh, surely she was in love, for nothing else could feel so beautiful as this!

Wanting to touch him, having viewed him from afar for so long, and not truly believing that she was actually with him in such a way, Maria raked her fingernails softly across his muscled chest, stopping at his nipples. She teasingly, slowly circled one nipple and then the other with her fingernails, realizing that in some way she was returning the pleasure she was receiving, for Shadow moaned sensually against her lips as he kissed her.

Feeling daring, enjoying the thought of causing him to feel the same as she, euphoric and happy beyond what she thought possible, Maria trailed her hands lower, feeling his stomach quiver as she pressed her fingers over him there.

Her heart pounded as she came to the waistband of his buckskin breeches. She had always wondered about the mysteries of a man, and this was the first time she had been with one in such a way. Her hand trembled as she inserted it below the waistband, slid it over the smooth material of the buckskin, then felt the strength of his manhood as it strained against his breeches, fully enlarged, almost frightening to her in its dimensions.

She gasped lightly as one of his hands clasped hers and held her fingers against his hardness. His mouth left her lips. He looked down at her with eyes filled with dark passion as he urged her hand to move over his hardness, guiding her in a slow, sensual motion. Her face flamed with heated embarrassment as he began to gyrate his body against her clutching hand, his breathing becoming first rapid, then erratic.

Maria sucked in a wild breath when suddenly his free hand sought and found the damp patch between her thighs and began caressing her in return. What she had thought was so pleasurable before seemed small in comparison to what his skillful fingers were arousing in her now. It was as though she was becoming awakened for the first time in her life. The bliss of his caress was giving her a wild sort of peace, melting her insides into something delicious!

But it was also suddenly frightening to Maria. She knew that she was no longer in control of her mind. She had already lost control of her destiny, she could not allow Shadow to own the even most secret part of her!

Jerking free, rudely aware of being nude from the waist down, Maria grabbed her skirt and hid the most private part of herself behind it. "I can't do this," she said, her voice thin and strained. "Please don't force me to. Never have I let a man do what you are doing to me! Never have I been so . . . so wanton as to desire it. I don't know what came over me. I am a . . . shameless hussy!"

Shadow ignored her and eased her skirt from her arms. In one swift movement he drew her blouse over her head, baring her full nudity to him now. Before she could fight him off, Shadow cupped her breasts, lowered his head, and flicked his tongue over a nipple until it grew hard.

Maria threw her head back in ecstasy and gritted her teeth, again fighting the need building up inside her. When his tongue began evoking a trail of fire downward from her breasts, across her quivering stomach, and even lower, she was lost to the ecstasy of the moment. She twined her fingers through his long hair and drew his mouth closer to the core of her womanhood as his tongue and lips caressed her. In the farthest recesses of her mind she knew that this was wrong, was most surely the ultimate intimacy between a man and a woman, but now that she had been introduced into this way of making love, she could not back away from it.

Thrashing her head, licking her lips, her fingers biting into the flesh of Shadow's shoulders, Maria felt the warmth of pleasure spreading. She drew a ragged breath when the smoldering ecstasy reached its peak inside her, spilling over, like the effervescent foam of a waterfall touching her all over.

Shadow stifled her cry of pleasure as he swept his body upward and sealed her lips with a searing, hungry kiss while he pushed his breeches down the full length of his lean, powerful legs. She framed his face between her hands, returning his kiss, accepting his tongue as it eased between her lips and entered the sweet recesses of her mouth.

Maria was only vaguely aware of Shadow's bare knee nudging her thighs apart, but became strangely thrilled when she felt the hardness of his manhood suddenly there, softly probing where his tongue and lips had just pleasured her so wonderfully. She moaned as his kiss deepened and his hands kneaded her breasts, unknowingly opening herself to him as his hardness moved into her, slowly . . . beautifully . . .

Then one maddening plunge of his manhood made a fierce pain reach into Maria's euphoric state. Her eyes widened and she cried out, but his mouth was again there, silencing her with a deep kiss, causing the pain to be quickly forgotten, magically changing it to something blissful.

She twined her arms around his neck and arched her body upward and accepted his eager thrusts, her pelvic movements matching his. The way he filled her with his hardness and the way it reached so far within her made her breathless with ecstasy. She let the incredible sweetness engulf her.

Shadow was becoming wild with the need of fulfillment, yet he was enjoying, also, the awakening of a woman in his arms, teaching her the ways of loving. He had hoped that Maria was virginal, and having found that she was made him love her even more. He had been attracted to her loveliness and her innocence. That he was the first man to lie with her was almost more than he could have asked for. He would now make sure that no other man ever touched her. He alone would teach her every way of making love. He would make her want it. She would forget the other world. She would live with the Navaho and become Navaho in thought, deed, and action. She would accept her new life because of her need of him. She had already proved that tonight.

Ah, how fiercely, how wildly she loved! Never had shadow owned a love slave who could compare with Maria in her ability to learn the ways of the body so quickly, so passionately. . . .

Scooping Maria fully into his arms, reveling in the touch of her breasts pressed into his bare chest, Shadow kissed her delicately tapered neck, then brushed a soft kiss across her ear, evoking a soft sigh from deep within her.

His body moved rhythmically, his thrusts even and deliberate now, ready to achieve that ultimate goal, wanting her to share it with him.

He curled his fingers through her long, fine hair and drew her lips into his, crushing her mouth with a feverish urgency. As their bodies tangled, the stars twinkling like a thousand eyes overhead, the peak of excitement reached, they took flight together.

Their bodies strained and shook, their mouths were on fire with burning kisses.

And then they lay in each other's arms, shaken and breathless, yet Shadow could not keep his hands from Maria's body. Slowly he caressed her, beginning at her breasts, moving downward across her tummy, then to the juncture of her thighs, where the proof of what they had shared lay like spirals of white spun silk across her body.

Smoothing the wetness away with his hands, Shadow began arousing Maria again with his fingers, glad to see her face take on a radiant glow as she closed her eyes and parted her delicate lips. He dipped his lips to a breast and nibbled on a nipple, then traced a path downward with his tongue until once again he was giving her pleasure that made her thrash her head, her hair perspiration dampened at the brows and temples.

Maria clenched her hands into tight fists, in wonder of how her body continued to be awakened by Shadow's skills at lovemaking. His mouth was searing her. She felt the nerves in her body tightening and then an onslaught of passion was once more enslaving her as her body shook and trembled. She accepted Shadow as he moved to lie above her, cradling her close as he entered her with his pulsing manhood. Again they rocked and swayed and kissed.

Then again Maria felt her body thrilling and knew that

Shadow was experiencing the same, for his body was a mass of tremors as he thrust more fiercely into her, his mouth now at the hollow of her throat, emitting a husky groan against it.

Totally at peace with herself, Maria laid her cheek on Shadow's shoulder and let her hands stray along the corded muscles of his back, then down to his buttocks. She dared to move her fingers around and was surprised to find his manhood small in comparison to what it had been earlier.

But then, everything that had happened this night within his arms had been a surprise to her. She had given herself totally to Shadow not once tonight, but twice! He had taken her to paradise many times! She should feel ashamed but she didn't.

It had all felt so right . . . so wonderful!

Shadow eased away from Maria and kissed her brow as he swept her hair back from her face. "Woman, are you glad you quit fighting what your body was hungering for?" he asked huskily, his eyes dark and passion-filled. "Did you enjoy being awakened into ways of a woman? Is Shadow a good teacher?"

Maria blinked nervously, feeling suddenly awkward. Strange how being asked to talk about it embarrassed her more than actually doing it. But in the throes of ecstasy's madness there was no thought or doubt. Shadow had played her body like a fine instrument, and she had responded in every way.

Sweeping up the buckskin skirt and dress, Maria hurriedly wriggled into them, not knowing how to answer Shadow's intimate questions. As she watched him slip his buckskin breeches up his wonderful body, she was thrust back into the real world, reminded of where she was, with whom, and why. She had, in a sense, betrayed her family twice in one day, first when she had ridden along with Shadow to steal her father's prized merino sheep, and now, when she had given herself to her father's enemy with hardly a fight.

Still, shame did not enter her heart, only anger at herself for not feeling shame!

"You are a skilled teacher," she finally said, glaring at Shadow. "But of course you must be quite practiced. *Señor*, just how many love slaves do you have at your stronghold who are there to satisfy your every whim, to pleasure you?"

Half smiling, Shadow gave Maria a sideways glance as he leaned over the rabbit, which was now golden brown. He tore off a leg, sat down close to the fire, peeled off a piece of meat with his white, straight teeth, and began to chew.

"Do you prefer not to answer me?" Maria said, eyeing the meat hungrily. "Are you afraid your answer would insult me because I became charmed by you so easily?"

"Eat," Shadow said motioning toward the rabbit with a flick of a wrist. "Food will do you more good than the answers you are trying to pull from me."

"Ha!" Maria said, her eyes dancing. "Your refusal to answer me is answer enough. You do have many slaves, don't you? I shall be just another love slave, worthless in every way to you except while being held in your arms."

"Eat!" Shadow flatly ordered, his jaw tight. "Then you must sleep. Tomorrow will be another tiring day for you. I have planned another raid against your father and you are to be a part of it. Tomorrow we steal his horses!"

Maria was taken aback. She paled at his words, his statement of fact that was so cold and calculating. She took a shaky step away from him, nervously running her fingers through her hair. "What?" she gasped, paling. "What did you say?"

Shadow threw the stripped bone over his shoulder and plucked the other leg from the rabbit. He rose to his feet and went to Maria and placed it beneath her nose so that she could smell its tantalizing aroma.

Then he placed it to her lips. "I said it is time to eat," he said dryly. He placed a hand behind her head and forced her mouth against the meat. "Now!"

Confused by his sudden roughness, Maria looked up at him wildly, her lips hurting from the pressure of the rabbit's leg there, almost cutting into her flesh. Anger raged inside her and she used the only weapon available to her. She dug her fingernails into the flesh of his chest and tore a path downward.

When Shadow jumped away from her, emitting a groan of pain, his eyes lit with fire, Maria covered her mouth with a hand, suddenly afraid. In the moonlight she could see tiny streamers of blood rolling down his stomach from the wounds she had inflicted, and a strange remorse tore through her for having inflicted them on his lovely bronze flesh.

Then her breath was snatched away when Shadow pounced on her, wrestling her to the ground. His eyes were two pools of black as he glared down at her while holding her wrists to the ground. She expected him to hit her, but his lips were suddenly crushing her mouth with a wild, savage kiss, his body bold and hard as it pinioned her to the ground.

Maria could feel Shadow's arousal against her thigh. She was hardly aware of when he lifted her skirt and lowered his breeches to his ankles, conscious only of their bodies locking and swaying together.

Soft sobs tore from deep within Maria's throat as she locked her ankles about Shadow's waist, meeting his every thrust with abandon. . . .

Blue Arrow held Pleasant Voice limply in his arms. He was glad that sometime back on the trail she had drifted into sleep. It was an escape from the pain of her wounds, but would she ever be able to forget the trauma of being shot and left alone to die? When Charging Falcon was found, he would die a slow, lingering death! Pleasant Voice would be avenged!

Soft ripplings of orange were evident in the sky as the early morning sun rose behind the boulders of the stronghold. Peace lay over the village of the Navaho. The only signs of life were the soft spirals of smoke emerging from the chimneys of the stone houses nestled along the river and within the caves.

Blue Arrow rode along the ledge with Pleasant Voice cradled close to him in the saddle until he reached her dwelling. Her mother and father had survived Charging Falcon's raid, but they did not feel fortunate. They lost much of their purpose in life when Pleasant Voice was abducted many months ago. She was their only child, their pride and joy. When they discovered that she was being brought to them today they would be happy that she was alive but tormented when they discovered that she was not well.

Blue Arrow hoped their love and medicinal powers would make her fight off the infection brought on by the arrow. Her wound was festering and she now had a raging fever!

Drawing his reins tight and looping them over his pommel, Blue Arrow slowly dismounted, still holding Pleasant Voice in his arms. The hoofbeats of his horse had alerted her parents to his arrival, and they ran from their house, eyes wide and tear-filled when they saw Pleasant Voice, her face blotched red with fever and her eyes closed.

"Daughter!" her mother cried, running to her. "Oh, daughter!"

Blue Arrow relinquished his hold on Pleasant Voice as her father took her into his own arms and looked down at her, sobbing. Blue Arrow wiped a tear from his own eyes as he watched Pleasant Voice being carried away from him and into her parents' stone house.

When her father returned outside and embraced Blue Arrow, that was all the thanks that was needed. He moved into the dwelling, sat down beside the fire, and began to explain exactly what had happened to his beloved, his eyes wavering as he looked toward Pleasant Voice, who lay snugly on her bed. Her mother removed the soiled clothes, revealing a body marred by the bloody wound.

Yes, he would make Charging Falcon pay. Many times over he would make Charging Falcon pay. He would receive much pleasure from listening to Charging Falcon beg for mercy when he had given none to Pleasant Voice. . . .

CHAPTER
8

Above, the sky gleamed with new morning light. Shadow stirred in his sleep, throwing an arm limply over Maria who lay beneath the sheepskin blanket with him. Feeling her so close, so desirable, made Shadow awaken to a feeling of expectation. He leaned up on an elbow and looked down at Maria, whose dark lashes lay thick on her cheeks and whose lips were seductively parted as she slept peacefully.

His fingers trembling, Shadow slipped his hand up inside her blouse and cupped a breast, causing his loins to begin a slow, nagging ache. His mind was filled with remembrances of the past evening. It would be torture to wait another full day before holding her and caressing her again as he so desired.

But the waiting would enhance the pleasure. That was one reason he had learned to value the use of restraint. The worth of anything was increased in waiting, even the loving of a woman.

Bending his head toward Maria, Shadow took a brief taste of her flesh, letting his tongue flick across her stiffened nipple. Then he moved away from her and stood over the gray ashes of the campfire and began reciting his dawn prayer. Though his people had been traumatized by the recent raid, he . . . *they* had much to be grateful for. They always learned from their misfortunes.

So did the ones responsible for the misfortunes, *always*. . . .

The deep resonance of Shadow's voice awakened Maria. Still comfortably curled beneath a sheepskin blanket, she rubbed sleep from her eyes and looked toward Shadow. He had slept in his buckskin breeches and moccasins, just as she had slept in her full attire, to ward off the chill of the night.

Rising up on one elbow, Maria was touched deeply by Shadow who was praying, looking toward the heavens. This made him look like anything but the savage that some called him. He seemed to be a man of many emotions and capacities.

To Maria, he was unique . . . fascinating.

A strange, slightly painful heat between her thighs and in her breasts made Maria recall what she had shared with Shadow the previous evening. Just thinking about it made her face flame with embarrassment. She had been with him in the most intimate way! More than once her body had responded with sheer abandon to every nuance of his lovemaking. She had surrendered fully to him!

Her hands went to her breasts and cupped them through the thin buckskin. Never had she thought to have such feeling in her breasts. They had come to life at the mere touch of Shadow's powerful hands.

Today they seemed swollen . . . hot. . . .

Shadow turned suddenly toward her, taking Maria off-guard. Her hands dropped from her breasts as though they were hot coals as she gave Shadow an awkward smile.

"You are awake," he said, moving to her to offer her a hand. "That is good. It is time to prepare for the arrival of my warriors, those who do not continue to the stronghold with the sheep. We will go and steal your father's horses; then we will return to my stronghold. My people will have cause to celebrate."

Maria took Shadow's hand and moved to her feet, stunned by what he expected of her. She had just awakened and he was going to make her leave so quickly? "I cannot believe that first you force me to accompany you to steal my father's sheep and now also his *horses*? And what about food?" she gasped. "I am *hungry*!"

Her gaze swept over her wrinkled attire and her fingers went to her disheveled hair. She was in need of a bath! She was thirsty!

She glanced over at the stream that looked so inviting, then looked up at Shadow with pleading in her eyes. "At least let me splash some water on my face," she said softly. "I never go a full day without a bath and . . . and it's now been . . ."

Shadow's eyes grew intense, his jaw became set. Grabbing Maria by a hand, he led her to her horse. "Ready the saddle," he said, thrusting a saddle blanket into her arms. "Then we leave. The luxury of a bath comes later when you are back at my stronghold! Not before."

Maria placed her hand over her stomach when it emitted a low, grating growl. She glared up at Shadow. "I am to go without a bath *and* without food, I presume," she said hotly. "Do you starve all of your slaves? That's what I am to you, isn't it? A slave?" Her eyes wavered. "A *love* slave, no less."

Shadow ignored her reference to being a slave because deep within him, where his desires were formed, he felt as though he was the one who was enslaved, not Maria. Having her totally was an obsession now. Hunger for her was always pressing in on him, as if he were being lashed by a whip over and over again! He had never before loved so deeply that it pained him.

Never!

Until now . . .

"You will not starve," he finally said, moving to the bank of the stream. He leaned over and broke off the furry brown spikes of several tall cattails. Taking them to Maria, he placed one in her hand and showed her how to peel it.

"It is good," Shadow explained, peeling one for himself. "It is nourishing. Eat well. We will not eat again until we return to my stronghold. It is not best to be away any longer than necessary to steal the horses today."

Maria's nose curled up with distaste as she crunched her

teeth into the cattail. It seemed so primitive to eat this wild plant that she had always looked upon as a beautiful weed that grew on the moist banks of rivers and streams.

Yet, to avoid starving she was discovering that she would eat anything.

Well, perhaps . . .

Maria turned with a fright when she heard the thunder of approaching horses. She gave Shadow a questioning glance.

"My warriors," Shadow said nonchalantly. He pitched the remainder of the cattails to the ground and hurriedly readied his horse for travel, scowling at Maria who had yet to saddle her horse.

Then his frown eased as she began scurrying around. He laughed to himself when she groaned as she placed the heavy Navaho saddle on the horse. His eyes watched and savored each of her movements . . . how her hips swayed as she walked, how her chest heaved when she breathed, causing her breasts to become even more defined beneath the thin buckskin of her Navaho blouse, and how her thighs were revealed to him as she placed a moccasined foot in the stirrup and swung herself up into the saddle.

Maria felt Shadow watching her and felt a blush rising to her cheeks when she saw what he was looking at. As she had swung herself up into the saddle, the motion had momentarily hiked her skirt most indecently above her knees.

She realized that he had seen that part of her anatomy before, had even caressed and kissed her there, sending her into a whirlwind of mindless bliss, but this was now and she was very much aware of what was happening. Had it not been for his kisses and caresses the previous evening, perhaps she would have had more control over what he had seen and touched. At least she was in charge of her life at this moment!

Pulling her skirt down, giving Shadow an annoyed stare, Maria cringed when he laughed throatily, for she suspected that his thoughts were also straying to last night. When he looked at her now, was he recalling the most intimate moments of their lovemaking?

Oh, for her to think of last night was to create so many tumultuous feelings inside her. There was no denying the thrill that coursed through her when she let her mind dwell on the wonders of it.

The horses were now so close that the riders could be recognized. Maria looked past Shadow, growing anxious when she saw that the lead rider was Blue Arrow! Surely he had news of Pleasant Voice or he wouldn't have joined Shadow's warriors with his own, to be a part of this raid today!

If only the news was good . . .

Blue Arrow, his copper face framed by long black hair held back from his brow with a scarlet handkerchief and with a disfiguring scar on his cheek, wheeled his horse to a stop next to Shadow's stallion. A colorful blanket had been drawn over his head, poncho style, and held in place at his waist by a belt of round silver medallions. His buckskin breeches were skintight with silver buttons shining down the sides of both legs. The breeches were tucked down inside his knee-high moccasins.

"It is good to see you again, brother," Shadow said, extending a hand to Blue Arrow, clasping his. "What news do you bring of Pleasant Voice? Did you find her? Did you find and kill Charging Falcon?"

Blue Arrow clasped harder onto Shadow's hand, his eyes wavering. "The news is good and bad," he said thickly. "It is good that I have returned Pleasant Voice to her parents. It is bad that I found her unconscious with an arrow piercing her tender flesh!"

Maria felt faint. She teetered in the saddle, fighting back the urge to retch. Placing a hand on her brow, she swallowed hard, not wanting to envision her special friend perhaps near death. If Pleasant Voice died, Maria's father would be responsible!

Maria was beginning to feel a quiet loathing for her father, the man she had been taught to respect so much. Little by little her respect was lessening.

"*E-do-ta*! No!" Shadow said, his voice drawn. "Will she be all right? Will she live?"

"Only time will tell," Blue Arrow said, lowering his eyes. Then once again he looked at Shadow. "When you return, to be with your people during the ceremony, a Singer will be sent into Pleasant Voice's dwelling. The Singer will win the help of the gods. He will sing many different songs and his fingers will paint many drawings in sand. Yes, surely in time Pleasant Voice will be well again. To ensure this, everything possible is being done for her!"

Shadow nodded. "That is good," he said hoarsely. "That is good." He released his friend's hand and placed his hand on Blue Arrow's shoulder. "You will marry her?"

"That is my plan," Blue Arrow said softly, his eyes shifting to Maria. He smiled over at her, then leaned closer to Shadow. "My brother," he said in no more than a whisper. "How was your night with the white woman? Some say they have more fire while loving than our women do. Is that so?"

Shadow gave Maria a half-glance over his shoulder, seeing how quickly she looked away from him, surely realizing that she was being spoken about.

Then he turned his eyes back to Blue Arrow. "There is much about her that intrigues me." That was all he would admit.

Shadow was again thinking of Pleasant Voice. His fingers dug into the flesh of his friend's shoulder. "You spoke of an arrow in Pleasant Voice," he said, his eyes two sparks of fire. "Was it Charging Falcon's?"

"None other," Blue Arrow growled.

"And were you able to find and kill him?"

"After shooting Pleasant Voice he knew enough to go into hiding. It may take a while to flush him out, Shadow."

"No matter how long it takes, once he is found, he will wish that he had never become my enemy!"

"Nor mine," Blue Arrow grumbled. "Nor mine!"

Shadow turned to face Maria. "It is time to go," he ordered. "Ride alongside me as before! It is only right that you be a part of the vengeance again against your father! That makes the vengeance much sweeter!"

Maria groaned, then pressed her knees into the sides of the horse and galloped away beside Shadow. Dread filled her for what lay ahead. First her father's prized sheep . . . now his horses! Would Shadow be able to find the hiding place of her father's prized Arabian horses?

She smiled wickedly. Perhaps she should tell Shadow where the Arabian horses were. Again she thought of Pleasant Voice and what had happened to her because her father had used her as payment to Charging Falcon for the raid against Shadow!

Wouldn't it serve her father right to suffer just a mite himself? He could acquire more horses. *No* one could set Pleasant Voice's life right again!

Fair was only fair!

Sí, perhaps she *would* lead Shadow to the Arabian horses. Her father would never know that she was responsible.

Edging her horse closer to Shadow, she twined her fingers through her tangled hair, smoothing it over her shoulders. "Shadow, there's something you might like to know . . ." she began, feeling wicked clean through for what she was about to do.

But her father deserved it.

Perhaps even worse!

The day had been long and grueling, but the Arabian horses had been successfully taken from their hiding place with not even one casualty. The Navaho warriors had sneaked up on the guards as though their feet were the paws of panthers and had rendered the guards helpless with only a slight blow to their heads. While the guards were being tied and gagged, the horses led away, Maria had watched, feeling torn by her decision to direct Shadow to them. She had betrayed her father, but at the same time she had strengthened the bond between herself and Shadow. He seemed to be looking at her differently because of her decision to tell him about the horses. It was as though he was dismayed at her!

Maria was dismayed at . . . herself. . . .

The sky was a brilliant orange along the horizon as the
sun crept lower, rimming the mountain peaks and canyon
bluffs with glorious color. Maria, limp with exhaustion,
rode relentlessly onward beside Shadow. She licked her
parched lips, tasting nothing but dust! Her hair was wildly
blowing across her shoulders, so tangled that she doubted if
she would ever be able to brush it out!

But Maria was not worrying about herself at this moment. Shortly she would see Pleasant Voice and would
know just how ill her friend was! The Indians could have a
different concept of health than the white people. Perhaps
Pleasant Voice was not as ill as Blue Arrow had said!

She hoped the wound was healing on its own, for Maria
did not believe that any Singer could work miracles over
her!

Glancing over at Shadow, she was at least glad that he
had taken the time—earlier that afternoon when they had
stopped to eat dried wild seeds from his leather pouch—to
explain exactly what a Singer was and what could be
expected of his magical powers.

Shadow had spoken with reverence when he explained
the Navaho curing ceremony, saying that when a Navaho
was sick, the family called in a Singer and gave him horses
or sheep in payment for conducting the ceremony. The
Singer had spent a great deal of time learning what to do, so
he had to be paid well.

The sick person's family, relatives, and friends gathered
at the hogan. The Singer arrived, knowing many different
songs and dances and prayers. He would often pray to
Changing Woman, the most important Navaho god, the one
who did good things and tried to help people. Her husband,
the Sun, wasn't always so helpful; there were prayers asking
him to do good instead of evil.

The Singer might also pray to the Hero Twins, the
children of Changing Woman and the Sun. They were
called Monster Slayer and Child of Water, and they often
did very mean things. Shadow said that the Navaho tried to
stay on the good side of these Hero Twins.

He then went on to say that the Singer conducted the ceremony to win the help of the gods, while the sick person knew that all the people were there, participating in the ceremony.

Maria had been given permission to attend the ceremony. She was skeptical but eager to see it.

The dust bathed from her face, her hair finally brushed, but still dressed in the dusty Navaho outfit, Maria approached Pleasant Voice's hogan, Shadow at her side, ushering her through the crowd of Navaho who stood around the door. The promise of a bath after the ceremony was pleasantly on Maria's mind, and she anticipated the feel of the fresh water on her flesh, but she was almost weak-kneed with anxiety over Pleasant Voice. After she had explained to Shadow exactly what Pleasant Voice was to her, Maria had been promised a private moment with her before the arrival of the Singer.

Maria gave Shadow a quick glance, his arm possessively around her waist. Ever since she had shared her knowledge of the Arabian horses with him, he had been receptive to everything she had said. He seemed ready to offer her the world because of her generosity and trust.

Perhaps he would offer her . . . freedom.

Or was she dreaming again?

Her pulse racing from being only a heartbeat away from seeing Pleasant Voice, Maria stepped into the dark hogan with Shadow. A few candles flickered on a table just ahead, and Maria clutched at her throat with a hand when she saw what the candles revealed. They cast golden light on a sheepskin-covered platform on which Pleasant Voice lay, ghostly pale and asleep. She was attired in a lovely doeskin dress adorned with silver ornaments, and she wore moccasins all new and pretty on her delicate feet.

As Maria grew closer she saw that Pleasant Voice's hair lay spread in a rich sheen beneath her head, like a black satin pillow. Dressed in such a special, lovely way, and lying so deathly quiet with her hands resting on her abdomen, she looked as though she had been readied to be placed in a casket!

Sobbing, Maria turned her eyes away and eased into Shadow's arms. "I didn't expect this," she whispered, clinging to Shadow. "She looks ! . . looks dead."

Shadow ran his hand down Maria's back in a soft caress. "She is only resting peacefully." He tried to reassure her as he looked past Maria's shoulder at Pleasant Voice. "Do you not see how peacefully she is breathing? She is awaiting the arrival of the Singer. That is all."

Maria shot Shadow a quick look; his eyes were filled with love as he looked down at her. "Do you mean that she would open her eyes and recognize me if I stood over her and spoke her name?" she asked, stifling a sob.

"Perhaps," Shadow said, nodding. He eased her from his arms and led her closer to Pleasant Voice. He took a step back from Maria as she now stood staring down at her friend.

Clasping his hands behind him, he watched, moved by Maria's sincere concern for her Navaho friend. He was learning much about Maria in a short time and most was pleasant. More and more he was deliberating over whether or not he should hold her captive, to be his love slave.

In truth, he felt more for her than that! In his heart he would like for her to be his wife.

But he did not trust any woman that much. His possessions would remain his. No woman would make him powerless by marrying and then divorcing him!

Tears threatening to spill from her eyes, Maria stood over Pleasant Voice, only vaguely aware of other people in the hogan besides herself, Shadow, and Pleasant Voice. In the darkest corner of the dwelling she could see two silent figures, observing her every movement, perhaps not trusting her. Maria had to surmise that these were Pleasant Voice's parents.

Ignoring their presence, Maria hoped to break through Pleasant Voice's seemingly unconscious state, not only to reassure herself that her friend was not dying but also to let her friend know that Maria was there to comfort her in her illness.

Slowly, Maria reached out and touched Pleasant Voice's hands. She sighed with relief to find that they were pleasantly warm. That had to mean Pleasant Voice was very much alive. But her hands were not hot, either. That meant she was no longer burning up with fever.

Gently, Maria cupped one of Pleasant Voice's hands with one of her own. Her heartbeat was rapid when she leaned down closer to her friend's pale and drawn face. Tears streamed from her eyes as she gained the courage to speak.

"Pleasant Voice, it is I, Maria," she said, her voice trembling. "I am here if you need me. Dear friend, you *must* get well. Do you hear me? Pleasant Voice, please hear me."

Pleasant Voice, her restful sleep having been induced by a potion given to her by her mother so that her shoulder would not pain her so severely, heard Maria's voice, but thought it was a dream. Maria would not be at the Navaho stronghold. She would not even know how to get there. The fact that Pleasant Voice herself was there was a miracle.

If it had not been for Blue Arrow . . .

Maria saw some soft movement behind Pleasant Voice's closed eyelids, indicating to her that she had heard. Her fingers squeezed Pleasant Voice's hand. She leaned down closer to her face. "Pleasant Voice, please open your eyes," she softly encouraged, her voice breaking with emotion. "I am here. Shadow brought me. One day soon I shall explain to you why. But for now just show me that you are all right by opening your eyes. Oh, please, Pleasant Voice, please show me that you hear me."

Pleasant Voice felt a warm pressure on her hand and sorted out through the fuzziness of her mind just what it was. Someone was holding her hand, and she had heard Maria's voice this time much more clearly!

Could it truly be . . . ?

Though her eyelids were heavy, Pleasant Voice began to force them slowly open. Through a silken haze she saw a face close to hers. Blinking her eyes, she tried to clear the haze away, and when it began to slowly fade, something sweet grabbed her around the heart as she saw that it was Maria! She didn't understand how she could have come here, but the fact that she was here was comfort enough for now.

"Maria?" Pleasant Voice whispered, her voice thick. "It . . . *is* you?"

"*Sí*," Maria said, half choking on a sob. "It is I. And you will be well soon. I know it!"

Pleasant Voice extended her free hand to Maria and touched her cheek gently. "My friend," she whispered. "My true, dear friend." Limply her hand fell away; she was exhausted from the effort it had taken to lift it. "I must sleep. I am . . . so . . . very, very sleepy."

Maria's insides grew cold; she was afraid for her friend. What if she went to sleep and never awakened? A part of Maria would die with her! They had become as close as sisters. If the same blood soared through their veins they could not have been any closer.

A strong arm slipped around Maria's waist, and she looked up into Shadow's dark eyes. Then her eyes caught a movement and were drawn back around to see what had caused it. She saw Pleasant Voice's parents moving to stand over their daughter, and she felt like an intruder. She glanced down at Pleasant Voice. Her eyes were closed, her lovely lips softly parted as she once again slept.

"It is time for the Singer," Shadow whispered, leading Maria away and helping her down onto a pad of sheepskin blankets in a far corner. "I must welcome others into the dwelling and then the Singer. I will join you soon."

Eyes wide, Maria folded her hands on her lap, feeling alien even to herself. . . .

CHAPTER
9

Maria watched spellbound as the Singer began his healing ritual close beside the platform on which Pleasant Voice still slept. He was an elderly Navaho with deep grooves in his copper face, attired in only a breechclout and with long, wiry hair hanging down to his ankles.

There was something in his majesty that made Maria feel he was separate from this world and its miseries. His face, though lined with age, was peaceful; his dark eyes had faded with time, but they were serene.

With an audience of many sitting in a circle around the bed, Shadow at Maria's side, the Singer spread a white doeskin blanket on the hogan floor. It matched Pleasant Voice's dress in color, design, and silver ornamentation.

While singing half beneath his breath, the Singer slowly covered the doeskin blanket with pure white sand, then made a bright sacred picture on the sand by slowly sprinkling it with earth dyed in various colors and with yellow pollen.

His fingers were skillful at making the beautiful painting in the sand, and he continued to paint different breathtaking designs. His voice rose in pitch with "The Holy Mountain Song," which Shadow had first heard when he was a child. On the day that his mother and father had been mortally wounded in a raid, the Singer had sat with Shadow, teaching the boy as he comforted him.

So immersed in remembrances, Shadow could not help but drift back into time to that day. . . .

Tall and just filling out into a man at age thirteen, and troubled by an intense sadness over the loss of his parents, Shadow sat across a fire from the Singer, an old man of character and great intelligence. To draw Shadow from his sad thoughts, the aged man had talked about "The Hozhonji Song," or mountain song, which he was transcribing on parchment paper, the skin of a sheep prepared for writing.

"It is good that our Navaho songs should be written, and it is now time, indeed, that this should be done," the Singer had explained, all the while transcribing the song onto the parchment. "So many of our young people grow careless of the songs, and mistakes will come into them. Unless the songs are written down, they will in time be forgotten. I know this; I have long known it."

The Singer had paused, then continued. "I will sing for you the oldest song I know," he said. "It was taught to me by my grandfather, who learned it from his father. It has been taught by fathers to their sons for no one knows how many years. Older songs than this were sung by an ancient people in the days before the coming of the Navaho. But those songs are all lost because the people themselves have perished. They grew wicked, and therefore, sandstorms and cyclones were sent to destroy them and their villages. There is nothing left of them but the ruins of their dwellings."

He had continued to explain that there were four worlds, one above another: the first world; the second world, which was the underworld; the third, which was the middle world; and the fourth world, the Navaho's own world.

In the underworld there arose a great flood, and the people were driven up to the middle world by the waters. They planted a hollow reed and came up through the reed to this world.

First Man and First Woman had brought with them earth from the mountains of the world below. With this they made the sacred mountains of the Navaho land.

To the east they placed the sacred mountain Sisnajinni. They adorned it with white shells and fastened it to the earth with a bolt of lightning. They covered it with a sheet of daylight, and brought the Dawn Youth and the Dawn Maiden to dwell in it.

To the south they placed Tsodsichl. They adorned it with turquoise and fastened it to the earth with a knife of stone. They covered it with blue sky and sent the Turquoise Youth and the Turquoise Maiden to dwell in it.

To the west they placed Dok-oslid. They adorned it with haliotis shells and fastened it to the earth with a sunbeam. They covered it with a yellow cloud and put the Twilight Youth and the Haliotis Maiden to dwell in it.

To the north they placed Depenitsa. They adorned it with cannel coal and fastened it to the earth with a rainbow. They covered it with a cloak of darkness and brought the Youth of Cannel Coal and the Darkness Maiden to dwell in it.

In the center they placed Tsichlnaodichli and adorned it with striped agate. Here were created the first Navaho.

So the mountains were placed and decorated. Before they were named, holy songs were sung, which told of a journey up the mountain where could be found everlasting life and blessedness. The Divine Ones who lived in and beyond the mountains made the songs, and they spoke of the journey as a homecoming.

When this song was sung over someone who was ill, the spirit of the person would make the journey that the song described. Upon the rainbow the person would move from mountain to mountain, for it was thus that the gods traveled, upon the rainbow.

While Shadow listened dutifully, the Singer had further explained that the rainbow was as swift as lightning and that man knew this to be true, for he could see clearly where the rainbow touched the ground, but before he could reach that spot, the rainbow always moved quickly away and far beyond. Man never could overtake it; it moved more swiftly than any one could see.

Shadow remembered the elderly Singer telling him that the mountains could protect a man. When a man sang of the mountain, through the singing, his spirit went to the holy place beyond the mountain, and he himself became like the mountain, pure and holy, living eternally, forever blessed. . . .

Shadow was drawn from his reverie and called back to the present when the Singer repeated the song that he had been singing for Pleasant Voice. This time he sang much louder, while looking down at her reverently.

In Shadow's heart he repeated the words quietly to himself along with the Singer, making him feel close to the spirit of his mother and father. He now believed beyond a doubt that Pleasant Voice would be well again. Had his parents not been killed so swiftly with arrows, they, too, would have survived after having been sung "The Mountain Song."

Though the Singer was singing in English, in Shadow's heart he was hearing the words being sung in Navaho:

> *Be-ve-la-naseya,*
> *Be-ye-la-naseyo,*
> *Be-ye-la-naseya,*
> *Ho-digin-ladji-ye-ye,*
> *Be-ye-la-naseya,*
> *Ka' Sisnajinni*
> *Bini dji-ye-ye,*
> *Be-ye-la-naseya,*
> *Sa-a narai*
> *Bini dji-ye-ye,*
> *Be-ye-la-naseya,*
> *Bike hozhoni*
> *Bine dji-ye-ye,*
> *Be-ye-la-naseya.*

Maria listened intensely to the English words of the song, touched by them:

> Swift and far I journey,
> Swift upon the rainbow.
> Swift and far I journey,
> Lo, yonder, the Holy Place!
> Yea, swift and far I journey

To Sisnajinni and beyond it.
Yea, swift and far I journey
To the Chief of Mountains and beyond it.
Yea, swift and far I journey
To Life Unending and beyond it.
Yea, swift and far I journey
To Joy Unchanging and beyond it.
Yea, swift and far I journey.

Suddenly the Singer turned on his heel and left the hogan. Everyone began leaving silently behind him in single file. Maria looked questioningly up at Shadow, then accepted his hand in hers as he urged her to her feet.

As he began guiding her from the hogan, she looked over her shoulder at Pleasant Voice whose father was carrying her to her bed in the far dark corner of the house.

Maria looked desperately up at Shadow as he led her from the house. "Is Pleasant Voice going to be all right?" she whispered, welcoming his arm around her waist, needing this reassurance that she was not alone. Somehow Shadow was taking her parents' place in her world and she did not at all mind the exchange. He brought so much into her life that she had never known before.

But the moments he was away from her were much too frightening to her.

"The Singer has worked his wondrous powers over Pleasant Voice," Shadow said, his voice revealing a more relaxed attitude. "Yes, she will be all right. Tomorrow you will see change in her!"

Maria sighed with relief. "Then perhaps I will rest more soundly tonight," she said, finding it odd that she thought less and less of herself as a captive. If she would allow herself, she could be content to stay with Shadow! While with him she was filled with wondrous expectations of when he would kiss her again!

He was becoming an obsession with her and she knew how dangerous this was. But it was true that she did not wish to even think of ever being without him. If staying near him meant being his captive, so be it!

But the word "slave" tormented her. The words "captive" and "slave" were worlds apart in meaning in her mind. Yet in her heart she knew they were the same and she should fight against having either captivity or slavery forced upon her!

But fighting enslavement meant fighting Shadow. She could not bear the thought. So she would put off resisting him, at least until she could bear her captivity no longer. At this moment, her life was filled with excitement and adventure that had been denied her until Shadow had rescued her from the solitude that her father forced upon her.

And wasn't the way her father had forced her to live a sort of enslavement also?

Sí, enslavement of her heart, body, and soul! She could hardly bear to think of returning to that way of life.

Could she return, if she was given the chance?

"Do you wish to sleep before or after that bath you have begged me for almost every hour of this day?" Shadow asked, drawing Maria closer to his side as they headed toward his hogan, the largest and most impressive of all the structures at this stronghold.

"A bath?" Maria said, her eyes wide. "You are serious, *sí*? I can have a bath?" She laughed softly, her dark eyes twinkling as she looked up at Shadow. "That would be most delicious, Shadow! Most delicious!"

Shadow forked an eyebrow. "Delicious?" he said, a half-smile playing on his lips. "How can baths be delicious? Do you taste them? If so, teach me how you do this!"

Giggling, Maria slipped from his arms and took off in a half-run to his hogan, again forgetting her position in life, forgot that she was a captive; instead, she felt like a schoolgirl.

Hurrying on into his house without hesitation she stopped in mid-step when several candles burning brightly all around the room sprayed their flickering light onto a great copper tub filled with steaming water. Floating on the top was a cake of soap in the shape of a rose. The sweet fragrance of the soap met Maria's approach as she went and stood over the tub, marveling at its presence in this village, much less Shadow's hogan.

Hands on the hem of her blouse, she raised it slowly up past her breasts, then took in a quick, nervous breath. She closed her eyes when lips began to stir fires along her back as her blouse dropped to the floor. And when Shadow turned her to totally face him, his hands now cupping her breasts, she could not deny that at this moment in time she was not at all embarrassed by being with him again in such a way. Instead, she was filled with a soft, warm ecstasy.

"Woman, your bath as promised," Shadow said, nodding toward the tub. "Are you not happy?" He brushed a light kiss across her lips. "Shadow wishes only that you are happy. In so many ways you have made Shadow happy."

Rendered almost speechless, becoming more and more lost to the soft spirals of passion that were weaving their way into her heart, Maria framed Shadow's face between her hands, drawing his lips close to hers again.

"Though most would think me daft to admit this to you, since I am a captive, I must say that, *sí*, Shadow, most of the time that I am with you I *am* happy," she whispered, flicking her tongue across his lower lip. "These feelings that you have awakened in me make me believe that I am in love with you. Am I wrong in letting myself love you? Am I?"

Afraid of that word "love," which made a man eventually speak the word "marriage" to a woman, Shadow stepped back away from her, ignoring her question. He looked down at her with heat in his eyes as he lowered her skirt on down away from her, then slipped the moccasins off her feet.

In one sweep he had her up in his arms and was holding her over the vat of water. "You like the tub I offer you a bath in?" he asked, trying not to see the hurt in her eyes, which he had caused by eluding her question. "Is it not a grand tub? The tub and the fancy soap were taken in a raid on a Spaniard's house long ago." He chuckled low. "You should have seen the trouble it was to bring this tub home into my mountain stronghold! It took four horsemen to carry it!"

Maria had noticed how he had ignored her mention of loving him, and that had sent a warning clean through her, yet surely he had to keep himself on guard at all times when talking of such feelings to a woman—a white woman at that!

And she must never forget why she was there! Only because of Shadow's hatred for her father! At times she had felt that it was more. When Shadow had made love with her, it had been genuinely sweet and most surely sincere!

Sí, she could keep that thought for the next hour or so, for she knew that things would not stop tonight at just her taking a bath! The sensual feelings had already begun to spin between them. With her heart pounding so hard that she thought it might break her breastbone in half, she knew that she could not back away from what had begun tonight.

Picturing in her mind's eye the Navaho warriors struggling to carry the heavy copper tub between their traveling horses made Maria forget her troubled thoughts and doubts. She laughed softly. "It is such a beautiful tub," she said, giving Shadow a sultry smile. "*Señor,* have you bathed in it, yourself?"

Then jealousy raged through her at another thought. "Or do you reserve it for women who, at your beck and call, share your hogan with you?" she asked, her lower lip curving into a pout.

"Will you believe me when I say you are the first?" Shadow said, lying. "It is for the most beautiful of women. It is for you, Maria. Only for you."

Wanting to believe him, yet finding his words too incredible, Maria began sliding her fingers slowly down his powerful bare chest. "And will this be the first time for you, also, *señor*?" she teased. "You do plan to take a bath with me, *sí*?"

Shadow smiled down at her and began lowering her toward the water. "That is my plan, yes," he said, chuckling. "Though I am not sure how much of a bath either of us will get. There is only room for you to sit on my lap. Perhaps as you bathe, I will be bathed at the same time?"

"*Puede ser,* perhaps," Maria said, giggling. The wonders

of the water, warm and refreshing, entered her body as Shadow set her down into the tub. She grabbed the soap and began rubbing it along her flesh while she feasted her eyes on Shadow as he began to undress.

Only a few short days ago she had never even seen a man naked and now she was actually watching a man undress in front of her. She was eagerly waiting to be with him, nude, again, to touch him all over, to be taught even more about how to make love with him!

When he came to the tub and eased her up to her feet, she felt no hesitation. There were no doubts in her mind that she wanted him with her.

As he then sat down into the water, holding her in place on his lap, facing him, Maria clung to him, her arms about his neck and relished the feel of his manhood rising to its full strength against her as she locked her legs around him.

Looping his arms around her neck, Shadow drew Maria's body into his so that he could feel the magnificence of her breasts pressing into his chest, then sought her mouth with his lips and gave her a kiss of fire.

Untwining his arms around her neck, he let his fingers trace her spine downward to the soft curves of her buttocks. Sinking his fingers into her flesh, he lifted her and then brought her back down, impaling her on his hardness.

His kiss stifled a soft moan on her lips as he began his even thrusts within her. When she began to move on her own, keeping up with the rhythm of his strokes, he moved his hands to her breasts to cup them.

Feeling them grow hot and responsive against his palms, he kneaded them, pinching her nipples between his thumbs and forefingers.

When Shadow lowered his lips, to flick his tongue around one of Maria's breasts, the soft glimmer of her hair billowed down her back as she held her head back and closed her eyes, desire gripping her. She clung to his sinewed shoulders, riding him, then felt a tremor beginning deep within her, building . . . building . . . until once again she was introduced to the peak of passion.

Breathing hard, she lowered her head and placed her

cheek on Shadow's chest, knowing that his sought-for release was near. She could sense it in the pounding of his heart against her cheek and in the way he moaned against the curve of her neck as his body moved into a feverish sort of rhythm.

His grip was like steel as his whole body shuddered, his thrusts reaching clean into her soul, causing her once again to reach the same sort of ecstasy that was taking over Shadow, mind and soul. The blood spun wildly through her veins as she closed her eyes and rode with the tide of pleasure, then lay spent within his arms, clinging.

"Shadow, tell me that you love me," she whispered, her voice foreign to her in that it was so passion-filled. "You can't make love so intensely without loving me just a little bit." She feathered kisses over his face, her hands splayed across his chest. "Tell me that I am more to you than a captive. Please don't give me the label of love slave. I don't think I could bear it!"

Dripping wet, having yet to actually take a bath, Shadow held Maria within his arms as he stood, then stepped from the tub. Carrying her to his bed, which was covered with soft sheepskins, he placed her on it then knelt down on the floor beside her. His hands trembled as he traced the perfect lines of her body, beginning with her toes, working their way upward.

"Today you did something for Shadow that made everything change between us," he said thickly, smiling down at her when she trembled as his hands moved to the juncture of her thighs, stopping to caress her there. "You proved your feelings for me by betraying your father. When you told me of the Arabian horses, you told me more than you will ever know! It made me know that you were worthy of being much more than a slave! But not now, Maria. Perhaps never. Never have I wanted to take a wife! Never!"

Without actually saying that he loved her, just the mention of the word "wife" was proof of how Shadow felt about her. He *did* love her! But something was holding him back. Something made him fear taking a wife!

And his speaking the word to her was frightening to *her*!

Though she now knew that she loved Shadow with every beat of her heart, it frightened her to think of actually marrying him. They were from two separate worlds. These worlds clashed in many ways. Wasn't the proof in the fact that she had just made love in a tub that had been stolen from one of her people, a Spaniard? Had not the need arisen for Shadow to steal again from her people? Even from her father?

The fact that she had aided him today made no true difference. It was a fact that there was war between his people and hers.

If worse came to worst, whom could she choose? Her father or the man she loved!

Just thinking about it gave her a sense of foreboding!

"After much careful thought Shadow has made a decision," he said, moving his hands on upward, gently molding her breasts with his palms. "You are no longer a captive. Tomorrow, after I make sure the sheep and horses are on higher, safer ground, I will deliver you close enough to your father's plantation so that you can ride safely on, alone. No longer will you be a captive! You are free to go!"

Maria's eyes widened. She leaned up on an elbow. "What?" she gasped. "Why, Shadow? Why?"

"I am not setting you free because I no longer want your company," he said, dropping a soft kiss on her lips. "You see, you will also have a choice of staying with Shadow. Be my woman. You will be free to come and go. My people will become your friends. You will be able to be close to Pleasant Voice! If you are here, she may get well much more quickly. It is obvious that you two are quite close."

"You want me to marry you?" Maria said, her voice a soft, surprised whisper.

"The word 'marriage' was not spoken, was it?" Shadow said in a growl, frowning down at her.

"No, it wasn't," Maria said, taken aback by his sudden sour mood. "But you asked me to be your woman. Isn't that the same thing?"

"No. Living with me and being my woman is just that," he said flatly. "You would not be my wife."

"You expect me to live in sin?" Maria gasped. "You do not love me enough to marry me?"

"Shadow did not say that."

"Then what are you saying, Shadow?"

"That I need you. Isn't that enough?"

Maria melted inside as his tongue began worshiping her body, beginning at her breasts, then leaving a trail of fire downward, across her abdomen. She sucked in her breath and felt as though he was using his ways of loving her to render her defenseless enough so that she would agree to anything!

But at this moment, she did not know what she wanted. It was too soon, too disarming to her, this mention of staying with him. It would be paradise, she knew, for at this moment he was showing her just how it would be.

Curling her fingers through his hair, she urged his mouth closer to her as he pleasured her in a way that she thought of as foreign, perhaps even forbidden. And she was surprised when he rose away from her and lifted her to her feet, then urged her to kneel down before him, her mouth to that part of him that knew the skills of taking her to heaven and back.

Looking dolefully up at him, her heart thundering inside her, she knew what he wanted and moved her lips slowly to him. When she kissed and gave him pleasure with her tongue and he moaned with bliss, she knew that she was doing exactly as he wished. Her mind became a blur of what was and should be, devoid of everything but the knowledge that she was giving pleasure to the man she loved.

But a question kept surfacing at the back of her mind, nagging her: What about tomorrow? What should her answer be? She had never expected to be given her freedom at all, and now that she had been, she truly did not want it!

Life without Shadow would be no life at all!

CHAPTER
10

Unsure about what she should do, afraid that if she left Shadow's stronghold she might never see him again, yet not wanting to live with him as his mistress, though that would be much better than living with him as a love slave, Maria had chosen momentarily to put it all from her mind by visiting Pleasant Voice. Candlelight was soft in the hogan as Maria sat comfortably on a pallet of sheepskins beside Pleasant Voice's bed.

"I am so sorry that this has happened to you," Maria said, her voice strained. "It is all my father's fault."

"But now everything is better," Pleasant Voice murmured. "I am home. That is all that is important."

"You *are* better this morning, *sí*?" Maria asked, placing a hand to Pleasant Voice's cool brow.

She marveled at the change in her friend, seeing how vibrant her eyes were this morning. Her dark, raven hair lay loose around a copper-colored face whose cheeks were blooming with pink.

Surely the pain had lessened in her shoulder, for Pleasant Voice, with a colorfully striped blanket drawn up to her armpits, had turned her body to face Maria as they talked.

"I soon will be well," Pleasant Voice said, her voice still weak. "But Pleasant Voice does not want to speak of self. What of you, Maria? Why are you here? How did you get here? You would not want your father to know where

Shadow's stronghold is. Shadow would not allow it. How is it that you and Shadow became acquainted?"

Seeing how the many questions had made Pleasant Voice breathless because of her weakness, Maria placed a finger to her lips, sealing them so that she would not continue rattling on. "Shh," she encouraged, uneasily aware of her friend's wound. It was not bandaged, and Maria could see the puckered, red indention in the shoulder just above the blanket. "I shall tell you everything, even more than you expect to hear, Pleasant Voice."

Maria eased her finger from Pleasant Voice's lips and glanced over her shoulder at her special friend's mother, who was standing over a large pot resting in the flames of the fire pit, stirring something that smelled wonderfully spicy. Pleasant Voice's father was outside, keeping watch with many other sentries. Shadow and several of his warriors had left the village to take the stolen sheep and Arabian horses into hiding farther up in the mountains.

So that only Pleasant Voice could hear her, Maria knelt close to the bed. She began speaking softly, but she could not hide the excitement she felt every time she thought about Shadow, much less spoke openly about him.

"Pleasant Voice, last night when you saw me here, to witness the Singer's healing performance, I was a captive," she said, watching her friend's slightly slanted eyes widen in wonder. "But today you see me as one who is *free*."

Pleasant Voice struggled to get up on an elbow, stunned by what Maria was saying. "Maria, I—" she began, but Maria interrupted her.

"Give me time to tell you everything," she said, laughing softly. "And I *will*. It is all so exciting, Pleasant Voice. You know I have always wanted to meet Shadow. And when I did the other day outside my father's study, I knew then that that was not enough. But never did I expect to have an opportunity to get to know him."

"Then how . . . ?" Pleasant Voice said, reaching for Maria's hand, squeezing it affectionately. Outside could be heard the thump-thump-thump of a weaver pounding down the threads in her loom. A distant child laughed. Someone was chopping wood. "And what did you mean by saying that you were a captive and now you are not?"

"You recall that my father threatened Shadow the day Shadow came to meet with him?"

"Yes, I recall. Shadow returned the threat."

"He not only returned the threat verbally, but he made the threat good."

"*E-do-ta*!"

"*Sí.*"

"How did he, Maria?"

"He came to my father's plantation in the darkness of night and stole back the Navaho who were enslaved," Maria said softly. "Also, he stole *me* away!"

Pleasant Voice gasped. "He . . . took you captive?" she murmured, her eyes wide.

"*Sí*," Maria said, nodding.

"And you? Did you fight him?" Pleasant Voice said, squinting her eyes, studying Maria. What she saw was a friend who had decisions in life to make, for had not she said that she was no longer being help captive? Had she not shown how happy she was to have made Shadow's close acquaintance?

Most who were taken captive were not happy! This had to mean that perhaps Maria's fantasies, her dreams, had come to life while with Shadow.

The thought of her best friend and one of the Navaho's most powerful leaders being in love pleased Pleasant Voice, for it would thrill her to see Maria become a part of the life of the Navaho in the capacity of Shadow's wife.

Pleasant Voice wondered if that would ever really happen. Everyone had seen his determination not to take a wife. Even the most beautiful Navaho women had not been able to change his mind. Would a woman of a different skin coloring and culture be able to do so? Would he be even more adamant against marrying Maria because of who she was? A . . . devilish Spaniard?

"At first I was too stunned even to think, much less fight off Shadow," Maria said, recalling the confused state of her mind when Shadow had entered her room in the middle of the night. His presence had been disarming! "Then the next thing I knew he had my hands tied and was carrying me from my room!"

"How did he escape with you?" Pleasant Voice asked, becoming more and more intrigued by Shadow's boldness. "Did he carry you through your house? Did your father or mother—"

"Neither Mother nor Father heard anything that happened," Maria said, taking in a deep, shuddering breath. "Shadow carried me out to the balcony and forced me to climb down the trellis."

"But your hands were tied."

"Shadow untied them."

"And you didn't try to escape?"

"It would have been futile to try."

Pleasant Voice again squeezed Maria's hand. "Something tells me that you wouldn't have tried even if he had given you the chance," she said, laughing softly.

Maria raised an eyebrow, then giggled. She leaned closer to her friend. "Oh, Pleasant Voice, I now know what being in love feels like," she said, her voice filled with awe. "I understand how you feel about Blue Arrow. Oh, how could you bear being away from him those many months after your abduction? How could you not speak of him often to me? How could you have kept it all inside? I feel as though I am going to burst I am filled with so many emotions! And it is all because of my love for Shadow. Oh, I do love him, Pleasant Voice. I do!"

"And he must feel the same, since he had decided to set you free," Pleasant Voice said, her voice becoming weaker as exhaustion set in. "If he did not love you he would make you his slave. He would enjoy using you nightly, Maria, as a love slave."

"He *does* love me," Maria said, sighing. Then she frowned. "But I am so confused by his loving me. He has asked me to stay with him, not as a slave but as one who returns his love willingly. Yet he will not even consider speaking of marriage." She wove her fingers through her hair in frustration. "I am so torn with what to do! Should I stay? Or should I return home? I do not want to live in sin. And why does Shadow wish me to? What does he find so distasteful about marriage?"

"He will have to explain that to you," Pleasant Voice said thickly. "It is not my place to do so."

Then Pleasant Voice reached out to touch Maria's cheek. "Would you marry Shadow if he did ask you?" she asked, fighting off her building weakness. "You know how you are used to living. Your family flaunts their riches and though Shadow is as rich a landowner as your father, he does not display riches in the same way. He shares his wealth with his people! You would not have the same comforts that you are used to as the daughter of a wealthy Spaniard!"

"*Sí*, I am aware of all the differences," Maria said, lowering her eyes. "I am so torn."

Then her eyes slowly lifted. "But Shadow has not asked me to marry him," she said softly. "And perhaps he never will. So it makes no difference that he and I are from different cultures. It makes no difference at all."

Pleasant Voice turned to lie on her stomach, breathing hard. She placed a hand to her brow. "I am suddenly so tired," she murmured, then looked anxiously over at Maria. "Let me say one more thing, my friend. Whether or not Shadow will marry you, stay with him. Find the happiness you have dreamed of by being his woman. Your father does not deserve your loyalty. Do not fret over not returning to live with him!"

"But my mother . . . ?" Maria said, sighing. "She will be shocked by my behavior. She will be hurt and embarrassed if I live with a man without a priest's words spoken over us! And that the man is Navaho will make her shock twofold. Oh, what *am* I to do?"

"Let your heart be your guide," Pleasant Voice said, her voice fading, her eyes closing. "I must rest, Maria. Please come later, and if you decide that you must leave this Navaho stronghold, do not leave without saying good-bye."

"Never," Maria said, moving slowly to her feet. "*Adiós* for only a short while, Pleasant Voice. I shall return again after you have rested."

"Yes, return soon," Pleasant Voice said, nodding. "And remember, my friend. Let your heart lead you into the right decisions. Life is short. Live it to the fullest now. Later may be too late."

"*Sí, sí,*" Maria whispered, backing away from Pleasant Voice. She turned and began tiptoeing toward the door, nodding a silent good-bye to Pleasant Voice's mother who looked up from where she still stood over the pot, stirring.

A strange sort of coldness touched Maria's insides when Pleasant Voice's mother failed to acknowledge her, instead continued to stir her food. Would this be the reception of all the Navaho should she decide to stay with Shadow? They all by now surely knew who her father was. Did they despise her for being the daughter of a man who had enslaved and tricked so many of the Navaho people? Did they blame her for what had happened to Pleasant Voice?

Ducking her head, not wanting anyone to see the sparkle of tears in the corners of her eyes, Maria rushed away from Pleasant Voice's hogan and made her way toward Shadow's. She felt the need to hide until he returned. And if this was how she felt now, would it ever change? Would staying with Shadow not only cut her ties with her family but also destroy her peace of mind? If she was hated at this Navaho stronghold, wouldn't she still be in a sort of captivity?

A determination not to let anyone make her feel like a criminal made Maria suddenly lift her chin. She wiped the tears from her eyes and began walking much more slowly, feeling eyes watching her from the doors of the hogans. Did they wonder about this white woman who was dressed in Indian attire, the skirt whipping in the wind, revealing the high tops of her moccasins? Did they mock her skin color?

Children scampering around began walking behind Maria, almost stepping on the heels of her moccasins. Low giggles followed along behind her as the children teased and talked about her.

Women, lovely in their buckskin skirts and blouses, were standing close to the wall overlooking the steep drop that led one's eyes down into the valley below.

Deciding to test these women's ability to be friendly,

Maria moved to the wall and stood beside one of the women. Her eyes wavered when she saw marks on the woman's arms that could only have been caused by a whip.

Maria shot a look upward, seeing a deep hatred in the dark eyes of the woman, who had surely at one time been the prisoner of a Spaniard. Perhaps even her father? She had not mingled with her father's slaves and gotten to know them personally. Her father had singled Pleasant Voice out for her to become acquainted with.

"*Buenas tardes,* good afternoon," Maria said, her voice breaking. "*Habla usted inglés*? Do you speak English?"

The lovely Navaho woman tossed her long hair back from her shoulders and looked haughtily at Maria. "Yes, I speak English, Spanish, *and* Navaho," she spat. "And you? Are you as gifted, *señorita*? Or didn't your father let you go into the city for schooling? Isn't it so that you were just as much a prisoner of Señor Zamora as the Navaho whom he enslaved?"

Maria paled and took a step backward, stunned by what the Navaho woman said, having had no idea the slaves looked upon her as her father's prisoner. The knowing made her speechless. And it embarrassed her.

Suddenly everything became a scrambling of feet and people whispering all around Maria. Something similar to birds' calls could be heard as the sentries alerted the people that all was not well in the valley.

Maria's eyes were drawn downward. She became numb inside when she saw a long line of horsemen coming into view, having been hidden earlier by the sheer cliffs and drop. At this moment they were almost directly below Maria, so close she could see the face of the lead rider. Though the man was dressed like all of those who were following him, in a colorful poncho belted at the waist, with a pistol resting on either hip, there was no denying that the man was her father! They had chosen to come searching for the stronghold dressed like Mexicans instead of Spanish soldiers. And it seemed that they were only a breath away from finding it.

Maria looked anxiously around her, seeing the Navaho sentries notching their bows with arrows. She looked desperately down at her father, knowing that at any moment he would be ambushed!

She nervously combed her fingers through her hair with frustration, thinking that, no, the Navaho would not make the first move. If the Spaniards passed on by without being shot at, they still would not know where the stronghold was.

Unless Charging Falcon was with them!

Searching with her eyes, going from man to man, Maria saw no sign of Charging Falcon. Her father had come on his own. He truly did not know exactly where he was. It was just a stroke of fate that had brought him there.

Lined up at the wall, children, men, and women alike watched in breathless anticipation for the horsemen to pass on by. Maria's heart pounded as she watched anxiously, for she knew the number of Navaho arrows that were pointed downward at the Spaniards. Most would be shot before they knew what had happened!

Maria watched her father, recalling how, as a child, she had idolized him. Only after she grew older did she realize that he was not deserving of such affection.

But she did not wish to see him killed! One slip of an arrow . . .

Maria looked slowly around her, again seeing the notched arrows and the waiting Navaho. None seemed afraid because this time they were ready for intruders! And this stronghold seemed safe enough. Its floor stretched in under an overhanging rock and in front of it was a natural rock parapet. People sitting behind the parapet could not be seen from below and those who were not looking down in wonder at the Spaniards were crouching, laughing to themselves as the enemy passed below them. No Spaniard had guessed there were Indians anywhere near, and the joke was too good to keep.

Out of the corner of her eye Maria saw the Navaho woman who had been her father's slave slowly climb out onto the edge of the overhanging rock. Maria's heart skipped several beats, and she reached for the woman, seeing the wicked gleam in her eyes and hearing her laughing throatily. In a matter of only seconds the Spaniards would know where the Indians were and the arrows would be flying!

"No!" Maria said in a hushed whisper, grabbing the woman's skirt. "*Por favor,* please! Don't!"

But the woman jerked her skirt free and ignored Maria. She stood up so that the Spaniards could see her. She flipped her skirt teasingly, raising it so that the soldiers would have full view beneath it.

Then she shouted. Her voice was loud and piercing, very mocking! "There go the men without eyes!" she jeered. "Señor Zamora, let me see your whip now! Soon you will get the taste of my people's arrows. I hope the one that enters your flesh will have poison on its tip!"

Maria felt a coldness splash through her. She covered her mouth with her hands. Her father and all the rest of the men had heard. The secret was given away!

In a hiss many arrows went flying through the air. In a state of shock, Maria watched them hit their targets and the Spaniards clutch at their bodies where the arrows were protruding.

She cried out when she saw an arrow enter her father's left arm, yet she felt thankful that, so far, it was nothing worse than that!

Wanting to go to her father, yet knowing that she would be in the line of fire, she watched and prayed as he and the others rode their horses quickly across the meadow and into the cover of the trees beside a stream.

And then she breathed much more easily when through the break in the trees she saw that they were riding onward, retreating. Though they had found the stronghold, they now knew that it was well defended. They would surely have to devise other ways to defeat Shadow!

"But how?" Maria whispered to herself.

She sank to the ground, leaning back against the wall as she lowered her face into her hands. Seeing her father in danger was causing her to become more and more confused about her feelings. She felt that she should go to him.

Yet he had not been mortally wounded. He was going to be all right!

But what about her? Shadow had said that he would return her home. How could he, now that the Spanish army would more than likely be watching for him, to capture him. It would be impossible for him to get Maria close to her house without being caught.

Now, whether or not she wanted to, she would have to stay with Shadow.

She shook her head. Her life was continually changing. . . .

Charging Falcon staked his horse out where uncropped spears of grass stood singly, each inches from the next, in brown sand. A beaten track toward an oak tree and a break in the rock caught the scout's eye. He followed it. Behind the oak, currant bushes grew in a niche of red rock, like a fold in a giant curtain. At the back was a full-grown, lofty fir tree. Behind the tree a cleft opened at shoulder height into dark shadow. The footholds were worn to velvety roundness. It would be a perfect place to hide a captive. He had received word that Maria Zamora had been stolen from her people by Shadow! Charging Falcon would prove his prowess by sneaking into Shadow's stronghold without being detected, to steal Maria away from him.

"And then I shall sell her to a Spaniard who in turn will sell her two ways—to her father *and* to Shadow!" He chuckled, kneeling down on a knee, tossing pebbles into a stream that snaked along beside him. "Yes, it will be profitable for everyone except the *woman*. She will wish that she had never heard the name Charging Falcon!"

He frowned, having also heard that Pleasant Voice had not died. She, too, was at Shadow's stronghold. When enough time had passed for her to be strong again, he would steal her also!

But he would keep her for himself this time. He had thought of nothing else since the night he had left her to die. He had been tormented by thoughts of wanting her as surely no man had ever wanted a woman! He would take her far away and leave his raiding days behind him. He would live only for her.

"Yes, only for her," he whispered, his heart aching for her.

CHAPTER
11

Maria eased away from Shadow's side and rose from the bed, wrapping a blanket around her shoulders. She went and stood over the ashes that had grown cold in the fire pit. Then, even though there was no fire, she sat down beside the pit on a thick mat of sheepskins.

She had spent a restless night, concerned about her father's welfare, and alarmed by Shadow's savage show of anger with Morning Flower for having alerted the soldiers. Because the woman had been so foolish, not thinking about what it would mean to her people to shout down at the soldiers who would now always know where the stronghold was, Shadow had ordered her hair cut short and then had banished her from the stronghold, forcing her to travel on foot down the mountainside.

The thought of Morning Flower wandering defenseless and alone all night had plagued Maria. The thought of her father suffering from his arrow wound had torn at her heart! Confusion of how she should feel about Shadow and of knowing the impossibility of returning home at this time, even if she desired to, made her feel imprisoned, even though she had been told that she was free!

Hands smoothing the blanket down from her shoulders made Maria turn with a start. Concentrating so hard on all that was troubling her, she had not heard Shadow move up behind her. As she turned, her blanket rippled away from her, settling on the floor.

"You are awake with the morning sun?" Shadow said, his hands claiming her body as though she were his possession. "Your night was a troubled one?"

A shiver coursed through Maria, the coldness of morning touching her flesh like clutching, icy fingers. She jumped to her feet, stepped away from Shadow, and bent to pick up her blanket, but once again his hands were there, holding her arms, urging her to stand before him.

"Last night you showed your displeasure with many things," Shadow said, pressing his fingers into her bare flesh. "Today it will be different. You must learn that though you are not my slave, while you are here at my stronghold, you must accept my decisions on all things, for everything I do is done after much thought. My people have learned to respect my judgment. So must you!"

His words reminded her that she had been taught to listen and obey her father. She'd had to stand by silently and watch him make horrendous judgments in life. Maria forgot how cold she was as her insides began to flame with anger. She did not want to be just an observer of the man she loved. She wanted to give her heart to him but not her mind or her freedom of thought and speech!

Yet to go against Shadow would produce terrible results. Again she was reminded of the Navaho woman who was now wandering aimlessly in the desert, thirsty and hungry, feeling alone and rejected. Maria had to guard her words carefully, for at this moment she had nowhere else to go. She could not return home just yet. Asking Shadow to take her there would be like handing him a death sentence. No matter how angry and disillusioned she was with him, she never wanted him to be harmed! And she would be just like the wandering Navaho woman if she set out to find her father's plantation all alone. She would never find it.

Challenging him with a set stare, only now becoming aware of his nudity, which seemed quite natural when they were together, Maria forced a smile. "Yes, I understand that decisions must be made by someone," she said softly. "And since you are the leader of your clan of Navaho, I understand that you are the one who must make the decisions. I will try to remember that, Shadow. I am sorry if I have not shown enough sympathy for your cause."

"But you *have*," he said hoarsely, his jaw lessening in tightness. "It is just that after I sent Morning Flower away you became so withdrawn." His hands left her arms and he placed them at her waist, drawing her closer. "You did not even let me love you last night. Do you not hunger for me as I do for you?" His lips sent butterfly kisses across her cheek and then her lips. "I love you, Maria. Please remember that every decision I make that affects you is made because of my love and concern for you."

A sensual tremor raced across Maria's flesh. She closed her eyes in ecstasy as Shadow's hands cupped her breasts and kneaded them softly. She sucked in her breath when his tongue flicked a nipple into a hardened peak.

She wanted to fight the euphoria he caused within her. She wanted to tell him that making love was not the answer to everything. It would not take away the tensions between him and her father. It would not make her less torn with indecision as to what she should do next.

While she was with Shadow, she wanted only him, but she knew that should not be enough for her. She was a seamstress! She had talents of sewing with Valencia lace that no one else could boast of. She had dreamed of using her talents in her own business one day. That would have been a way of winning her independence from her father.

But now?

If she gave herself wholly to a man, even though he was the man she loved and would love forever, what then of her independence?

There would be none. Shadow was even more demanding than her father!

"Love me, Maria," Shadow whispered, picking her up and carrying her to his bed. "My day will be easier if it begins in your arms. I have much to do. Now that the Spaniards know the location of my stronghold, the young men of my village must begin more vigorous training in raiding and fighting. You are to witness. You will see the determination of my people to be independent of all people with the white skin."

His words stung Maria's heart. As he knelt over her, placing his knees on either side of her, his hands moving sensually over her body, she looked up at him. "You talk of wanting to be independent of all white people, yet you speak of loving me," she said softly, trembling when one of his hands went to the soft valley at the juncture of her thighs and began to caress her. "How can you love me when you despise all Spaniards? How can you separate me from the others in your heart?"

"Do you not know the difference yourself?" Shadow said, twining his fingers through her hair, drawing it from beneath her head, spreading it out on the sheepskin around her face. His eyes devoured her; his heart was soaring with want of her. "You have feelings for the Navaho. Did you not choose a Navaho for your best friend? Did you not choose me with your eyes long ago, even before you knew my name? Have you not secretly watched me from afar? Maria, you were then filled with compassion for the Navaho. This compassion led you into loving the Navaho, loving not only me but my people as a whole. This is how you are different."

He brushed her lips with a soft kiss. "You proved your feelings for my people when you led me to your father's Arabian horses," he said thickly. "At that moment, I understood more about you than you will ever know about yourself!"

"*Sí*, I believe that is possible," Maria whispered, running the palms of her hands across his hairless chest. "Lately I have been very confused about my feelings. When you abducted me, you changed so much in my life. And even though you have offered me my freedom, that does not mean that things will be the same again. I don't even want them to be. *Sí*, Shadow, perhaps you do know me better than I know myself."

She began circling his nipples with her forefingers then tweaked them between forefinger and thumb, drawing a husky groan from between Shadow's sculpted lips. "I hope one day to know at least half as much about you," she whispered. "I do love you so, Shadow. I do."

"Then let us not waste any more time trying to reason things out in our minds," he said huskily, bending over her, pressing his lips softly against hers. "Let us wander together to a place that has no frustrations. Let our minds become filled with peace and joy. Let our bodies come together as one."

He cradled her close as his knee nudged her thighs apart. She became breathless with desire when she felt the wonders of his manhood softly probing, then plunging inside her, beginning his masterful strokes.

"*Sí, sí,*" she whispered, moving her hips with each of his thrusts, marveling anew at how his hardness so filled and thrilled her. Locked together, their bodies moving in unison, it was as though they were becoming one body, one mind, and one soul.

She relished these moments with him, treasuring them in her heart, as though she were entering them in a precious diary to be read over and over again by her alone.

Maria's lips throbbed with his kiss. Her breasts pulsed beneath the pleasuring of his hands. A delicious tingling heat was spreading through her and as his tongue surged between her teeth, she felt that she was melting. Her hands became wild, touching him all over. She clasped his buttocks and urged him even closer to her, becoming breathless as the passion began to peak.

Shadow felt the fires raging within him. His mouth moved from Maria's lips and, as if in a frenzy, tasted first one breast and then the other, his fingers now digging into her hips, lifting her so close he felt as though his manhood had reached the deepest recesses of her soul.

Never had he felt such warmth envelop his hardness as he stroked deep within her. He wanted to delay that ultimate of feeling, to enjoy holding Maria and sharing the pleasure they both were savoring.

The day would be long before they could be together in this way again. It would be hard to concentrate on teaching the young men their duties, knowing what awaited him at day's end.

More than ever, Shadow did not want to let Maria go. In a sense, Morning Flower had done him a favor by drawing the attention of the Spaniards. It was going to delay Maria's departure from the stronghold!

Maria twined her fingers through Shadow's hair and urged his lips lower, recalling the wondrous feelings that waited to be enjoyed because of his different ways of pleasuring her. When he reciprocated and inched his manhood from inside her, moving his head lower and parting her softness at the juncture of her thighs to let his tongue and lips discover anew the wonders of her there, Maria thrashed her head back and forth, becoming mindless with bliss. She cried out softly when the pleasure mounted and spread, then encouraged him back up, so that she could reach the ultimate of feelings along with him.

Again Shadow entered her. While he kissed her with a blaze of urgency, his thrusts became demanding, no longer wanting to hold off that moment of ecstasy. He was beyond the point of waiting. His manhood was pulsating with the need for release.

And when it began, he locked Maria against him in a solid embrace. He kissed her hard and long, smiling to himself when he felt her body trembling with the same sort of pleasure that he was finally letting himself enjoy.

For a moment, there was only their bodies straining together, sharing that supreme feeling.

And then it was too soon over.

Maria clung to Shadow, raining soft kisses across his face. "My love," she whispered. "My love."

His mouth slipped down and fastened gently on her breast, his hands caressing her womanhood as he slipped his spent manhood from inside her. He could tell that sparks of passion were still kindled inside her, for she moaned as his fingers brought her to another brief, fleeting climax.

"How is it possible that my body is ready so often to feel this pleasure that you have introduced me to?" Maria asked, smoothing her hair back from her eyes as Shadow moved to lie beside her, his hands now folded and resting on his stomach.

Maria turned on her side to face Shadow. She began tracing his chiseled features with her forefinger. "Darling, would it be the same if I tried this with another man?" she said, teasing him.

Shadow's eyes widened with horror. He grabbed Maria by the waist and drew her up, so that she was lying on top of him. He looked up at her with brooding eyes. "Do not even consider trying to *see*," he warned. "You are mine. Remember that, Maria."

Maria laughed, but then his words sank in, and she frowned and tried to get away from him, as though a threat had been handed her.

But his hand on her wrist held her immobile, her breasts pressed hard into his chest. "I was only jesting," she said angrily. "Don't you ever jest, Shadow? Do you always have to be so serious? Do you not even see that you are behaving brutally to me at this moment? First you say that I am no longer your prisoner; then you treat me like one! Let me go, Shadow. You're hurting my wrist."

Taken aback by her anger, shaken out of his trance, Shadow dropped his hand away from her and watched her as she scurried away from him. He rose up on an elbow, still watching her as she quickly donned her buckskin blouse and skirt.

When she began angrily drawing a brush through her hair, he continued to watch her. She was many things, and a spitfire was one of them. This he would have to grow used to, for he had never allowed such behavior in any other women. He was spoiled, it seemed, for his love slaves had never argued back. They had let him do as he wished, any time that he wished.

Maria was different. . . .

Now more amused than shocked at Maria's behavior, beginning to enjoy her more challenging side, Shadow rose from the bed and hurried into his own clothes.

As he sat back down on the bed and drew on his knee-high moccasins, he watched Maria look down into the

fire pit where ashes lay spread and cold. Since he had
ordered his love slaves not to enter his hogan while Maria
was there, and since he had grown used to his slaves
keeping the fire going, the flames had been allowed to burn
out.

"The women of the house usually keep a fire burning in
the pit all the time because it is hard to make sparks with the
fire drill," Shadow said, rising to his feet. "But in *my* house
my slaves tend to the fire."

The mention of his slaves made Maria turn to look at
him, having wondered where all of these slaves were that
she knew he had. How many did he own? Did he miss a
particular love slave while Maria was there? Had he been
truthful when he told her he loved her? Could he, in truth,
ever love only one woman? Was this why he never wanted
to enter into a discussion of marriage?

"Where are they now?" she blurted, watching Shadow
saunter across the room and take the fire drill from the wall,
where it hung beside a smaller stick with a pointed end,
which he also grabbed. The fire drill was a smooth piece of
yucca with holes pierced along one side, each with a little
channel leading from it.

She followed Shadow with her eyes as he knelt on the
ground beside the fire pit with the long stick in front of him.
He placed the point of the smaller stick in one of the holes,
then twirled the stick rapidly back and forth between the
palms of his hands. The quick rubbing soon brought a
spark.

"Hurry and bring me some shredded bark," Shadow said,
giving Maria a quick glance. He nodded toward a wooden
box that sat beside the door. "In there. In the box. Grab a
handful of the bark and place it where you saw the sparks.
There will be more."

Having forgotten that Shadow had not answered her
question about where his slaves were, and having been
anxious for a fire to get the chill out of the hogan, Maria did
as Shadow asked. She carried two handfuls of the bark to
the fire pit and sprinkled it around where Shadow twirled
the stick.

"More," Shadow ordered flatly.

Maria got some more of the bark and sprinkled it on the other as more sparks appeared. She knelt and began to blow on a trace of a flame that a spark had caused, and in a moment's time flames spread and a nice fire was started.

Smiling, Maria moved to a sitting position as Shadow set his fire-starting tools aside and began laying small limbs in the fire.

"That is how it is done in the Navaho hogans," Shadow said, rising to his feet and going to the door, to lean outside.

Maria was taken by surprise when he returned carrying a big pot of steaming food. "How did that get there?" she gasped. "Who . . . ?"

Then she grew silent. Of course it would be a slave. The slave must have been ordered to have the food there at daybreak.

"It matters not who prepared this for us," Shadow said flatly. He reached for two wooden bowls and spoons and with a ladle dipped stew into the bowls. "It is important to take nourishment, for today much energy will be used up."

Maria nodded a silent thank-you to Shadow as he gave her a bowl of food and a spoon. She took a bite and savored its rich texture, surmising this must be made of rabbit and of vegetables from the gardens she had seen growing in the fertile ground in the grooves of the canyons.

"Must I go with you today?" she asked, taking another bite. "Why? Surely you trust that I will be here upon your return. I would not dare leave for home without direction."

"So you have decided that you will return to your family?" Shadow asked, already knowing her answer. There had been too much in their sharing for her to want to leave him, even if it meant staying with him out of wedlock.

Scooping a large bite of stew into his mouth, Shadow stretched one long, lean leg out before him and leaned back on an elbow. It was time to relax, for the hours that lay before him would be taxing. Training the Navaho youth made him quite aware that he was twenty-nine years of age. He wasn't sure if Maria could keep up with them this entire day.

But it was a test of her endurance that Shadow needed at this moment. If she stayed and lived with him and his people, many challenges would be put before her. And if they ever had a son, it was best that she know now what would be expected of *him*.

The very idea that Shadow had gone so far in loving her as to consider the possibility of their having a son jolted him for a second. He rested the spoon in the stew, looking at Maria, letting his gaze move over her, reminding himself just why she had this power over him. She was vibrant, she was beautiful, she was intelligent! She was everything he wanted in a wife!

It was easy to overlook her stubbornness and her challenging nature! For, in truth, even this he liked about her!

"You ask if I am going to return home," Maria said, blushing under his close scrutiny. She lowered her eyes and toyed with the food in her bowl, yet she could not avoid his question forever. Nor could he avoid hers. She *was* going to ask him again.

"Do you truly wish me to stay with you?" she asked, lifting her eyes, melting beneath the dark passion in his. "If you do, Shadow, why don't you marry me? I would marry you if you asked. I would stay with you forever!"

Shadow's eyes wavered, hearing the sincerity in her voice, touched by how deeply she felt about him. Her love was sincere! But would it stay sincere? How could he be sure that it would? If she grew tired of living away from the comforts of her family, would she turn her back on him and their marriage and leave?

Setting the bowl down on the floor, Shadow rose to his feet and began pacing. Maria grew cold, seeing how torn he was by her question. But she would not let him get away with not answering her this time. She angrily set her bowl down and went to him. Stepping in front of him, stopping his fitful pacing, she framed his face between her hands.

"Why are you afraid of marriage?" she murmured. "Is it because I am white? Does that make your trust in me so much less than if I were a Navaho woman? Darling, when

I give my heart to you, it will be totally yours. Forever it will be yours. Why do you trust me so little? Why?"

His heart pounding, her dark eyes reaching clean into his soul, Shadow could not help but be swayed by her words. He reached up and took her hands from his face and kissed the palms, then drew her over to the bed. Laying her down he knelt over her, kissing her with tender kisses, his body pressed into hers so that he felt her breasts through the buckskin of his shirt.

"My sweet one," Shadow said, cupping her breasts, seeing how doing so lit fire in her eyes. "Once we are married there will be no divorce. Do you understand that? Never shall you place my saddle outside my door. Do you understand that? Never shall you gather up what is mine and take it away. Do you understand?"

"I would never do those things," Maria said, smiling up at him. "I have never believed in divorce. It is ugly to me! Once I give my heart to you, it will no longer be mine to bargain with in any way! It will be yours, only yours."

She placed her hands on his face and drew his lips to hers. "Are you saying you will marry me?" she whispered, kissing him in quick, sweet kisses. "My darling, are you?"

"I have never put trust in a woman before," Shadow said softly, his loins heating up as Maria swept her hand down and touched his rising hardness.

"You had never met *me* before," Maria said, her heart racing as her hand cupped his hardness through his buckskin breeches.

"That is true," Shadow said huskily, laughing. "That is true."

He slipped a hand up inside her skirt, causing Maria's pulse to race when he splayed his fingers across her mound, which was pulsing with building passion. "Shadow," she said, his lips at the hollow of her throat, kissing her. "Tell me there will be no more slaves to serve you. I despise slavery as much as I despise divorce." She wove her fingers through his hair. "Especially love slaves. Please tell me you will need none. Tell me that my lovemaking will be enough for you."

"We shall see," Shadow said, laughing throatily. When Maria tensed and tried to wriggle from his embrace, he placed his hands on her cheeks and drew her close to him. "You said that Shadow never jests. My woman, Shadow just proved that he *does* jest. No love slave will ever enter my hogan again." His eyes twinkled as he gazed down at her. "That is, unless *you* request one."

Maria's eyes widened. She looked up at Shadow, stunned, then began to laugh softly. He *was* capable of joking.

Then she raised an eyebrow questioningly. He *was* joking, wasn't he?

His mouth claimed hers in a fiery kiss, erasing all thoughts of love slaves, reviving within her the wonders of *him* and of what he could do to her with a mere kiss.

Oh, and wasn't there always so much more?

And he was going to be her husband!

Her husband!

CHAPTER
12

Maria sat stiffly in her saddle, riding alongside Shadow and his magnificent stallion, watching with fascination as Shadow went from hogan to hogan, shouting, alerting the young Navaho braves that it was time to get up and resume their education in raiding and fighting.

As he came to each hogan he would stop before the door and repeat the same order: "Wake up! Be lively! If you are not up early, the enemy will come and kill you while you sleep!"

Maria had never seen so much scampering in her life. She watched the young Navaho braves scurry from their hogans, attired in only breechclouts and moccasins, their sleek raven hair hanging to their shoulders, their copper bodies shining beneath the early morning sun.

Obedient to Shadow, they raced through the village of hogans to the flat stretch of meadow that reached from one high canyon wall to the other. There they awaited Shadow in silence.

Just as obedient, Maria continued to ride alongside her lover, but her eyes were drawn to the women of the village, who were busy with their daily duties.

Some women were baking wheaten bread in outdoor ovens made of adobe bricks. As Maria passed by, one of these women raked out a fire that had already been built, then slid the flat loaves through the side door of the oven, where they would bake for hours in the hot clay. The wheat used for the bread had been reaped with sickles; horses were then driven around on top of the stalks to trample the seeds.

Going farther, Maria saw a woman making a water-bottle basket, pitched with *jícara*, piñon gum. Several others were busy weaving just outside the doors of their hogans. Because of her own skills in sewing, Maria recognized two kinds of looms, a belt loom and a blanket loom with an upright frame four or five feet square, used for making blankets and shawls.

Maria had learned from Pleasant Voice that before the arrival of sheep to their land the Navaho had done all of their weaving in cotton, which they carded, or combed, into straight threads with thistles. Now they used European-style cards—two blocks of wood studded with nails, like very coarse steel brushes. The Navaho women spun the thread and wove it on their old looms. Sometimes cloth was painted with earth colors or dyed with plant juice in green, yellow, or brownish pink. The brown or black blankets were made from the natural wool of dark-colored sheep.

Maria became absorbed in thoughts of home and of the many hours she had spent sewing. She longed to have her own sewing equipment with her. But as long as Shadow and her father were at war with each other, she could never return home to get it. She had made a decision, one that only included the man she loved. Her home was with him now! He had even promised to marry her.

But *when* had not been discussed! She hoped it would be soon, for if her father came for her again—whether he intended to bargain for her or take her by force—he would surely not separate a woman from her husband.

That Maria would be Shadow's wife could even assure Shadow a measure of safety, for surely her father would not want to make her a widow so early in life!

Smiling, feeling much more comfortable about her own future and Shadow's, Maria nudged her heels into the flanks of her horse, a gentle white mare, and rode her in a lope toward the meadow where the boys awaited their teachings only a heartbeat away. Maria wished she could feel comfortable about being asked to observe the day's activities. She had to wonder why Shadow would insist that she did. Her observations told her that she would be the only woman present. The other women who were this far from the hogans were busy working together planting corn, beans, and squash beside the river and the little streams that trickled down from the mountains.

Shadow inched his horse closer to Maria's and looked at her with his fathomless dark eyes. "You observe carefully what the young warriors will be taught," he said thickly. "This instruction is required to guarantee strong, capable warriors when they become men. It is the young braves' ambition to be thought good enough to go on a war party. In the days of old, if a brave managed to kill an enemy, he became a full-fledged warrior. Today, to be able to join in the raid and defend himself and others is all that is required to become such a warrior. If a brave shows cowardice he may be called ever after by the dreaded name 'crow.' Crows are afraid of everything so to call a man crow is a deadly insult."

His eyes became darker and more intense. "When you and I bring a son into the world, this training will be required of him," he said hoarsely. "It is important that you know this, Maria. All Navaho boys are educated for raiding and fighting. The training begins when they are seven years of age. This is part of our culture that you will have to grow accustomed to."

Maria looked at him in wonder, surprised at his having spoken of a son so suddenly. Until only a few hours ago he would not even speak of marriage!

He was a complicated man, but surely she would get to learn everything about him. If he wanted her to learn about the way their son would be trained, even before they were married, surely he would be as generous in revealing everything about himself to her.

And now she understood why he was requiring her to watch this performance this morning. He was preparing not only the young braves but also *her* for the future.

Suddenly she felt much promise in their future, together.

"*Sí*, I shall watch," she said, reaching out to touch him gently on the cheek. "For you, anything."

Shadow's eyes twinkled and a soft smile lifted his lips. "Never promise so much, my love," he said, taking her hand, kissing the palm. Then he released it and wheeled his horse around and rode away from her.

In a state of peaceful euphoria, Maria swung herself out of the saddle and secured her horse's reins, then settled down on a thick bed of grass and began watching. Shadow dismounted and began mingling with the young men, clasping his hands on their shoulders, giving them individual attention and encouragement while he spoke to them.

Then from out of nowhere, it seemed, many horses were brought by Shadow's Navaho warriors close to the throng of youths. Great shields and lances were placed on the ground. Many bows and arrows were placed beside them.

And then began hours of vigorous activity. The young men practiced with their bows and arrows, learning how to dodge arrows, to take advantage of any cover, to stand and hold the shield so as to give smallest possible target to an enemy.

The boys mounted their horses. The world became full of a roar of hooves and noise rushing together, the boys leaning forward over their horses' necks, their mouths wide as they shouted, "E-e-e-e!"

They met in a great swirl of plunging, dodging horses and swept on, all together, whooping for dear life, with some holding lances, others grasping shields.

And then they dismounted and ran to the icy waters of the streams and splashed into them, shouting and laughing.

Shadow came to Maria. He swung himself from his saddle and stood square-shouldered as he offered her a hand. "It is time to teach the young braves how to hunt for small prey," he said, drawing her up from the ground. "You will ride with us to observe how this is done. What is caught will be brought home for their mothers to prepare for a feast that will be held in honor of what the young braves have learned today. We will rest and then you must return to the village, for the young braves will have to take a long run in the sun and then be instructed in how to build sweat houses in which to take sweat baths. They will be made to vomit after their baths, to purify them. This is not something you will want to witness."

He looked into the distance, then back down at Maria. "I will send one of the youths with you, to see that you will arrive at my village safely," he said.

Maria's eyes widened at the thought of what he had described. It gave her a sick feeling in the pit of her stomach to envision the boys being forced to vomit. But her main concern lay elsewhere. "But if you have one of the young men accompany me, he will not benefit from the rest of today's teachings," she said, looking up at Shadow adoringly. "I can return alone. It isn't that far."

"It may be, if we have to travel far to find the holes that house the prairie dogs, the animals that I have chosen for the young braves to hunt and kill today," he said, frowning down at her. "If I do not send one of the young braves with you, perhaps one of my warriors will escort you home."

Maria looked at the warriors who were absorbed in teaching the Navaho youth. If one of them was pulled away from the activity, he would be denied so much and he could hate her because she was the cause.

She gazed determinedly up at Shadow. "No, not one of your warriors, either," she said stubbornly. "It is enough that they have to grow used to having me around; they mustn't be asked to cater to me as though I were a helpless ninny. Shadow, I *can* travel back to your village alone. I *shall*."

"You test me often, woman," Shadow growled. He led her to her horse and helped her into the saddle. "So shall I continue testing *you*."

"Testing me?" Maria said, arching an eyebrow. Then she smiled down at him as she wrapped her reins around her hand. "*Sí*, I guess you are. I presume that today is just the beginning. Am I right?"

Shadow did not answer her, only smiled up at her, then turned and mounted his stallion. While waiting for everyone else to mount, he stole glances at Maria, becoming more and more aware of how much of a challenge she continued to be.

But he had always loved challenges. They made him come alive!

Never had he felt more alive than now.

Thrusting his heels into the flanks of his stallion he rode away, glad when he heard Maria quickly gaining on him. As she drew up next to him, riding skillfully, he was proud to be able to boast that she was his. And as time went on, she would make him more and more proud of her. Though she was as slight as a wisp of grass, she seemed capable of doing anything that was set before her. . . .

Maria's hair blew in the wind, the tail of her skirt whipped about her legs, all of her senses were vibrantly alive as she clutched the reins. Knowing that she might never have to answer to her father again, she had never felt so free.

Throwing her head back, she sighed, then lowered her chin and let herself enjoy riding through the deep canyon where the high plateaus and steep gullies wound snakelike through the bottomland, clumps of juniper and piñon adding their dark, dusty green to the landscape, over which hung the most brilliant of blue skies.

But the ride was a short one, for the Navaho were suddenly dismounting, gathering together, carrying flat, shiny pieces of mica and clubs up a slight slope of land where she, after drawing her own horse to a halt, saw several colonies of prairie dogs' burrows, characterized by funnel-shaped entry mounds.

Not leaving her saddle, afraid to see how the clubs would be used, Maria felt her insides tighten when she saw the first prairie dog stick its head up from a hole and emit a sharp, barklike call.

Just as quickly it disappeared into the hole again. Maria tensed up as several young Navaho braves fell to their knees and began to crawl along the land toward several of the holes. She leaned forward in the saddle just a bit when the braves placed shiny pieces of mica outside the holes so they would catch sunlight and shine into the holes.

Before Maria could turn her eyes away, several prairie dogs emerged from their holes. Blinded by the light reflecting off the mica, they were easily prey for clubbing.

Shouts of victory rang through the air. Maria sat in her saddle, feeling ill, as the youths walked away from the burrows with their catch—several short-tailed yellowish-brown animals, about twelve inches long, with small ears and short legs.

Maria turned her eyes away. She had never enjoyed seeing anything her father caught while hunting. And to see so many at once was almost more than she could bear! If she were one of the mothers, back at a hogan, it would be her duty to prepare the animal for eating!

Oh, could she ever do that?

"Maria?" Shadow said, suddenly beside her.

Maria turned her head with a start and looked down at him, her face warm with a blush when she realized that he had seen her distaste at the performance by the Navaho youths. This was not the best way to impress her future husband!

"So I see that the young men will present their mothers with gifts for dinner tonight," she said, forcing a smile. "How nice, Shadow."

Shadow had seen her reaction to the hunt and knew she was trying to pretend that she had not been sickened by the killing. He decided not to question her about it. She was new to the Navaho life. It would take time. He was luckier than she in some respects: He already knew the customs of the Spaniards; she still had to learn everything about the Navaho.

"It is time for the young Navaho braves to begin building their sweat houses," he said, smoothing a hand over the buckskin that covered her leg. "You are sure you do not want someone to accompany you on your return journey to my village?"

"No, it isn't necessary," Maria said, glad to leave these rituals behind, no matter if it could be dangerous for her to travel alone. "I shall be just fine."

"This is my valley and mountain," Shadow said in a

growl, gesturing with a sweep of his hand around him. "You should be safe. No one will dare to trespass. My sentries can spy the most elusive person, except for one man . . ."

He looked up at Maria. "Only Charging Falcon is skillful enough to elude my sentries," he said. "But I doubt if he will ever come this way again. He surely knows that Pleasant Voice didn't die and has told everything she knows about his thieving ways. His death will be slow and agonizing if he is caught anywhere near my stronghold!"

A chill coursed across Maria's flesh when she heard the venom in Shadow's voice. At times he did seem so savage; at others, as gentle as a lamb.

She leaned down and placed a soft kiss on Shadow's brow. "I shall be awaiting your return to your hogan with an anxious heart," she murmured. "I shall keep the fire burning for you, my love, in both the fire pit and my heart."

Shadow chuckled, snaking a hand up her skirt to give her a gentle caress at the juncture of her thighs, then withdrew it and reached up to frame her face between his hands. "Shadow will be only half alive until tonight," he whispered, his tongue flicking out, tracing her lower lip sensually. "Until then, my love. Until then . . ."

Maria's insides were melting dangerously. Her whole body felt the wonder of how Shadow could affect her. She smiled once more down at him, then wheeled her horse around and rode back in the direction of the village nestled between the boulders of the mountain. Her stomach growled, attesting to how long it had been since she had eaten.

But she wanted to cover some ground before stopping to rest and eat. And she knew the exact spot. If she followed the stream, she would come across several broad-leaved yucca plants known as Spanish bayonets.

There she would rest and eat. . . .

Bone-weary from her trying day in the saddle, having only recently been forced to ride on a horse for so many hours at a time, Maria lay on soft moss beside the cool stream where rocks, piñon, and the sky were reflected in the translucent water beside her. She had taken only a few nibbles of the fruit of the yucca, having been more tired than hungry at this point in her journey back to the village.

Folding an arm up over her face, shielding her eyes from the light, Maria let herself drift into the sweet escape of sleep. As soon as she awakened she would hurry on with her travels.

But for now she needed rest. . . .

Ignoring the nervous neighing of her horse, reined close beside her, Maria felt her slumberous state deepen.

But then something drew her quickly awake. It was the answering neigh of another horse. She turned on her side and looked toward her horse, which was shaking its head and snorting, pawing the earth with its right hoof.

Then she froze in place when a hand was clasped around her mouth and another pinioned one of her wrists to her back.

"*Señorita*, I will kill you if you try to escape," a familiar voice said in a low growl. His breath was hot on her ear as he drew her to her feet and leaned his body against hers from behind. "Since Shadow already intends to kill me, it would not matter at all to me if I had to silence you with a knife. Now, I would rather not have to do that, for alive you are much more valuable to me."

Maria was stunned by Charging Falcon's cunning and daring to come into the mountains that were so closely guarded by Shadow's warriors. But if he had come this far unnoticed, could he not leave just as freely?

The thought of him taking her with him made panic rise inside her. What did he mean when he said she was valuable to him? Maria did not believe it meant that she was going to be valuable to him as a love slave. From all she knew about Charging Falcon, he looked to wealth as money, not human flesh!

He judged a captive's value according to the size of the payment he could get for that person.

Caramba! He was going to use her as a bargaining tool. But with whom? Her father or Shadow?

Squirming, trying to get free, even trying to bite the hand
that was clasped over her mouth, Maria soon learned that
was not the way to accomplish anything with Charging
Falcon. His fingers tightened on her wrist, paining her
terribly, and his fingers bit into her mouth, causing her teeth
to grind into her lips until she tasted the salt of blood inside
her mouth.

"My hands will not be my weapons the next time you try
to get free," Charging Falcon said, jerking her around to
face him. His gaze went over her as he appraised her with
his eyes. "Yes, Maria, I can see why Shadow stole you
away to be his love slave." He placed a hand on her breast
and squeezed, repelling her. "Perhaps I am wrong not to
keep you all to myself."

His dark hair bounced on his shoulders as he shook his
head. "No, that is not why I have risked my life to come
here for you," he said, his eyes gleaming. "If I want a lady,
there are many to choose from. You are only one of
thousands in this land of beautiful women."

Now free of his grip, but afraid to try to escape because
he had a knife handy at his waist, Maria steadied herself and
glared up at him, wiping blood from her lips with the back
of a hand. "I'll have you know that I am not Shadow's love
slave," she snapped angrily. "He has more respect for me
than that."

Charging Falcon's eyebrows rose inquisitively. "That is
so?" he questioned, then chuckled. "Then, woman, that
makes you more valuable than I would have ever imagined.
If Shadow cares for you so much that he did not place you
into slavery, he will pay twice as much to get you back!"

Maria took a step back, paling. "You plan to sell me back
to Shadow?" she gasped.

"No, not exactly," Charging Falcon said, laughing,
pushing her toward his horse. He nudged her in the ribs with
an elbow. "Get up into my saddle. One horse used for
escaping through these mountains will be less detectable
than two." He untethered Maria's mare and set it free.

Maria placed her foot in a stirrup and eased up into his
saddle, questioning him with her eyes. "First you say that

Shadow will pay twice as much to get me back and then you say that you do not intend to sell me to him," she said, flinching when he swung himself into the saddle behind her and held her firmly around the waist with an arm of steel. "What *are* your intentions?"

"I know of a wealthy Spaniard who is an enemy to your father because of rivalry in the past," Charging Falcon said, lifting the reins and snapping them. "*He* will pay me for you and then safely deal with both Shadow and your father. He will get paid twice for you. Then whomever he chooses to give you to will be up to him."

"Who would be foolish enough to try such a trick as that?" she gasped, hanging onto the pommel of the saddle as the horse began traveling down a steep embankment. "The man he *doesn't* give me to will be ready to kill him."

"I doubt that," Charging Falcon said, chuckling.

"And why are you so smug about this?" Maria asked, glancing at him over her shoulder.

"Neither of them will know that the other is involved in the transaction," Charging Falcon said flatly. "After the money is paid, the Spaniard plans to set you free and let you wander in the desert. Neither your father nor Shadow will know whom they have paid, since the deal will be made secretly. How can they retaliate against the Spaniard if they don't know who he is?"

Maria's heart plummeted to her feet. Either way she looked at it, if Shadow did not rescue her quickly while Charging Falcon was stealing her away, she would die! She would never see Shadow *or* her parents again if Charging Falcon had his way.

And it seemed that . . . he did. . . .

CHAPTER
13

Maria's head was bobbing as she fought sleep, Charging Falcon's arm still tight around her waist as they rode onward across a straight stretch of desert. The sun was just rising in the distance behind the mountains. Though tired and hungry, Maria was thankful that Charging Falcon had not stopped to rest and eat since having abducted her. She did not trust him and felt much safer on a horse with him, than taking the time to rest and eat.

But how much longer could she endure this punishment to her body? They had been traveling an entire night. Where *was* he taking her? With whom would she spend the next full night? Was she going to be treated like a slave—raped and then taken out into the desert to die? Somehow she had to find a way to escape.

But even if she did, in which direction would she travel to get back to Shadow's stronghold or her father's plantation? At this moment, her mind was so disoriented she could not see anything familiar about the terrain around her. It was barren wasteland with only an occasional jackrabbit suddenly appearing out of nowhere, or a lone buzzard flapping its ugly wings overhead, its beady eyes watching . . . watching . . .

"*Señor*, how much longer?" Maria asked, giving Charging Falcon a weak stare across her shoulder. She would not complain of being tired and hungry. She would not give him

the satisfaction of knowing that she was suffering, nor
would she give him an excuse to stop, for she sorely feared
that he would take advantage of her. If he raped her, she
would want to die! She wanted no one but Shadow to touch
her.

But she no longer had control over anything that happened to her. Charging Falcon was in charge of her destiny
now, not herself, or Shadow.

The knowing made a slow ache circle her heart. And
what of Shadow? What was he doing now that he realized
she was missing? Did he have his warriors searching for
her? If so, just how much time had passed from the moment
he had discovered her missing to when he had set out to
search for her?

Surely many hours!

Oh, but it was all so hopeless!

"You ask how much longer?" Charging Falcon said,
smiling smugly at her. "You are anxious to get away from
Charging Falcon? Do you feel that you will be better off
with the Spaniard? Soon you will see that you are wrong!
You will be thrown into the slave house with the rest of the
slaves. Then you will be taken out to the desert and left to
die. So you see? Compassion the Spaniard does not have!"

Maria turned her eyes away from Charging Falcon,
feeling cold inside. She squinted as the morning sun rose
higher in the sky, the horse traveling directly toward it.
Wondering just which Spaniard Charging Falcon could be
speaking of, in her mind she began sorting through the ones
whom she and her father had become acquainted with after
having arrived in New Mexico, trying to find the one who
could hate her father so much that he would be willing to
treat her so unjustly.

But no particular man would come to mind. When her
father had commanded men, while he was a colonel in
the Spanish army, he *had* made enemies. *Many*! Because he
had been chosen for a top rank, *many* who had wanted the
position had envied him.

But would envy cause them to react in this way?

Maria gave Charging Falcon another quick glance.

Everything *he* did against Shadow was done because of envy, and they had once been best friends.

Sí, there *could* be Spaniards who could go as far against Maria's father, for he had never been a true friend to any of them. Trust had been too lacking among them all to make close friends . . .

Maria felt Charging Falcon's arm tighten around her waist and realized that he had tightened the reins, urging his horse to slow down. A thundering of hooves approaching them made her glance quickly upward. She swallowed hard and squirmed in the saddle when she saw many Spanish vaqueros approaching, the silver ornaments on their bridles flashing in the sun.

"Say nothing," Charging Falcon growled. "The wrong words used now could get us both killed!"

Maria cringed as she watched the men draw rifles and make a circle around her and Charging Falcon when the Indian drew his horse to a shuddering stop. Scarcely breathing, she looked from man to man, wishing that because they were Spaniards she could feel safe. But the look in their dark eyes made her grow numbly cold inside. The well-armed vaqueros with their rifles shining in the morning light were threatening.

"Charging Falcon, why are you here, on land that belongs to Señor Gironella?" one of the vaqueros said, his shoulder-length dark hair blowing in the breeze, his buckskin outfit fitting his muscled figure like a glove. His gaze met and held Maria's, as though in recognition. "What are you doing with *her*?"

"She is to be offered to Señor Gironella for a price," Charging Falcon said, smirking. "He knows of the transaction. I discussed it with him. Let me pass or you will pay for interfering!"

Maria's breath was stolen away when the vaquero placed the barrel of his rifle against Charging Falcon's side. "Injun, you sometimes forget your place," he growled, again glancing at Maria, looking her slowly up and down. He dropped his rifle away. "But this time you can pass. Just watch your words in the future, *comprende*?"

Charging Falcon glared at the vaquero, his eyes narrowing angrily, then nodded. "Vaquero, do not get so brave
with your words that some night you will be rendered
unable to speak again," he said in a whisper, yet loud
enough for the man to hear. "My knife has cut out many a
tongue, vaquero. Do not tempt me!"

A shiver coursed across Maria's flesh. She had been
warned by Charging Falcon not to say anything, yet here he
was making threats! Surely the only reason he felt safe in
doing this was that José Gironella was expecting him and
would not want the business transaction to be interfered
with.

José Gironella . . .

. Maria did not know the man, but more than likely he
knew her father well enough to do this vicious thing for
spite!

"Ride on," the vaquero growled, nodding to his companions to make way for Charging Falcon to pass. "But,
Charging Falcon, make no more threats to me. You are
alone, without warriors. Do you think that wise?"

Charging Falcon urged his horse forward. "José Gironella depends on Charging Falcon for many things," he
warned. "He would not be happy if anything happened to
Charging Falcon!"

Slapping his reins with one hand and hanging on to Maria
with the other, Charging Falcon urged his horse into a hard
gallop toward a plantation house that was becoming visible
on the horizon.

"You are not very smart!" Maria shouted above the roar
of the hooves. "We both could have been killed. You are
not a very smart warrior, Charging Falcon."

"And why do you care?" he shouted back at her. "In a
short time, you will wish you were dead." His laughter
echoed across the land, trailing along after him as he sank
his heels into the flanks of his horse, urging it into an even
faster gallop.

Fear soared through Maria at the thought of what might
happen in the next few hours. She watched the large
two-story plantation house grow closer and closer. The

desert had changed—almost magically, it seemed—into fertile green land where sheep grazed peacefully as far as the eye could see. A mountain slope reached down at the far end of the land, where streams were mountain-fed.

She looked at the assortment of outbuildings behind the house, knowing that many of them were used to house the slaves. Soon she would be thrown into such a house! In the distance she could see Indians toiling in the fields, tending sheep, planting seed!

Then her insides recoiled when she got a closer look and saw several Spanish women among the Indians, working side by side with them. It was the habit of this Spaniard to take his own people into slavery! How was it that she had never heard of such a practice?

But she knew why: Her father had kept her shielded from too many things in life. Even *this*!

Her spine stiffened when Charging Falcon rode his horse up to a wide porch where a tall, thin man dressed in a white suit, with diamonds glittering on his fingers and on the ascot at his throat, stood waiting. Maria's eyes went quickly over him, stopping at his face, seeing nothing familiar about the long, narrow nose, wide lips, and beady gray eyes, with black hair cropped short.

No, this was not a man she knew.

But surely her father did . . .

"Bring her to me, Charging Falcon," José Gironella said, clasping his hands behind him, rocking back and forth, from his heels to his toes and back again. "Let me see what I am paying you for. Let me see if she is worth it."

Charging Falcon swung himself down from the saddle, then yanked Maria from it, causing her to stumble. She frowned up at him and steadied herself, then jerked away from him when he grabbed her wrist.

"Keep your filthy hands off me," she snapped. "It's enough that I have had to spend the full night with you in the saddle. Now that you have me here, ready to hand me over for whatever this man is going to pay you, I am no longer any concern of yours."

Gironella's eyes danced with amusement. He moved

down the steps and began walking around Maria, appraising
her with his eyes. "I like them with spirit," he chuckled.
"While she's here, she'll liven up the place just a mite."

Maria's eyes followed him. When he stepped out of eye
range, she turned, still watching him. When he grabbed her
wrist and she tried to yank herself free, he pulled her up
close to him and spoke down into her face.

"I will tolerate only so much from you, though," he
growled. "I am sure your daddy has ways of teaching
obedience to his slaves, doesn't he? Well, I have my own
ways."

Maria's face paled. She stood quiet, looking up at him.
"Do you know my father?" she asked guardedly. "Do you
know him personally?"

"Everyone knows Esteban Zamora." He laughed, reaching out to pinch her buttocks with his free hand. "But
scarcely anyone knows he has such a vivacious daughter.
He has kept you well hidden, *sí*?"

"What has my father done to you for you to treat me so
unkindly?" Maria asked, shivering when his free hand
traveled down the curve of her buttock. "Or perhaps you
don't have a grudge against him at all. Perhaps you will buy
and sell *any* woman's flesh."

"The *señorita* is smart also," Gironella said, laughing
boisterously, his free hand now touching one of Maria's
breasts where the buckskin fabric strained against it. "You
see, you are right. Though I led Charging Falcon to believe
I wanted to purchase you because of hatred for your father,
that is not so. I hate no one. I just love *women*."

His deep, throaty laugh sent chills up and down Maria's
spine. She gave Charging Falcon a beseeching look, now
realizing that she would have been better off with *him*. He
had had every opportunity to take her sexually and he had
not. Perhaps he had some loyalty to Shadow left after all.

Oh, if only he would see what this Spaniard has planned
for her and take back his offer to sell her to him.

She could see a rising fear in Charging Falcon's eyes.
Was he thinking that he might not leave this man's planta-

tion alive? The vaqueros had arrived and were looking on, enjoying her humiliation.

But the one vaquero's eyes were on Charging Falcon.

Only . . . Charging Falcon . . .

Releasing his hold on Maria and giving her a shove, José Gironella frowned down at her. "You are familiar with plantation properties," he snarled. "Go and find the slaves' houses. Choose one. Go inside. And don't try to run away. As you see, my grounds are heavily guarded. I will give you to whichever man catches you in an attempt to escape! I don't have to draw a picture to describe what fun he will have with you before he gives you back to me."

Maria flipped her hair back from her eyes and shoulders and glared at him, then at Charging Falcon. "One day both of you will be sorry," she said, her voice breaking. "If Shadow doesn't kill you, my father will."

Turning on her heel, she began running, the tears bitter and hot at the corners of her eyes. She bit her lower lip in frustration when she reached the back of the massive plantation house and saw the long line of slave dwellings. Several women were outside, bent over tubs, washing clothes. As she approached, their attention was drawn to her, their eyes questioning and sad.

Wiping a tear from her cheek, sniffling, Maria stopped running and walked toward the women with her chin held high. Then, showing those men who were watching her that she did not set herself above the others who had been enslaved, she offered to help with the laundry.

Soft smiles and silent nods welcomed her. Maria sank her arms elbow-high into sudsy water and glared at José Gironella as he looked at her, amusement dancing in his dark eyes.

When the women began clamoring around her with questions, she looked away from Gironella, but not before she had seen Charging Falcon go into the mansion with him. In a matter of moments she saw Charging Falcon leave. He tucked a small leather drawstring pouch into his saddlebag; inside it were surely many coins in payment for his spineless deed this day.

She had to wonder if sometime soon that money would be back in Gironella's safe, or had the Spaniard given his men strict orders not to harm Charging Falcon? It seemed that the Pueblo was more valuable to him alive than dead.

Night had fallen and the oil lamps had just been lit. José Gironella stood at the window in his study, peering toward the slaves' quarters, seeing the flicker of lamplight at a small, curtainless window. He watched the slight silhouette of a woman's figure pace back and forth before the window, and he had to surmise that it was Maria Zamora. It was taking all of the willpower he could muster up not to take her from the slaves' quarters and go to bed with her.

But first, she must be made to feel degraded by having to eat and sleep with the slaves for several days and nights. Though she had tried to prove a point earlier by doing laundry along with the rest of the women, he had known that it was just an act of open defiance for him to see. Surely, deep within, she hated every minute of being with the other women who had never known the meaning of being as rich as Maria Zamora.

And her father would pay *much* to have her returned. In truth, the payment would be made, but Zamora would never get her back!

Perhaps José would keep her for himself instead of turning her out to the desert to die! He had not known how beautiful she was. She could be worth much to him. Perhaps he would not send her to her death.

Hearing footsteps behind him, Gironella turned and smiled down at two Mexican boys who were paid well to be his messengers. But this time orders had been handed down to kill both of the boys after the messages were delivered. They must not be traced back to Gironella. He knew Shadow's cunning ways, and perhaps where his daughter was concerned, even Zamora could be determined to find her abductor!

No, the boys must be killed! The one after he used his own prowess to get a message to Shadow, and the other when he left Zamora's plantation after giving the message to him.

"*Buenas noches*," Gironella said, smiling smugly from one boy to the other. "It is good that you have come. I will pay you well for delivering messages." He walked to one boy and clasped his shoulder. "Lad, you will travel to Señor Zamora's plantation and tell him that his daughter is being held prisoner and that payment is required for her return to him. But do not tell him who has sent the message. Tell him to place one thousand gold coins in a bag and take it to the same spot where payment to me has been made before. Tell him to come alone. And if he tells anyone and he is followed, Maria will be killed. He will never see her again. *Comprende*?"

"*Sí*," the boy said, nodding anxiously.

José Gironella went to the other boy and clasped his shoulders. "And you," he said, his eyes narrowing. "You will pass the same message on to the Navaho leader, Shadow. Now I know you do not know exactly where his stronghold is, but that does not matter. Keep watch until you see one of his warriors traveling across the land. Then give the message to him and tell him to take it to Shadow. *Comprende*?"

The boy swallowed hard. "*Sí, sí*," he said, his voice thin and terrified.

"Good," Gironella said, going to his desk. He picked up two folded slips of paper and slipped one into each boy's hand. "Then, lads, be on your way and *que le vaya bien*, good luck to you! A vaquero will find you later and pay you well for your services."

"*Gracias*," the boys said in unison.

Gironella watched them depart, frowning. He would have trouble finding two such cooperative young men again. But he had no choice but to have these two killed. . . .

Charging Falcon stole across the land, only a slight shadow in the night, having watched for a good portion of the vaqueros to retire in their bunkhouses for the night.

There weren't enough guards left around the plantation grounds to cause him any threat. He moved swiftly and silently. His prowess was extraordinary at night; no Spaniard he had ever met could compare with him.

Having thought over his arrangement with José Gironella very carefully, Charging Falcon had decided that he had been wrong to leave Maria with him. Even though Charging Falcon had known from the first what her fate would be in the end, he could not allow it to happen. He had seen the pleading in her eyes. He had had fleeting remembrances of his youthful days with Shadow and how they had learned to hunt and ride horses. How could he have let things go this far? Why had he let jealousy break the bonds between two boys who had been closer than most brothers?

He knew very well when it had happened. When their boyhood challenges had become challenges of men, the Pueblo had placed more importance on winning than on friendship. When Shadow began to win at everything, Charging Falcon had felt worthless. This had eaten away at his gut and his self-confidence until he could stand it no more. That was when he had begun working against Shadow rather than with him.

His footsteps light, his movements stealthy, Charging Falcon raced behind the slaves' quarters, having watched which one Maria had chosen before he left the plantation grounds earlier in the day. Creeping along the wall of the cabin, he glanced in all directions to be sure he wasn't seen. Then he leapt through the open window, glad that everyone was asleep. If he made any commotion at all, he was the same as dead!

As he crept from bunk to bunk, the moonlight through the windows bathed most faces with its faint light. Charging Falcon's muscles tightened and his breath slowed when he finally found Maria. She was lying on her side, sleeping soundly, still fully clothed, as were all of the other slaves, since no blankets were given them to use.

Trembling, knowing that if Maria cried out the rest of the women would also be awakened, Charging Falcon quickly clamped his hand over her mouth and grabbed her wrist

with his other hand. When she opened her eyes and looked
wildly up at him, he couldn't explain what he was doing. It
would have been dangerous even to whisper.

Stunned, now wondering what Charging Falcon wanted
of her, Maria felt she had no choice but to do as he asked.
If she cried out, the guards would come. She felt she would
be safer with Charging Falcon. It was in the way he was
looking at her, as if apologizing for having brought her
there. Or did he have other devious plans for her?

Whatever his reason, it appeared that he was helping her
to escape! She would cooperate with him. Fully!

Going to the window, Maria climbed through it and
waited for Charging Falcon to follow behind her. Crouching, they ran together behind the other outbuildings and
then across the barren land until they were in the safe cover
of trees.

When they stopped to catch their breath, Maria questioned Charging Falcon with her eyes; then she spoke.
"Why are you doing this?" she whispered. "You know the
danger. You will be killed instantly if you are caught!"

"Charging Falcon will not be caught," he said blandly.
"And why do I do this? Charging Falcon does not understand too clearly himself. The fact that I am doing it is all
that should matter to you."

"Are you taking me back to Shadow?"

"No."

"Are you taking me to my father?"

"No."

Maria grew cold inside. "Then where?" she asked, fear
lacing her words.

"I have brought another horse," Charging Falcon said,
glancing over at her, seeing her loveliness beneath the soft
splash of the moon. "I cannot take you to Shadow or your
father. But I can take you far enough away from here for
you to go on horseback alone to find your way either to your
father's plantation or to Shadow's stronghold. That is all I
can do for you. If I took you either place, I would be killed.
You know that."

Maria trembled from realization that she could not find

her way to either place. She was not that well acquainted with the desert, mountains, and meadows of New Mexico. She would be lost forever!

But she would not tell her fears to Charging Falcon. She most certainly did not want to stay with him! Being set free was the only answer. She would just have to pray that she would be led, somehow, safely to Shadow or her father.

"*Gracias*, for doing this," she murmured, then fire lit her eyes. "But, Charging Falcon, you shouldn't have stolen me away in the first place."

"Charging Falcon does many foolish things for money," he admitted, lowering his eyes. Then he took her by the wrist. "Come. We must hurry onward. We are not free yet."

"*Sí*," Maria said, running along beside him. Her eyes were adjusting to the darkness and just up ahead she saw two horses grazing peacefully on a slight slope of land. When they reached them, Charging Falcon helped her up into the saddle, then swung himself onto the other horse.

"We are safe now," he said, grasping his reins. "You follow. We have a long ride ahead of us, and then I will leave you alone."

The thought sent spirals of fear throughout Maria, yet she was learning the art of survival.

Sí! She *would* survive!

She would concentrate hard on Shadow and how it would feel to be held in his powerful arms again. *He* would be her reason to find her way back to civilization again once she was set free in the desert!

CHAPTER
14

The morning sun streaming in through the window beside the bed, his wife still in a deep sleep, José Gironella rose from his bed and drew on a pair of velveteen breeches. Going to the window, he stared out at the slaves' quarters, having been unable to get Maria out of his thoughts the entire night. Dark circles beneath his eyes attested to a night of restlessness.

Smoothing a hand over his whiskered face, yawning, he studied the cabin where Maria Zamora more than likely still slept. His loins aching, hungry for a woman, he decided not to wait any longer until he had her sexually. She was in his blood. He could not wait any longer!

Glancing at his wife as he turned to face the bed, he smiled to himself. It was always this time of day that he needed a woman the most and this was when his wife chose to sleep! He had learned to accept, even welcome her habit of sleeping until lunchtime, for this was when he would choose a slave and take her to a cabin apart from the others, where he would have his love games without interferences.

Today his choice was Maria Zamora!

Slipping his feet into slippers, drawing a velveteen shirt over his head, he crept from the bedroom, down the stairs, and through the house, then strolled confidently . . . eagerly, hungrily . . . across the lawn to the slaves' quarters. Boldly, authoritatively, he opened the door and went from bunk to bunk, looking for Maria.

His heart turned cold when he did not find her anywhere and then discovered the vacant bunk. Anger flared in his eyes as he emitted a loud shriek, causing the women in the room to awaken with alarm and scurry from their beds, looking wildly at Gironella.

"Where is she?" he shouted, motioning toward the empty bunk. "Surely one of you saw her leave! Tell me or each and every one of you will bend beneath the whip. Twenty lashes to each of you if someone doesn't speak up!"

A frail woman stepped out away from the others, her head humbly lowered. "*Señor*, an Indian helped her escape," she said, her voice trembling. "I did not cry out because I feared the Indian might kill, then scalp me! *Lo siento*, I am sorry, *señor*. But I was afraid."

Gironella went to the woman and grabbed her long, black, sleek hair and jerked her head up so that her eyes could meet his. "Which Indian?" he shouted. "Surely you know Charging Falcon when you see him. He's been here enough times, transacting business with me. Was it he?"

"*Sí*, it was," the woman said, her words strangled with fear.

José Gironella dropped his hand away from her and stepped back, jolted by the news. "Charging Falcon?" he whispered, staring at the empty bunk, then at the window that had no bars or glass to stop escapes. The slaves never attempted to escape because they knew that the plantation was well guarded and that if they managed to elude the guards, desert stretched out on three sides of the plantation, mountains on the other.

Escape meant death!

But Charging Falcon knew ways of eluding the best of guards, and he also knew the desert and the mountains.

"But *why*?" he asked, scratching his brow.

Maria forced her eyes to stay open. Her backside felt numb in the saddle; the ride across the barren desert had been long and grueling. All night she had followed Charging Falcon. They had changed horses twice, but hadn't stopped to eat or rest, fearing being followed. Maria was nearing a state of total fatigue from being hungry and tired, yet she fought to ride onward.

She flinched when Charging Falcon wheeled his horse around and reached out to take her horse's reins, stopping her. She licked her lips, parched from thirst. She combed her fingers through her wind-tossed hair, looking at Charging Falcon, knowing that they had more than likely come to the place where they were to part.

Maria squinted up at the sun, which had reached the midway point in the sky; then she looked toward the mountains. Somewhere in them was Shadow's stronghold. Could she ride that far alone? Or should she try to find her way to her father's house?

She seemed not to truly have a choice at all, for she did not think that she could arrive at either place alive. She was weak from lack of food and water. She was beginning to feel a strange lethargic spinning in the head, caused by hunger, thirst, and fatigue!

Perhaps this was what Charging Falcon had planned for her all along! He had only pretended to care that she should not be left under the care of the evil Spaniard! He had brought her to this place of all sun and sand and was going to leave her to die; surely this was just another way to get back at Shadow!

"This is as far as I can go with you," Charging Falcon said, his eyelids heavy over his dark eyes. "I cannot take you on to Shadow's stronghold. He would not understand why I chose to steal you away, then rescue you. He would not understand why I shot Pleasant Voice and left her to die, then rescued you. I do not have answers myself, Maria. Perhaps it is because I am beginning to lessen in resentment toward Shadow. After I shot Pleasant Voice and left her, I began to have feelings of guilt for the first time in many moons. These feelings have been following me around like a ghost. I tried to fight this emotion by abducting you to prove to myself that I am not lessening in hard feelings toward Shadow. But after I left you with the Spaniard I could not live with more guilt. Too much plagues my heart already."

With a sweep of the hand, he motioned toward the mountains. "It looks like a far way to go, but it is not," he said, trying to reassure her. "Just set your sights on the mountains and ride toward them. By tonight you will be there. You will be seen by Shadow's warriors. They will take you to Shadow. Tell him how my heart is suffering, Maria. Tell him I am ready to repent all that I have done to his people. I shall do nothing more against him. The fight is over for me."

Maria was stunned by his confession. She was speechless as he wheeled his horse around and rode away from her. She watched him until he became only a speck on the horizon. Then, fearing the solitude and the long journey ahead, she thrust her heels into the flanks of her horse and rode on toward the mountains.

The lethargy and dizziness seemed to be worsening . . .

Shirtless, a bandage wrapped securely around his shoulder and across his chest, Esteban Zamora sat at his desk in his study, poring over his ledgers. But his heart wasn't in his work. His thoughts kept drifting to Maria. He had failed to free her from the wretched Navaho, Shadow. His wound was a constant reminder of Shadow's manpower, and he would not try to rush the stronghold with force again, for Maria would surely be killed because of it!

He was biding his time until he was well enough to ride again. Then he would come up with a peace offering to Shadow. If the two men could reach an agreement, perhaps Maria would be returned home.

But until then what was her fate?

Knitting his brow, frowning, Zamora tried to block such thoughts from his mind. His hands were tied for now. Damn the shoulder wound. It was healing much too slowly!

A commotion just outside the door of his study caused him to raise his head in a jerk. One of his guards ushered a young Mexican boy into the room, his face flushed, his eyes wild.

"What is this?" Zamora said, rising slowly from his chair, wincing when a sharp pain shot through his shoulder.

"This boy says he has a message for you," the guard said, roughly grasping the boy's arm. "He says it has something to do with Maria, so I brought him to you."

Zamora's gut twisted with the mention of Maria. He stepped around his desk and went to glower down at the boy. "What *about* Maria?" he snapped. "What message have you brought to me? Have you come from Shadow's stronghold? Is Maria all right?"

"*Señor*, I know nothing except that I was given this message to bring to you," the boy said shallowly, breathing hard. "I do not even know who sent the message," he lied. "A vaquero paid me to bring it to you. Now that I have, I would like to leave." He gave the guard an uneasy glance. "I have done nothing except be kind enough to bring you the message about your daughter. Now I wish to go."

Zamora studied the boy, then grabbed him away from the guard and gave him an angry shake. "You know more than you are telling me," he shouted. "I am sure you cannot read, yet you know the message is about my daughter! Tell me how you know this."

The boy dug his hand into his breeches pocket and pulled the note from it. He held it out. "*Señor*, take the note," he said, his eyes wild. "Read it. The vaquero told me it was about your daughter Maria. That's how I know what the note was about. I was told to tell you, also, where to take the *money*."

Zamora paled. His hand trembled as he took the note and slowly unfolded it, afraid to read it. What was this about a vaquero? Shadow did not have vaqueros under his command, only Indian warriors.

Holding the note up, Zamora began to read the distinct handwriting, in perfect Spanish. He began to feel ill at his stomach the more he read, realizing that Maria was no longer at Shadow's stronghold, but being held captive by one of his Spanish foes. It was apparent that Maria had been abducted from Shadow's stronghold and sold to this Spaniard. The Spaniard in turn was going to sell her to *him*.

Rage tore through him as he continued to read. He was to leave one thousand gold coins in a certain spot. Maria would be returned later. He alone was to deliver the money, or Maria would be killed!

The pain in his shoulder seemed intensified at this moment, for his whole body was racked with emotions that were tearing him apart!

Refolding the note, he glared down at the Mexican boy. "All right," he growled. "Tell me where I am to take the money." He had not planned to ride on a horse just yet, his shoulder wound having only begun to heal, but for Maria, he *must*.

Riding along the golden sand of the desert on his chestnut stallion, his warriors following obediently behind him, Shadow felt only half alive. He had searched and searched for Charging Falcon's hideout, planning to kill him the moment he saw him, for having stolen Maria away. He knew beyond a shadow of a doubt that Charging Falcon had captured her. Only he could elude Shadow's sentries! He also knew the skills of hiding in the mountains, for not even one trace of him or Maria had been found.

Shadow hung his head, disillusioned about life. "Will it ever end?" he whispered. "Charging Falcon, will your hatred for me ever be appeased? Do you forget so easily those times we were together as children? Oh, how could you? We were closer than brothers!"

"Someone comes!"

A warrior's shout broke through Shadow's quiet, brooding grief. His head jerked up and he straightened his shoulders when he saw a slight figure of a boy on a horse just ahead, moving toward him. His hand moved easily down to the knife he had slipped into a sheath on his thigh. He squinted his dark eyes, wondering what the boy would want out here on the desert, wandering all alone.

Holding a fist in the air, a silent warning for his warriors to stay behind as he proceeded toward the Mexican boy, Shadow went ahead until he was side by side with the boy.

When he saw no weapon, he relaxed and gave the boy a frown.

"What are you doing out in the desert alone?" Shadow asked, looking past the boy for signs of anyone following, seeing none.

"You are Shadow?" the boy asked, his eyes wide.

"Yes, I am Shadow," he said in monotone. "Why do you ask?"

The boy sighed with relief, his brow beaded with perspiration. "I have been searching for you," he said, withdrawing from his pocket the note intended for Shadow. "I have been paid to bring you this." He handed the note to Shadow.

Shadow forked an eyebrow and took the note, glad that he had been taught to read by his mother who had learned it from a holy man who had for a time lived with the Navaho. Shadow unfolded the note and began to read.

The hair at the nape of Shadow's neck bristled with anger when he read that Maria was with a Spaniard instead of Charging Falcon.

Yet, why should this surprise him? Surely Charging Falcon had received a large payment to deliver her to this nameless Spaniard who dealt in human flesh. Now the Spaniard, in turn, was demanding money from Shadow to have her returned to him!

His eyes lit with fire, Shadow crumpled the note up, making his hand a tight ball around it. "Who sent you?" he growled. "Who has Maria?"

The boy looked innocently up at him. "*Señor*, I do not know who wrote the note," he lied. "A vaquero gave it to me and paid me well to bring it to you. Now I must tell you where to drop the money. *Comprende*?"

Shadow leaned over and with his free hand locked his fingers around the boy's throat. "You lie," he said between his clenched teeth. "You tell me the truth or *die*."

The boy squirmed uneasily in the saddle, breathing hard. "I . . . do not lie, *señor*," he said, pleading up at Shadow with fearful eyes. "Please let me go. I am innocent! Innocent!"

Having never made it a habit of killing children, even those who were developing into men, Shadow moved his hand away from the boy's throat. "Tell me where I am to take the money," he said, his voice strained. He leaned closer to the boy. "But be forewarned that if anything happens to Maria, I will search the earth high and low for you and I will not have pity the second time you plead for your life!"

Again swallowing hard, the boy slouched in his saddle, then nodded eagerly. "*No se preocupe*, don't worry," he said in a rush of words. "The woman will be safe enough. I give you my word!"

Shadow laughed sarcastically. "Your word?" he said sourly. "It is worthless, I am sure!"

The boy proceeded to tell Shadow where to take the money while Shadow listened, hate searing his insides. Charging Falcon would be found and dealt with.

For having done this to Maria, Charging Falcon *must* be found. His death would come slowly . . . painfully . . .

Hardly able to hang on to the horse's reins, her vision blurring from hunger and lack of rest, Maria felt herself slipping from the saddle. She grabbed for the pommel and looked into the distance, but was only able to see a haze of green ahead. It was trees . . . the trees that lay at the base of the mountains! She was not that far from the stronghold! Surely she wasn't . . .

Too weak to hang on to the pommel any longer, Maria cried throatily as she felt herself falling . . . falling . . . falling.

When she hit the ground with a loud thump and pain soared through her, she took a shallow breath, closed her eyes, and welcomed the void of unconsciousness. . . .

Zamora placed the satchel of money at the foot of a stack of rocks beneath a cottonwood tree. Pain tore through his shoulder as he fit his foot into the stirrup and eased himself back into his saddle.

Rubbing his bandaged shoulder through the velveteen

softness of his shirt, he sat for a moment, peering intently in every direction, looking for any signs of those who would be coming to get the ransom money.

But all that he could see was the yellow sand contrasting with the blue of the sky and, on his right, a line of cottonwoods edging along beside a meandering stream.

His head bowed, Zamora swung his horse around and began riding back in the direction of his plantation, filled with despair. Something told him that though he had done as he had been instructed, he still would not see Maria.

But he could not have taken the chance of refusing to pay the money. Just perhaps he was wrong! He must grasp on to at least a measure of hope for his daughter.

Shadow was riding alone, carrying a buckskin bag filled with money, his intent to deliver the money as he had been instructed, though to do so went against everything he had been taught as a warrior. It was best not to deal with those who would make you pay ransom. Those sorts did not know the meaning of honesty! They had no feelings for humanity. If Maria came out of this alive, he would be surprised.

But he had to chance it. And he was planning to track the one who picked up the money. He would find the person responsible and hang him by his toes from a tree. This person would tell Shadow where Maria could be found, then beg for mercy, but Shadow would give none!

"If she is harmed at all, *many* will pay!" he growled, seeing all Spaniards as responsible. He would send his warriors on raids that would be talked about for generations to come. It seemed that this was the only way to make the Spaniards understand that the Navaho could no longer be pushed around.

"Having to pay to have my woman returned to me is the last straw!" he said to himself, his heart paining him to think that Maria might have been raped, perhaps even repeatedly!

He would make it all up to her. He would love and protect her as no woman had ever been protected and loved before! He felt that it was his fault that she had been put through such traumatic experiences, for he had been the first to abduct her . . .

The landscape just ahead seemed to be shimmering, the heat beating down on the sand was so intense. But something else was disturbing the landscape. Shadow rose up in the saddle and placed a hand over his eyes to shield them from the bright rays of the sun, then stiffened when he saw something on the ground.

It was a body.

His gaze swept around him, searching for a horse, but finding none.

A sense of foreboding stung his insides, wondering how long this person had been lying there, seemingly unconscious, and most surely scorched by the sun.

Sinking his knees into the sides of his horse, Shadow sent it into a gallop, then grew numb inside when upon closer observation he saw that the person lying so deathly quiet on the sand was a woman. When he came alongside her and slid from the saddle, he saw the face only partially hidden by an arm held up over it, apparently to protect it from the sun. His heart seemed to be tearing in shreds, for it was not just any woman lying there . . . it was Maria!

"*E-do-ta*, no!" Shadow gasped, falling to his knees beside Maria. He eased her up so that her head was cradled in his arms. "Did you escape? How?"

His gaze swept over her face, seeing her parched, white lips, her sunburned cheeks, and her eyelashes heavy with dust as they lay closed. Still attired in the Navaho skirt and blouse that she had worn to accompany him and the young Navaho braves to witness the young men learning ways of fighting and raiding, he hoped that she had not been molested. It seemed that the main things wrong with her were heat exhaustion, thirst, and hunger. If he did not get her into the shade and get water and food down her parched throat, he might lose her forever this time!

"Maria," he whispered sorrowfully, lifting her up into his arms, carrying her to his horse. "My Maria. I shall kill Charging Falcon for this! I shall!"

Maria was suddenly hearing a voice and feeling movement. Was she also feeling strong arms holding her? Had she prayed so hard for Shadow to come that he *had*?

Slowly opening her eyes, she looked up at the sculpted face of the man she loved as he placed her gently on his horse. She moved a hand to his cheek as he steadied her on the saddle with one hand while pulling himself up on the saddle behind her with the other.

"Shadow?" Maria said, her throat burning from dryness as she spoke. "Darling, is it . . . really you?"

Taken off guard by her voice and her hand on his cheek, Shadow flinched as though shot. He looked down at Maria, his insides warming when he saw that she was awake and had the strength to speak to him!

"My woman," he said, drawing her fully into his arms as he positioned himself on his saddle. Long, lean fingers moved through Maria's hair; lips rained soft, comforting kisses along her brow. "You will soon be where you can rest and where you will have food and water." He frowned. "And then, once you are strong again and I feel that it is safe to leave you, I will hunt for Charging Falcon until I find him. He has been my enemy for way too long now. Soon he will be *no* one's enemy!"

Maria looked quickly up at Shadow, torn with how she should feel about Charging Falcon. He *had* rescued her from José Gironella. But hadn't Charging Falcon been responsible for her having been there in the first place? Hadn't he left her to travel to Shadow's stronghold alone?

She was recalling Charging Falcon saying that he no longer wanted to work against Shadow. Which side of Charging Falcon should she believe? Was he sincere?

At this moment, she felt so weak she wasn't sure if she would even be alive tomorrow!

"I'm so tired," she whispered, too weary to worry about Charging Falcon and Shadow's plans for him. She closed her eyes and leaned into Shadow's embrace, drifting . . . drifting . . .

Shadow held tight to Maria as he swung his horse around and headed toward his stronghold. He looked down at the buckskin bag bulging with money, and smiled. The person who went to pick up the ransom money would be surprised. He would think that Shadow cared not what happened to Maria, since no money was left to pay for her when, in truth, he had her *and* his money!

Chuckling low, he urged his horse into a strong gallop across the land. . . .

CHAPTER
15

When Maria awakened, a damp cloth was being drawn gently across her brow and the tantalizing aroma of broth filled her nostrils. Weak, she blinked her eyes and looked slowly around her, seeing not only Shadow but also Pleasant Voice and Blue Arrow, their faces etched with worry.

Maria soon realized that she had been brought to Shadow's hogan and was on his bed, covered by a comfortable layer of sheepskins. A fire burned pleasantly warm in the fire pit and a large pot hung over the flames, emitting fragrant steam.

Pleasant Voice was smoothing the damp cloth over her brow, her eyes filled with concern.

"Pleasant Voice?" Maria said in a low gasp, reaching trembling fingers to her friend. "You are all right? You are well enough to be out of bed?"

"I am well enough to come and be with you," Pleasant Voice said, dropping the cloth into a wooden basin of water. She squeezed Maria's hand affectionately. "You must eat or you will never be well. Shadow did not stop to feed you and give you water in the desert because you were sleeping so soundly once he placed you in his arms on his horse. He brought you here. Now that you are awake, let me feed you broth. You will get your strength back only if you eat."

"But do you feel well enough to do this?" Maria asked,

her voice slight. She looked up at Pleasant Voice's face, seeing how gaunt and pale she was. "Your wounds? Are they healed? Has your strength returned?"

Shadow rose up from his haunches and came to kneel down beside Maria. He placed a hand gently on her cheek and pressed a kiss on her brow. "You ask too many questions," he said thickly. "Eat. Get nourishment into your body. Then we can talk as long as you like."

He smiled over at Pleasant Voice. "As for Pleasant Voice," he said, his eyes warm with love, "soon she will be totally well. She is well enough now to be with a friend. She insisted on it."

Pleasant Voice ducked her head, blushing, then went to the large kettle that hung low over the fire and ladled out some broth into a wooden bowl. She tingled all over inside when Blue Arrow came and took the bowl from her while she got a spoon, and they both went back to Maria's bedside.

Blue Arrow looked down at Maria and smiled. "If you would rather not have me here, just tell me to go and I will go," he said, holding the bowl as Pleasant Voice dipped the spoon into it. "I do not want to interfere. It is just that you mean so much to Shadow and Pleasant Voice, I want you to mean the same to *me*."

Feeling blessed that so many people cared about her, Maria felt tears burn at the corners of her eyes. She choked back the urge to cry and looked up at Blue Arrow. "Please stay," she murmured. "I am honored that you want to." She bit her lower lip and looked from Shadow to Blue Arrow to Pleasant Voice, then back at Blue Arrow. "My father is your enemy. It is so kind of you to care about me, his daughter."

"You did not choose your parents," Blue Arrow said. "It is the choices you made later that count. You chose Pleasant Voice to be your best friend and Shadow to be your husband. That is what matters, Maria. Only that."

"I am glad that—" Maria began, but was interrupted by Shadow.

"You have talked enough," Shadow scolded, stepping

aside to make room for Pleasant Voice. "Eat. Getting your strength back is what is important, Maria. Without that, you have nothing!"

Maria eagerly accepted the broth, enjoying its warmth and flavor as it trickled down her throat and into her gnawingly empty stomach. She coughed when for a moment she found it difficult to swallow, then resumed accepting the broth as it was placed to her lips.

Her eyes moved to Shadow who was again on his haunches beside the fire, gazing at her with worry, causing minute lines to appear on his handsome copper face.

Approaching horses outside drew Shadow to his feet. He looked toward the door of his hogan when a warrior stepped inside, attired in only a breechclout, his copper body shining with perspiration.

Maria's insides grew tight when she heard the message that the warrior had brought. Some of Shadow's men had followed the young Mexican boy who had brought Shadow the note about Maria, in an attempt to find out who had sent it. The boy had been shot through the head by someone hiding in the hills, and Shadow's warriors were not able to find the assailant.

While they were pursuing the killer, they had found the body of another Mexican boy who had been shot in the same way, apparently with the same gun.

Maria rose quickly to an elbow, her free hand holding the sheepskin blanket up to hide her nudity. "Good Lord!" she gasped. "José Gironella must be responsible! Don't you see? He sent ransom notes to both you and father, but he never intended to release me to either of you. He killed those innocent boys so that no one would ever know who ordered this done. He intended to take advantage of me then turn me loose in the desert to die! Oh, what of my father? Surely he was killed when he took the ransom money to the drop-off place! Shadow, you would have been murdered, too, if I had not gotten in the way before you arrived! Oh, Shadow! I must go and see if my father is all right! Please take me to him!"

Shadow ushered the warrior from the hogan, then came

back inside and knelt down beside Maria, Pleasant Voice
and Blue Arrow making room for him as they went to stand
before the fire.

"It is not good for you to be so upset," he said, taking her
hand, holding it. "It is not good to talk so much, but now
that you have said much that I find is dangerous, I must
have more answers, my love."

"My father," Maria said, tears rolling down her cheeks.
"If José Gironella killed those boys, surely he will have
given orders that my father is to be killed after he delivers
the ransom money. My father may have already stepped
right into a trap!"

"Shadow is confused about many things," he said,
frowning. "Who is this José Gironella you are talking
about? It was Charging Falcon who abducted you from my
stronghold, wasn't it? Only he would know such skills!"

Maria took a deep breath and wiped tears from her eyes.
"Charging Falcon abducted me not only from your stronghold but also from José Gironella's slaves' quarters," she
said, her voice trembling. "After Charging Falcon took me
from your stronghold, he sold me to José Gironella.
Gironella in turn sent ransom notes not only to you but also
my father. But he never intended to give me back to either
of you. As I said, he was going to turn me loose in the
desert to wander and die!"

"You say Charging Falcon stole you from the slaves'
quarters?" Shadow said, raising an eyebrow inquisitively.
"He took you there and then stole you away? Was it his
intention to keep you for himself? Did you manage to
escape from him? I am confused, Maria. Confused!"

Maria licked her parched lips and swallowed hard, then
looked softly up at Shadow. "I am also confused," she
murmured. "I don't know what to think about Charging
Falcon." She glanced over at Pleasant Voice, recalling what
Charging Falcon had done to her, then how he had felt about
it later. It was because of Pleasant Voice that Charging
Falcon had changed his mind about what he was doing to
Shadow. He had said that he was sorry.

She looked back up at Shadow. "Charging Falcon abducted me from José Gironella because he regretted having stolen me from you," she said in a rush of words. "He regrets much that he has done to hurt you, Shadow. He seemed sincere when speaking of his regrets. And he did come and take me from the slaves' quarters."

Shadow turned his eyes away from Maria, in his mind's eye recalling two young warriors learning the skills of riding horses and shooting arrows. They had been very close as children. Charging Falcon's family, along with many other Pueblo Indians, had brought much knowledge of weaving to the Navaho villages.

But when Charging Falcon's mother and father were killed in a raid—the same raid that took the lives of Shadow's parents—things changed quickly for them. The competition became too keen and fierce between them as each tried to be the richer and more powerful. The lack of family support had always kept them close, but it became a major cause of their going their separate ways when they were old enough to lead their own warrior groups.

Somewhere along the line, Shadow had proved to be more cunning, and it was then that they had become enemies!

Could it ever be any different now? Charging Falcon had slain many of the Navaho in his attempts to prove that he was more cunning than Shadow. Charging Falcon had been paid, over and over again, by the Spaniards to work against the Navaho. Because of this, Charging Falcon had been labeled *traitor*!

E-do-ta, no. Charging Falcon could not be forgiven, no matter what he did now to make amends!

"Shadow, you have grown so quiet," Maria said, placing a hand gently on his cheek. "Was it what I said about Charging Falcon? Are you as confused about him as I?"

Shadow took her hand and kissed the palm. "He is not worth worrying about," he said darkly. "He chose unwisely the road he would travel in life. He is a traitor. Always shall he be! Do you not see Pleasant Voice and how pale she is? That is because of Charging Falcon! Do you not know of the many fresh graves on the hillside? Those people died

because of Charging Falcon! He has waited too long to try
to salvage our friendship. He has done too much that is not
good. That he rescued you proves only one point. He used
you as a pawn to get to *me*. He did not save you out of the
kindness of his heart. Do you understand, Maria? Do you?"

He swept her into his arms and cradled her close. "You
could have died because of him," he said thickly. "He was
not brave enough to bring you to me! He left you in the
desert! Even now he does not know if you are alive or well!
He is *hogay-gahn*, bad, Maria! *Hogay-gahn!*"

Thoughts of her father suddenly outweighed anything
that Shadow was saying to Maria about Charging Falcon.
Her concern kept her from feeling total peace while being
held within her lover's embrace.

She swallowed hard, then slipped away from Shadow, to
beseech him with her eyes.

"Shadow, I am so worried about my father," she said, her
voice breaking. "I must go home. I have to see if he is all
right. I must prove to my mother that *I* am all right. Surely
by now my mother believes I am dead. If my father did pay
the ransom and return home alive, he will, by now, believe
that I am dead, for he will know that he has been swindled!
I cannot leave my parents in the dark about this. It would be
cruel, Shadow. Please understand."

Shadow rose quickly to his feet. He glowered down at
Maria. "First I have you, then I don't?" he snapped angrily.
"If you love me, if you are going to be my wife, only I
should be important to you. How can you want to leave?
How can I let you? Your father is my bitter enemy now. I
am his."

Maria licked her lips and closed her eyes slowly, torn by
conflicting feelings. She drew the sheepskin blanket around
her and sat up, watching Pleasant Voice and Blue Arrow
slip quietly from the hogan, realizing that Shadow and
Maria needed privacy for the discussion at hand.

Then she looked up at Shadow, again pleading with her
eyes. "My darling, I know that you and my father are
enemies, but I cannot let that stop me from returning home
to let my parents know I am all right," she said softly. "I

would like to return for more than one reason. I want to set
things right with my parents before I enter into a marriage
with you. While riding alone in the desert before passing
out from exhaustion and hunger, I had much time to think.
Though I desperately want to be your wife, I need my
parents' blessing, or at least my mother's. She has so little
happiness in life, and losing me will shatter her. At least I
owe her an explanation of what I plan to do. If she knows
I am going to marry you because I desperately love you, I
believe that she will understand."

She lowered her eyes and swallowed hard. "You see, my
mother has never known this kind of love herself," she said
in a near whisper. "My father gives her earthly possessions
but not the love that a woman needs to make her feel vital
and alive! He has always managed to get what his body
craved elsewhere. I guess . . . it was more exciting for
him that way. My mother understood my father's weak-
nesses, but stayed with him so that I would have stability in
a home, with both a mother and a father."

She looked up at Shadow, eyes anxious. "I *must* go
home, Shadow," she repeated. "I want enough time to
make things right and then I shall return to you. We can be
married then."

"Everything that you ask is dangerous," Shadow said,
moving to his haunches beside her. "Your father will now
have guards posted around the plantation. It will not be as
easy to return you as it was to take you away from there.
And, my love, when your chore there is done, how will you
find your way back to my stronghold? How will you know
you are not being followed? How do you know your father
will *let* you return?"

He rose quickly to his feet. He kneaded his brow as he
began feverishly pacing. "*E-do-ta*! No!" he grumbled. "I
cannot do it."

Maria felt panic rising within her. Was she going to be a
prisoner of the man she loved? Wasn't she ever going to
have control of her own life? Why were all men alike?

Though she was still weak and undernourished, Maria
swept the sheepskin blanket away from her and swung her

legs off the bed, placing her bare feet on the floor. Teetering, feeling light-headed, she rose to her feet and moved toward Shadow, stopping him when he turned to pace in her direction. Placing her hands on his shoulders, she steadied herself and looked determinedly up at him.

"Shadow, I must return home," she said. "You will accompany me only halfway. I can make it the rest of the way by myself. You will lend me a few of your poison-tipped arrows after you teach me how to shoot them. I can defend myself quite well."

Shadow's gaze swept over her, his loins suddenly on fire at the sight of her ripe body. It seemed so long since they had made love. Perhaps they would have only one more opportunity if he allowed her to do as she wished! He would make love to her before he set out on the journey with her, and perhaps never again!

"Maria, Shadow cannot . . ." he said, but she drew angrily away from him and looked up at him with fire in her eyes, silencing the rest of his complaint and denial.

"Then, Shadow, I cannot be your wife," Maria said, glaring up at him.

Her knees weak, her head throbbing, she turned and inched her way back to the bed, feeling empty. Shadow did not understand her now. He never would. It was hopeless. Perhaps it was best that she had discovered his true intentions now instead of later, when it would have been too late.

Like her mother, she believed in the marriage vows! Once spoken with a man, the bond lasted forever! It was good to have discovered that marriage to Shadow meant keeping a woman prisoner!

Well, she would have no part of it! When she was well enough she would leave. If he kept her guarded, she would devise a way to escape!

Even if leaving him tore her heart in shreds, she would leave him. . . .

Shadow was stunned by her stubbornness and her willingness to give him up. His eyes followed her, hungering for her body, for her gentle kisses and touches, as she crept toward the bed. Then he could bear no more of the rejection and went to her and grabbed her by a wrist and swung her around to face him.

"Maria, it will be up to you to find your way back to me," he said huskily, his free hand cupping her breast, then trailing a path of fire down to the triangle of hair between her thighs, to softly caress her. "If you do not, that will be what fate has wanted for both you and me. I shall not interfere in your plans. Do you understand?"

Surprised that he would be willing, suddenly, to let her do as she wished, then in the same breath the same as tell her that if she could not find her way back to him, he would not care, Maria was numb with wonder.

Then her heart began to pound because of the pleasure his hands were arousing within her. It made her numbness fade, to be replaced by wondrous bliss. She closed her eyes and threw her head back as his lips trailed kisses along the curve of her throat, then moved down to cover a nipple, his teeth sinking in, stirring her insides into an inferno of desire!

But then her head began to spin, and her knees buckled, reminding her that she was not up to lovemaking. She laughed softly as Shadow caught her and carried her back to her bed, then continued to feed her the broth.

"You are a most stubborn woman," he said, his eyes gleaming.

"You are a most frustrating man," Maria said, her eyes twinkling. "I cannot believe that you would not care if I got lost in the desert to die, only because I had insisted on seeing my parents to reassure them that I am all right and to explain why I so desperately want to marry you."

"It will be time-consuming for my warriors to keep watch over you, to make sure you return to me safely," Shadow teased. "There are much better things for them to do, like raid your father again and again."

"You would raid while I was there at my father's plantation?" Maria gasped, her eyes wide.

"Whenever the opportunity arises, my men raid," Shadow continued to tease. "Perhaps if you see them, you will assist them again? You proved to me that you are skilled at raiding, as though you had been born Navaho yourself!"

"Had I been, that would have been perfect," Maria sighed, gently pushing the empty bowl away, her stomach comfortably full. "There would be no obstacles to prevent us from becoming man and wife. *Sí*, that would have been perfect."

Shadow placed the bowl on the floor and drew Maria into his arms, cradling her close. "But there *are* obstacles," he said thickly. "Like your father not letting you return to me when you are ready. What then, Maria? What then?"

Maria grew quiet. . . .

CHAPTER
16

The days of recuperating had been slow for Maria, who was filled with worries about her father, and hating it that her mother more than likely thought she was dead, but now Shadow was accompanying her partway back home.

It was dusk; purple rivulets rippled the sky as evening began to turn to night. A turtledove sang its soft, mournful song in a cottonwood tree close by, and the water of a creek gurgled over rocks as Maria cozied into Shadow's arms close beside a slow-burning campfire.

Maria was going to revel in every minute of Shadow's closeness, for she knew as well as he that she was taking a chance by returning to the Zamora plantation. Unless she convinced her parents that she loved Shadow with every fiber of her being, they could forbid her to return to him.

But she also loved her parents, she had to take that chance. They deserved to know that she was all right, and they had to be told whom she was going to marry and when the ceremony would be performed.

She had been stifled while living with her parents; her father was overbearing and overprotective of her, but she could not deny that in other ways she had been blessed.

She owed them a lot.

Because of this, she had to take some chances.

"You are so quiet," Shadow said, turning to face her. He placed his hands on her waist and drew her to him, their lips close. "Are you changing your mind? Would you rather we return to the stronghold? That is best, you know."

Maria placed her hands on his hair and twined her fingers through the sleek blackness, her lips grazing his in a soft, swift kiss. "I haven't changed my mind," she whispered, mesmerized by his dark eyes and the magic of his hands as he moved them from her waist to her breasts, softly kneading them through the buckskin blouse.

A soft laugh, similar to a gurgle, rose from deep within her. "Even a maddening loving won't make me change my mind," she murmured. "But I hope knowing that doesn't dissuade you from doing it. Please love me, Shadow. Love me fiercely. I hunger for you."

Shadow laughed throatily as he looked down at her, his eyelashes heavy with building passion. "Sometimes I believe you are insatiable," he teased. "My woman, this morning we made love. Now you are ready to love again tonight? What will you do tomorrow night when I will not be available for you? Dreaming is not the same as doing."

He slipped a hand up inside her blouse and circled her breast, feeling the nipple hardening against his palm. "Though you may dream of me caressing you in such a way, the thrill will not be the same," he teased, lightly pinching her nipple, causing her to emit a soft moan of mixed pleasure and pain.

His other hand slid up beneath her skirt and began inching its way up her leg. "Will you also enjoy this in your dream?" he further tormented. "I fear you will cry out in your sleep when you ache so fiercely for me to be at your side! What will your parents say, my love? What will you tell them when they come to your room to see if you are in pain?"

Going wild with his teasing and tormenting, his breath hot on her mouth as he kept his lips just close enough, yet not kissing her, Maria drew away from Shadow and rose to her feet. The sky was dark overhead now, the moon only a sliver of white, surrounded by the reverberating light from the stars that looked like sequins against the dark, velveteenlike heavens.

"I'm glad you alone are accompanying me," Maria said, her voice foreign to her in its huskiness as she teasingly, slowly began to raise her blouse. "This time together is enhanced by being alone."

Shadow rose to his feet and looked down at her as she slowly lifted the blouse so that her breasts were gradually exposed to him. He smiled down at her and placed his hands on his hips, letting her have her way and enjoying her chosen method of teasing him.

"We are alone, yet not totally," he said, chuckling. "Do you think I would travel without my warriors, with so many waiting to assassinate me? No, my woman, that would not be wise."

Maria jerked her blouse back down and looked behind her, toward the mountains, then to one side, at the cluster of cottonwood trees that lined the creek. She hadn't seen the warriors following. She hadn't even heard the horses as they had traveled across the land. All along, she had thought they were alone. Even when she and Shadow had been making love at the crack of dawn this morning? Had they been watched? Was nothing private?

"Why didn't you tell me," she said in a whisper. Her face colored with a blush. "I would never have—"

Shadow grabbed her by the wrists and drew her against him, his eyes twinkling with amusement. "My darling, my warriors do not make a habit of watching me make love," he said, laughing softly. "They are far enough away not to see us, yet are positioned so that they can see anyone approaching us from all four sides. What we do is not being observed by anyone."

He lowered his hands and grasped the hem of her blouse and began raising it along her flesh. "Whatever we choose to do is only *our* concern," he reassured her. "Let us make love all night, for tomorrow and all tomorrows after that until we are together again will be lonely."

His fingers grazed the flesh of her breasts as he continued to raise the blouse. "Let us give each other the ultimate of pleasures tonight, Maria," he said huskily, her breasts now fully exposed.

As he raised the blouse on over her head, his mouth went to her breast. He flicked a tongue over it, tossing her buckskin garment to the ground.

Maria's breath was stolen away when Shadow began inching her skirt down away from her, his fingers teasingly stopping at the downy patch of hair between her thighs, to slide up inside her, where she ached so to receive his manhood within her.

As he began moving his finger as though it were his manhood, Maria bit her lip to keep from crying out with pleasure, combing her hands through her hair as she closed her eyes and threw her head back in ecstasy.

And then she felt herself being lowered to the ground where Shadow spread her out on a sheepskin blanket beside the fire and removed her moccasins. Her naked body was golden in the dancing light of the fire as Maria welcomed Shadow. His lips met hers in a fiery kiss, his hands again arousing her by caressing her at the juncture of her thighs.

She squirmed, she arched, she returned his kiss with ardor, all the while pulling at his buckskin shirt, wanting to feel his sleek chest against her own.

But Shadow had no thoughts just yet of pleasing himself. He only had Maria's pleasure in mind. She must be made to want to return to him. He must give her many reasons to want to return! He knew of no way better than loving her, teaching her all the methods of loving!

Slipping his mouth from Maria's lips, Shadow knelt down over her and began trailing his tongue from the hollow of her throat downward. He stopped at her breasts and caressed first one and then the other, then moved lower, making her stomach quiver sensually as his tongue left a wet trail there, stopping where her soft hair tickled his nose as he positioned himself so that he could give her a loving she would never forget.

While his hands clung to her breasts, softly kneading them, his tongue made lunges inside her, then caressed her. Maria's mind became blurred with the passion that was building within her. She felt as though something inside her was beginning to glow, spreading . . . spreading. . . .

She arched her body upward. She placed her hands on the back of Shadow's head, pressing his lips and tongue closer, feeling as though she could not get enough of him as he made love to her again in what she felt was surely a forbidden way.

Breathing hard, gyrating her hips, Maria felt the wondrous spinning of her senses and cried out as the rapture peaked and her whole body became a river of sensations that she did not want to end. . . .

Shadow smiled to himself, glad that she had again responded with abandon, then quickly undressed before she came down too far out of the clouds of pleasure.

Quickly he mounted her and thrust his hardness inside her. He quieted her gasp of ecstasy with a stormy kiss, his body feverishly working inside her, his hands again claiming her breasts, tweaking her nipples into a renewed hardness.

Maria's moans of pleasure fired Shadow's passion. He felt the tension building within his loins, then slowly changing to something similar to a melting. He kissed her hungrily, his strokes became maddening, and soon they trembled against each other, having found the ultimate of feelings together, shared, wonderfully shared. . . .

Maria clung to Shadow as their lips parted. She thrilled as he kissed the slender column of her throat and then a breast. She sighed and rocked with him as he once again began his slow thrusts inside her.

Again she responded with abandon, feeling the bliss overwhelming her.

Again they reached that plateau of desire.

When they came down from the clouds, Shadow drew away from Maria. He placed a hand in hers and helped her up from her back.

"That is not making love the entire night," Maria teased, drifting toward him again. He welcomed her at his side as they moved closer to the fire. "I feel as though I have just begun, Shadow. Until this morning's wondrous moments with you, it had been so long, darling, so very, very long."

"The night is young," Shadow said, smiling down at her

as he drew a sheepskin blanket around her shoulders and
his, covering them both with the same blanket. "We rest,
then make love. By morning, you will wish that you had
slept."

"Never," Maria said, giggling softly. "All I want is you.
Rest can come later."

"If you wanted only me, we would not be making love
many miles from my stronghold," Shadow said, suddenly
brooding. "We could be married tomorrow! As it is, we are
the cause of the delay of the marriage not only between you
and me but between Pleasant Voice and Blue Arrow as well!
They are waiting until your return so that we can all be
married during the same ceremony."

Maria looked quickly at Shadow, surprised by the news.
"Pleasant Voice didn't tell me," she said in a slight gasp.
"They are actually waiting for me so they can get married
with us at the same time?"

"Yes, and then we will all live *ka-bike-hozhoni-bi*, happy
forevermore," Shadow said softly, nuzzling her neck with
his lips. "Remember that, Maria. Happy forevermore. You
and I . . . Blue Arrow and Pleasant Voice."

"That sounds wonderful." Maria sighed, then melted
inside when Shadow twined his arms around her waist and
eased her back to the ground.

She closed her eyes and laced her arms about his neck,
their lips kissing softly this time. . . .

The sun hung midway in the sky; the desert sand had
given way to rich, wondrous pastures fed by mountain
streams. Maria questioned Shadow with her eyes when in
the distance she could see sheep grazing . . . her father's
sheep. Somehow Shadow had managed to go in a large
circle, seemingly hardly any farther from the mountains
than before, yet this stretch of the land was her father's.

But this was a long way from the plantation house. Maria
gathered that he had brought her here so that the herdsman,
Manuel, could lead her safely to her home.

"All along you had planned this, hadn't you?" she said,
flipping her hair back from her shoulders. "You never did

intend to leave me alone in the desert to find my way home, did you? You brought me here so that Manuel could see that I got home safely. Why didn't you tell me, Shadow?"

"This is safer in all respects, is it not?" Shadow said, reaching for her hand as their horses came to a halt. "No one but the lone herdsman stands guard here, so I am safe. The herdsman can see to your safety when he leads the sheep closer to your house, so that *you* can be safe. *E-do-ta*, no, I did not plan to abandon you. Never would I do that."

"But you led me to believe that you would, Shadow," Maria fussed, lifting her chin angrily.

"Shadow would try anything, even a small lie, to persuade you not to return home," he said, frowning at her. "If you became frightened of being left alone, of traveling alone, and chose to return to the stronghold with Shadow instead, would not the lie have been worth it?"

Maria pulled her hand free. "Perhaps for you," she said. "But not for me. I feel strongly about letting my parents know how I am and that I am going to marry you. You know as well as I that you could not send a message by any of your warriors. They would have been shot on sight!"

"Then go in peace, my love," Shadow said, reaching out to draw her face to his. His lips met hers in a savage, fierce kiss; then he let her go, his eyes dark and fathomless as he wheeled his horse around and rode away from her.

Maria felt a sudden surge of apprehension race through her. A soft cry rose from deep within her as she reached out for Shadow, but he was riding away from her so quickly and determinedly that he was already becoming a speck on the horizon.

A part of her wanted to ride after him, forget the mission that she was on.

A part of her knew that it would not be fair to her parents! They had suffered enough by not knowing where she was or whether she was alive!

Her poor mother! She was living on the edge of her sanity anyhow. Worry about her daughter might push her over the edge, into the pit of total darkness that came with mental illness!

And her father? Was he all right? Had he been slain by
José Gironella's vaqueros?

"I have made the right decision," she said, setting her
jaw firmly. She gave Shadow one final look, then sank her
heels into the flanks of her horse and rode on toward
Manuel. Sometimes in life one had to think of someone
else's welfare, and Maria felt good that she had chosen to
place her parents' before her own.

But what of Shadow? How did he feel about her decision
to do this? Would he decide not to welcome her back?
Would it not be simpler for him to choose one of his own
Navaho women to love, so that he would be able to lead his
people with fewer complications?

Brushing such a horrible thought from her mind, Maria
rode on toward Manuel. When the sheepdogs raced toward
her, barking, Manuel turned and looked at Maria with
alarm, then ran toward her, waving.

Tears sparkled in Maria's eyes as she recalled the day she
had helped Shadow steal the sheep from the elderly herdsman.

But of course Manuel had known that she had been
forced. . . .

CHAPTER
17

Tears blinded Maria as she clung to her father, relieved to see that he was all right. The way his arms cut into her flesh as he hugged her made her realize the extent of his happiness to see her.

"Maria, I didn't think I would ever see you again," Zamora said, his voice breaking as a sob surfaced. He held her at arm's length and looked her up and down. "You weren't harmed. I have your abductor to thank for that, at least. When did he release you? Who abducted you, Maria? I only knew that you had been kidnapped and that I paid to have you released."

Maria reached out one hand to her father's shoulder where the bandage was still bulky beneath his shirt. "First, tell me how you are," she said softly. "Is the wound healing all right? You still have it bandaged."

"I am fine," her father said in a low growl, his hate for the Navaho more intense than ever before. If Shadow had not abducted Maria, she wouldn't have had to go through all of this trauma. He also hated this person to whom he had paid ransom money for her. How was it that she had been with him and not Shadow?

In his heart, his main hate would always be for Shadow!

"And mother?" Maria asked. "How is she?"

"She is her same old self," Zamora said, his voice strained. "She just goes on each day doing nothing special.

I continue giving her trinkets that seem to make her happy enough."

His fingers bit into Maria's shoulders. "We can go and see your mother later," he said. "You must tell me everything. Who did this? Why weren't you with Shadow?"

Then his face drained of color and he took a wide step away from Maria. "You never did say that it was not Shadow who asked for the ransom money . . ." he said, his words trailing off, wondering why he had not thought of that earlier. "Was it the Indian, Maria? Did he abduct you from me only because he wanted to get payment for you?"

Maria emitted a low gasp and placed a hand to her throat. "Father, never would Shadow do that," she said shallowly. "It was not Shadow. It was José Gironella. Surely you know him. He is a Spaniard just like you and me. He buys and sells human flesh as if he were bargaining over animals! It was *he* who did this. No! Never Shadow!"

A pained expression creased Zamora's brow when he listened to how ardently Maria defended the Indian. Why would she do so unless she had special feelings for him?

And if she did . . . ?

"José Gironella?" he said, blocking from his mind further thoughts of Maria's interest in Shadow. He would not believe that she could feel anything but hatred for the marauding Navaho! Only hatred! "José Gironella did this to you? But how? You were with the Navaho."

"I was until Charging Falcon abducted me from Shadow's stronghold," she said, looking up at her father, seeing so much confusion in his eyes. "I know it seems incredible, *Padre*, that all of these things keep happening to me, but they do. But I have survived it all. Let's not worry ourselves about how it all has happened."

Zamora wove his fingers through his hair nervously. He turned on a heel and slouched down in his chair behind his desk, his eyes dark with anger. "Charging Falcon?" he growled. "First he turns traitor to the Navaho and Pueblo and then he turns on *me*. I never should have trusted him. Never!"

Maria went to her father and placed her arms about his

neck. "*Padre*, Charging Falcon also *rescued* me from José Gironella," she said softly. "So do not condemn him too severely. Somewhere inside him there is some good. It was just for a moment hidden behind a wall of *bad*."

He looked up at her quickly. "Then it was Charging Falcon who took you to Manuel so that you could be brought home safely?" he said, raising an eyebrow inquisitively.

"No, it was not Charging Falcon," Maria said, feeling uneasy beneath his close scrutiny. "It was Shadow! After my escape from José Gironella, I made my way to Shadow's stronghold."

She tensed when her father rose slowly from the chair, his eyes still on her, questioning her. "You chose to go there instead of coming here?" he said. "Maria, I don't understand."

"I knew you wouldn't," Maria said, lowering her eyes. Then she challenged him with a set stare. "I would like to explain, but I wish to do so in Mother's presence. There will be much for you to grasp. I think it will be best if Mother has you there, for at least some measure of support, *Padre*."

"What could you have to say to us that would require you to be so . . . so cautious about telling us?" Zamora said, placing a hand on Maria's shoulder and again looking her up and down. "Did the Navaho or Charging Falcon or José Gironella rape you? Is that what you are finding so painful to tell us? That you were . . . raped?"

Maria looked at her father, stunned by his assumption, then shook her head. "Good Lord, *no*," she gasped. "I wasn't raped by anyone. And what I have to tell you is not painful to me. Perhaps it will be to you, but never to me."

Zamora slipped his hand away from her and pressed it to his brow, again studying her. "I don't like this," he said hoarsely. "Not one bit."

"Let us go to Mother and get the telling over with," Maria said, flipping her hair back from her shoulders. "That would be best, Father."

Zamora's eyes darkened as he focused on her Indian attire. He smoothed a hand over the buckskin material.

"This won't do at all," he grumbled. "Your mother has been traumatized enough by your abduction at the hands of Indians. Seeing you in Indian attire could really upset her."

He waved a hand toward the door. "Go to your room and get presentable," he ordered. "Then come to the sewing room. That's where your mother is. She is at least doing something with her hands today. She is embroidering."

"*Sí, Padre*," Maria said, swallowing hard. "I shall do whatever I can to make things easier for Mother. I shall go to my room and change into something appropriate, then come immediately to the sewing room."

Lunging into his arms, Maria savored his nearness, knowing that once she was married to Shadow, she would have to forfeit all hugs and embraces of both her mother and her father, unless Shadow and her father could come to some sort of peaceful understanding.

Perhaps *she* could bring them together. . . .

The red velveteen blouse made Maria's recent tan more noticeable. Her long and flowing skirt of bright calico rustled as she walked down the narrow corridor toward the sewing room, her thick, coal-black hair hanging down to her waist, drawn back from her delicate, lovely face with combs encrusted with jewels.

Zamora held Maria gently by an elbow, walking alongside her. There was a strain in the air as they both stopped before the closed door and exchanged troubled glances.

"Are you sure you want your mother present when you disclose whatever needs to be said?" her father asked, looking down at Maria with troubled eyes. "She's not at all strong."

"Mother must be present," Maria argued softly. "She doesn't know yet that I am all right. That should make anything else I say to her far less upsetting. She will be so happy to see that I am home and well."

"Well, we'll see," Zamora said, shrugging. He placed a hand on the doorknob and slowly turned it, then stepped aside and silently watched Maria walk ahead of him into the room.

Maria's pulse was racing when she looked across the spacious room and saw her mother sitting beside a window in a plush chair, her fingers nimbly drawing needle and thread through a linen fabric that was held tight in a round wooden frame.

Since the last time Maria had seen her mother, she seemed to have aged. She looked pale, but perhaps it was the brightness of the afternoon light pouring in on her delicately chiseled ivory face that made her look so frail and drew the wrinkles out more prominently than when she was sitting in a more subdued light.

Sucking in her breath, still not having been noticed, Maria covered her mouth with a hand, stifling a sob behind it, still studying her slight mother. Her mother's hair, graying at the temples, was drawn back from her face in a tight bun. She wore a lace shawl over her bent shoulders, and a skirt with lace ruffles fell from her waist in gathers and covered her tiny feet where they rested on the floor before her.

As though her mother had sensed her presence, she lifted her eyes. Shock registered in her face when from across the wide room she saw Maria. She dropped her embroidery hoop to her lap and grabbed the arms of the chair so hard that her knuckles were rendered white by the pressure.

"Maria?" Letha said, her voice trembling. "Maria, daughter?"

Maria choked back a sob and rushed across the room. She dropped to her knees before her mother and hugged her legs, tears wetting the skirt of the ruffled dress where her cheek pressed hard into her mother's lap.

"Oh, Mama, it *is* I," she sobbed. "Did I have you so terribly worried? *Lo siento*, I am so sorry if I did. But so much has happened that I had no control over. Please understand."

Letha stroked Maria's back with trembling hands, tears streaming down her face. "Do you think that I would blame you for the sins that ignorant men commit for money?" she said, her voice thin. "The ransom was paid. You were returned to us. That is all that matters."

Maria looked quickly up at her mother. With the back of her hand she wiped her face clear of tears. "The ransom was paid?" she said hoarsely.

"*Sí*, it was," Letha said, placing her hands on Maria's waist, urging her to her feet as Letha slipped out of the chair. She hugged Maria with all of her might. "I feared that after the money was paid, you would not be returned anyway. I thought they might kill you!"

"I am very much alive," Maria said, trying to sound lighthearted, yet hating José Gironella, for he had known quite early on that she was gone from his premises, but he had sent the ransom note anyway!

Letha stepped away from Maria and held her hands, looking her up and down. "*Cómo le va*? How are you, darling? Did anyone harm you?" she asked, her voice breaking with emotion.

Maria started to speak but was stopped when her father stepped to her side and slipped an arm around her waist. "She's fine, and no, no harm came to her," he said thickly. "But she has much to tell us. Let's let her do it now, Letha. Perhaps then you should rest. You seem more pale today."

"I do not feel frail or pale now that Maria is home," Letha said stubbornly, looking angrily up at her husband. "Stop fussing over my health. I am fine. Just fine!"

Zamora slipped an arm around Letha's waist and guided her and Maria to a colorful sofa, looking like a garden with its spray of flowers in all the colors of springtime on a backdrop of white linen. "I see, I see," he said. "I am glad you are feeling better. But who wouldn't? Our daughter is home!"

Maria cringed as she settled between her parents, both of whom believed that she was home to stay. When she told them the truth, that she wanted their blessing so that she could have a clear conscience when she married Shadow, what *then* . . . ?

Maria smiled awkwardly at her mother and father when each took one of her hands and held it on either side of her.

The room was so quiet, Maria knew that if someone dropped a pin, it would sound as loud as a gun firing.

"Tell us, Maria, what is bothering you," her father said, squeezing her hand affectionately. "Tell us now."

Maria focused her eyes straight ahead, on the mantel over the fireplace where gold candle holders held tapers, waiting for the darkness of night to fall, to be lit.

But in her mind's eye she was seeing Shadow and kept him in mind as she began to tell her parents about her feelings for him. "Much has happened since I was abducted," she said in a monotone. "Some that was unpleasant and some *wonderful*."

"Wonderful?" her father gasped, leaning forward to study Maria closely. "How could anything that has happened to you since your abduction be wonderful?"

Maria gave her father a nervous smile, then again focused her eyes straight ahead, not wanting to let her father's overbearing nature take away the courage she needed to reveal her feelings about her father's enemy, a Navaho leader!

"I met a man who I wish to marry," she finally blurted, tensing up inside when she heard her father and mother gasp over that statement.

"You what?" Letha asked, dropping Maria's hand as though it were a hot coal. "How *could* you? Who, Maria? Who?"

Maria swallowed hard and eased her hand from her father's grasp. She clasped her hands on her lap, still keeping the picture of Shadow in her mind, loving him so much and missing him with every fiber of her being!

"It just happened," she said softly. "I imagine it is fate. But it *has* happened and I want to marry him."

Her father leapt to his feet. He doubled his hands into tight fists at his sides and glared down at Maria. "Who in the hell *could* you be talking about?" he shouted. "Don't tell me it's the Indian. He is the only one you have spent considerable time with since you were taken from your room that night. Tell me it's not Shadow, Maria." He reached for her and grabbed her up from the sofa and shook her. "Tell me it isn't so! Tell me!"

Maria was numbly cold from her father's violent reaction. Her head and body ached from him shaking her. She cried out when his fingers dug into the flesh of her arms.

Letha jumped to her feet and clasped her husband's arm. "Esteban, don't!" she cried. "What are you doing?"

Zamora's face grew pale. He let go of Maria and stepped away from her, nervously weaving his fingers through his hair. "*Lo siento*, I am sorry," he murmured. "I don't know what got into me."

Maria rubbed her burning arm, studying her father with wonder in her eyes, and then she grew angry. "I expected this, yet I put myself through it because I love and respect you," she cried. "*Padre*, I didn't have to come and tell you. I could have married Shadow and lived with him peacefully without your interference, and you would never have known the difference. I *did* care! I *did* come home. But I came only to tell you then leave again. I intend to marry Shadow as soon as I return to his stronghold. If you don't want to give us your blessing, so be it!"

She whirled her skirt around and began stomping from the room, then stopped when she heard her father emit a cry of alarm. She turned around and her heart skipped a beat when she saw that her mother was lying unconscious on the sofa, in a dead faint.

Rushing back to her mother, Maria fell to her knees before her and tried to revive her by talking to her and rubbing her hands briskly. "Mother, *lo siento*, I am so sorry!" she cried. "But I had to tell you the truth. I love him, Mother. I love him."

Maria was shoved aside roughly as her father stooped to sweep Letha up into his arms. He glowered at Maria. "Go to your room and wait for me there," he said darkly. "I think the rest that needs to be said must be said only between the two of us. Go, Maria. Now."

Maria rose to her feet and edged toward the door, then flinched when her father hurried past her, carrying her mother.

Then, downhearted, feeling as though gloom was casting a gray shadow over her, she went to her room and sat down on the edge of her bed and hung her head in her hands. She wept softly, then grew tense when she heard a key turn in the keyhole.

Jumping from the bed she went to the door and tried to open it, but it was locked. She grew cold inside when her father spoke through the locked door.

"Until you come to your senses, you won't be allowed to leave the house," he said blandly. "For now, and every evening after this, you will be locked in your room. Then through the long daytime hours, except when you are dining with me and your mother in the dining room, you will be locked in the sewing room. Soon you will grow tired of this and will agree to forget Shadow. That is the way it has to be, Maria. You will not shame your family by going to live with an Indian in *any* capacity!"

Anger grew inside Maria, making her feel hot all over. She splayed her hands against the door and spoke through it. "Do you think you can keep me prisoner forever?" she cried. "For, *Padre*, that is how long it will be before you will hear me say that I will not marry Shadow."

"Guards will be doubled around the plantation grounds," he shouted back. "Your Navaho friend won't get a chance to come and rescue you. He won't even get a chance to steal any more of my sheep or Arabian horses. Maria, how could you care for a man who stole from your own father? From *you*? What he steals from the estate, he steals from you, for it is your inheritance!"

"I care nothing for any inheritance!" Maria said, tears streaming down her face. "Nothing! Do you hear?"

"In time, you will come to your senses," Zamora said, bowing his head as he turned to walk away.

Maria slumped down to the floor and sat there, feeling empty and defeated. She would have to find a way to get free, and when she did, and was back in Shadow's arms once more, she would never leave again!

She shook her head in despair. "But I may never see him

again, much less be with him," she cried, cursing the day she had decided to be fair to her father.

He was *never* fair to her! Never!

Zamora stormed into his office, buckled his holstered pistols around his hips, then rushed out to the quarters of his vaqueros. Opening the door with an angry jerk, he went from bunk to bunk, waking those who had come in to rest after guarding the house and livestock all night.

"We've got someone to kill!" Zamora shouted. "The one responsible for this whole damn mess! I want you to ride out and don't come back until you find and kill Charging Falcon. Bring his head to me to prove that you have killed the son of a bitch!"

He glowered from man to man. "And after we see that he is no longer a bother to us, we will go after Shadow," he said dryly. "But first we'll see if that is necessary." He hoped Maria would come to her senses and realize that the Indian was not the right man for her to marry. "My shoulder still hurts like hell because of my last attempt to get into his stronghold."

The men stumbled from their bunks, but much too slowly for Zamora. He shook a fist in the air. "Hurry up," he shouted. "I intend to ride a ways with you today."

He lumbered over to two men who were already dressed. He pointed to one and then the other, instructing one to guard Maria's room from out in the hallway, and the other to guard the balcony outside her bedroom. He instructed others to position themselves around the plantation grounds. The others were to ride with him.

"One of these days all Indians will learn their place," he said, his brows gathering together in one line as he frowned. "Perhaps killing Charging Falcon will set the example that has been needed for some time now!"

He looked away from them, recalling how he had been humiliated and cheated at the hands of José Gironella. One day, after all of this with the Indian was settled, he would set things straight with that Spaniard. Gironella would make payment in full for his humiliation and for the money he had stolen from Esteban Zamora.

But that was too far in the future. For now, he was going to concentrate on Charging Falcon, then Shadow. . . .

Shadow was sitting before the fire in his hogan, his thoughts varied. First he would think of Maria, then of Charging Falcon. He was recalling what Charging Falcon had said to Maria. The Pueblo had even rescued Maria. His attitude was changing about warring and stealing from Shadow! Could it be that old friends could be friends again? Was Shadow foolish for wanting this? Charging Falcon had betrayed Shadow many times over! How could anyone forgive someone for such a betrayal?

Yet, how could he not forgive, if Charging Falcon sincerely regretted what he had done?

"My friend, your thoughts are filled with many things tonight, are they not?" Blue Arrow said, stepping into Shadow's hogan with Pleasant Voice at his side, seeing Shadow's face filled with many emotions, one battling the other. He helped Pleasant Voice down onto a thick bed of sheepskin blankets beside the fire, then sat down beside her. "Is there something you need to tell me? Talking helps lift many burdens, you know."

"I cannot stop thinking about Charging Falcon and how he seems to be changing back to the man I knew when he was my friend," he said hoarsely, giving Blue Arrow and then Pleasant Voice a sideways glance.

When he saw pain enter Pleasant Voice's eyes, he recalled the wound in her shoulder that was still struggling to heal. "I have many decisions to make about Charging Falcon and none are easy!" he growled.

He rose quickly to his feet and walked toward the door, speaking over his shoulder. "My mind is made up," he said, stopping to look from Pleasant Voice to Blue Arrow. "I am going to have my warriors search for Charging Falcon, find him, and bring him here to meet me face to face. It may take many moons to do this. I will tell my warriors not to return home until Charging Falcon rides beside them."

Blue Arrow and Pleasant Voice exchanged quick glances, then nodded to Shadow.

"You do what your heart leads you to do," Pleasant Voice said, breaking the strained silence. "I have always said that one who forgives is blessed for eternity. If you can forgive Charging Falcon, I will try to forgive him also."

Blue Arrow said nothing. He gave Pleasant Voice a worried look, having only recently discovered that Pleasant Voice at one time, many moons ago, loved Charging Falcon. Did she still . . . ? Was this why she could forgive him anything? Even that he left her to die?

Shadow nodded silently and left the hogan. He looked up into the dark heavens and breathed in the mountain air, glad that he had reached his decision and relieved that Pleasant Voice understood.

Yet why would she not? For many reasons she could want Charging Falcon brought home to the stronghold. A long time ago she had vowed never again to speak of once having loved Charging Falcon. She had vowed that she would not even let her thoughts stray to him. She had told Shadow that when Charging Falcon had left her to die after shooting her with the arrow she had not spoken to him of what had been between them at one time that had been so dear. Self-discipline had made her cool and contained where Charging Falcon was concerned.

But now? If he was no longer an enemy?

If she still loved him just a little bit, what of Blue Arrow . . . ?

CHAPTER
18

Several days had passed. Filled with tumultuous thoughts, hating her father for imprisoning her, and loving and missing Shadow so much, Maria could not concentrate on sewing.

Setting aside the dainty lace she was gathering to sew on a pillowcase, she rose from the chair and went to the window of the sewing room and looked down at the guards her father had positioned around the house. They were heavily armed, and she could see no way to escape.

"There *must* be a way," she said, throwing her head back in exasperation. "But *how*?"

Trying to steady her nerves, she began to walk around the sewing room, touching the softness of the bolts of material lining the shelves. Her thoughts went to the Navaho women and their love of sewing. Though they did not work much with fancy stitches and did no embroidery at all, they loved to weave in bold zigzag designs and diamond shapes. But they lacked brilliant colors. Their earthen and vegetable dyes gave only brownish and pinkish shades to their fabrics. They surely longed for the bright scarlet they saw in flowers and feathers, but did not know how to copy it!

"They have never been introduced to *bayeta*!" Maria whispered, her eyes widening.

Maria went to a woolen cloth, colored a soft crimson with cochineal dye, and ideas began to multiply inside her head. This precious cloth was made in England, where it was called *baize*, and then sold to Spain in quantities. Spain, in turn, sent bales of it to the new world for use as a gift and a bargaining tool.

Maria decided to suggest that her father use it for bargaining with the Navaho, but she would do the actual bargaining . . . with her father. And he would not know that she was doing it! While she was encouraging sales of baize, or *bayeta* to the Navaho, she would actually be encouraging him to release her from her imprisonment and allow her to travel with him to Shadow's stronghold.

And she would be convincing enough. He *would* do as she suggested, for the thought of acquiring more money, no matter how, was all the incentive that he would need.

"I must be convincing!" Maria whispered, going to the locked door. On the other side, in the corridor, stood an armed guard whom she had learned to despise these past several days. To leave the room, for even the most personal reason, she had to ask the guard's permission! Every day she was becoming more humiliated by her father's mistrust in her. Even her mother had not spoken up in her defense! Did her mother condone her imprisonment?

Oh, how could her mother? She knew the meaning of imprisonment without being locked away from the world! Being married to Esteban Zamora was imprisonment enough!

"Diego?" Maria said loudly, doubling a fist at her side. "I must see Father. Will you unlock the door? It is important. Unlock the door. Now!"

"*Señorita*, I cannot do that," the guard said, his voice loud and distinct. "Your father gave me orders. The door is not to be unlocked except for . . . for—"

"Except for what?" Maria shouted, waiting to see if he would say the embarrassing word *inodoro*, toilet!

"*Señorita*, I will go and tell your father that you wish to have an *audiencia* with him," the guard said.

Maria turned with a whirl of skirt and petticoat. She shook the long streamers of her hair down her back as she looked up at the ceiling, fuming. "*Idiota*!" she whispered.

She looked over at the *bayeta*, hope swelling inside her. She thought about what she planned to say to her father, then began nervously pacing.

And when her father did not come right away, she went back to the door and banged on it with her fists.

"Diego! Are you there?" she shouted. "Did you speak to my father? Did you?"

Silence was her only reply. Screwing her face up in a frown, Maria went to the window and looked down, a keen sadness impaling her heart as she ached to be free. If she ever was again, she would not do anything so foolish as to return home for *any* reason, even to see her mother. Letha had let her down by not speaking up in her behalf. This time her mother was almost as responsible for Maria's imprisonment as her father!

"I shall never forgive either of them," Maria whispered. "Never."

The key clicking in the lock made Maria's heart skip a beat and her knees grow weak. Turning slowly, she watched the door open and her father walk into the room.

"You asked to see me?" Zamora asked, closing the door behind him, yet never taking his eyes off Maria. She looked beautiful today in an aqua velveteen blouse and a skirt with bright red and blue flowers in its gathers. Her hair was not held in place by jeweled combs, but instead hung long and free down her perfectly straight back. Although she had been cooped up in the house for several days, she retained the tan she had acquired on her adventures in the desert and mountains, and today her cheeks were rosier than usual.

And weren't her dark eyes unusually bright and vivacious today? Was she ready to cooperate? Had she learned her lesson?

Surely she had!

Maria cringed inside at the thought of what she must do to convince her father. But for freedom and for Shadow, she must force herself to do many unpleasant things, not only today but also tomorrow.

Rushing across the room, Maria lunged into her father's arms. She hugged him heartily, then kissed his cheek. "*Padre*, I'm so glad that you have come," she murmured. "I've much to tell you."

She turned away from him and gestured to the sofa.

"Please sit down and listen," she said, almost breathless with anxiety. "I have such a fabulous idea! It can make you a lot of money! *Lots*, *Padre*!"

Her father rubbed his chin warily, raising an eyebrow as she took his free hand and half dragged him to the sofa. He stumbled as she pushed him down onto the plush cushion, reminded of when she had been a small girl, always filled with ideas of this or that, to take away the boredom of being an only child.

"What is it, Maria?" he asked, laughing nervously as he watched her plop down on a chair opposite him. "What on earth has made you so excited? I haven't seen you like this for years."

"Wait until you hear," Maria said, smiling smugly over at him. "You will see the worth of my idea. I know it!"

"Well? What is it?" Zamora asked, leaning forward, placing his elbows on his knees as he leaned his chin into his hands. "Perhaps what you have in mind is worth something. Tell me what it is."

Maria cleared her throat nervously, suddenly feeling not so sure of herself. "*Padre*," she said, her voice shallow, "I have noticed how you have your slaves busy making mantas, narrow woolen blankets that are wrapped around the body and fastened on the right shoulder. I know they are being made by the hundreds and sent to market. You are making a fortune, *Padre*. A fortune!"

"*Sí*, so I am," Zamora said, leaning back on the sofa, resting his back. "So what does that have to do with what you have to tell me?"

"I know another way of making money with a product used by the Spaniards," Maria said, breathless. "The Navaho, Father. They would pay dearly for *bayeta*! They do not have colorful cloth and thread. Their blankets and clothes are drab in color. If you introduced the Navaho to *bayeta*, Shadow would pay dearly for it. His people could produce much of it and sell it back to you. Then *you* could take it to market, perhaps in Mexico, double the price you paid for it, and make an even greater fortune."

Zamora frowned over at Maria. He stared icily at her.

"Do you think me foolish?" he said. "Don't you know that I understand that this is a way for you to get back with that Indian?"

He rose hotly to his feet and began walking toward the door. Panic rose inside Maria. She rushed to her feet and went to her father and grabbed him by a wrist, stopping him.

"That is not so," she said, hating to lie. "I have had a lot of time to think. I understand how wrong I was to be taken in by Shadow."

She pleaded with him with her eyes. "*Padre*, what I have told you today about how you could make money is for my own benefit also," she said in a rush of words. "I need something for myself in my life. I would like to supervise all sales of *bayeta*. It would be a way for me to become a businesswoman. You don't have a son. Wouldn't you like to see me take the place of a son? I could learn all ways of your businesses. I am good with figures. You know how good I am at sewing! I could be the seamstress I always dreamed of being *and* run my business at the same time."

She lowered her eyes and swallowed hard, then raised her eyes slowly to her father. "*Padre*, I truly want this," she said. "Give me a chance. Please? And if there is any doubt at all in your mind about me still thinking about Shadow, keeping me and my mind occupied is the best way to make sure that I forget everything and everyone else."

Her father's eyes softened. He placed his hands on Maria's shoulders. "I want to believe you," he said hoarsely. "But I find it very hard to believe that you could be determined to go to Shadow one day, to be his wife, then decide against it the next. How am I to believe you? How?"

"I was just being stubborn," Maria said, laughing softly. "Now I am being wise."

"You know that Shadow and I are bitter enemies," Zamora said, pondering her idea, liking it more and more as the moments passed. "He recently stole my prized merino sheep and my valuable Arabian horses! He stole *you* away and some of his warriors even shot me! How can all of that be rectified, Maria? How? Surely not by my going to Shadow with bright cloths to offer to his people!"

"You would not be offering only the cloth," Maria said softly. "You would offer friendship as well! Peace! *And* you would be giving Shadow's people a way to make money for themselves. How *can* he refuse you? How?"

"He would not let me or my men get near his stronghold," Zamora said, moving to a window, staring down at the guards, hating their presence. It would be nice to be able to trust Maria again. Dare he?

Maria moved smoothly to his side and gently touched his arm. "*Padre*, he would admit you if *I* were with you," she said, forcing her voice to remain calm, though her insides were jumping with fear that her father might see right through her scheme.

Her insides splashed cold when he moved his eyes slowly to her and looked at her, as though boring a hole through her. "I would personally introduce *bayeta* to the Navaho women," she quickly added. "I would make them want it so badly that Shadow would not dare refuse it!"

"And what about Shadow himself?" her father said dryly. "How would you convince him that refusing to marry him was your idea, not mine? Would he truly let you leave?"

"There is much about Shadow that you do not know," Maria said, her voice even. "He does not trust women. He has not married because he has not found a woman he trusted enough. You see, Navaho marriages can be dissolved by the wife merely placing the husband's saddle outside the door of the hogan. And when the woman divorces the man she gets his worldly possessions. Shadow would not marry me if he had the slightest doubt that I would not want to marry him. He would not risk losing all that he has worked so hard to accumulate through the years. No. Once I tell him that I do not wish to be his wife, he will let me return with you gladly."

Her father stroked his chin and raised an eyebrow. "Maria, how can I be sure of you?" he asked shallowly. "*How*?"

"I guess that is a chance you will have to take," Maria said, lifting her chin stubbornly. "*Padre*, I believe you have gambled on less certain things than your daughter's word."

"*Sí, sí*, I guess I have," he said, chuckling low.

"Then you will do it?" Maria asked, her heart pounding.

"*Puede ser, puede ser*, perhaps, perhaps," Zamora said, walking toward the door. "I shall let you know."

Maria wrung her hands as she watched the door close. She gritted her teeth angrily as she heard the key turn in the lock.

"I am still a prisoner, *Padre*?" she shouted. "Even now?"

"It can't be helped, Maria," he said through the locked door, slipping the key back inside his pocket. "As I said. I shall let you know about your proposition. Soon. I do like the idea of you taking on the role of a son. *Sí*, I like that idea a lot."

Maria nodded. "*Sí*, I was sure you would," she whispered. "Anything to keep me from the man I love!"

She strolled limply to the window and gazed toward the mountains. Her fingers went to the windowpane and scraped aimlessly against it. Shadow was so far, yet in spirit forever so close to her heart.

"I did all that I could think of, darling, to help get me free to come to you," she whispered. "If that doesn't work, I just don't know. . . ."

Charging Falcon rode quickly over the land, having seen the approach of Shadow's warriors from one side and Spanish vaqueros from the other. He was being penned in. He could be caught in crossfire between the Spaniards and Navaho, for they were ardent enemies!

Bending low over his horse, his dark hair flying in the wind, Charging Falcon spurred his horse faster, yet he knew that he had been seen by both of his enemies, for both groups were riding toward him, their weapons drawn!

He looked toward the Navaho, sorting Shadow out from the others, as he led his men onward. Perhaps if he shifted his direction and rode toward Shadow, he would have a measure of mercy, whereas many Spaniards would want him killed because he had of late deceived not only one but many of them.

Realizing that death could come more slowly at the hand of the Navaho, Charging Falcon understood that they would like to see him suffer. This gave him some hope, however, for while he was awaiting his death, perhaps Shadow would remember their youth, how they had loved and learned the ways of warring together. If Charging Falcon had a chance, he could remind Shadow that he had helped Maria escape from José Gironella. His having helped Maria escape might make Shadow forget exactly who had taken her from Shadow's stronghold in the first place!

Then he grew cold inside. There was no guarantee that Maria had made it back to Shadow's stronghold alive. If she was dead, Shadow would show no mercy whatsoever!

Drawing his horse to a halt, fear rushing into his heart, Charging Falcon looked from the Spaniards to the Navaho; he was now definitely trapped between them. He scarcely breathed as Shadow and his warriors drew their horses to a shuddering halt on the one side of him, the Spaniards on the other, weapons drawn and threatening.

Shadow raised his fist in the air, glowering from Charging Falcon to the Spaniards. He glanced over his shoulder at his braves, seeing hatred burning in their eyes. "Remember Maria!" he shouted. "Do not fire upon the Spaniards unless they fire upon you. If we do not move wisely here, I may never see my woman again!"

Shadow's warriors nodded, but their arrows remained notched into the strings of their bows.

The lead vaquero raised one hand and looked cautiously over at Shadow, seeing that he was not giving any command to shoot. In fact, he had heard Shadow caution his men against shooting.

He then looked at the notched arrows. He had no idea whether they were poison-tipped, and he did not desire to find out. He had come for Charging Falcon. He wanted no problem with Shadow!

"Do not fire upon the Navaho," he shouted, his finger tight on the trigger of his own rifle. "All we want is Charging Falcon. Fire only if we are fired upon."

Shadow inched his stallion away from the rest of his men,

his bow and arrow ready for battle. He watched the lead vaquero begin inching away from his men, also.

He then looked at Charging Falcon, who was cowering like a cornered animal. And he had cause to. Shadow had heard the Spaniard say that all the vaqueros wanted was Charging Falcon! That was all that Shadow and his braves wanted, also! It seemed that Charging Falcon had made too many enemies and no friends!

Somewhere deep inside Shadow, where memories were cherished and sweet, he felt sorrow for Charging Falcon and what he had become. And at this moment he was torn by tumultuous feelings for him. Charging Falcon seemed ready to repent of his evil ways, and if possible, Shadow wanted to forgive.

But it was not that simple. First Charging Falcon must be taken back to the stronghold and held captive while Shadow pondered over what was best between old friends who were now enemies.

"And what is it you want with Charging Falcon?" Shadow asked, side by side with the vaquero, with Charging Falcon only a few yards away. "I have come for Charging Falcon. I shall take him away, not the Spaniards!"

The vaquero once again looked at the Navaho warriors and their weapons, their faces etched with hate, then looked slowly over at Charging Falcon and Shadow. "We have come for Charging Falcon because he has betrayed Señor Esteban Zamora. He must pay. We have been searching for the scoundrel for days and we will not give him up to you or anyone. Do you understand, Shadow?"

"So you know my name?" Shadow said, his lips curling into a smug smile.

"Hardly any Spaniard does *not* know you," the vaquero said.

"Then you know that it is not wise to take from Shadow anything that Shadow believes is rightfully his?" Shadow said, his words clipped. "My warriors and I have been searching for many days for this scoundrel! He should pay for his evil deeds the Navaho way!"

"We do not want to fight over the likes of him," the

vaquero growled, nodding toward Charging Falcon. "But I have been given orders to bring him back. If I go against orders, I will turn into the hunted!"

"If you do not do as Shadow says you will not live long enough to be hunted," Shadow said, motioning to his braves to aim their arrows at the Spaniards. "Now it is understood that you have powerful firing sticks, but you would have time to fire only once. After that my men would put many arrows into your chests. Now what will you choose—death or giving up Charging Falcon to Shadow?"

The vaquero blinked his eyes nervously and lowered his rifle. "*Señor*, Charging Falcon is not worth dying over," he said, backing his horse away from Shadow. "Take him. It won't be a surprise that I return to the Zamora plantation empty-handed. No one was expecting us to find Charging Falcon anyhow."

Shadow's eyes glimmered in the afternoon sun as he watched the vaqueros ride away, leaving a thick veil of dust in the air behind them.

He turned and faced Charging Falcon while replacing his bow and arrow in their cases, then rode slowly toward him. Without a word Shadow reached out, plucked Charging Falcon's weapons from his body, and tossed them to the ground.

"You are now stripped of your pride," Shadow growled. "Now you follow me. There are many in my stronghold who will enjoy seeing you stripped naked and tied out in the sun to suffer while I make up my mind as to what to do with you next!"

Charging Falcon lowered his eyes and rode off beside Shadow, shamed. . . .

Maria tossed in bed, finding it hard to sleep. She drew the satin comforter up beneath her chin and tried to force her eyes to stay closed, but they would not. She could not get her mind off the talk between her and her father. He had not yet told her whether he agreed with her.

But as greedy as he was, and with the possibility of cheating the Indians while transacting business with them, he would surely see that what she suggested was a sure way of making a lot of money.

Tired of trying to sleep, Maria rose from her bed and in the soft glow of a dripping candle drew on a robe and went to the window to look out into the darkness.

Then she looked toward the doors that led out to the terrace. Her heart thundered wildly when she recalled the night that Shadow had come and forced her down the trellis.

Oh, if only he could come tonight!

But there were too many guards . . . too many risks, and he did not know that she was being held prisoner. How much longer would he wait for her? Would he come for her when he realized that she was not going to come to *him*? Or did he think that she had changed her mind, that she no longer wanted to be his wife?

Maria went to a chair and picked up her embroidery from a table and began furiously passing the needle back and forth through the fabric. She was going to go insane if things did not change! Oh, how could her father be so unfair to her? How much longer would he keep her prisoner?

A slight tapping on the door caused Maria to prick her finger with the needle. She winced with pain, then set the embroidery aside and rose to her feet. Her father softly spoke her name as he turned the key in the lock.

Maria stood with her chin lifted haughtily as her father entered the room, yet her pulse was racing. Had he come to say that he agreed with her plan? It would be just too perfect! Little did he know that once she got him halfway between their plantation and the stronghold, she would slip away from him in the night while he slept, and go on to Shadow alone! He would awaken and find her gone and would know by then that he had been tricked, and he would be so disenchanted with her that he would turn around and head back to the plantation.

"So you are still awake, I see," her father said, his maroon velveteen monogrammed robe sleek and expensive-looking as he walked toward Maria, his hands in his pockets. "Is it because you are thinking about *bayeta* and the Navaho?"

"*Sí*," Maria said, every nerve in her body moved to a keen excitement, believing that she had won with her father! "I was. I do believe much money could be made, *Padre*, by introducing it to the Navaho. And Shadow is an astute businessman. He will see the worth, also! And because *I* would offer it, he would be more apt to agree with how we approach them with how the bargaining should be done."

"Even though you are not going to be his wife after all?" Zamora tested, his eyes narrowing as he watched Maria's reaction.

Maria knew that she was being closely observed, so barely batting an eye, she met her father's stare. "I have explained how Shadow feels about women and marriage," she said smoothly. "Once he knows that I do not want a marriage with him, he will not want it, either. He will look to me as a passing fancy. That's all. Now, *Padre*, please say that you are ready to go to the Navaho stronghold! It would be profitable. It would!"

"Tomorrow your door will no longer be locked," Esteban said, taking Maria's hands. "Get together whatever you think will be required to make a good impression on the Navaho, especially Shadow. Maria, I see this as a way to come to a peaceful solution to many problems. Perhaps Shadow will eventually return my sheep and horses!"

"I hope so, *Padre*," she said, shielding her lie with a convincing, soft laugh. "I do hope so."

Her father yawned and released Maria's hands. "Now do you think you can go to sleep?" he asked, his eyes twinkling.

"*Sí, Padre*," Maria said, lunging into his arms. "I do. *Muchas gracias, Padre*, for giving me the chance to prove myself to you."

"*Que le vaya bien*, good luck to you in this adventure," Zamora said, caressing her back with light strokes of his fingers. "If it should fail, much else will also fail."

Maria tensed and fluttered her eyelashes nervously. . . .

CHAPTER
19

The moon was a perfect circle overhead against the back-drop of the black velvet sky. Maria squirmed uneasily on her pallet of blankets on the ground close beside a campfire that was flickering into ashes. She had waited forever, it seemed, for her father and his men to drift off to sleep. Even the guard who was supposed to be watching over them was fast asleep, propped up against a cottonwood tree, his rifle having gone lax in his hand.

Breathing hard, filled with both fear and excitement over what she was about to do, Maria rose slowly to an elbow and looked cautiously around her to see if everyone was still asleep.

Her gaze went to her father, guilt plaguing her when she was reminded of how she was so willfully deceiving him and her mother.

Yet she had no choice!

Though her father had agreed to go to Shadow's strong-hold, it was not for *her*. The trip was for business purposes only. Had she not thought up a way for her father to make money off the Indians, even though her willingness to do it with him *was* only in pretense, she would still be imprisoned by him!

Sí, this was the *only* way. . . .

And she didn't think that he would storm Shadow's

stronghold when he discovered her gone. He would be too humiliated by her escape to draw undue attention to it!

No, once she was gone, he would more than likely return to the plantation as quietly as possible, not wanting everyone to know that his daughter had made a fool out of him by feeding on his weakness—money.

She could be wrong, however. Perhaps he would proceed to Shadow's stronghold and demand her return, the threat of being killed by the Navaho hanging over his head.

No matter, she had devised this scheme that would at least get her back in the arms of the man she loved. Whatever the result of her decision, she would let fate take its own course.

Having gone to bed fully dressed, Maria inched her hand across the ground to get her valise. Her fingers slowly circled around the handle of the bag, then even more slowly slid it across the ground toward her. Her eyes wide, she watched anxiously for any signs of movement, but the only disturbances were the snores of those men who were sleeping most soundly.

She tucked the valise in the crook of her left arm; inside it were some swatches of the precious *bayeta* that she was going to introduce to the Navaho without making any monetary demands of them. Maria rose to her feet, breathless. She squinted as she looked ahead to where the horses were peacefully grazing close beside a creek, a makeshift corral having been quickly erected by stringing ropes from one cottonwood tree to another.

Her eyes settled on one horse in particular. It knew her. It would go with her easily, without making a commotion that could awaken someone.

Moving stealthily through the night, Maria frowned up at the moon. She felt it was her enemy this night, for it illuminated her like a lighted candle.

Then she once again focused on the horses, relieved that the one she had chosen on which to make her escape was grazing away from the others. It would be easy to slip the corral rope over the horse's head and lead him away from the others, but she could not take the time to saddle him.

She would have to make the rest of the journey to Shadow's stronghold bareback.

Taking a brief glance toward the beckoning mountain, which did not look so far away in the darkness, Maria was glad that her father had brought her farther than they had originally planned before stopping for a night of rest. She was feeling confident that she could find her way alone.

She hoped this would be the last time that she would have to travel alone at night. From this night forth, she would have Shadow! If everything worked out as planned, she would be his wife.

Smiling, thinking of marriage to Shadow a balm to her troubled mind, Maria went to the rope corral and slipped beneath it. Smoothing her hand over the horse's sleek white neck to comfort him, she saw the reins hanging loose from the bridle, which had not been removed. So far she was in luck.

Grabbing the reins, she led the horse toward the rope. Securing her valise more securely in the crook of her arm, she managed to get the rope up high enough for the horse to slip beneath it. Then she eased herself onto the horse and bent low over its back and sent it into a quiet lope across the grassy land.

She did not turn to look back. Her sights were set straight ahead, and none too soon. Daybreak was just appearing along the horizon, as though a line of contrast between dark and light had been drawn by a skilled artist.

As soon as she could dare to, she would have to send the horse into a fast gallop. She *must* reach the mountains before her father awakened. She was becoming familiar with the canyons and valleys that led to Shadow's stronghold. She knew them much better than her father, for he had only found the stronghold once and that had been by accident. She had been taught much about the mountain by Shadow.

Eventually she would know everything about it, for it would be her home. . . .

* * *

Attired in only a breechclout and moccasins, Shadow stood on a steep bluff not far from his village, a hand cupped over his eyes. It was early morning and he was surveying his domain, in awe of the beauty of the land and of the eagles that were soaring across the sky, then dipping to seize prey in their sharp talons.

Yet there was something missing in this moment of contentment. Maria! She had been gone for too long now. It should not have taken her this long to reassure her parents that she was all right.

His sculpted face wrinkled into a deep, brooding frown, for he knew that it might take Maria an eternity to convince her parents that she should be free to marry a Navaho!

"Perhaps she has changed her mind and no longer wishes to be a part of my life," Shadow worried aloud, running his lean fingers nervously through his long and flowing, sleek black hair. "Was I wrong to trust her? Is she no different from other women? Should I go and see if I was wrong? Should I go to the Spaniard's plantation, risk being slain, to see why she has not returned to me?"

He hung his head in a hand. "Is she worth it?" he whispered harshly. "Is any woman worth all of this grief and torment?"

A cry of agony tore through the silent morning, wrenching Shadow from his thoughts. He turned and looked toward his village where Charging Falcon was tied naked to a stake. His resolution wavered, seeing the humiliation of this Pueblo who had at one time been such a close friend. Many Navaho and Pueblo women were now tossing pebbles at him and calling him names.

Shadow's gaze shifted and his jaw tightened when he saw Pleasant Voice standing back away from the crowd of women, silently watching, wringing her hands. He looked into her dark, intense eyes and saw tears. Was she also recalling many wonderful moments with Charging Falcon? Did she still love him, despite what he had done? Was her love for Blue Arrow so frail?

Nodding, his shoulders slouching, Shadow saw this as an

example of why he had never given his heart solely to any one woman until Maria. Seeing Pleasant Voice torn between two loves made him wonder if any woman was capable of true love, even Maria! If she loved him, where was she now? She should have come to him. She had much to prove to him now, just as she had once felt that she had much to prove to her parents.

Shadow's insides grew tight when he saw an elderly Pueblo woman make her way through the crowd of women. "Little Doe!" he whispered, stiffening his arms at his sides. His heart cried out to both her and Charging Falcon when she raised her eyes to her nephew and glared up at him, then suddenly spit in Charging Falcon's face.

"You are no longer of my family of Pueblo," Little Doe declared, then spun around and waddled away, the buckskin dress loose and flowing on her bulky shape.

Shadow turned his eyes away and once more stared across the land below, then his eyes widened when he caught sight of a lone traveler heading toward the mountains on horseback, her dark hair flying in the wind, her skirt whipping up past her knees.

"Maria?" he whispered, his heart racing. "Could that be Maria?"

He watched as several of his braves rode into view, riding toward the woman, surrounding her with arrows notched into the strings of their bows.

Swinging around, he ran to his stallion and swung himself up into his saddle and rode away, his hopes high. . . .

Maria became cold with fright as she peered from one warrior to the other, recognizing none of them. They were clothed in only breechclouts, their bows and arrows ready, their eyes filled with loathing. She did not think that any of them recognized her.

Or perhaps they did and they saw an opportunity to rid their lives of her. Since Shadow was not among them, they could kill her, do away with her body, and he would never be the wiser! Would not life be much easier for the Navaho if a white woman did not live among them?

Or had Shadow given up on her and decided that she was no longer of any worth to *him*? Had he given his braves orders to kill her if they caught her anywhere near the stronghold?

"Good morning," Maria said, forcing a smile. She again looked guardedly from man to man. "I am on my way to see Shadow. He will want to see me. Surely you remember me. I was with Shadow at your stronghold only a short while ago. He took me home to meet with my parents. I am returning now to his stronghold to stay."

When there was no response, Maria swallowed hard and felt nervous perspiration beading her brow. "I have come to marry Shadow," she dared to say, then flinched when one of the warriors grabbed her horse's reins and looped them with his and urged her horse into a steady gallop across the land, on toward the mountain.

Filled with anxiety, fear lacing her heart, making her every heartbeat feel as though it might swallow her whole, Maria clung to the horse's mane with one hand and her valise with the other. She looked up at the sheer cliffs that grew closer and then she felt herself slipping from the horse as it was being led up a steep slope of land with loose gravel beneath the horse's feet.

Clinging to the horse, bending to wrap her arm around its neck, Maria held her breath as she continued her ride upward. . . .

Esteban Zamora stood apart from his men, feeling empty, feeling betrayed! And his own daughter had done the betraying! She had cleverly persuaded him to bring her along with him to transact business with Shadow, only to help her *go* to him, to be his wife!

Zamora bent his head and held the note before his eyes again, reading his daughter's written words of apology and her plea for him to understand and not hate her.

Crumpling the note into a tight ball and tossing it into the wind, he cursed his ignorance in not having seen the scheme for what it was before letting it get this far! And his daughter had the nerve to ask him not to hate her? At this moment, he hated no one any more. And he would pay her back for having humiliated him like this in front of his men.

Somehow she would pay. No daughter was so important that she could humiliate a father over and over again. . . .

Swinging around, his face drawn and pale, his hair windblown, his sleek breeches clinging to his long, lean legs, Zamora marched solemnly back to the waiting men, all eyes on him.

"Let us return home," he said, stopping before the camp-fire, clasping his hands together behind him. He looked over the heads of the men as he continued to speak. "We must gather more men. Many vaqueros will be required to storm the Navaho stronghold. This time we know where we are going and will not be surprised by an attack with bows and arrows. We shall attack *first*."

His heart sank at the thought of Maria being there in the middle of the attack. But she was no longer his concern. She had chosen a Navaho over him. . . .

Zamora was losing faith in his ability to make life go his way. His vaqueros had not found Charging Falcon, and now Maria was also lost to him.

All of this was Shadow's fault, for he had surely captured Charging Falcon and he most certainly had captured Maria . . . her heart, at least. . . .

Maria saw more familiar terrain as the Navaho warriors led her higher up the mountain, and her fear lessened. If the Navaho warriors had planned to kill her, they would have done so by now. It was apparent that they were taking her to Shadow! In only a short while she would be with him, but would he welcome her back? They had been separated for many days now. Surely his trust in her was lacking! Could he ever trust her again?

Maria's breath was stolen away from her when suddenly just ahead Shadow appeared in the path on his beautiful

stallion, his eyes so dark and fathomless that Maria could
not read the expression in their depths.

But his set jaw and tight lips made fear once more
envelop her. Shadow did not look happy to see her! Had she
been right to think that he had lost faith in her?

Surely after he heard that her father had imprisoned her
he would welcome her into his arms and love her even more
for what she had gone through because of him.

Her love for him was never ending . . . was forever!

Surely he would believe her and love her as much in
return!

Shadow's braves stopped their ascent up the mountain
when they saw him, and Maria took this opportunity to slip
from her horse and take off in a mad run toward him,
holding on to her valise for dear life, for if she dropped it
over the edge of the cliff, she would not have the opportunity to introduce the Navaho to the bright crimson *bayeta*!

"Shadow, oh, Shadow," Maria cried, holding her free
hand out to him, her feet threatening to tangle in the hem of
her skirt as she raced up the steep slope of graveled land.
"My darling, I have returned. I did not mean to worry you.
Lo siento, I am so sorry, my love!"

Shadow sat stiffly on his fancy Navaho saddle, the silver
ornaments reflecting the sun in dancing flames along the
wall of the canyon that rose up on one side of him. He
watched Maria moving hurriedly toward him, hearing
her, seeing the sincere pleading in her dark eyes. His gaze
swept over her, seeing the familiar lines of her delicate,
lovely body through her clinging blouse and glimpsing her
tapered ankles as her brightly flowered skirt first threatened
to trip her, then hiked up past her ankles as she ran even
faster.

His love for her spoke in the way his heart thundered
against his ribs, as though a thousand drums were beating in
unison inside him. The burning in his loins attested to how
much he needed Maria . . . how much he had missed her.
When he awoke in the night and did not find her cuddled
against him, it was as though a part of his identity was
missing!

Never had he loved so intensely! Never would he again!

Maria stopped when she reached Shadow's horse. She panted hard, her breasts heaving as she harshly breathed. She placed her free hand in one of Shadow's and intertwined their fingers. "Tell me that you are happy to see me," she said, her pulse racing, his presence overwhelming in that he was so breathtakingly handsome.

Her gaze swept him up and down, his partially nude body disturbing her to the core! Oh, how she had missed their shared passion . . . the rapture of lying with him, tasting the wonder of his kisses . . . feeling the magic of his hands!

Oh, never had she loved so intensely! Never would she again!

"You have been gone a long time," Shadow finally said. "You have become *anaye*, stranger, to me. Why?"

Shadow withdrew his hand, causing Maria to grow tense. "Never could I be a stranger to you," she cried, pressing her hand to her throat in despair.

She started to explain, then squared her shoulders stubbornly. "Did you even think to come and discover why I was detained?" she said dryly. "I know there are dangers in that, but you came the other time, Shadow. You stole me away! You have enough braves under your command to make another successful raid against my father. Why did you not come and see just why I did not return to you? Am I of so little importance to you?"

She gestured toward him and his horse. "You sit there so smugly on your horse, as though I am nothing!" she cried. "Was I wrong to risk everything, even my relationship with my parents, to come and be with you? Oh, please don't tell me that I was wrong to do that, for I don't believe things can ever be the same again between me and my father. After today he will hate me! Totally!"

Shadow's eyes wavered and his gut twisted, for he was reading much into what she was saying, without her having to explain exactly what had happened. She had said enough to let him know that she had gone against her father's wishes by coming here. Surely she could not have returned earlier! He had been wrong to doubt her! She did love him; she *did* want to be with him, regardless of how it affected the rest of her life . . . her relationship with her family!

Shadow bent over and with one sweep of an arm lifted Maria up on the horse with him and held her on his lap. Paying no heed to his warriors who were watching, he wove his fingers through Maria's hair and drew her lips to his, firing passion between them anew.

With her free arm, Maria clung to Shadow, emitting a soft sob of joy against his lips, savoring his muscled arm that held her close to his powerful chest, inhaling the outdoor fragrance of his body, which she had grown so accustomed to and had missed while they were apart.

Things were going to be all right! Shadow *did* love her. He did have faith in her! Oh, surely within the next few days they could seal their bond of love and speak vows between them!

Then she would show him ways to make money that he never dreamed of. And it would be an *honest* living, not booty obtained by raiding.

They could begin taking journeys together to Mexico to purchase the precious *bayeta*. *She* would benefit from the Navaho's knowledge of the *bayeta*, not her father. But when she benefited, the Navaho would also. What was hers . . . was theirs!

Shadow inched his lips away from Maria's. He looked down into her dark eyes, his filled with love. "*Ukehe*, thank you," he said thickly.

Maria was touched by his words, having been taught by him that the Navaho very seldom said thank you. Instead, they gave gifts in return for very great favors. Ordinary gifts and kindnesses were offered and accepted in silence.

She placed a hand on Shadow's smooth cheek. "You thank me," she murmured. "For what?"

"For being you," he said, his voice deep. He wheeled his horse around and headed toward the stronghold. "For being you and for loving Shadow!"

Maria smiled sweetly up at him and leaned her cheek against his chest, clinging around his waist, happy, so very happy. She would not think of her father and mother, for she did not want guilt to ruin her contentment at this moment. Perhaps one day she could make up with her mother; she was not sure if she wanted to make up with her father. He was a rogue!

"My woman, what *did* delay your return?" Shadow asked, interrupting Maria's train of thought.

She looked up at him, solemn. "I was held prisoner in my own house, Shadow," she explained. "My father did not allow me to go anywhere without being watched. It was horrible. Missing you was horrible, Shadow!"

"How did you manage to get free?" he asked, glancing down at her.

Maria laughed softly and snuggled deeper into his embrace. "Just wait until you hear what I did!" she said, proud. "I was very clever, Shadow. Very!"

"Tell me," Shadow said, almost afraid to hear. Whatever it was must have angered the Spaniard. If Maria was not allowed to return with her father's blessing, vengeance could lie heavily on Zamora's dark heart!

Leaning away from him, watching Shadow's expression change from curiosity to delight and then to worry, Maria explained exactly how she had fooled her father.

Then she grew tense when Shadow's ensuing silence began to unnerve her. "Shouldn't I have done it in that way?" she asked. "Shadow, it was the *only* way. I would still be prisoner today!"

"Shadow is glad that you are here," he finally said. "But Shadow does not welcome the thought of many vaqueros coming to the stronghold again. It will now be necessary to double all sentries at their posts. If your father comes, Maria, this time he will have to *die*."

Maria's insides went cold at the thought. Then she looked up at Shadow. "Perhaps he won't come," she murmured. "Perhaps he hates me too much to care what I do anymore."

Shadow's lips quivered into a smile. "My love, how can anyone hate you?" he said hoarsely. "Even a father who is betrayed could not hate you. He will come. He . . . will . . . come."

Feeling numbly cold inside, Maria rested her cheek against Shadow's copper chest again, trying not to think of anything but the pleasure of being with him. But, truly, should she want him so badly that she was willing to see her father killed because of him?

As she had since she had fallen in love with Shadow, she felt torn . . . absolutely torn. . . .

CHAPTER
20

Wide-eyed, Maria clung to Shadow as they rode into the village. Stunned, she looked at Charging Falcon tied to a stake at the edge of the village, and then she blushed, for he was *nude*.

When her eyes met and held his, a sadness tore through her, for she recalled how sincere he had sounded when he said he was sorry for what he had done to Shadow.

Apparently Shadow had not found room in his heart for forgiveness, and Maria did not know whether he should have. Charging Falcon had been disloyal to Shadow's friendship and to their people who lived as one in the stronghold. Charging Falcon was lucky to be *alive*. Maria knew the torment he had put Shadow through, and it was up to Shadow to decide whether the Pueblo would live or die.

Turning her eyes quickly away, Maria was relieved when Shadow took her on toward his hogan. His braves now scattered, going their separate ways as their family members came and heartily greeted them.

Still clutching the valise, Maria was glad to be back on solid ground when Shadow helped her down from the horse.

Then her eyes filled with happiness when Pleasant Voice ran toward her and lunged into her arms and hugged her.

"It is good to see you!" Pleasant Voice said, her voice quavering with excitement. "Maria, I had given up on your returning. I am so glad that you are here. So glad!"

221

With her free arm, Maria returned Pleasant Voice's enthusiastic greeting. "You know my father," she murmured. "He did not make returning easy. He forbade me to return."

Pleasant Voice stepped away from Maria. "How is it that you managed to come back if he forbade it?" she gasped. "I know your father *very* well. When he sets his mind, no one can dissuade him!"

Shadow pressed a gentle kiss on Pleasant Voice's cheek. "It is a long story," he said, giving Maria a soft smile. "Why don't you go into my dwelling and visit with Maria while I order special foods to be brought to us?"

He touched Maria's dust-laden cheeks. "Also, bathwater will be brought," he said, chuckling. "After you take nourishment, you can cleanse yourself of the desert dust and change into appropriate attire for living with the Navaho, not the white man."

Pleasant Voice nodded eagerly and grabbed Maria by a hand. "Come," she encouraged. "What he suggests sounds good to me. Surely it does to you, also. *Sí?*"

"*Sí, sí,*" Maria said, laughing softly as she watched over her shoulder as Shadow walked away from her.

Going on into the hogan, dimly lit by a slow-burning fire in the fire pit and a candle almost burned down to its wick, Maria swung her valise to the floor and sighed as she sat down on a thick pallet of sheepskin.

Closing her eyes, she wove her fingers through her thick, wind-tangled hair, then became aware again of a presence when Pleasant Voice touched her arm.

"Maria, tell me everything," Pleasant Voice encouraged. "How did you persuade your father? How?"

Maria opened her eyes and smiled at Pleasant Voice. "I didn't," she said, her voice thick with a laugh. "Pleasant Voice, I was very clever in my scheming against my father and I succeeded!"

"*E-do-ta,* no!" Pleasant Voice gasped, paling. "How could you be so brave?"

"I'm not sure whether I was being brave or foolish," Maria sighed, stretching her legs out before her, slipping her shoes off. She wriggled her toes, loving the freedom she had just given them. It was as delicious as she felt all over inside because she was free again!

"What do you mean?" Pleasant Voice asked quietly.

"I don't know what my father's reaction was when he found my note," Maria said, inching her skirt up past her knees, letting it rest there. "I don't know if he will come after me or be glad to be rid of me, since he knows that I can never be loyal to him as long as he forbids me to be with Shadow. Shadow is doubling the sentries around the stronghold."

She rolled the sleeves of her blouse up past her elbows, grimacing when she saw the lines of dust at her wrists. *Sí*, a bath would be greatly welcomed.

"What if because of my scheming I lose both my father and Shadow during a bloody battle?" she said, looking slowly over at Pleasant Voice. "What then, Pleasant Voice? What then?"

Pleasant Voice shook the long streamers of jet black hair that fell across her shoulders and down her back. "You and I are facing many questions in our lives at this time," she said solemnly. A haunted look rose into her dark eyes as she gazed down into the slow embers of the fire. "Why is life so hard . . . so complicated, Maria? You don't know what is best for you. I don't know what is best for *me*."

She looked hurriedly over at Maria and grabbed her hand. "Did you see Charging Falcon?" she said, almost choking on the name, for every time she thought of him imprisoned in such a humiliating way she wanted to die a slow death inside.

She had forgiven him for what he had done. Why couldn't Shadow? Did Shadow not see the remorse in Charging Falcon's eyes? Had he not humbled himself to Shadow by apologizing for all the wrong that he had done?

"*Sí*," Maria murmured. "I saw Charging Falcon. Did he come to Shadow and give himself up or did Shadow search him out?"

"Shadow found *him*," Pleasant Voice said, her voice hoarse as she fought back a throat-tearing sob. "Shadow had preached to me about forgiveness, but Shadow himself does not forgive so easily. Now when Charging Falcon is released, he will have to go away in shame. Everyone in the village will remember him as he hung on the stake. He knows this! The humiliation is too great for him. I ache for him, Maria. What am I to do?"

Maria took both of Pleasant Voice's hands and squeezed them affectionately. "Pleasant Voice, don't tell me that you love Charging Falcon," she said, her voice strained. "What about Blue Arrow? You and he were to be married. Where is he now? Does he know you feel this way about Charging Falcon?"

Pleasant Voice lowered her eyes and blushed. "I once loved Charging Falcon with all my heart," she said almost in whisper. "Then he left the village to take money and gifts from the Spaniards. He began raiding the Navaho and Pueblo. I had to force myself never to think of him again!"

Pleasant Voice slowly lifted her eyes. "Then I met Blue Arrow and I thought that I had placed Charging Falcon from my mind and heart," she said. "I do love Blue Arrow, but perhaps in a different way than I loved Charging Falcon, who was my first true love. He gave me feelings of excitement by the mere touch of his hand! I gave myself to him only! He was the first! My love for him was a wild love. My love for Blue Arrow is a peaceful one."

She covered her eyes and began to sob. "When Charging Falcon shot me with the arrow, I wanted to die because it was *he* who had done it," she cried. "How could he? How? I know he loves me still! Yet, to prove to himself that he did not love me, he shot me? That is what he says! Do you know that? He says he shot me to prove to himself that he *could*!"

Maria wrapped her arms around Pleasant Voice. "There, there," she crooned.

Pleasant Voice clung to Maria. "I so want to love Blue Arrow in the way I once loved Charging Falcon," she continued to cry. "But with Charging Falcon here, how can I?"

"You never said where Blue Arrow is," Maria said,

holding Pleasant Voice away from her as she framed her face between her hands. "He wasn't with Shadow. Where *is* he?"

"He left, to be with his own people, to give me time to think," Pleasant Voice said, blinking nervously. "So you see, he *does* know. In a sense, he has been as humiliated as Charging Falcon, who hangs on a stake. I may have lost Blue Arrow forever, Maria! Forever!"

Maria drew Pleasant Voice into her arms. "Just listen to yourself," she said softly. "I believe you have just proved to me *and* to yourself which man you love and want to marry. You are in much distress over Blue Arrow! Don't you hear the distress in your voice when you speak of him? Pleasant Voice, it is *he* you love now, not Charging Falcon. It is just a memory that makes you feel anything about Charging Falcon. It was a torrid young love affair that is now only a part of the past. Your future is with Blue Arrow. He deserves your love, not Charging Falcon."

Pleasant Voice's eyes were wide as she drew away from Maria to stare at her. "It *is* Blue Arrow I wish to spend the rest of my life with," she said in a rush of words. "It is! I do see that now. And I feel it. All over inside me I feel it! It was just pity I was . . . I *am* feeling for Charging Falcon."

Pleasant Voice's buckskin skirt whipped around as she rushed to the door. "I must go to Blue Arrow!" she said across her shoulder. "I shall have some Navaho warriors escort me to Blue Arrow's stronghold. I will convince him of my love for him. I hope he won't let his pride stand in the way of our love!"

As Pleasant Voice hurriedly left, Maria relaxed her shoulders and sighed heavily, then smiled widely when Shadow returned, carrying a large wooden tray of all sorts of food. Behind him were two braves, carrying the copper tub that she had used the one other time, and several young warriors carrying buckets of water.

"How wonderful!" Maria sighed, clasping her hands together before her. Everything was falling into place. Her life. Her future . . .

Surely nothing would spoil her happiness now. She prayed that her father would not cast a shadow of gloom on her life. . . .

Warmed all over with tantalizing food and revitalized by her bath, Maria snuggled into Shadow's arms on his bed covered with a thick, comfortable layer of sheepskins. His lips were sweet as he kissed her while rolling her closer to him, fitting their bodies together so that her breasts were crushed into the hardness of his chest. She moaned sensually as his hands began to move over her, her every intimate place becoming his. She snaked a leg over his leg, opening herself more to his caressing fingers, feeling the pleasure mounting within her, spreading.

With care she began to move her hands over his taut body, reveling in the feel of his muscled shoulders, back, and hips. She reached around to his manhood, which had risen and was now resting against her thigh until the moment he would fill her with its hardness, to take her to wonderfully beautiful moments of bliss.

Her hand trembling, Maria circled his manhood and began slowly moving her fingers up and down. She was happy that she could give him a small measure of pleasure in this way. She knew that she was pleasing him by the way his breathing had quickened and his groans of pleasure were being breathed against her lips as he kissed her with more passion . . . more fire.

She swallowed hard as his free hand cupped one of her breasts and began kneading it, his thumb slowly circling the nipple, causing it to harden against his flesh. His tongue flicked between her softly parted lips, exploring the sweetness of her mouth, making Maria's heart pound with building rapture. She met his tongue with flicks of her own and arched her hips upward when he began probing with his manhood and entered her with a quick thrust.

Locking her legs around his waist, her hands clasped around his neck, Maria began to ride with Shadow, his lips now at the hollow of her throat, kissing her there, then lower, so that his tongue could circle one nipple and then the other.

Maria swept her hands down his back and dug her fingernails into the tautness of his buttocks, encouraging him to send his strokes deeper within her. She wanted to feel all of him. She wanted to experience the ultimate of ultimates! And as he stroked, she followed him with her body, taking him, savoring him.

A thick, husky groan rose from deep within Shadow. He twined his fingers through Maria's hair and drew her mouth to his, giving her another fiery kiss, feeling the heat of his body reaching a feverish pitch. The power of her body was draining him of everything but the need of her. He could not think any further than this moment, this miracle that they were together again, soon to be husband and wife. He could not ask for more than that, to have the woman his heart had directed him to, no matter that she was white. The color of her skin did not matter. All hearts were the same color . . . all desires were formed of the same passions. Their love was meant to be. It was . . . meant to be!

Feeling the thickening of need burning in his loins, Shadow slowed his body so he could enjoy the time just prior to the moment when total release would claim him, body and soul. He framed Maria's face between his hands and rained gentle kisses along her brow, the tip of her nose, and her chin.

Then once again he kissed her with a hot possession and resumed his eager thrusts, ready to take what his body was crying out for. He placed his hands on Maria's hips and lifted her so close to him that it was as though she had become a part of him. When the spasm of joy racked his body, so did it rack Maria's. When he cried out with bliss, so did she, their lips touching . . . tasting. . . .

Filled with marvelous tingling sensations, although the pleasure had already peaked and been enjoyed, Maria looked up at Shadow, oh, so loving him. "My darling, it is so good to be with you again," she purred, tracing his sculpted facial features with her forefinger. "I never want to be parted from you again. Never. Don't allow it, Shadow. Keep me safe within your arms forevermore. Please?"

"You will be *sa-a narai*, living forever with Shadow," he said huskily. "We will be *ka-bike-hozhoni-bi*, happy ever-more. While with you, *daltso hozhoni*, all is beautiful!"

"I will learn your language, will I not?" Maria asked, placing a finger on his lips, trembling sensually when he sucked it into his mouth and very slowly, calculatingly, circled his tongue around it, then sucked on it again.

The gnawing ache for Shadow was beginning between Maria's thighs again. She felt as though she could make love all night! Would she always want him as much, as deeply, as now?

Oh, *sí*, surely she would. He was her every heartbeat. Her soul!

"You will learn many things from Shadow," he said, chuckling low as he took her finger from his mouth and placed her hand on his manhood, which was renewing in strength against her abdomen. "But for tonight, let us reacquaint ourselves, over and over again, with that which we already know so well."

He bent and sucked one of Maria's nipples between his teeth and chewed softly, then kissed her as he rolled on top of her and thrust his hardness deep inside her again. "You are a skilled lover," he whispered as he placed his lips to her ear, breathing heatedly against her flesh. "And Shadow is responsible, is he not?"

"*Sí*," Maria said, closing her eyes as rapture began to soar through her. She tossed her head back and forth as Shadow's hands molded her breasts, his tongue flicking over one nipple, then the other.

"Good Lord!" Maria cried, reaching the peak of passion quickly this time as her body shimmered and shook against Shadow's while he experienced the same passion along with her.

Once again they clung to each other, their bodies covered with a wet sheen of perspiration from their exertions. Maria laughed softly and wove her fingers through her damp hair as she drew it out from beneath her, to lie in a dark shroud around her head.

"I am so deliriously happy!" she cried, her eyes twinkling as she looked up at Shadow, whose face was a mask of contentment. "I don't have to ask if you are, for I see it in your face, Shadow."

She threw her arms around his neck and hugged him fiercely. "Isn't it wonderful to be in love?" she murmured, a tear wetting his shoulder as she pressed her cheek against it. "Isn't it wonderful to be together? Oh, how I missed you, Shadow. It was beginning to look as though we would never be together again. My father was so cold and cruel. He hates you, Shadow, hates you!"

Shadow looked past her, her words having brought him back down to earth and made him see what real life was. What did the next several days have in store for him? For Maria? And for his people? Would Esteban Zamora come with a multitude of vaqueros and spread blood over the land?

Shadow had to make sure that the vaqueros did not get that close! He would post sentries far from the stronghold. Word of the first signs of approaching Spaniards would be brought to him. The warring would take place away from his mountain. If blood must be spilled this time, it would not be that of the precious women and children of his village. Especially not his woman's blood . . .

Esteban Zamora dismounted, downcast. He gave the reins to his stable hand and strolled listlessly toward the house, having given orders for his men to round up many soldiers. It would take a few days, but then he would return and kill Shadow! He would kill many Navaho! They would all pay for the foolishness of one man . . . their leader! How dare he fall in love with a Spanish lady, the daughter of a proud *patrón*? Shadow must pay. His people must pay!

Zamora could not fool himself into believing that he wanted Maria to be among those slain. He *did* love her. With all of his heart he loved her! The fact that she had betrayed him ate away at his gut. She had humiliated him in front of his men.

The worst task of all still remained before him: He must tell Maria's mother that she was gone again, perhaps for good this time.

Stroking his chin nervously, he frowned as he ran up the wide front steps to the house. His frail wife might bend under the pressure, but she had to be told. There was no way around it.

The wide oak door opened as Zamora stepped up on the porch. He paled and his eyes became distantly haunted when he looked down upon the pale face of his wife, worry causing deep wrinkles on her brow.

"Maria?" Letha said, wringing her hands nervously, looking past her husband, then up into his eyes. "When I heard the horses and looked from my window, something within me became very cold. You should not be back this soon. And where is Maria? She is not with you. *Por qué*, why, Esteban? *Por qué*?"

His dark brows knitted together in a frown, Zamora took Letha by an elbow and guided her back into the house. He walked her to the parlor and stood her before the fireplace, where huge logs were burning on the grate. He took her hands and squeezed them affectionately.

"Letha, there is much to tell you," he said thickly. "It seems our daughter has betrayed both of us. She used me, Letha, to get out of the house so that she could go to that damn savage Indian, Shadow! After we stopped for a night of rest and everyone was asleep, Maria slipped away and rode to the Indian's stronghold. She has chosen to live with the Navaho instead of us, Letha."

Letha gasped and teetered from the shock. Tears burst from her eyes as she jerked her hands away from her husband. She stiffened her back and began walking away, her gait unsteady.

Zamora rushed to her side and placed an arm about her waist. "I'm going for her, dear," he said, almost choking on the words, knowing that such an action could cause his daughter's death!

But his pride was at stake here. If he did not get his daughter back, he might never be able to face anyone again!

"No, don't do that," Letha said, her voice strangely calm. She stared straight ahead as she moved from the parlor toward the staircase. "Our daughter is no longer our daughter. Leave it at that, Esteban. There is no sense in fighting what the heart has led her into doing."

Zamora stepped away from Letha and watched her ascend the stairs, stunned wordless by her reaction.

The moon was hidden behind dark, scudding clouds. The village was quiet except for neighing horses, bawling sheep, and barking dogs. Charging Falcon's head was limp as he hung on the stake, his hope gone that Shadow might release him and forgive him his past evil deeds.

But of course Charging Falcon understood why Shadow could not. He was a man of pride. He was a leader! If Shadow showed himself to be weak by forgiving a man who had murdered and stolen from his own people, he could very well lose his position of leadership!

No. This was Charging Falcon's fate, first to be humiliated for several days, to be taunted and tormented by the gawking, grabbing women, then to be put to death. At this moment he welcomed death! There was nothing else for him. As for Pleasant Voice, he had lost her that first day he had chosen to raid the Navaho people! Then when he had shot her, to prove something to himself, oh, what had she thought of him? She must hate him with all of her might!

But he could not be mistaken about the way she had been looking at him since he had been tied to the stake. There had been more than pity in the depths of her eyes. There had been traces of the love that she had felt for him at one time, long ago.

Yet it wasn't truly that long ago. Only three years had passed since their last embrace. She had been twenty, he twenty-five. His loins ached even now when he recalled their shared passion. No other woman could fill him with such excitement.

And he had exchanged that love for money and gifts from the Spaniards?

He had been a very unwise Pueblo! And he was paying dearly for his mistakes!

Sobbing to himself, the pain in his bound wrists searing as though his flesh had been set on fire, his body cold from the mountain air that grew so frigid at night, Charging Falcon closed his eyes, hoping to escape from his torments by sleeping.

Then his head jerked up and his heart skipped a beat when he saw a figure stealing through the darkness. He watched, afraid; then his breathing became even again when he saw that it was only his feeble aunt, Little Doe, coming to stare up at him again, as she had done so often through the long day. She had spit in his face and told him that he was no longer a member of their family. That had been the worst of all humiliations.

As now, while the clouds slipped away from the moon, lighting everything around Charging Falcon, Little Doe was so close he could see the hate etched across her face, her expression livid.

"Little Doe, what do you want?" Charging Falcon said, his voice dry from lack of water. "It is late. You must go home and stay by the fire. You don't want to become ill from the night air."

When she did not speak, but instead reached up inside the wide sleeve of her buckskin dress and brought out a knife, its blade reflecting dangerously beneath the shine of the moon, Charging Falcon gasped and stared disbelievingly down at her.

"You hate me this much?" he said, his voice breaking.

Little Doe said nothing. She moved closer, her knife raised.

"Do you think I will beg for mercy?" Charging Falcon said, his heart pounding with fear he did not want to show. "I welcome death, Aunt Little Doe. You are doing me a favor. Kill me. Kill me now!"

Little Doe plunged the knife into Charging Falcon's heart. He willed himself not to cry out, fear no longer a part of him. Relief washed through him. He closed his eyes as his life's blood rolled down his chest and dripped from his toes.

Little Doe stepped closer. She pried the knife from her dead nephew's chest and removed the part of him that would have disgraced the family if he had ever had children.

Then she walked away, her shoulders slouched, her head bent. She went inside her hogan, sat down comfortably beside the fire, and leaned into the knife herself.

CHAPTER
21

The cry of a mourning dove awakened Maria. The first signs of dawn were rippling in spirals of light down through the smoke hole in the ceiling, the fire had turned to glowing ashes within the fire pit.

Deliriously happy, Maria turned toward Shadow and rose on an elbow and gazed down at him as he slept, his raven hair framing his handsomely sculpted face. Unable to help it, loving him so much, unwilling to resist the temptation of being so close to him, she lowered her lips to his mouth and kissed him softly, then lost her breath with surprise when he threw open his arms and wrapped her within their iron strength.

Maria looked at him, seeing eyes seething with heated passion looking back at her. "Darling, you frightened me," she said, laughing, rearranging herself against him as he rolled above her.

She touched his cheek gently. "But wasn't I foolish?" she giggled. "I should never expect anything *but* surprises while in bed with you. First you are asleep; then you're awake with hunger in your eyes."

She kissed his shoulder, then the column of his powerful neck. "Do you hunger for me so early in the morning, even before you have eaten?" she teased. Her lips strayed to his mouth. She traced the shape of his lips with her tongue.

"My, but you taste good this morning, darling. I would like to eat you whole, if you would allow it."

Shadow chuckled and rolled away from Maria, to stretch out on his back. He wove his fingers through her hair and urged her to kneel over him, her lips close to his chest. "Pleasure me, woman," he said huskily, urging her head lower. "If you are hungry, feed your hunger! You will at the same time feed mine."

Her heart thundering, her breasts touching his manhood, brushing against it as she slid down to rest her elbows between his outstretched legs, she looked up at him and smiled seductively, then circled his hardness with a hand. Slowly she moved it over him, arousing a husky groan from within him.

Then she bent her mouth to his pulsing hardness and pleasured him in what she would always feel was a forbidden way, but she enjoyed performing this deed for him, because he enjoyed it so much.

She could not deny that wondrous ecstasy soared through her, also, to know that she was able to give him such pleasure. He was all that was important to her now. Only him. Whatever way she could feed his desires, she would do it.

In a sense she was a slave . . . a slave to her own heart!

Her fingers crept around him, and she dug her fingernails into his buttocks as she urged him closer to her. His lusty moans made her continue to pleasure him with her mouth with vigor, but when his hands came to her shoulders and urged her away from him, she knew that he had almost reached the point at which he would no longer be able to hold back. He wanted to reach that peak of rapture while riding the tides of pleasure in the same age-old way that man and woman had loved each other from the beginning of time.

Shadow looked up at Maria, smiling, as he lifted her into a sitting position above him. With her legs straddling him, she let him fill her with his magnificence. She bent and placed her hands on his shoulders and let him move inside her, all the while moving her hips rhythmically with him.

When he reached out and cupped a breast, tweaking its nipple until the pain became pleasure, Maria closed her eyes in ecstasy and threw her head back in a low moan.

She rode him until she felt the world melting away. . . .

Feeling the curl of rapture still encasing her, Maria rose away from Shadow and slipped on the loose-fitting buckskin dress that he had given her the previous night. Her wardrobe was now Navaho, not Spanish, and she accepted this heartily, as she would the forthcoming changes in her life.

But there was something she had brought with her from her home. The precious *bayeta*! She eyed the valise with hope in her heart, knowing that it could mean so much to the Navaho.

Maria went to the bag as Shadow drew on fringed buckskin breeches and bent low over the fire pit to place wood in the simmering ashes. As he bent to blow on the coals, Maria removed the colorful *bayeta* swatches from her bag and laid them out on the floor so that Shadow would see them as soon as he turned around to face her. He was familiar with the colorful clothes worn by the Spanish people, but he would never accept bribes of *bayeta*. He had not stolen the fabric, either, perhaps not wanting his people to hunger for that which the Spaniards flaunted.

He wanted his people to remain happy in a simple way.

Would he want to change now?

Could Maria convince him of what this fabric could do for his people? The money earned by sewing colorful garments could buy them food and supplies in abundance. The Navaho would never again want for anything!

Except peace, but peace was the hardest thing to acquire, and she had not been able to manage that for them.

If only her father were to—

"What do you have there?" Shadow asked, interrupting Maria's train of thought.

He stood over the display of bright cloth. The crimson was like heat lightning in his eyes. The fabrics were so beautiful and tempting!

Maria locked an arm through his, looking anxiously up at him. "Shadow, I have a grand idea that could make much money for your people," she said, breathless with anxiety. "Do you see the bright fabrics? We could make sure your people have as many as they wished. They could sew beautiful clothes. They could use the colorful thread to weave wondrous blankets that could be sold in either Mexico or another market. Just think what the money could do for your people, Shadow."

Shadow slipped away from Maria and turned his back on the collection of cloth. Frowning, he dropped to his haunches before the fire that was just taking hold. "Shadow does not wish to tempt his people with such fabrics and thread," he growled. "It is best to live simply, as we are now living. Shadow makes sure they are provided for. They want for nothing."

Maria was stung by his words, yet she was not surprised, nor would she give up so easily. She knelt beside Shadow and placed a finger on his chin, urging his face around so that their eyes could meet.

"I understand your pride," she said softly. "But there could be so much more, Shadow, if you would let me help you! I know where the clothes can be sold. My father let me and my mother accompany him to New Orleans and Mexico. I know the market well. And I am a Spaniard. I can buy the material cheaply. I have brought some of my jewels, which I can sell to raise money to buy our first shipment. Or we can *steal* the first batch, whichever is the quickest way to acquire it."

Shadow was taken aback by her suggestion of stealing. Then he chuckled as his eyes danced with amusement. "You are this determined?" he said, placing a hand on her cheek, caressing it softly.

"*Sí*," Maria said, her eyes wide. "Shadow, you and I could do it. But if stealing is required, I will do it only once. I want us to go into a legitimate business together. I think it would be wonderful!"

"It sounds simply done," he said, his eyes filled with doubt. "But Shadow has learned in his twenty-nine years that nothing is easily done or achieved. I will have to ponder this, Maria. I'll see. Be patient until I decide. Until then, you have *me* to fill your lonely hours, do you not? I will make you want nothing *but* me."

Maria crept into his arms and hugged him. "Darling, I do not offer this idea to you for myself," she murmured. "I offer it to you and your people because you deserve so much more in life than what you have."

"My people are content enough," Shadow grumbled, easing her from his arms, to look down at her. "I hope that what I have to offer you is enough, for once you are my wife, do not ever decide to place my saddle outside my door. Never would I allow it! You will not get a chance to divorce me!"

Maria paled and her knees grew weak as she watched him busy himself with dressing, drawing his buckskin shirt over his head, slipping into his moccasins, tying a red bandanna around his head.

She went to him and framed his face between her hands. "Do you think I would ever consider divorcing you after what I have given up to come to you?" she asked. "Please get that out of your head, Shadow. I am yours as long as you will have me."

He looked down at her, his eyelids heavy. He slowly placed his arms around her waist and drew her into the hard contours of his body. "My woman, never would I want to give you away," he said, his lips beckoning to her as they drew closer to her mouth. He kissed her gently. "My woman, never will I cast you aside for another! Never!"

A shrill scream from somewhere outside wrenched Maria and Shadow apart. They stood looking at each other with curiosity in their eyes. Then Shadow raced toward the door of the hogan, Maria close behind him.

Stepping outside, where twilight laced the sky in blues, grays, and whites, Shadow surveyed the village with his eyes, then looked at the far edge, where a crowd was assembling around Charging Falcon.

"*E-do-ta*, no!" Shadow cried, focusing his eyes on the blood covering Charging Falcon's body. "Today I was

going to pardon him! Today I was going to welcome him
into my hogan as a friend! Forgiveness came too slowly!
Someone has killed him!"

Maria covered her mouth with her hand, now also seeing
the lifeless body. When Shadow started running toward
Charging Falcon, she followed, to give him support if he
asked it of her, for she could hear how distraught he was.
She had been wrong to think that he would not forgive
Charging Falcon. It had just taken time for him to be sure
that it was the right thing to do.

And now someone had taken that decision away from
him.

Someone had murdered Charging Falcon!

Her moccasins silent as they ran across the dusty rocks
behind Shadow, Maria watched as the women who had
come to survey the death scene turned quickly away, some
going away from the crowd, retching.

Maria's footsteps faltered, now wondering if she was
wise to go on. She had never been able to stand the sight of
blood. Was that why the women were vomiting? Were their
stomachs weak also? Or was it something *worse* that was
causing such a reaction?

A great space opened up for Shadow as he reached the
death scene. Maria stopped in mid-step when she saw not
only the knife wound and blood, but also that Charging
Falcon's private parts had been severed from his body and
now lay in a strange purplish-red heap on the ground at his
feet.

"My . . . God!" Maria whispered, feeling her stomach
rebeling at the sight.

She turned her eyes away, then froze inside when in the
distance she saw Pleasant Voice returning to the village on
horseback with Blue Arrow riding proudly alongside her. If
Pleasant Voice saw Charging Falcon, there was no telling
what her reaction would be! It appeared that everything had
been ironed out between her and Blue Arrow. If Pleasant
Voice began blaming herself for what had happened to
Charging Falcon, although she bore no blame for the

tragedy, this could cause the end of her relationship with Blue Arrow.

"I must stop Pleasant Voice from seeing Charging Falcon," Maria whispered, turning to glance over her shoulder at the dead man, relieved to see that Shadow had removed him from the stake, placed him on the ground, and covered him with a blanket.

Turning her eyes back to Pleasant Voice, Maria began to run toward her. When she met the approach of the horses she reached out a hand to her friend. "Pleasant Voice, why don't you and Blue Arrow come into Shadow's hogan and let us talk about our upcoming marriages?" she said anxiously.

She glanced over her shoulder again, knowing that Pleasant Voice and Blue Arrow had noticed the commotion. She looked up at Pleasant Voice and reached for her hand, urging her from her horse. "Pleasant Voice, come on," she said almost wildly. "Let's go inside Shadow's hogan. I have so much to tell you! Don't you want to hear?"

Pleasant Voice slid from the saddle, her eyes riveted straight ahead, seeing the empty stake, the blanket covering someone on the ground. She became numb inside, knowing that Charging Falcon was dead!

She sucked in her breath and questioned Maria with her eyes, afraid to ask, not wanting to know the answers. Many of the Navaho and Pueblo had grown to resent, even to hate, Charging Falcon. Any one of them could have killed him.

The fact that he was dead made Pleasant Voice feel empty. Remembrances of their young love swept over her like a raging tide, then left just as quickly when she looked up at Blue Arrow, who was gazing devotedly down at her.

Though a part of her wanted to run to Charging Falcon, to cradle his head on her lap, another part of her cautioned her not to. She had a future ahead of her that could be beautiful, and it did not include Charging Falcon, except for brief remembrances of times that had been so sweet, so passionate. . . .

"*Sí* Maria, let's go into Shadow's hogan," she murmured. "Let us talk." She gave Blue Arrow a sweet smile. "My love, will you join us?"

Blue Arrow looked down at her, then at Shadow, seeing how distraught he was, and Blue Arrow knew why: Charging Falcon was dead.

He again studied Pleasant Voice, wondering how she was accepting this death. There was a trace of sadness in her eyes, but it was controlled, as she was controlling all of her emotions at this moment in her life. She *did* care that Charging Falcon was dead, but she did not want to show her grief because of her love for Blue Arrow!

This pleased Blue Arrow. It made his heart swell with love and compassion for her. He would make her so happy she would never regret having chosen him as her husband!

He dismounted and went to Pleasant Voice, touching her softly on the face. "You go ahead," he said thickly. "I must see what I can do for Shadow."

"Yes, I understand," Pleasant Voice said, leaning her face into his hand, reveling in the warmth radiating from him to her. "Go to Shadow. Your friendship means much to him."

Blue Arrow nodded, then walked boldly away from her, his breechclout flapping in the wind, his dark hair fluttering on his shoulders.

Maria went alongside Pleasant Voice into the hogan. She spied the display of *bayeta* and smiled over at her friend. "Do you see what I have brought?" she said softly. "Pleasant Voice, I have such plans! Do you want to hear?"

Pleasant Voice knelt down beside the fabrics, running a hand over the softness of the *bayeta*, enthralled by the crimson color, envisioning a blouse of that color for herself. She had wanted one for oh, so long. . . .

"*Sí*, tell me," she said, looking up at Maria, trying to block remembrances of Charging Falcon from her mind, finding it hard. . . .

Esteban Zamora buckled his heavy pistol holster around his waist. He went to a hat tree and grabbed his hat, wide-brimmed and dark brown. Brown leather boots shone from a fresh waxing; his rifle had been polished, and it glittered beneath the soft light of the early morning fire as he pulled it from the gun rack on the wall. He was confident that enough vaqueros had gathered to aid him in his planned vengeance. The Navaho would not have the upper hand this time.

He had left the bedroom before Letha awakened, feeling that she needed as much rest as possible since she had been in a depressed mood since Maria had chosen to live with Shadow . . . even marry him. He dreaded leaving his wife alone while he traveled to Shadow's stronghold. In her state of mind, he did not want to think of what she might do. She had lost a daughter, the most important person in the world to her. . . .

Glancing out the window of his study, Zamora saw that the vaqueros were congregating on their horses, waiting for him. Slapping the rifle into his other hand, he moved in long, confident strides from the room and up the staircase, then on to his bedroom. He leaned his ear to the door, hearing no sound from within. He scratched his brow, debating whether or not to awaken Letha to say good-bye. She knew that he was going. Why disturb her?

Knowing that he owed it to her to bid her farewell, he placed his free hand on the doorknob and slowly turned it, then pushed the door open and was met by total darkness.

Grumbling about the thickness of the curtains closed over the windows, half stumbling to the bed for lack of ability to see where he was going, he finally came to the bed and reached out with his hand for his wife, to gently shake her awake.

His insides recoiled and he jerked his hand quickly away when his fingers came in contact with a sleek wetness on his wife's wrist. Panic rose inside him.

Dropping the rifle to the floor, scrambling to the window to draw the curtains aside, he felt faint when the bright light revealed to him an ivory-handled razor in Letha's limp right hand, while her other arm hung over the side of the scarlet-stained bed.

A deep sob surfaced from within him. He teetered for a

moment, then steadied himself against the back of a chair as
he continued to look at his wife, disbelieving.

"Why, Letha?" he said, choking on a sob. "Why was life
so unbearable for you? Why couldn't I make you happier?"

With shaky knees, he went to the bed and kissed her
softly on the brow, then covered her with a satin comforter,
her beautiful face now forever passive.

Zamora's eyes widened and he looked toward the window, which had a marvelous view of the distant mountains.
"Oh, my God," he whispered, covering his mouth with a
hand. "Maria! What of Maria? She must be told. She must
be present for her mother's funeral!"

Sinking down into a chair, hanging his head in his hands,
he shook his head slowly back and forth. "I can't blame
Maria for this," he said thickly. "I can't. This was coming
for a long time. A very long time. I *must* go and tell her. She
will want to see her mother one last time."

Pushing himself up from the chair, for the very first time
feeling age pressing in on him, he walked heavy-footed to
the window and peered down at the waiting vaqueros. The
mission had suddenly changed. He would not be riding to
attack the Navaho after all. He would be riding to carry a
message to his daughter! Fighting would come later.

It was now time for loving, compassion, understanding . . . and mourning. . . .

Shadow had ordered that Charging Falcon's body be
taken away and given a quiet burial, and he did not want to
know where. The ties had been broken forever, and he did
not want the bond between them revived by knowing where
Charging Falcon was buried. He did not want to have cause
to pay his respects. Charging Falcon was gone.

The burial would be final!

Walking gloomily back to his hogan, he was stopped by
another scream. His head jerked around. His gut twisted
when a young Navaho girl ran from Little Doe's hogan, her
face streaked with tears.

Shadow met the young girl's approach and welcomed her
into his arms as she came crying to him, clutching him.

"She is dead!" the girl cried. "Little Doe is dead! She died by knife wound! She inflicted it herself. Oh, Shadow, she is . . . dead."

Shadow's eyes grew misty, understanding how this could have happened. He understood now who had killed Charging Falcon. Little Doe, who had found it hard to accept a nephew who had betrayed so many. She had rid the earth of her disgrace and Charging Falcon's. Then she had taken her own life.

Shadow gave comfort to the young girl, wondering if life would ever be beautiful again, as it had been for a short while when he was a young boy of five before warring had been taught him. Only then in his life had there been a measure of peace . . . of innocence. . . .

He looked over the girl's shoulder at the wall of the stronghold. Below it, the land stretched out as far as the eye could see. Surely Maria's father would be coming soon. Shadow had no choice but to practice the ways of being a headman again, though the thought of doing so filled him with sorrow.

Of late he had learned to want some quiet, some time to enjoy the wonders of loving a woman. He wanted to give Maria quiet moments and a sense of security.

But how?

He felt helpless. . . .

CHAPTER
22

Shadow and Maria stood on the rim above the canyon, which was bathed in sunlight. Behind them in thick shadow people moved and smoke rose from tiny fires. Shadow listened for omens in the sounds around him. If he heard a horse or sheep, that meant success. The cry of an owl, crow, or coyote meant bad luck.

Shadow wrapped an arm around Maria's waist and looked down at her. "There is much sadness in life, yet there is also much happiness within the grasp of those who are determined to have it," he said, pressing a kiss on Maria's brow. "Let us be lucky ones. Let us be happy no matter what happens. One can be alive today, dead tomorrow."

He ducked his head, swallowing hard. "Little Doe is dead. Charging Falcon is dead," he said hoarsely. "So many Navaho and Pueblo died in the raids! Who will die tomorrow, Maria?"

Maria placed a hand gently on Shadow's cheek. "Let us not speak of death and unhappiness," she murmured, her thick, long hair billowing from her shoulders in the wind. "There is so much awaiting us, Shadow. The world is ours. Ours! Let us take advantage of it. Let us speak of *bayeta* again. There is such a future in the business adventure that I have offered you."

She smiled mischievously. "When I escaped from my

father in the desert, he was on his way to offer you *bayeta*, but not in the same way I propose," she said softly. "He was thinking only of himself and of the fortune he could make at the hands of your people. *I* am thinking of *you*, Shadow, *and* your people. Please tell me that you have thought of what I have offered and will agree to it."

She eased into his arms and pressed her cheek against his powerful, sleek chest. "You see, Shadow," she murmured, "if you would agree to go into business with me, I would have you with me both day and night."

She drew her head back and looked up at Shadow, fluttering her eyelashes. "But, of course, you must see me as selfish," she murmured. "I guess, in a sense, I *am* thinking of myself."

Giggling, she twined her arms around his neck. "But wouldn't any woman who loves you want to be with you day and night?" she said, her eyes sparkling. "You make me feel more alive than I ever thought possible, Shadow. When I'm not with you, I feel so very, very empty. Love me forever, Shadow. Never be far from me."

Shadow did not respond with words. He dropped his hands to her waist and drew her roughly into his arms and kissed her with fire, his tongue darting through her parted lips, tasting her, savoring her. . . .

Then wild shouts and cries rose from the straight stretch of land beneath the canyon, wrenching Shadow and Maria apart. Shadow took a step closer to the ledge of the canyon, and his eyes narrowed when he saw many of his warriors riding toward the stronghold.

"Your father must be near," he said, circling his hands into tight fists at his sides. "My warriors have come to warn me. I must alert my other braves and get my war gear on! This time Shadow is ready for the fight!"

Maria was numbly cold inside, his words tearing pieces of her heart away. She placed a hand over her mouth to stifle a sob. Only moments ago she had spoken of death, and now it was so near! She could lose Shadow before nightfall! Could she bear it? She had just found happiness for the first time in her life!

She began following Shadow to his hogan, now immersed in thoughts of her father. She could also lose him.

Yet, in a sense, hadn't she lost him already?

But still, she did not want to believe that he could die at the hands of her lover. The thought of that could haunt her for eternity!

Grabbing Shadow's hand, she stopped him. "Darling, I am so afraid," she said, looking wildly up at him.

Shadow pulled his hand free. "Fear is for children," he growled. "Do not waste it on yourself!"

Maria stared numbly up at him, then again followed him as he shouted out orders when he passed the hogans, drawing the warriors from within them. There was a sudden scurry in the village. Dust swirled as horses were brought and saddled, their silver ornaments jangling and gleaming beneath the bright rays of the sun. Eyes brightened as the men prepared themselves for the fight ahead, painting their bodies with magical symbols, including snakes and bears. Blue Arrow stepped from Pleasant Voice's hogan, carrying a long lance. His warriors awaited his command where they had been camped out close to the stronghold.

"Let me go with you," Maria begged, following Shadow into his hogan, watching him hurry into his war shirt which was made of the thickest buckskin obtainable and was longer than the shirts Shadow usually wore. This garment was meant for fighting on horseback and was made of eight buckskins—four in front and four behind. It came to the knees but was slit in front and back to permit straddling the horse.

He wore sturdy moccasins and hide leggings tied with garters, and a war cap made of badgers' skin, the wet hide having been stretched, placed over a man's head, and fitted. Wool had then put in it so it would hold its shape while drying. When dry, a chin strap had been attached, and the feathers of eagles and owls had been put on top, abalone and white shells in front.

The bow Shadow chose to carry with him was like the ones used in hunting, but he made sure it had new sinew backing and a new bowstring. He placed fifty arrows in his quiver, all of them treated with poison. He slid a club with a stone head and wooden handle into the waist of his breeches.

Maria followed Shadow around, wringing her hands nervously. "Please let me go with you," she pleaded. "I don't think I could bear the waiting, to see if you survive or die! Shadow, can't you speak to my father first, to try and reason with him? Why does there have to be fighting at *all*? Surely you can reach an agreement between you. Can't you try?"

"It is too late to reason with that man," Shadow grumbled, marching solemn-faced toward the door. "If I delay in defending my people, many could die. I will not let that happen, Maria."

He grabbed up his shield, heavy with two thicknesses of buckskin decorated with feathers and painted with magic symbols. When he reached the door he turned abruptly and locked an arm around Maria's waist and drew her into his hard-framed body. He looked down at her with eyes dark with determination.

"You wait for me," he said flatly. "I assure you that I will return. I cannot speak for your father. His skills at warring will decide whether he dies or lives!"

Shadow's lips bore down upon Maria's. After giving her a deep, passionate kiss, he swung away from her and fled outside, leaving her staring blankly ahead, feeling as though she had already lost him.

Going to the fire pit, she sank down onto a thick layer of sheepskins and hung her head in her hands, praying harder than she had ever prayed in her life. . . .

Shadow, with Blue Arrow devotedly at his side, led his men across the great stretch of yellow sand, the distant mountains cast blue in shadow behind him, and then rode into a canyon, its cliffs harsh by daylight, yet looming soft with coolness.

Knowing that Esteban Zamora and the vaqueros were heading in this direction, Shadow ordered his men up a steep incline that overlooked the valley. He spat out orders to his men to take cover and wait. They would ambush the Spaniards! If any of the white men got away alive, they would do so with terror in their hearts and with remembrances of their comrades dying with poison-tipped arrows and lances tipped with the ends of Spanish sabers piercing their flesh!

His heart pounding, echoing in his ears, his breathing harsh, Shadow took his position behind a fallen tree. He looked eagerly around him at the many other fallen trees, which had been blown over in a recent storm. He eyed the circumference of the trees, then smiled and waved to several of his warriors who came and dismounted beside him.

"When the Spaniards get close enough, we will roll the trees downhill toward them," he said, smiling smugly. "As they are taken off-guard some of you will rush in with clubs and lances. We others will enter on horseback. But remember to watch out for the deadly bullets of the Spaniards. If you are skilled at your craft, your arrows will kill faster!"

Hands were clasped, eyes flared with hungry intent for the fight; then the braves took their positions and watched the valley. The sound of horses approaching echoed from the canyon walls. Shadow swung himself up into his saddle and grabbed his club, holding it along with his shield, his jaw tight. When he saw the first signs of the Spaniards making their way toward him, he raised a fist to warn his warriors and watched and waited until the Spaniards were close enough for the trees to be rolled down the incline.

"Now!" Shadow shouted, dropping his fist. He smiled as his men shoved the trees in unison and the trees began to rumble down the sides of the canyon toward the enemy. He laughed throatily at the look of utter shock on the faces of the Spaniards when the great trees hit several of the horses' feet, causing the animals to rear and empty their saddles of the men, then stampede.

"It is time!" Shadow shouted, sinking the heels of his moccasined feet into the flanks of his stallion, thundering down the incline, his eyes searching for Maria's father, yet not able to single him out from those who were scrambling around in confusion.

His heels under his stallion's belly, as though lifting him clean off the ground, Shadow urged his horse at a tearing gallop, facing the Spaniards, shrieking.

"*E-e-e!*" Shadow cried, now a part of a big, spinning wheel of mounted warriors and Spaniards, horses tossing their heads and dust flying. Some Spaniards trying to flee, were headed off by the Navaho, who caught up with them and clubbed them to death.

Shadow dodged a bullet by using an old Indian technique—riding while hanging over the side of his horse away from the enemy. Then he remembered how long it would take the gunman to prepare his weapon for firing again at him; the Spanish musket had only a single barrel, so the gunman had to get out his powder horn and use both hands to ram another bullet and powder charge down the muzzle of his gun. Meanwhile Shadow wheeled his horse around and headed toward him.

Smiling, his eyes gleaming, Shadow leapt from his saddle and grabbed the Spaniard from the horse and wrestled him to the ground. While horses plunged all around him and men cried in pain as they died, Shadow started to raise his club to kill the victim, then stopped his arm in midair, recognizing the man.

"Zamora!" Shadow gasped, one hand at the Spaniard's throat. He loosened his grip, having noticed how purple Maria's father's lips had become, then lowered the club, unsure what to do. If he, personally, killed Maria's father, perhaps she would not be able to live with the knowing.

Yet if he did not kill him, would not Shadow one day regret it?

"Shadow, order your men to stop killing!" Zamora said in a low gasp, his throat raw where Shadow's fingers had pressed into it. "We did . . . not come to fight. These men accompanied me to give Maria a message. Her mother is dead, Shadow. I have come to tell her. We have come in peace this time. In peace!"

Hearing the chaos on all sides of him and the gurgles of

men in death's grip, Shadow was taken aback by what Maria's father had said. Could he be trusted? Were these deaths today all in vain?

For Maria's sake, he decided to give Zamora the benefit of the doubt.

Shouting in Navaho, leaning up away from Zamora, yet not before he grabbed the knife that was belted at the Spaniard's waist, Shadow rose to his feet. He helped Zamora to his feet and listened as he shouted for his men to quit fighting. It had all been a mistake on both sides!

The ensuing silence was filled with foreboding. Dead warriors cluttered the land, Navaho and Spaniards alike. Horses pawed at the bloody ground nervously, weapons were lowered, faces were grim.

Zamora combed his dark hair back from his perspiration-laced brow with one hand, while the fingers of his other hand nervously twisted the tip of his mustache. He looked over at Shadow, his eyes dull with a deeply hidden pain. When he had raised his musket to fire at Shadow, he had known it was the Navaho leader and had been ready to rid his life of the bastard. Though he had come in peace to spread the terrible news to Maria, never would he have total peace while Shadow was alive. Shadow had stolen his most precious commodity away from him—his *daughter*.

Shadow squared his shoulders and nodded toward Zamora's horse. "You may ride peacefully with me to talk with Maria," he said thickly. "But your time with her will be short. And remember this. I allow you to go to her only because I know the pain of losing one's parents. It is right that you should tell her. Not I."

"*Muchas gracias*," Zamora said, half bowing. Then he looked up at Shadow, wondering if the Navaho would allow Maria to leave the stronghold for her mother's funeral. Seeing how possessive he was of her, Zamora doubted it.

But that was where Maria would have to work her magic on the Indian. Surely if Maria asked this of Shadow, he would not be able to refuse her. And once she was away from the Navaho again, Zamora would send her back to

Spain, where she would have no means of escaping to be with the Indian again.

Smiling smugly over at Shadow, Zamora grabbed his horse's reins and swung himself into his saddle. He waited for Shadow to climb into his fancy Navaho saddle, stunned when he saw the gentle side to the Indian as Shadow went to his fallen comrades to hang his head over them, to softly weep. . . .

Maria and Pleasant Voice stood on the rim of the canyon, peering into the distance, anxiously watching for Shadow and Blue Arrow's return. Day was slipping into evening, with streaks of orange splashed across the horizon where the sun was dipping low behind the hills.

So worried she felt ill, Maria shook her head despairingly. "Though we are watching for their return I am afraid to see them," she said, stifling a sob behind a hand. "What if Shadow and Blue Arrow do not return riding in their saddles? What if they are brought back, slain?"

She closed her eyes for a moment, thinking of her father, but refused to speak his name out loud to Pleasant Voice. She did not want her best friend to know that she feared for him almost as much as for Shadow. Though she had come to loathe, even at times hate, her father, she could not bear the thought of him dying, especially at the hands of Shadow or men under Shadow's command. It would make her betrayal of her father something that she perhaps could not live with. It would be *her* fault if he died. He would not have traveled to the stronghold with warring on his mind if it had not been for her!

"Maria!" Pleasant Voice gasped. "I believe I see them. Look yonder. See the cloud of dust in the distance? It must be them!"

Maria's eyes opened wildly. Her heart began to pound as she looked intensely at the dust cloud moving quickly across the land toward the mountain that sheltered the Navaho, yet something deep within her sent out a warning. The dust was hiding the riders. Perhaps it was not Shadow at all, but the Spaniards, who could have been victorious over the Navaho and Pueblo warriors! Did not the Spaniards have more powerful and precise weapons? Weren't their guns the most deadly?

If many vaqueros with rifles had ambushed the Indians, none of the Indians' lives would have been spared. Her father could be riding victorious, coming to give orders that the rest of the community of Navaho be killed. He would take her away, perhaps never to release her from imprisonment again!

"I can bear this waiting no longer!" Maria blurted, lifting the buckskin skirt into her arms, running toward the horse corrals at the far edge of the village. "I am going to meet their approach. I must see if Shadow is all right."

She would not tell Pleasant Voice of her fear that the Indians had been defeated and that the Spaniards were on their way to finish what they had started. If this was true and she went to meet her father halfway, perhaps he would spare the lives of the remaining Indians at the stronghold. She had to believe that she was all he wanted, especially after having killed Shadow.

Pleasant Voice began to run after Maria. "Wait!" she shouted. "I shall go with you. The waiting is tearing my heart apart. If anything should happen to Blue Arrow, I would want to die also!"

Maria stopped and turned to face Pleasant Voice. She grabbed her hands. "No," she said. "You can't do this. *No está bien*, it is not all right. It is not safe! I'll go alone."

Maria swallowed hard, now having no choice but to say what she had been thinking. "If it is my father approaching instead of Shadow and Blue Arrow, you would be taken and put into slavery again," she said, her voice breaking.

Maria lunged into Pleasant Voice's arms and hugged her. "Do this for me?" she pleaded softly. "Stay? I don't want you ever to suffer at the hands of my father again. Stay with your people. Hope that I am wrong and that Blue Arrow will come to you soon."

"If this is what you think is best, I will stay," Pleasant Voice said, feeling the desperation in the way Maria clung to her, and hearing the same desperation in her voice. She

leaned away from Maria and looked at her with tears
burning her eyes. "*Que le vaya bien*, good luck to you,
Maria."

Tears streamed from Maria's eyes. She choked back a sob
as she nodded to Pleasant Voice, then turned and rushed
toward the horses. Choosing the gentle mare she had grown
used to, she led the horse from the corral, quickly slipped
the bridle and saddle in place, then stepped into the stirrup
and swung herself into the saddle. Lifting the reins,
snapping them against the horse's mane, she rode toward
the narrowing path that led downward, fear riding with
her. . . .

The steepness of the mountain had always been intimi-
dating; Maria was relieved now to be riding over flat
terrain. Her heart pounded as she saw riders approaching.
She squinted, trying to see who they were. Were they Indian
or Spanish? She would soon know if she had lost the man
she loved or her father. What if she had lost both of them
in one blow? She feared that she would fall into a snake pit
of despair and never emerge again; perhaps she would
remain on that narrow margin of sanity where her mother
lived day by day. . . .

The dust from the riders cleared away as a brisk wind
swirled it around above their heads. Maria gasped and felt
a keen relief sweep through her when, unbelievable as it
was, she saw Shadow and her father, riding side by side like
allies instead of enemies.

"*Caramba*, good Lord!" she whispered harshly, thrusting
her heels into the mare to urge her into a gallop. "They are
both alive! They are riding together! What has happened to
make them appear to be friends? It makes no sense at all.
They hate each other with a passion!"

When she drew closer to the procession of warriors,
Maria slowed the mare, seeing that many of the Indians
were stretched across saddles, lifeless, blood covering their
bodies. Other Indians were slumped over, barely able to
ride upright in their saddles, wounds on various parts of
their bodies.

Growing numb inside, knowing that an intense battle had been fought after all, she surveyed the lead riders again.

Shadow . . . her father . . . Blue Arrow . . .

And then she looked beyond them again and was able to make out several vaqueros trailing along behind the Indians; they, too, showed casualties and wounds.

"Has Shadow taken the vaqueros and my father captive?" she gasped, her reins growing limp within her hands. "Why else are they riding together? Why?"

She wheeled her horse into an abrupt stop when she was close enough to be seen and recognized. She watched as Shadow and her father broke away from the others and rode toward her. She looked from one to the other, seeing that both were covered with dust and in disarray, their hair wildly tousled. It was apparent they had been a part of the fight, but luckily had not been killed in the process.

Shadow drew his reins taut as he came to Maria's side. Zamora did the same on her other side.

"What are you doing out here all alone?" Shadow growled, his eyes flashing angrily.

"Daughter, you know the dangers," Zamora growled, drawing her attention to him. "Why can't you behave like other genteel ladies?"

Maria felt trapped between these two scolding men. She glowered from one to the other, and then saw a hidden pain at the depths of her father's eyes. "*Padre*, what are you doing here with Shadow?" she asked, then looked slowly toward Shadow. "Shadow, is my father now your captive? Is that why you ride together?"

Glancing from Shadow to her father, Maria became fearful of the answers. What could this mean? "Tell me!" she demanded. "Why are you together? Why?"

Shadow gave Maria a quiet stare, then wheeled his horse around and rode a few feet away from her, leaving her alone with her father.

Panic rose inside Maria, knowing how unusual this was. She pleaded with her father with her eyes, paling as she saw the pain deepen in his. "*Padre*, what *is* it?" she asked softly. "It's as though you have something terrible to tell me. What could it be? You are all right. Shadow is all right. That was all that I was worried about."

Zamora reached out to touch Maria's cheek gently. "Maria, it's your mother," he said thickly. "She's dead. I was coming to tell you and Shadow mistook our approach to be hostile. Thank God things were straightened out before everyone was killed on both sides."

Maria was grief-stricken by the news of her mother. She choked on a sob that was rising from within her. She paled. She teetered from a strange sort of weakness sweeping through her, having not yet lost anyone close to her.

And now her own mother . . . ?

She hung her head and wiped tears from her eyes, then looked back up at her father. "*Padre*, mother wasn't ill when I last saw her," she said, her voice strained. "How did she die?"

Zamora looked away from her momentarily, then gave her a set stare. "She killed herself, Maria," he said hoarsely.

Maria was stung by his words. Though she had known the weakness of her mother's mental state, never had she believed that she would go this far to rid herself of her daily misery!

She shook her head, her eyes wild.

"Don't blame yourself," her father said, reaching for Maria's hand. "You did not know she was capable of doing this. Just because you left—"

Maria knocked his hand away. She looked at him with fire in her eyes. "How dare you blame me for Mother's death!" she cried. "If anyone is at fault, it is you! You are the reason I left. Had you been more understanding, I would have never betrayed you. In a sense, the true betrayal was yours. You betrayed me and Mother!"

"Maria, you can't mean that," Zamora choked.

"Oh, but I do," she said, her insides aching for her mother. She rode to Shadow. "Shadow, I must return home. I must keep vigil at my mother's side until her burial. Tell me you understand. I *must* do this, Shadow. It is my duty as a daughter."

Zamora looked on, watching guardedly. Once he got Maria home, everything would go his way. Before Shadow had a chance to abduct her again, he would put her on a ship for Spain!

Shadow lifted Maria from her saddle and placed her on his lap. He hugged her gently, kissing her reassuredly on the nose, cheeks, and lips. "You go," he said, glancing at Zamora, speaking loud enough for him to hear, knowing that the Spaniard had schemes swirling around inside his head as far as Maria was concerned. Shadow would not allow it! Never!

"But Shadow and many warriors will accompany you there," Shadow added quickly. "We will be close by, waiting until your duties are over. Then you will return to the stronghold and become my wife. Your life will be bonded with mine forever, darling. Forever. I will protect your from all sadnesses, my love."

"My darling," Maria murmured, clinging to him, taking from him all of the love and compassion that he was giving her. "Oh, my darling."

Zamora gritted his teeth. His hair rose at the nape of his neck when he heard Shadow say that he would accompany Maria. Together with Blue Arrow's warriors, there would be many Indians guarding the plantation. The Spaniard would have no opportunity to take Maria away.

He felt defeated.

He had lost everything these past several days—his wife, his pride, his daughter. . . .

CHAPTER
23

The sky was a dull gray with the threat of an impending storm as Maria stood near her mother's grave alongside her father. The casket, strewn with flowers, was being lowered into the ground.

The dark, lacy veil hiding Maria's tear-streaked face fluttered in the breeze. Her long black dress with its high collar and full sleeves looked stark against the backdrop of weaving grass on the hillside where sheep grazed peacefully. The picket fence that surrounded the grave smelled fresh and new with white paint. The priest who had celebrated the requiem mass, clad in funeral vestments, leaned over the casket before it disappeared into the ground and plucked a single rose from atop it.

He held the rose out to Maria. "A remembrance of your beloved mother," he said, his green eyes sympathetic.

Maria gazed at the rose, seeing it as a symbol of grief, since it had lain on the casket within which her mother lay. She shuddered, sobbed, and turned her eyes away. "No," she said thickly. "I cannot take the rose. Take it away."

Zamora, attired in a black suit, accepted the rose. "*Muchas gracias*," he mumbled. "My daughter does not know what she is saying. She is distraught."

"That is understandable," the priest said, then with his head bowed left the small cemetery, clutching his missal.

Zamora slipped an arm around Maria's waist. "Come,"

261

he encouraged. "Let us go home. Perhaps a cup of tea will help you feel better."

Maria lowered her eyes and let him guide her away from the cemetery, where grave diggers were shoveling earth into the open grave. "Nothing will make me feel better," she said, her voice thin and drawn. Her gaze moved to the hills, where she could see many horses grazing and the smoke of a campfire. "Except Shadow."

She glanced at her father and saw him grimace at the mention of Shadow. She let him help her up into the carriage, then flinched when a clap of thunder in the distance reverberated across the land. Strange how it seemed only appropriate that it should storm at such a time as this, when she felt as though a part of her world had been taken from her.

Her need to be with Shadow grew stronger. She needed his arms around her, to give her strength. Though she had never been close to her mother, the loss was overwhelming!

Maria had vowed never to let distance come between her and Shadow's children. She would be their friend as well as their mother, she hoped . . . soon . . .

His shoulders slouched, Zamora slapped the reins against the horse and directed it toward the house. He did not know how to give Maria encouragement at this time. She had made it clear that only the damned Indian would know how to do that. It grated on his nerves to know that his daughter was going to live with Shadow as his wife.

But an idea had begun to form. It would be a way to avoid losing Maria altogether. And hadn't she been the one to instigate the clever plan? The *bayeta* could prove to be more valuable to him now than before. It could be the instrument that would keep his daughter at least a small part of his life.

The thundering of hooves approaching made Zamora stiffen and jerk his head around. Everything in him rebelled when he sorted Shadow out from the rest of the riders. Their eyes met and held in a silent challenge. But the challenge had been met and the victor chosen! Shadow! He had won. Zamora had lost!

"Shadow," Maria whispered, lifting her veil. She had not expected him to come for her so soon after the funeral.

But it had been several days since they had parted. She could understand how he could be anxious to get their future back on course. And she knew that he would not want to leave his stronghold without his protection much longer. Although he had sent many of his warriors back to protect the Navaho in his absence, he felt that his people depended on him too much for him not to be there more often than not.

"That damned Indian," Zamora growled, tightening the reins, drawing the horse to a shuddering halt. "I would say he's damned impatient, wouldn't you? Does he expect me to give you up so soon after burying your mother? I hate the thought of being alone in that house." He gave her a heavy-lashed look. "Don't go with him, Maria. Reconsider. I will make all wrongs right for you. You can have all the freedom you desire. I will see to it that friends are brought to the house all the time. I will give dances!" He lowered his eyes. "That is, after proper time has passed for mourning your mother's passing."

Maria looked at him disbelievingly. "Father, all those things you mentioned are things I wanted so badly while growing up," she said, stifling a sob by swallowing hard. "But now it is too late. I have Shadow. He is all I want to fill my lonely days and nights. And one day we will have children. The thought makes me radiantly happy, *Padre*."

She cleared her throat nervously when she saw pain enter his eyes and tears stream down his cheeks. "You are too late," she murmured. "I have been forced to find my happiness elsewhere."

She placed a hand on his arm. "And while I'm with Shadow I am happy," she said softly. "Be happy for me, Father. Please?"

Zamora ignored her request. He looked away from her. His eyes were drawn around again when Shadow rode up next to the wagon and put an arm out for Maria. His gut twisted when she let Shadow lift her from the carriage onto his lap. When she embraced him and kissed him, he felt a sickness sweep through him, yet he knew that he must keep his composure or lose her forever.

Leaning over, Zamora looked up into the Navaho's eyes as Shadow's and Maria's lips drew apart. "Shadow," he said thickly, "since you are going to be my son-in-law, I think we should behave civilly toward each other. When I want to send a messenger to you, let him pass. When you want to send one to me, he will also pass unharmed. Do you agree to that arrangement, Shadow? I don't want to lose touch with Maria. She is . . . all I have left, you know."

Shadow looked down at Maria. "This that your father asks. Do you approve?" he asked, glad that she was removing the veil, freeing her hair and perhaps a portion of her grief.

"*Sí*, that would be wonderful," Maria said, looking at her father, seeing a side of him that warmed her clean through. "*Padre*, I am so glad you want peace with Shadow and his people."

"Maria, I won't pretend to approve of this savage," Zamora said, frowning at Shadow. "You know it is you I want to keep peace with, not the Indian."

Maria blushed and lowered her eyes. "In time I hope you will change your feelings about Shadow and his people," she said. She raised her eyes, looking from Shadow to her father. "You will be welcome at the wedding, if you desire to come. Isn't that so, Shadow?"

Shadow glowered at Zamora. "You are welcome," he said bluntly, "but only long enough to observe the ceremony. Your presence will make my people uncomfortable. They remember much that will never fade from their minds." He leaned closer. "So do *I*, rich Spaniard!"

Zamora squirmed uneasily. He raked his fingers through his sleek raven hair. "When should I arrive?" he said, never having guessed that the man he gave his daughter to would be a damned savage. And he had no choice but to let it happen. If he fought this marriage, he would lose Maria altogether. It would be easier to watch her marry Shadow than to wait for her to visit him, knowing that she never would.

"Begin your journey to our mountain after I send for you," Shadow said. "I will pass the word among my people that you are coming in peace."

Shadow wheeled his horse around and began riding away. Maria looked over Shadow's shoulder at her father, who was watching her from the carriage. She spoke a silent goodbye to him, then snuggled into Shadow's arms.

When they rode past the cemetery plot where the grave was piled high with beautiful flowers, she spoke another silent good-bye.

Warm and cozy after a full day and night of rest in Shadow's hogan, another night upon her now, Maria crept into Shadow's arms as they lay beside a low-burning fire on a thick pallet of sheepskins before retiring for the night in their bed.

"I feel filled with peace," Maria said, smoothing her hand over Shadow's hairless chest. "I have you to thank for that, darling. When I am with you, everything ugly in the world becomes blurred in my mind. Will it always be that way?"

Shadow rolled over and positioned himself atop her. Their nude bodies were pressed together as they looked into each other's eyes. "I have promised you that, haven't I?" he said huskily, a hand sending fiery sparks along her flesh as it traveled from her breast down over her stomach. He leaned away from her as he placed it on the juncture of her thighs and began his gentle caresses.

"And when will we be married?" Maria asked, becoming breathless with ecstasy as his fingers aroused her. "You did not give my father a date. Are you still afraid of marriage? I thought I had helped to dispel your suspicions of women, Shadow."

She framed his face between her hands and drew his lips to hers. "Tell me if I have done something to anger you, Shadow," she whispered against his mouth. "I want to make you happy in every way. I want to be the one who causes peace within your mind and heart."

Shadow kissed her softly, his eyes alight with heated

passion. "My love, at this moment I feel anything but peaceful within my mind and heart," he chuckled. "My heart is going wild with want of you. My mind is spinning!"

Maria giggled, then sucked in her breath when his lips moved to one of her breasts and he flicked his tongue around its nipple. "That's not what I'm talking about and you know it," she said, her voice thick with passion. "Darling, you *know* what I mean."

"Yes, Shadow knows," he said, twining his fingers through her hair, his mouth now at the hollow of her throat. "And the wedding must be delayed for only one reason."

Maria's eyes opened wide. She looked at Shadow as he looked at her, amusement lighting his face. "Why must it be delayed?" she gasped. "And for how long?"

Shadow leaned away from her. "My love, it is the practice of the Navaho to shower gifts upon the father of the bride before the ceremony," he said, smiling down at her. "Though your father is not Navaho, this still will be done, since he has shown signs of wanting to make peace between our families. I will make that first gesture of peace by giving him gifts. It will be a way of thanking him for you and of showing him that I am serious about wanting peace!"

Maria leaned up on an elbow, stunned by his generosity. Then she plunged into his arms, drawing his body fully down upon hers. She hugged him tightly. "You prove so often what a generous and kind man you are," she whispered against his cheek. "My father will soon know also. He will see why I have fallen in love with you. *Muchas gracias*, Shadow."

"*Ukehe*? Thank you?" he said, forking an eyebrow. "For *what*?"

Maria rained kisses across his sculpted face. "For . . . being you," she said, tears of joy sparkling in her eyes.

Shadow placed a hand on the back of her neck and guided her lips to his mouth. Kissing her with a fierce possessive heat, he slid his manhood deep inside her and began his rhythmic strokes, trembling with building passion when she arched her hips and moved rhythmically with him as she locked her legs around his waist.

Maria was soon lost in wondrous desire as warm flesh met warm flesh and hands explored and touched. She parted her lips and welcomed his tongue within her mouth. Her blood quickened when his hand molded and kneaded a breast. She slid a hand down the full length of his back, reveling in the touch of his flesh against the palm of her hand, then moaned as his mouth left her lips and his teeth nipped the sharp peak of her breast.

Placing her hands on his buttocks, sinking her fingernails into his muscled strength, she drew him more tightly into her and let the euphoria begin to take hold. He stroked her maddeningly, his mouth on her body hot and demanding. She moaned as the passion crested, sensing that the familiar explosions of sensations were near.

Gripping Shadow, she opened herself fully to him and let the heat of desire spread throughout her like lightning flashes, knowing that he had reached his peak also, by the way his body stiffened and then trembled like an earthquake against her, his moans of pleasure blending with hers.

Lying together in the aftermath of bliss, lips meeting, hands touching, it did not seem right that at this moment gunfire and war cries should split the air with their savagery.

But there was no denying the sounds of battle as Maria and Shadow drew apart, wildly looking toward the door of the hogan.

"What is happening?" Shadow gasped, gathering his senses enough to leap to his feet and pull on his buckskin breeches.

Maria's flesh became clammy, for she feared the answer to Shadow's question. No, it couldn't be! Surely her father had not been toying with Shadow *and* her! While making promises of peace, had he been scheming to come to the stronghold and take her away from Shadow? Had he rounded up enough soldiers to make sure he succeeded in this venture of vengeance?

Pale, Maria rose to her feet and slipped a dress over her head. Then she ran after Shadow, who had grabbed his bow and arrow and left the hogan without another word to her.

She knew that he suspected the same thing. He was surely thinking that he had been tricked by the man he had planned to shower with gifts!

"No," Maria cried as she ran blindly through the darkness behind Shadow, this time knowing that nothing would keep her from going with him. The shouts and gunfire still poured up from the valley, ugly in their meaning. Cries of death stung her heart, causing tears to blind her as she followed Shadow into the corral, where he quickly saddled his horse while his warriors were scrambling around, saddling their own.

Shadow turned to Maria as she grabbed a saddle and prepared her own mare. She saw puzzlement in his eyes as he came to her to clutch her shoulders.

"If it is your father, much will be changed," he said. "If he lies so easily, can his daughter also lie? Maria, you had best pray that your father is not among those who have come to take the lives of many Navaho! If he is, I shall kill him; then I shall send you away!"

Maria looked blankly up at Shadow, disbelieving what he was saying. Could his trust in her be so little? How could he blame her for what her father did? Would she always have to worry about him having such lack of trust in her, if it *wasn't* her father leading this attack tonight?

When he dropped his hands from her shoulders, Maria stepped back away from him, too stunned to mount the mare and follow him. In a sense she felt betrayed by the man she loved. She had gone through so much to prove herself to him. Had her efforts been in vain?

Lowering her eyes, she would not allow herself to watch Shadow ride away from her. Hearing the hoofbeats scattering rock was enough. In a sense, whether or not he returned alive, she felt as though she had lost a part of him tonight.

"Maria?" Pleasant Voice said, rushing toward her in the night. "What is happening? Who is attempting to attack the stronghold?"

Maria turned tearful eyes to Pleasant Voice, then leaned into her arms and began crying. "It could be my father," she sobbed, clutching her friend. "How could he do this? How could *Shadow*?"

"Shadow?" Pleasant Voice questioned. "It is not his fault the stronghold is being attacked. What do you mean, Maria?"

"He does not trust me," Maria cried. "He blames me for my father's madness! How can he? He is even talking of sending me away if my father is the one coming to break the peace tonight. How could he, Pleasant Voice? I am only my father's daughter. Nothing else!"

"Be patient with Shadow," Pleasant Voice encouraged softly. "He is thinking of his people when he says these things to you. He does not want them to suffer because of his decisions. If he is wrong about you, he could be damned in the eyes of his people! He must be sure you are loyal."

"I thought he had already decided that I was," Maria said, drawing away from Pleasant Voice. "Now I find out that I am wrong." She cringed when she heard more gunfire and screams and cries of death. She held her head in her hands. "And was I wrong about my father, also? Moments ago I felt at peace with myself . . . with the *world*. Now I feel nothing but confused!"

Pulling away from Pleasant Voice, Maria ran blindly back to Shadow's hogan and stretched out on the bed, pounding her fists against the mattress of sheepskin hides. At this very moment Shadow and her father could be face to face.

Oh, dear Lord, who would be the victor *this* time?

Either way, *she* would be the loser . . .

The gunfire had ceased. There were no more cries of pain and death. There was a strained silence in the air as Maria sat beside the fire, awaiting the return of those who were victorious. She was torn, not knowing how to feel or what to expect. It was apparent that the Navaho had defeated the attackers, whoever they had been, but had Shadow come through the attack unharmed? Had her father been the leader of this attack? Had he been killed, as Shadow had threatened?"

Rising to her feet, the hem of her buckskin dress swirling around as she began to pace, Maria bit her lower lip nervously. "Why is it taking so long?" she whispered. "If Shadow *is* all right, he should be back by now. What if he is . . . dead?"

The thought causing her to feel numb all over, Maria rushed from the hogan. Just as she was about to walk to the rim of the canyon, to peer over it, she heard the approach of horses.

Paling, she turned and watched for the horsemen to appear, the twilight of morning illuminating everything in a soft pale gray. Maria's knees grew weak when she recognized the lead rider.

"Shadow!" she whispered hoarsely. "Oh, thank you, Lord. Shadow!"

She turned and began to run toward Shadow, then stopped in midstep when behind him, tied and gagged on a horse, she saw José Gironella. She would never mistake him for anyone else. She saw him as no less than a devil for what he had done to her and to others of his own kind.

Then relief flooded her senses! If José Gironella had been taken prisoner by Shadow, that had to mean that her father was not implicated in this latest raid against the Navaho stronghold. Maria's father and José Gironella would never work together. They were not the same breed of men. José Gironella was a traitor to his race. He bought and sold the flesh of innocent Spanish women. He had even planned to rape Maria, then turn her loose in the desert to die.

Maria's and Shadow's eyes met and held when he rode up beside her and looked down at her apologetically. She understood the look. No words were required. She loved him so much and was so glad to see that he had not been harmed, she would not worry about the threat he had made just before he left to defend his stronghold. It was enough that he was there, alive!

Maria moved her eyes slowly to José Gironella and glared at him. Shadow followed her gaze, seeing whom she was looking at with hate, then studied her again.

"You know this Spaniard?" he asked, slipping out of his

saddle. He placed an arm around Maria's waist and led her to the captive. "You look at him as though you know him. Maria, do you?"

"*Sí*," she hissed, her eyes narrowing angrily as Gironella looked down at her. "He is the man who demanded money from both you and my father as payment for my release. He bought me from Charging Falcon! I am sure he has found your stronghold under the direction of some of Charging Falcon's warriors who were a part of the raid that killed many of your people." She flipped her hair back from her shoulders haughtily. "He is a snake, Shadow. *Very* evil!"

"He is the one who deals in Spanish women's flesh, is he?" Shadow growled, looking up at Gironella with hatred. "What should his fate be? How should he die, Maria?"

A chill coursed through Maria's veins at the thought of having to see this man tortured, to watch him die a slow death while she stood witness. Would Shadow require this of her, since she was to learn the habits and customs of the Navaho? She had seen how the women had taunted and teased Charging Falcon while he hung nude on the stake.

It was not in her to do this, though she did hate this man with every fiber of her being. It was not that she did not wish to see him suffer; she did not wish to be a part of the suffering. It would humiliate her to humiliate him.

"My people have their own ways of dealing with traitors," she blurted, challenging Gironella with a set stare, seeing his eyes wavering. "You see, he *is* a traitor to our people. Buying and selling Spanish women makes him a traitor! Return him to my father. *He* knows ways of punishment. José Gironella owes my father not only heartfelt apologies for having bought *me* but also the money he forced my father to pay for me."

"This is what you want?" Shadow asked, tightening his arm around her waist, drawing her closer. "For this man to be taken to your father for punishment?"

"*Sí*," Maria said, recalling the whip that her father was so fond of using. "He will teach the traitor many lessons, then hand him over to the proper authorities."

Shadow smiled smugly. His eyes gleamed as he looked

up at the Spaniard, then again at Maria. "Tomorrow many gifts will be taken to your father for our wedding transaction with him," he said. "I give your father the prized sheep and Arabian horses that I stole from him, and also this Spaniard! Will your father approve of these gifts, Maria?"

Maria was stunned by his generosity. She knew how highly Shadow had valued the sheep and horses. Even though they had originally belonged to her father, they would be cherished gifts accepted by him. But the full meaning behind the gifts was how Shadow would feel about losing them to the rich Spaniard again.

"*Sí*," she murmured. "He will approve. *I* approve."

She warmed up to him as they walked away from Gironella, who still sat on the horse, staring at them.

"Strip the Spaniard and let the women have fun with him until we leave in the morning to take him to Esteban Zamora," Shadow said over his shoulder as his warriors dismounted. "Do not bother me or my woman until time comes to ride to her father's plantation."

He stopped and turned to face his warriors. "After securing the Spaniard on a stake, go and round up the Arabian horses and the merino sheep," he said. "They are to be taken to Esteban Zamora."

Silent stares were the only response. Tears of happiness sparkled in Maria's eyes as Shadow swung her around and held her to his side as they walked toward his hogan.

She had learned much about her man tonight, and all of it was good.

CHAPTER
24

Sipping from a glass of wine, Esteban Zamora moved listlessly through his house, from room to room, feeling the emptiness and quiet press in on him, causing an almost overbearing loneliness to plague him. He and his wife had never had long conversations, sharing their likes and dislikes, nor had Zamora spent enough time with Maria, talking about problems with her. But now that they were both gone—the only family he had in the world—he was saddened.

His hair disheveled, his brown suit crumpled from having been slept in, he walked into his study and sat down at his desk, to try to concentrate on the figures in his ledgers, but was drawn quickly back to his feet when he heard the approach of horses outside.

Grumbling, not wishing to have an audience with anyone today, lonely for what he could not have, he angrily set the tall-stemmed wineglass down on his desk, splashing wine from it, and walked heavy-footed to the window and peered out.

Seeing several Navaho warriors accompanying a white man who was gagged and bound, secured on a horse with ropes holding him in the saddle, Zamora's head jerked back in surprise.

"Whom do the Indians have as captive?" he gasped, paling. "And why have they brought him here?"

He had told his guards to let any Navaho pass who might approach the plantation grounds, but he was surprised that they had a white prisoner with them.

Turning on a heel, running his fingers through his hair to straighten it, he rushed from his study, down the narrow corridor, and out to the porch. He stopped and assessed the situation at a much closer range, seeing that the Indians had not yet dismounted, as though they were waiting for him to appear.

Moving cautiously down the steps, he grew tense when he felt the eyes of the Indians turn to him. Zamora's eyes moved over the prisoner, recognizing the clothes as those worn by a Spaniard, a *patrón* just like himself. With his dark eyes and hair he looked Spanish, but he was not someone Zamora had ever had the opportunity to meet.

"*Buenas tardes*," Zamora said, going to the warrior who seemed to be the leader of this group of Navaho, whom he now recognized as Blue Arrow! He was stunned by this turn in events. All that he had expected from Shadow was a message brought to him to tell him when the dreaded wedding was to be performed. What did this hostage have to do with anything?

Blue Arrow slipped from his saddle and went to stand before Zamora, folding his arms across his muscled chest. "Shadow sends a message that you are to come with me, to have council with him," he said thickly. "There you will receive gifts from Shadow."

Zamora was taken off-guard by what Blue Arrow had said. "Gifts?" he gasped. "What sort of gifts? Why?"

"It is the custom of the Navaho to give gifts to a father when a daughter is taken from him for a marriage ceremony," Blue Arrow said matter-of-factly. "Shadow wishes to give you gifts today." He gestured with a wide sweep of one hand. "Not so far away Shadow and Maria await you. The gifts shall be presented to you there."

"Gifts? Maria?" Zamora said, his voice trailing off as he tried to see in the distance, where Blue Arrow was motioning to, but seeing nothing.

Then he looked at the captive. "And who is this?" he asked. "Why have you brought this man to me?"

Blue Arrow explained who José Gironella was. Then he untied him, pulled him from his horse, and shoved him roughly toward Zamora. "He is yours to do with as you wish," he growled. "It was your daughter who suggested that you choose the way in which this Spaniard is to be punished. So it is done. Your vengeance will be Shadow's and Maria's as well!"

Stunned almost wordless by this new development and feeling the hatred building up inside him for Gironella, now that he knew who he was and what his crimes were, Zamora just stood there for a moment, looking the prisoner up and down.

Then he grabbed Gironella by the throat and yanked him close to him. "You are nothing more than a pig," he said heatedly. "You will regret ever having paid Charging Falcon for my daughter. And where is my money? I paid you well for the return of my daughter, and all along you knew that you would not return her to me. I will spare your life just long enough to recover my money and then, after you bend beneath many lashes of my whip, I will hand you over to Governor Castillo to see that justice is done!"

Fear entered Gironella's eyes. He fell to his knees, but he could not speak, for he was still gagged. He tried to talk through the foul-tasting buckskin, but only muted ramblings emerged.

Zamora gave the prisoner a kick, causing him to tumble over on the ground, then shouted to his guards to come and get him. He smiled at Blue Arrow. "My daughter was wise to send him to me," he said smoothly. "He will be taken care of in the right way."

Nervously he ran his fingers through his hair as he looked toward the beckoning hills where his daughter awaited him. A part of him felt hopeful again, for it was apparent that Shadow had been sincere when he spoke of peace, and Maria wanted to be with him.

"I won't be long," he said, as he turned to go back inside

the house. "I want to look decent when I meet with Maria and Shadow."

Blue Arrow nodded, then swung back up into his saddle and surveyed the riches of this man's land and house. Many Spaniards were equally rich. Most of the Navaho were equally poor.

He turned his eyes away, not wanting to be reminded of the plight of his people.

Perhaps one day it would change and everyone would be equal. Perhaps the beginning lay right here, with the peace being offered between Shadow and this rich landowner. Perhaps Maria was destined to be the catalyst.

Mesas of brightly colored rock jutted up from valleys covered with soft gray-green sagebrush. A deep canyon gashed the high plateau, and steep gullies wound snakelike through the flat bottomlands, with clumps of juniper and piñon pine adding their dark dusty green to the landscape. Over it all hung the most brilliant of blue skies.

Maria was lying beside Shadow on the ground on a plateau where a spring flowed under a big cottonwood tree. Thousands of sheep were grazing close by. The Arabian horses stood with their heads dipped, enjoying the lushness of the knee-high grass where they grazed.

Striped blankets, thrown over the horses' saddles, glimmered through a cloud of dust as Maria caught her first glimpse of approaching horsemen, one in particular catching her eye, since he was the only one attired in a velveteen suit; the others wore only breechclouts.

"*Padre!*" Maria gasped, leaping to her feet. "He's coming, Shadow." She clasped her hands together behind her, the breeze lifting her hair from her shoulders, whipping it about her face. "I can hardly wait to see his face when he catches sight of his sheep and horses. He never expected to see them again."

"He is not aware of this gift just yet," Shadow said, wrapping an arm around Maria's waist. "I told Blue Arrow not to tell him. I want to see the man's eyes when he recognizes the gift."

Maria swung around and hugged Shadow. "No other gift could thrill him as much," she said excitedly. "The sheep were a special gift to him from the king of Spain. The horses were also special. You will make a friend of my father forever, Shadow."

Shadow eased her away and placed his hands on her waist, looking dark-eyed down at her. "That is good," he said hoarsely. "I am glad that he will want to accept my gift in the manner in which it is given, as my attempt to restore peace between us."

He bent to kiss her nose. "But you are wrong when you say that no other gift could thrill him as much," he said softly. "My love, *you* would be the best gift of all for *any* man, be it a father or a lover."

Maria ducked her head, her thick lashes touching her cheeks. Then she jerked her head back up when she heard the closer approach of the horsemen. Pulling away from Shadow, she turned and waved to her father, but he did not see her. He had already seen the sheep and the horses.

The moon was cold and remote overhead, the air brisk. Maria snuggled closer to Shadow where they were making camp beside the spring. The others had gone on ahead, to make camp farther up in the mountains.

"This is your last night of freedom." Maria giggled, placing her finger beneath Shadow's chin, directing his eyes to hers. The glow from the campfire made his eyes take on a golden sheen, hauntingly beautiful to Maria. "What do you wish to do, my love, on your last night of freedom? This is your last chance, you know."

Shadow placed his hands on Maria's narrow waist and drew her close, their bodies pressing against each other on the pallet of sheepskins. He had erected a lean-to of sheepskin above them, to give them some measure of shelter from the evening mountain air.

"Woman, freedom means many things to many people," he said huskily, gyrating his risen hardness into her abdomen, silently cursing their buckskin clothes, which impeded him at this moment. "Do not you see? I do not lose my freedom tonight. Nor do *you*. Together we are one. One heartbeat . . . one soul."

He snaked a hand up inside her skirt and claimed the damp patch between her thighs, caressing her as she arched herself closer to his callused fingers. "We are one body," he said huskily, his lips hot on her ear. "As one, we soar together over the mountains. Shall we go there now, my love? Except for you and me, is not the world and everything about it an elusive place? Are not all woes and cares erased from your mind at this moment? *That* is what freedom is for us, Maria. The moments when we soar together to find bliss in each other's arms."

Maria's blood felt near to boiling as it flowed through her veins. She closed her eyes and held her head back so that Shadow could kiss the hollow of her throat while his free hand lowered her dress over her shoulders, revealing to him in the moonlight the dark tautness of her nipples.

"*Sí*, my darling," she whispered, moaning when he flicked a tongue over a nipple, causing her to begin a slow melting inside. "Let us make love tonight, as we can every night from now on. Oh, Shadow, it is too wonderful to believe."

"Even your father accepts this truth," Shadow said, leaning away from her, rising to draw her to her feet. As Maria looked up at him, her eyes filled with passion, he pushed her clothes on down away from her, then dropped to his knees and removed her moccasins.

While on his knees he gave her a sly smile, then placed his hands on her hips and drew her close to his mouth, letting his tongue elicit fire where his fingers had already skillfully aroused her.

Maria chewed on her lower lip. Her hands wove through her long, streaming hair. She closed her eyes and let herself enjoy this way of making love that seemed to excite Shadow as much as it did her. As his tongue and lips pleasured her, a wondrous thrill shot through her as she reached the pinnacle of rapture without him. It did not matter, for Shadow was now trailing kisses upward, his hands cupping her breasts as he rose slowly to his feet.

"Shadow will teach you every way of making love," he said, now standing over her, drawing her against his powerful frame. His hands swept her hair back from her face. His mouth came down upon her lips, kissing her with a gentle passion, his body once more gyrating against hers, his manhood pressing almost unbearably tight against the inside of his buckskin breeches.

Shadow stepped away from her. He spread his legs and beckoned to her with his arms. "I undressed you; now you undress me," he said, his voice deep and resonant. "Then touch me all over with the velvet of your hands, Maria. I want you to know every inch of my body so that in the middle of the night, when it is dark, you can reach out to me and touch me and know that it is your man at your side."

His gaze swept over her, the moon silvering her body with its light. Again, as so many times before, he saw the magnificence of her breasts, which seemed to have developed even more since he had first touched and fondled her, the flatness of her stomach, the narrow waist, and the tapering thighs. His eyes became two points of fire as he savored the view of her beckoning triangle, where only moments ago he had not only touched but tasted the sweetness of her.

Hardly able to bear the waiting, he took her hands and placed them on his chest. "Begin there," he said thickly. He sucked in his breath at the mere touch of her hands. "Go slowly. We have all night. Do not forget," he said, "the wedding cannot begin until we get there."

Maria smiled up at Shadow, his mention of the wedding evoking remembrances of her father. Although at this moment she did not want anything to invade this precious time with Shadow, it was because of him that she could not erase her father from her mind.

While she ran the palms of her hands over Shadow's powerful, sleek chest. moving downward, to circle his nipples with her fingers, she could not help but feel an immense happiness that included her father. He had been so shocked and happy when his sheep and horses were returned to him! There had been a sincerely peaceful look in his eyes when he had shaken Shadow's hand to seal the friendship. The animals had been her father's in the first place, but Shadow could have kept them forever, had he chosen to. That made the return of the animals an even more precious gift.

Sighing, feeling more at peace with herself and the world than she had in years, Maria banished further thoughts of her father from her mind and leaned closer to Shadow as she continued to circle his nipples, pinching them between her thumbs and forefingers. Bending her head, she imitated Shadow's skill at teasing and tormenting her nipples with his tongue. A thrill soared through her when she heard him gasp and moan with pleasure. And while her tongue continued to tease and torment him, her hands strayed lower, his stomach quivering beneath the feather-light touch of her hands. When she found his manhood, a small droplet of wetness at its tip, she smoothed the wetness along the full length of his hardness and then cupped her hand around him and began to move her fingers over him, evoking a sensual snarl from deep within him.

When she felt his hands twine through her hair and urge her to her knees before him, she did not hesitate to do what he so obviously wanted. She splayed her fingers across his abdomen and bent her mouth closer . . . closer. . . .

Shadow's insides seemed to be all aglow. The pleasure she was giving him made him feel as though he was almost out of control, yet it was the sort of mindlessness that he savored while with her. He guided her head in easy movements at first, then much more quickly as he felt the heat rising, threatening to spill over.

"*E-do-ta,* no," he said huskily, drawing her to her feet, then locking his arms around her waist as he lowered her to the pallet on the ground. "I want to be inside you when I reach that culmination. I want not only to receive pleasure at that moment but to give it as well." He lowered himself over her. He pressed his lips to hers and whispered her name almost meditatively. "Maria, oh, my Maria. I love you . . . so much."

He thrust his hardness deep inside her with a solid plunge

and began his determined strokes, his mouth on her lips, wildly kissing her, his hands on her breasts, cupping them. As he moved within her, she met his eager thrusts, arching her body upward, opening herself as fully as she could to feel all of him.

Maria was beginning to feel the ecstasy that came with being with him in such a way. A marvelous bliss overtook her, as though her body was separate from herself, a being in itself.

She clung. She kissed. She could not keep her hands still, for she loved the feel of his muscled shoulders and the hardness of his buttocks as he became more aroused and neared a mind-bursting climax that would match her own.

Sucking in her breath, Maria let the warmth spread in wondrous splashes as she reached that moment of intense pleasure, arching wildly upward as his body hardened and then quivered, releasing the warmth of his love-seed deep inside her.

And then they lay breathless in each other's arms, Shadow lying limp atop her, his hands framing her face between them. His lips came to hers in a gentle, sweet kiss; his eyes were peaceful. . . .

Zamora was filled with a strange peace after being with Maria again and realizing that the man she had chosen to marry was not a savage in any sense of the word, as he had originally thought. Shadow had shown a sincere effort to have peaceful relationships with him again, and being so alone, so empty, Zamora had eagerly accepted it.

He climbed the staircase slowly to the second floor of the house, to prepare himself for his journey to Shadow's stronghold. By nightfall he would be witnessing a marriage that he had never thought to be able to give a blessing.

But now?

Sí, he was ready to give his blessing and accept the fact that Maria would no longer be a part of his household. His plans to steal her away were abandoned when he had been touched by Shadow and Maria being together, so openly admiring each other, so loving.

"And then there are my horses and sheep," he whispered, reaching the second landing of his house. "Shadow did not have to give them back to me. I can't believe that he did. His having done so proves much to me . . . and it is all good!"

Zamora did not head for his bedroom, but went instead to the sewing room, his mind having toyed with an idea that could in a small measure keep Maria a part of his life. . . .

After opening the door and stepping into the quiet, dark room, he lit a candle and held it up so that its golden rays would move around the room and reveal the many bolts of material, beautiful webs of lace, the loom, the embroidery work half finished as it lay on a table beside the chair.

"And then there is the *bayeta*," he whispered, going to the brightest colored bolts of material of all. "Maria's idea to share this with the Navaho could still come to pass."

A smile flickered across his narrow face, making his mustache quiver. "Shadow has proven his intentions of peace to me," he said, smoothing his hand over a bolt of crimson cloth. "It is now time for me to prove mine. When I arrive at the stronghold I shall bear *many* gifts."

He again looked over Maria's prized sewing materials. "She has given up her dream of being a famous seamstress," he said. "But she does not have to give up sewing altogether! I shall take everything to her. She can sew to her heart's content!"

Nodding, feeling good for having settled this inside his heart and mind, he left the room and summoned his guards and gave the orders that several mules be brought to the house, readied for travel.

Smiling, he later watched as the mules were loaded down with all of the sewing equipment, including several bolts of *bayeta*.

Maria rode proudly into the village with Shadow. When she saw Pleasant Voice running toward her she slipped from the saddle and met her approach. Hugging each other, they laughed and cried with happiness.

"By nightfall we both will be married," Pleasant Voice said, sighing. She leaned away from Maria. Her brow furrowed into a frown. "Your father? Did he meet you? Did he come peacefully? Did he not send the army to take you away from Shadow?"

Maria took Pleasant Voice's hands and squeezed them affectionately. "My father has reconciled himself to the fact that I am no longer his little girl slave," Maria giggled. "He understands now that no matter what, I *will* be Shadow's wife. He was very touched by Shadow's gift."

"But they were your father's—"

Maria interrupted. "Until Shadow stole them, they were father's," she corrected. "They then became Shadow's, just the same as all of the things my father has stolen from Shadow have become *his* personal possessions. That Shadow willingly parted with anything that he had gotten while raiding surely came as a surprise to my father." She giggled softly, her eyes dancing. "As it also did to me," she said.

"But never will he give *you* up," Pleasant Voice said, smiling. "And *you* were *also* taken in a raid."

Maria flipped her hair back from her shoulders and walked alongside Pleasant Voice as they turned toward Shadow's hogan. "*Sí*, and so I was," she said, lifting her chin haughtily. "So I was."

Shadow watched Maria walking ahead of him as he slid from his Navaho saddle. His eyes proudly followed the seductive, soft sway of her hips and the billowing hair that hung to her waist.

CHAPTER
25

Never was Maria more aware of the colorful cliffs and canyons, the warm rock, than now, as she sat among Shadow's people, a part of it. The sun was comfortable upon one's bones; the breeze was too soft to feel.

Sitting beside Shadow, Pleasant Voice and Blue Arrow on his other side, Maria awaited breathlessly the moment when she would become Shadow's wife. Silver and stones with soft highlights and deep shadows hung around her neck, glowing against her buckskin dress. Oval plaques of silver surrounded her waist; ceremonial jewels were sewn in the fringes of a sash that was draped across one shoulder. She wore moccasins with silver buttons shining at their sides.

Maria's hair was drawn back from her face and adorned with wildflowers of the mountain; her cheeks were rosy with excitement.

Yet her eyes were troubled, glancing now and then toward the path that led up from the valley below.

Where was her father? Had he decided not to come after all? Had he seen his gesture of friendship toward Shadow as too hasty, perhaps as even foolish? Once he had had time to think about it, had he decided that he hated Maria because she had chosen Shadow and his way of life over all that she had been taught from birth?

286   *Cassie Edwards*

The humiliation of this could have made her father decide to forget that she even existed.

She did not want to think of unpleasantness this afternoon. The sun was sending its gilded rays across the tips of the mountain as it lowered in the sky. Maria looked proudly over at Shadow. Tonight he looked more savage than not, dressed in only a breechclout, even his feet bare of moccasins, his hair devoid of its usual colorful handkerchief twisted into a headband to hold his hair in place. He was wonderfully seductive with all of his bare skin gleaming in the light of the campfire around which everyone was positioned, celebrating the upcoming marriage.

Maria could not help but feel a sensual fluttering in the pit of her stomach when she looked at him slowly, from his broad, squared shoulders, downward across his muscled, powerful chest, lower still past his flat stomach, his navel round and perfect, lower still to where she could see how well defined his manhood was beneath the thin fabric of his breechclout.

She swallowed hard, controlling her breathing, which always became erratic when she thought of the moments that he had pleasured her so wonderfully with that part of a man's anatomy that she had never become acquainted with until Shadow. She was glad that he had been the first, that he had been her teacher of the mysteries of making love. It surely could not have been the same with any other man!

Maria blushed when two small naked boys brought ears of roasted corn on a wooden platter and set one platter before Maria, the other before Shadow, doing the same then for Pleasant Voice and Blue Arrow. Several women came and placed broiled goats' ribs and corn bread before them.

When he offered her a platter of food, Maria smiled a thank-you to Shadow, following his lead when he ate the baked root of the wild potato, taking a mouthful of the root, then a mouthful of alum, which looked like white clay. She had been taught by Shadow that the strong taste of the root would make one vomit; the alum prevented this. She had also learned that wild mountain celery was peeled and baked, then ground into flour. Wild onions were gathered and rubbed in hot ashes to singe and remove their strong taste before they were used in cooking.

Then as she nibbled on corn bread she became absorbed in the activities around her. One Navaho was rapidly beating a small drum, and the young men, wearing only breechclouts, danced gracefully.

Maria watched intently the slender golden brown bodies, the bodies of perfect boys, under the dark color a glow of red showing. Each wore a horsehair roach and a feather on his head. They danced all together or by turns, without fixed order, laughter coming readily among them. Bare feet thumped, raising dust from the ground.

It was a feast of sights and sounds for Maria, the Indian costume accentuating her whiteness.

Yet her eyes continued to stray to the path that led downward from the mountain. Where was her father? Was he going to try to ruin this special day for her deliberately? Did he hate her that much?

Placing her wooden spoon on the platter, following Shadow's lead, Maria smiled at another nude boy as he came and took the platters away.

Then she warmed all over inside when she felt a warm, comforting hand circle hers. She turned her thankful eyes up to Shadow, knowing that he had sensed how ill at ease she was, and had surely guessed why. He had been glad that things were smoothed out between himself and her father. Was he going to be disturbed when he discovered that things were not right at all and that they were still enemies?

When Shadow had time to think about having given up the sheep and horses in a sincere gesture of friendship, would he feel foolish for having done so?

Would he, in the end, think that Maria was not worth any of this bother?

"Do not despair," Shadow said, leaning closer to her, looking down at her with devotion and love. "It is our wedding night. Nothing should be in your mind but happiness and joy. Listen to me, my love, and let your heart be filled with gladness. There is only you. There is only *I*."

"You are not upset that my father again spoke with a

forked tongue?" Maria murmured, fluttering her lashes
nervously up at him. "This does not cause you to wonder
again about my sincerity? My trustworthiness?"

"If there was any doubt in my mind about you, do you
think I would be sitting here, a part of the celebration that
leads up to the wedding ceremony?" Shadow said, chuckling low. "*E-do-ta*, no. I think not. My love, we are going
to be *ka-bike-hozhoni-bi*, happy evermore, you and I."

"*Sí*, you and I, happy evermore," Maria whispered, her
insides melting with happiness. She would cast all thoughts
of her father from her mind. She must! To be happy, one
must not dwell on the past. Only the future mattered and her
father had now obviously chosen not to be a part of that
future!

So be it!

The sun was down. The fires burning outside the hogans
were golden spots in the blue dusk, the larger, communal
fire a burst of sunshine in the pending darkness, everything
around it gay and wonderful.

A clamor, the sound of horses approaching, made Maria
turn her head. She rose slowly to her feet, her pulse racing,
when she saw several of Shadow's warriors escorting her
father on horseback. Trailing along behind him were several
mules packed high with supplies.

"*Padre*," Maria whispered, placing her hands on her
throat, her eyes misting with tears. She smiled up at
Shadow. "He has come, Shadow. He *has*."

Shadow placed a hand on her arm. "Go to him," he said.
"I understand."

Maria rose up on tiptoe and gave Shadow a grateful,
fierce hug, then spun around and began running toward her
father. When she got to him, she waited anxiously for him
to dismount, then flew into his embrace, laughing softly.

"*Padre*, I had given up on you," she murmured, fighting
back the urge to cry. "I thought you had decided not to ever
see me again, to cast me aside, as though you had no
daughter at all. I'm so glad that I was wrong."

Her father looked past her at the celebration, then smiled

at Shadow as he approached, walking tall and dignified, though attired only in a breechclout, which did not seem at all fitting for a wedding ceremony.

But Zamora had to remind himself that many things were different between these two cultures of people marrying.

He hoped Maria could adjust to the changes.

"I promised I would come, didn't I?" he said, holding Maria away from him, looking deep into her eyes. "Just how many times have I broken a promise to my very special daughter? How many times?"

"None that I recall," Maria said, thrilling inside when Shadow laced a strong arm around her waist, showing his possession of her. She glanced up at Shadow, then back at her father. "He has come in time to see us married, Shadow. Isn't that wonderful?"

Her smile faded gradually when her father stepped into the light of the campfire and revealed just how extremely tired he appeared to be. There were dark, deep circles beneath his eyes, and his shoulders were slouched as though it was a great effort to keep them held back in a more dignified fashion. His face displayed a thin film of dust, as though he wore face powder, and his clothes were dusty and wrinkled.

"You are welcome here," Shadow said, extending a hand to Zamora. "Come. It is time for the wedding. Though a short ceremony, it should not be delayed any longer."

Zamora grasped Shadow's hand and patted it with his other one, glancing at the loaded mules, then back at Shadow. "Perhaps just a few moments longer won't hurt?" he asked. "You see, Shadow, I have brought you and Maria many gifts. I would like for you to know what they are and then give permission that they be unloaded so that your whole community will see them and realize that I have come to offer true friendship."

Maria and Shadow exchanged questioning glances; then Shadow broke away and strolled casually toward the mules. He kneaded his chin as he walked from one to the other, unable to see what was beneath the thick layer of sheepskins that covered them.

He then turned around and nodded to Zamora. "Yes, there is time for you to explain what you have brought and for you to display it for my people to see and to understand that these wedding gifts are brought in the name of friendship," he said, anxious, himself, to see what the Spaniard felt was good enough to bring to the Navaho people who had never accepted any bribes from the Spaniard.

Shadow did not look to these gifts as bribes and would accept them in the spirit in which they had been brought to him.

Zamora found the strength that had not been totally drained of him due to fatigue and went square-shouldered to the mules and one by one began uncovering them.

Maria stepped up to Shadow's side, her pulse racing when she saw the many bolts of material, the wondrous lace that looked like delicate cobwebs, and many bolts of *bayeta*! This had to mean one thing to her! Her father had forgotten his plan to trick Shadow and his people into making money for him. He was being generous in that he was actually giving this to the Navaho out of the goodness of his heart.

He uncovered the last display of sewing materials and turned to face Maria and Shadow. "These I bring to you to share with your people," he said, then focused on Maria. "With these you can resume your sewing and become the best damn seamstress in the territory."

He went to her and placed his hands on her shoulders. "You recall our plan to bring the *bayeta* to the Navaho?" he said. "If you wish, we can do it so that it will benefit the Navaho instead of me."

Maria's eyes wavered. "You would do this?" she gasped; then she smiled up at him. "But, of course, you would do this only because I am to soon be a part of the Navaho."

"*Sí*," Zamora said, chuckling low. "It would not be something I would do unless my daughter would benefit by the transactions."

Maria looked up at him, tears again misting her eyes; then she threw her arms around him. "*Padre*, you have just proved so much to me that I had been doubting," she softly cried. "*Muchas gracias, Padre. Muchas gracias.*"

"Then you think Shadow will agree to such a business arrangement?" Zamora said, running his fingers down the clinging buckskin material along her back, looking questioningly up at Shadow.

Shadow reached for Maria and eased her from her father's arms. He drew her next to him, his arm locked around her waist. "If Maria sees a benefit in what you say, then no more is required," he said, his voice smooth and even. "It is my goal to make both my Navaho people and my wife happy. If she chooses to engage in a business venture with you, which will also benefit me and my people, then it will be done."

He swung Maria around and began walking her back to the fire. He tossed his head toward several warriors who were silently admiring the colorful bolts of material. "Take the gifts and display them so our people can see them," he said. "Do it quickly. It is now time for the marriage ceremony to begin!"

Maria smiled at Pleasant Voice as she met her and Blue Arrow just rising from their pallet of sheepskin, to accept Shadow and Maria back among the others. Pleasant Voice smiled weakly at Maria, also seeing Zamora lumbering along behind her. When Pleasant Voice saw him she was reminded of everything ugly in the world and she regretted that he had come to be a part of one of the most precious moments in her life, when she married the man she loved.

Gritting her teeth, Pleasant Voice looked quickly away from Zamora and clung to Blue Arrow's arm, now watching the gifts being placed close beside the light of fire so that everyone could get a close look. Her own heart pounded when she saw the brilliant colors of several bolts of material. She adored lace, having watched Maria sew it onto many of her fancy gowns while sharing time together in the sewing room at the plantation. Her fingers itched to touch it, to sew with the precious fabrics, and she knew that she would be allowed to. Maria was her best friend and would share everything with her. She was even sharing her wedding day with her.

Turning her eyes back to Maria, Pleasant Voice became

all warmed inside, so glad that all the ugliness of their lives was finally behind them. What remained was a future of beautiful moments.

The wedding ceremony was held in Shadow's hogan. As many as possible crowded inside to witness the double marriage. A Singer, an elder Navaho with floor-length gray hair, wearing a loose buckskin gown, had performed many songs, blessing the two couples, who were sitting on separate blankets before a small fire in the fire pit.

The Singer now handed a medicine basket to Maria and Pleasant Voice. They rose to their feet and went to two large platters of corn mush they each prepared earlier in the day for the ceremony. Placing the corn mush in the baskets, they took them back to the Singer and gave them to him, then settled back down on the blankets beside their loved ones.

The Singer divided the mush into four portions, then prayed for each couple. When the prayer was over, Shadow and Maria, then Pleasant Voice and Blue Arrow, partook of the corn mush, ceremonially. Then Shadow sang his prayer song:

Daltso hozhoni, all is beautiful,
Daltso hozhoni, all is beautiful,
Daltso hozhoni, all is beautiful indeed.
Naestsan-iye, now the Mother Earth,
Yatilyilch-iye, and the Father Sky,
Pilch kaaltsin sella, meeting, joining each other,
Daltso hozhoni, all is beautiful.

Blue Arrow then sang his portion of the song:

Kanatan-alchkai-ye, and the white corn,
Kanatan-alchtsoi-ye, and the yellow corn,
Pilchka altsin sella, meeting, joining each other.
Daltso hozhoni, all is beautiful.
Daltso hozhoni, all is beautiful indeed.

The Singer sang the last portion of the song:

Kasa-a narai, life that never passeth,
Kabike hozhoni-ye, happiness of all things,
Pilch ka altsin sella, meeting, joining each other,
Ho-ushte-hiye, helpmates ever, they.
Daltso hozhoni, all is beautiful.
Daltso hozhoni, all is beautiful indeed.

The Singer went from Shadow to Maria, then to Pleasant Voice and to Blue Arrow, touching them one at a time. "In beauty it is finished," he said solemnly. "In beauty it is finished."

Maria's eyes widened when Shadow drew her around to face him, his face brimming with a smile. "We are married?" she whispered. "All that simply?"

"Was not the ceremony beautiful?" Shadow said softly, cupping her chin tenderly in the palm of his hand, tracing a circle beneath her chin with his thumb. "*You* are so beautiful, Maria. So very, very beautiful."

He swept her up into his arms and without hesitation carried her from his hogan, on past her gawking father, to the outside and began running with her through the village until they came to an isolated, grassy knoll that overlooked the valley below, which was now only elusive shadows of gray and blue beneath the light of the moon.

Shadow laid Maria down beside a rambling brook, frogs croaking, crickets singing. The smell was sweet where wildflowers grew across the banks of the brook, all colors of the rainbow.

"We are now man and wife," Maria sighed, placing her hands on Shadow's cheeks, drawing his lips to hers as he knelt down over her, his knees on either side of her. "Love me, husband. Show me if it feels different to make love with a married man."

Her soft giggles were stifled beneath his lips. Her mouth trembled as his tongue surged between her teeth, setting her on fire inside with need of him as he thrust his tongue in and out of her mouth, as though seducing her in a new way.

Maria sighed deeply when he lowered her skirt away

from her and then held her up so that he could slip her blouse and all of her jewelry up over her head so that she was lying sleekly nude beneath him, beckoning for him to come to her with her outstretched arms.

"In time, woman," Shadow said, placing his fingers at the band of his breechclout, slowly shoving his garment down, taking his time to reveal to her how ready he was for her in the strength of his distended manhood.

When Maria saw his readiness she extended a hand to him and encircled his shaft with eager fingers as he kicked the breechclout away from him. She felt her heart begin to thunder inside her as she moved her hand on him, marveling anew at his size and at how seeing him naked thrilled her clean to the soul.

Tossing his garment aside, he took Maria's hand away from him, feeling as though he might burst from the pleasure she was inflicting on him, Shadow pressed himself against her. Their bodies molded together, Shadow entered her with one swift movement and began his strokes within her, savoring how tight she was around his manhood, like a cocoon.

Rocking with him, Maria twined her arms around his neck and enjoyed the rapture spreading throughout her, causing a headiness to claim her. The baying of a distant wolf did not dissuade her from taking from Shadow what she was eagerly giving him, suddenly unaware that they were outside, an audience of millions of stars blinking down at them.

It was all perfect—the peaceful solitude of the mountain; the wondrous, fresh smell of the water bubbling over rocks; the touch of the soft grass beneath her hips, cushioning her body as Shadow continued to plunge inside her, setting her afire, the warmth glowing inside her, surely as bright as a torch!

"My love, my *wife*," Shadow whispered huskily as he felt the fire burning within his loins, growing hotter . . . hotter.

He kissed her hard and long, his fingers digging into her buttocks, lifting her higher so that he could penetrate deeper, her needs tonight matched by his in the way she was responding with such abandon.

"I love you so much," Maria whispered, flicking her tongue across his bottom lip as he withdrew his mouth to look down at her. "To be your wife! Oh, Shadow, tell me it is not a dream!"

"It is real," he chuckled, sucking her tongue between his lips, again kissing her with an open, hot mouth. His hands moved along her flesh and around, to cup her breasts. He kneaded them as he emitted a husky groan, then drove even harder inside her and quivered and quaked when the release was finally at hand, and savored. . . .

Maria clung to him. Her breathing became harsh, her heartbeat erratic. She dug her fingernails into the flesh of his back, her teeth nipped at the tautness of his shoulder, and then she felt her head swim as the pleasure soared and peaked, causing her to moan and throw her head back in ecstasy as it claimed her, body and soul.

Too soon the wondrous bliss melted away, yet the memory of it still clung to Maria, causing her to hug Shadow tightly to her. "I shall always remember this night," she whispered. "The marriage ceremony . . . the songs were beautiful. And now? The first time we made love after our marriage was just as beautiful. It was *wonderful*!"

"Tonight is only the beginning, Maria," Shadow said, leaning away from her. He reached for her waist and drew her up from the ground and onto his lap, so that her legs were straddling him where he sat close beside the brook. "There is much promise in the wind tonight, is there not, my love? Promises of a future so sweet and perfect between us? It was our fate . . . our destiny that we should meet and marry. Let us celebrate every night what we have found together."

Maria giggled as she locked her arms about his neck and drew his lips close to hers. "Why only celebrate at night?" she teased. "When you are available through the day, so will *I* be. Would that be wicked, Shadow, to make love in the middle of the day?"

"Wicked?" he said, chuckling. "*E-do-ta*, no. Never wicked. Just daring on your part, a *woman*. Yet you are not just *any* woman, are you? You are my wife, the chief of this clan of Navaho. Whatever you ask for, you will receive. Even if it is time alone in bed with your husband during the noon hour!"

"Much of my day will be spent in doing chores that are expected of me, your wife," Maria said, on a more serious note. "I want nothing more than to make you happy."

"You will also spend time with the colorful fabrics brought by your father?" Shadow asked, eyeing her cautiously.

"*Si*, but only if you approve," Maria said blandly.

"I have already given my approval," Shadow said, cupping her chin within the palm of his hand, drawing her lips to his. "Anything you wish, my love. Anything."

Again he kissed her long and passionately, his hands on her hips, guiding her onto his manhood. He smiled to himself when she showed that she knew what to do by moving with him, sending messages of endearment directly to his heart. . . .

CHAPTER
26

Sitting outdoors close to the hogan, under a "shade," a roof of brush held up by posts to keep the sun off, Maria was enjoying some peaceful time with her friend. Pleasant Voice was teaching her the art of weaving and they were working intricate designs into handmade blankets. They were using wool that they themselves had sheared from sheep, and twisted into yarn by hand. Maria was weaving a saddle blanket for Shadow, a red background with the black and white interlocked fret of designs of lightning.

"You will find what looks like a mistake in my blanket somewhere," Pleasant Voice said, holding her colorful blanket close to Maria. "Every real Navaho rug and blanket has a 'mistake.' The weaver leaves one place that is not finished and perfect, so that his spirit will not be trapped inside the garment. There must always be a way for the weaver's spirit to get out."

"How interesting," Maria said, arching an eyebrow inquisitively. She rested her hands for a moment, studying her own blanket, which was taking shape. "My mother always taught me to make *no* mistakes when I was sewing."

"And because of her teachings you are a wonderful seamstress," Pleasant Voice said, resuming her weaving. "But now you are of the Navaho culture and must do as we do so as to make Shadow proud, Maria." She smiled over at Maria. "He is already happy, happier than I have ever seen him."

Maria sighed, looking into the distance, seeing nothing but the blue sky and the rim of the canyon, wondering what was taking Shadow so long today. He had left with his warriors to ride across the vastness of the valley below, to see that nothing was there to threaten their peaceful existence. Her father had left several days ago. She hoped he had arrived home safely enough. He had refused to let any of Shadow's warriors accompany him on the journey.

Although he had made peace with the Navaho, he still seemed to want to distance himself from them whenever he could.

Perhaps one day even this would change, for if her father was to have much contact with Maria, he would have to associate with many Navaho.

"It is wonderful that your father brought bolts of *bayeta* to our people," Pleasant Voice said, rambling on as she sewed. "Already many women are sewing with it. Soon enough garments could be ready to take to the market. The money from the sale will buy many supplies for our village. Strange how it is your father who shares the *bayeta* with us."

"*Sí*, strange," Maria said, resuming sewing.

Maria's frown revealed to Pleasant Voice that she was troubled by something, and Pleasant Voice gathered that it was the talk of her father. Perhaps she missed him and did not want to admit to such a truth. Living with the Navaho was a traumatic change for Maria, since she had been used to all of the luxuries that were showered upon the daughters of rich Spaniards. The hogans left much to be desired in comparison to Zamora Manor.

"Do you wish to hear more about my people while we sew?" Pleasant Voice asked, wanting to draw Maria into the mystique of the Navaho, to intrigue and interest her.

Maria looked quickly over at Pleasant Voice. She forked an eyebrow. "*Sí*, please," she said softly. "I am always eager to listen."

"Has Shadow spoken to you of monster slayer?" Pleasant Voice said, smiling over at Maria.

"*Sí*, once. When we first met," Maria said, her fingers eagerly working on the blanket, anxious to finish it to get not only Shadow's approval but that of the other women of this village as well. "But I forget. What is monster slayer?"

It seemed to her that if she wove this blanket as the Navaho expected it to be done, and it was accepted by them, *she* would be accepted as well. For now, she still felt vague, questioning looks when she strolled through the village. Even while she was with Shadow or Pleasant Voice this lack of acceptance by Shadow's people unnerved her.

It *had* to change!

She must make it so!

"Monster slayer is the war god," Pleasant Voice said matter-of-factly. "When he killed the evil creatures who made the world unsafe, he made their remains into something useful. He scattered their fur and feathers to the winds to become small birds and animals, and as he did so, he said, 'Earth people shall use you,' and they did. They used every seed and root and food animal. That is how the Navaho have survived from the beginning of time."

"That's a beautiful story," Maria said, her eyes wide. "I love hearing the Navaho lore."

"Snakes are the guardians of our sacred lore," Pleasant Voice said, straightening her back proudly. "They will punish those who treat it lightly! Neither snakes nor frogs are harmed by our people. They are rain-bringers and any harm to them will mean bad luck."

Maria continued to listen, spellbound.

"Coyotes and crows are not often killed, either," Pleasant Voice said softly. "They are hunters like the Navaho themselves, and they often show the Navaho where game is to be found. Bears are regarded as almost human, since they walk on hind legs and use their front paws like people. Bears are killed only on special occasions, when needed for ceremony or when people are starving. In that case hunters speak to the bear before touching it, explaining what the need was, and they sing and pray over its dead body. Bears are killed by striking them with a wooden club, never by drawing blood."

Maria's intense concentration on what Pleasant Voice was saying was interrupted when she heard the approach of horses, and then she dropped her blanket to the ground and rose shakily to her feet when Shadow appeared. Beside him, draped over a horse, was the lifeless body of her father. There was no denying that it was Esteban Zamora, for his face was turned toward her, drained of color, his eyes fixed in a death trance.

Feeling light-headed, her knees weakening, Maria did not have the strength to move. She pressed her hands to her mouth to hold back a scream that seemed to be strangling her at the base of her throat. She felt an ache embrace her heart. The pit of her stomach was suddenly strangely empty.

Shadow caught sight of Maria standing there beneath the shade and saw her sudden distress. He had not expected her to be outside to view his arrival in the village with the remains of her father. He had wanted to go to her and explain in a quiet way that her father was dead.

Anything could be running through her mind! At this moment she could even be silently accusing Shadow and his warriors of the murder when, in truth, the murderer's identity was not known!

Or would she trust Shadow enough to know that he would not be responsible for this horrendous crime, especially horrendous now because he had vowed friendship with this Spaniard. Shadow did not vow friendship one minute and kill the *next*.

Surely Maria knew this. Her trust in him had been earned!

Maria stared disbelievingly at her father's body, the blood splattered on his brown shirt evidence of a gunshot wound, not an arrow. But, of course, she had not suspected that Shadow could have done this! She should not even have looked for it to be an arrow wound!

Swallowing hard, tears splashing from her eyes, Maria finally found the strength to walk toward the approaching horses. When she met them, Shadow quickly dismounted and drew her into his arms, trying to shield her eyes from further viewing of her father.

"Do not look," he said thickly, pressing her face against his chest. "It is not a pleasant sight. He has been dead for many days now. He more than likely was attacked the night he left after the wedding celebration. Had he stayed the night, as he was advised, perhaps he would not have ridden into an ambush. Or perhaps someone was waiting for him and would have killed him then or later."

"Who?" Maria sobbed, clinging to Shadow. "Everything was just looking so perfect for us all. Who could want to see my father dead?"

"As I see it, it must have been another Spaniard," Shadow growled. "The Navaho never carry fire sticks! Your father was shot by a white man's rifle. I am sure even your father did not know who his assailant was before he took his last breath."

"It's so horrible," Maria cried. She doubled her fists and pressed them into Shadow's chest. "It's so unfair."

"Much in life *is* unfair," Shadow said, again trying to keep Maria from turning to look at her father, but this time she would not be discouraged from doing what she felt she must. Shadow watched her as she half stumbled over to her father.

Her fingers trembling, Maria reached out to touch her father's pale face. When she came in contact with his flesh, she flinched, for never had she felt anything so cold, so horribly cold.

"*Padre*, I am so sorry," she sobbed, caressing his cheek with the palm of her hand. "If it had not been for me, you would not be dead now. I am to blame. I *am*!"

Shadow's insides grew tight when he heard what she was saying. If she truly believed that she was at fault, her future with him and the Navaho would not be a pleasant, peaceful one. He had to give her cause not to believe such a falsehood. She could not believe that loving Shadow, marrying him, and living with him had caused this to happen to her father. She would be haunted by this forever!

Walking determinedly to Maria, Shadow took her hand
from her father's face and led her away from him. "Never
blame yourself for what has happened to your father," he
said. "Just as you saw that you were not to blame for your
mother's death, you must also see that you are innocent of
your father's! To be happy, to make sure your dreams are
sweet at night while you are sleeping in my arms, you *must*
dispel such thoughts from your mind, Maria. Your father is
dead because someone hated him and wanted him dead.
Your father made enemies easily. You know that. You
cannot blame yourself for your father's enemies. *He* made
them. Not *you*."

"But had he not come here for the wedding—" She
sniffed and looked wide-eyed up at Shadow as he covered
her mouth with a hand to stop her from talking foolishness
to him.

"That was a *happy* occasion for your father," he said
encouragingly, as he removed his hand. "He was here
because he wanted to be. Not because he was forced. He
more than likely died with happy thoughts of you on his
mind. Remember that, Maria. He died *happy*."

Maria glanced at her father, feeling a strange sort of
peace flow through her, for he *had* been happy the last time
she had seen him, perhaps happier than he had been in a
long time. Perhaps he *had* died with peace! With love!

Blinking tears from her lashes, she looked back up at
Shadow. "*Sí*, I believe you are right," she murmured.
"Shadow, you are so wise. You always know the right
things to say."

Again she looked at her father. "We may never know
who killed him," she said, choking on the words. "But we
must take him home, and bury him beside Mother. And it
must be done soon."

"We shall leave now," Shadow said hoarsely. "You get
what you want for the journey and we will leave soon."

Maria hugged Shadow. "*Muchas gracias*," she whispered. "Thank you so much, Shadow. Thank you for being
you."

* * *

Heavily guarded, Maria rode alongside Shadow, her father's body on a travois behind them. Among her belongings when she had gone to live with Shadow were the lacy black veil and the long-sleeved black silk dress that she had worn to her mother's funeral. Too soon she was wearing the same outfit again. She had lost both her parents within a short time, and she was finding it hard to accept. And the way they had died made this acceptance much harder. Her mother had taken her own life. Her father had been brutally murdered!

She looked at Shadow, thanking God that she had him. Without him, her life would have been worthless. He gave her strength. He gave her courage. In a sense, he breathed life into her by his mere presence!

The wind whipped her long skirt up past her ankles and made her veil flutter around her chin, causing Maria to direct her attention to the sky. Dark, billowing clouds were building in the heavens, adding to this feeling of foreboding that was encompassing her. Bright flashes of lightning forked across the sky, resulting in a loud rumble of thunder reverberating through the ground at her horse's feet, causing him to shake his head and whinny with fear.

And then there was a hostile fury to the silence that ensued, the steady rhythm of the horses' hooves on all sides of Maria muted by the yellow sand. They were now in a part of the country of desert and canyon where dwarf pine trees called piñon dotted the hillsides and red rocks stood up in weird shapes against the darkening sky.

Just ahead was the wide range of fertile land where grass was abundant and sheep could be seen grazing far and wide. Sad and abstracted, Maria rode onward, now staring into space, as though dead herself. This should have been a time of celebration and loving. She had just become a wife. She was married to a man she loved so desperately that sometimes the intensity of it frightened her.

But now everything had been overshadowed by another death. Who would be next?

Again she looked at Shadow and prayed silently to God that *he* would not be taken from her!

The day turned into dusk and the outreaches of the Zamora plantation were reached. There was no excitement in returning home as there would have been if life had been fair to Maria. As it was, she was just going to be adding another mound of dirt to the family cemetery.

And then what?

Zamora Manor would now be hers, but she did not want the responsibility of it! She had made her choice: She had chosen Shadow and the life he offered her. She was settling easily into the ways of the Navaho. She was happier than she had ever been at the plantation!

Oh, what *was* she to do . . . ?

She could not let her father's dream die. And what of all the slaves and servants who had been under his direction?

She wanted no slaves!

She wanted no servants!

An aroma of smoke drifted through the air, stinging Maria's nostrils. She lifted her veil and stared ahead, growing numb inside. At this point she should have been able to see Zamora Manor standing tall in all its grandeur. But there was nothing! Only . . . space . . .

Shadow and Maria exchanged a quick glance. Then she looked at her father's body wrapped in blankets on the travois behind Shadow's horse. She stared ahead again, curious about what had happened to the house. She had to ride faster. She had to see what had happened. The closer they drew to the plantation, the stronger became the smell of smoke that filled the air!

"Shadow, I must ride on ahead!" she shouted, not caring when her veil slipped from her face and head, and her skirt hiked way above her knees as she sent her horse into a mad gallop. "Zamora Manor! I cannot see it on the horizon. And do you smell that smoke? Oh, Shadow, what has happened?"

She ignored his command to stay with him. At this moment she was not ready to listen to anything but her heart, which told her that something was terribly wrong. She came to the wide gate that led to the house and stifled a sob behind a hand when she saw the glowing ash remains of the house. She looked on past it and saw that the slaves' quarters, the bunkhouses, and the stables had also burned to the ground. There was nothing left but ashes and smoke blowing in the wind!

Only moments ago she had been fretting over having to take responsibility for the plantation, and now there was nothing left to oversee! Surely whoever had killed her father had also burned everything that had belonged to him!

But who . . . ?

As she approached the house she was startled when several men on horseback suddenly appeared from behind a long row of cottonwood trees that stood back from the grounds near a stream. She wheeled her horse to a startled halt and sucked in her breath when she recognized one of the men: Governor Castillo! The others were soldiers in full military uniform.

"Maria, I see that you received word of what happened here," Governor Castillo said, moving his horse alongside hers. "I'm damn sorry, Maria. Damn sorry." He lowered his eyes. "Maria, everyone but your father is accounted for. Seems he may have perished in the flames. Once the ashes cool down we can search for—"

"*Señor*," Maria said, interrupting him. "You need not do that. I came here today to bury my father. He was shot out on the desert. And I had no idea someone had burned Zamora Manor and everything that was a part of it." She paused and met his steady gaze. "Since you are here, perhaps you know who is responsible for all of this? If you know, please tell me."

"Several of your father's men brought José Gironella to me the other day," he said thickly. "He was imprisoned, awaiting trial. A couple of nights ago the bastard escaped. It seems he has wreaked havoc on your family. He took all of your father's slaves and placed them with his. They will be returned to you soon. The men under your father's employ . . . well, none of them came out of this attack alive. Gironella was caught and has confessed to stealing the slaves, killing all of the men, and destroying this property but he never said a word about killing your father."

"But you know that he did, if he is responsible for doing *this*," Maria hissed, clutching the reins more tightly within her hand. "Where is he now? I, personally, want to loop the noose around his neck!"

"He is under heavy guard," Governor Castillo said, stroking his pointed chin. "Let us take care of the bastard. We will first beat a confession out of him for killing your father. And then he will stand before a firing squad. No trial is needed. Not this time."

"Thank God," Maria said, sighing heavily. "And as for the slaves, return them to my care. I will take them with me to Shadow's stronghold and they will become a part of the community, free spirits."

She glanced over her shoulder as Shadow came up behind her. Slipping out of her saddle she went to him as he dismounted, and fell into his arms. "Shadow, everything is gone," she murmured. "Everything."

Then her breathing shortened and her eyes widened. "Everything but the sheep that we saw grazing in the meadow," she said, looking anxiously up at Shadow. "And the Arabian horses. They are surely safe, also! Father told me that they are hidden in a valley. I know which valley. Shadow, we must go and get them and take them and the sheep home with us. We will sell the land and purchase more *bayeta*. My father would approve. I know he would."

"Who did this?" Shadow said, framing her face between his hands.

"José Gironella." Maria's eyes were snapping. "But he is imprisoned. He is to stand before the firing squad. If I were given the chance, I would pull the trigger on the guns that will release the shots into his body!"

Shadow drew her into his arms and hugged her. "*E-do-ta*, no," he said thickly. "My woman, that would not give you the satisfaction that you may think that it would. Forget revenge, Maria. Live for tomorrow. Not yesterday.

So much good will come to you . . . to us. Think on that, Maria. Think on that."

Maria sobbed, clinging wildly to him. She knew that he was right. It seemed that he was always right!

Maria knelt between two graves, touching each one with a tender hand. Wildflowers from the meadow in colors of the rainbow lay on each of the mounds of dirt. As raindrops began to fall in a fine mist, Maria's tears mixed with them, and she bent to kiss first her mother's grave, then her father's.

When a great burst of thunder echoed across the land, Shadow bent and placed a hand on Maria's elbow, helping her to her feet. "My wife, let us go home," he said hoarsely. "Things are done here. And do you not feel the peace? Your father and mother are walking together on the road to the hereafter at this very moment. Their hands are clasped. Their hearts are again as one. Envision it in that way, my love, and you will be much happier for it."

Sniffling, wiping a torrent of tears from her eyes, Maria looked up at Shadow. "*Sí*, it is a beautiful thought," she said softly, hoping that perhaps in death her mother and father could find a much more treasured happiness than they had found in life. "I shall carry that with me at all times, Shadow." She leaned into his embrace. "Take me home, my love," she murmured. "I am so very, very weary."

The earth shook beneath them as thunder again rumbled across the land. Maria let Shadow lift her up onto her horse. She took a last lingering look at the graves, then ducked her head and rode away as the rain continued to spray its fine mist in the air. . . .

CHAPTER
27

While Shadow was tending to his horse, Maria sat back from the fire in their hogan, sewing, while things stewed and bubbled in a great iron kettle over the flames. Several months had passed since their marriage. It was spring and there was a nip in the air outside, but her house was cozy and warm, the air was sweet, and the adobe walls and clay floors were clean.

Resting her sewing on her lap, Maria looked proudly around her, seeing all the reminders that this was now her home as well as Shadow's. Around the fire pit she kept kitchen utensils made of wood, clay, and basketry. There were four smooth sticks, tied together with strips of yucca leaf, which she used to stir soup. Close to the fire pit was a hearth brush, a bundle of stiff spikes from the narrow-leafed yucca known as bear grass. This was tied near the middle with the butt ends all at one end, the spiked ones at the other. The stiff butt end served as a broom to sweep the earthen floor; the spiky end was used as a hairbrush.

Across her shoulder she saw the bed, which at one time had been covered only with sheepskin. It now revealed a smooth pink satin comforter that she had purchased on her last trip to market to sell the wares made by the Navaho.

Glancing around her, Maria smiled to herself, seeing all sorts of oddities that she had brought home—things that reminded her of her mother in their daintiness, and of how she had once lived. It had not been easy to cast thoughts of her luxuries from her mind. It had been fun to purchase a few such items and bring them back to the hogan.

A beautiful gold vase here, a gilt-edged mirror there, and gold candle holders with long white tapers, which she placed on the small table she had brought to the hogan for a special meal by candlelight.

Shadow had not forbidden these things, yet Maria knew there had to be a limit. She would, for now, be content with her small treasures.

She reached out to touch the blanket folded neatly at her side. Finally . . . the saddle blanket that she had been weaving for Shadow was finished. She would present it to him tonight. She would be able to tell by reading his eyes whether or not he approved. If *he* approved, so would his people!

If he did not, Maria would just begin all over again and try to make the next blanket better!

Without having to look toward the door of the hogan, Maria knew that Shadow was there. There was something in his presence that she had learned to detect, as though a force were there, invisible to the eye, yet allowing her always to be aware of his presence.

Smiling, she turned and watched him walk toward her. Grabbing the blanket up from the floor, she rose to her feet, holding it behind her back. She caught the glimmer of curiosity in Shadow's eyes. He had seen her place the blanket behind her.

"And what have you there?" he asked smoothly, going to Maria, weaving his long, lean fingers through her hair, drawing it back from her face. "Is it a present for your husband?"

"*Sí,* a present," Maria said, her eyes dancing. Slowly she withdrew the blanket and held it out before her, seeing the approval as Shadow's eyes widened and lit up. He took the blanket and held it out between his hands.

"My wife, this is a beautiful blanket," he said, surprise in his voice. "When did you make this? I have never seen you laboring over it. Not once!"

Maria placed a hand on his cheek, bubbling over with happiness. "Darling, never did I feel that I was laboring over the blanket," she said, laughing softly. "It was done out of *love*. And I did it when you were away tending the sheep and horses. Is it a surprise, darling? Do you truly like it? Will your people approve?"

Shadow folded the blanket up and placed it on the floor so that the light of the fire picked up its brilliant red color. "I approve," he said, drawing her into his arms. "My people will be impressed. My woman can do anything. Anything!"

Maria cast her eyes downward, feeling suddenly bashful, something unique to her now that she had been married so long to such a wonderful, caring man. But the news that she had to tell him was of a different sort tonight. Even she could hardly believe the reality of it!

"You say that I can do anything," she murmured, slowly lifting her eyes, melting beneath the wondrous warmth of his as he gazed down at her. "Do you truly mean that?"

"Yes, anything," Shadow said huskily, smoothing his hands over the buckskin material of her dress, cupping her breasts through it.

"Even bear you a child?" she said, her voice quivering with emotion.

Shadow dropped his hands away from her and took a step backward, his eyes registering shock. "A . . . child?" he said in a low gasp.

Maria swallowed hard, not knowing how to interpret his reaction. It was not exactly what she had expected. "Shadow, are you not happy?" she asked, her voice wavering.

Shadow stared down at her, and then his face broke into a sudden smile. Laughter then rang out as he grabbed Maria up into his arms and held her close to him. "Are you with child?" he asked softly, looking down at her with a pride she had never seen before. "You are positive that you are?"

Maria twined her arms around his neck and laid her cheek against his bare chest, sighing. "I couldn't be more positive," she said, laughing softly. "And I don't have to wonder any longer whether or not you are glad. Darling, now I know that you are happy and that makes me so very, very happy. A child is forever, also, my darling, just like our love for each other."

Shadow carried Maria to their bed and gently placed her on it. Meditatively he removed her blouse, skirt, and moccasins, then began tracing her body in soft caresses with his hands, stopping at her abdomen. He framed it between his hands, his eyes aglimmer.

"A child grows there," he said thickly. "*Our* child, Maria."

"*Sí*," Maria said, tears welling up in her eyes. She covered Shadow's hands with her own. "It is already a beautiful child, Shadow, because you are the father."

Shadow smoothed his hands upward and cupped her breasts gently. "Our child will one day taste the wonders of its mother just as I have so many times," he said, flicking a tongue over a nipple, causing it to grow tight. His lips moved along her flesh, higher, across the hollow of her throat, along its column, and then to her lips.

"Maria, you have made my hogan a house of happiness," he whispered against her lips. "*Ukehe*, thank you, my love. *Ukehe*."

Maria's lips quivered as Shadow kissed her with sweetness. For so long she had dreamed of him before she had ever been given the pleasure of meeting him, but never had they been savage dreams. They had been beautiful, as her life was, now that she was living it with Shadow, the man she would love, forever.

Daltso hozhoni, at long last, all *was* beautiful. . . .